THE TITAN

THE TITAN PROPHECY

Rise Of
The Dark One

A. M. CRAWFORD

Murray McLellan, Edinburgh
www.thetitanprophecy.com

First published in Great Britain 2011
by Murray McLellan
Edinburgh

ISBN 978-0-9570091-0-3

Murray McLellan
43-45 Circus Lane Edinburgh EH3 6SU

www.thetitanprophecy.com

For Alastair and Matthew

CONTENTS

Cover illustration & Maps copyright **CHRIS DUGGAN**

PROLOGUE

PARSEUS hurried towards the palace, the sound of his footsteps echoing off the flagstones as he made his way through the quiet, winding streets, his mind racing. He had been summoned. But why? At first he had thought it had come from the Division — they usually did. Then he spotted the royal seal: the summons was from the king himself. The message could not have been clearer. It read: *COME AT ONCE.*

He quickened his pace, there was an urgency to his step now as his mind spun with all manner of dreadful possibilities. A king's command was never given lightly. But he could not recall a summons as stark as this one.

He stopped outside the palace gates. They rose up in front of him, proud and bold, gleaming in the late afternoon sun. The avenue stretched beyond, perfection in precision, not a tree out of place. He expected no less.

The gates opened and he slipped through, picking up his pace once again. Reaching the palace steps he slowed down, the guard straightening as he neared. But there was not the usual greeting. Parseus sensed trouble.

As he reached the top step, the doors swung open and the guard motioned him in. Parseus swept inside. The palace hall was huge. Passages branched off to the left and right, stretching as far as the eye could see. Marbled walls shimmered in the flickering light and columns ran up and down the corridors, like soldiers standing to attention.

But there was friction in the air. Parseus could feel it. He quickly set off down one of the passages, his feet thundering across the floor, shadows dancing on the walls as he passed. He strode on towards a huge, brass door, intricately carved with symbols and figures. Two guards stood impassively on either side, like statues.

Parseus stopped in front of them.

'I'm here to see...'

'We know.' One of the guards replied, his expression grave. Leaning down he turned the handle, opened the door and ushered Parseus into the room.

Parseus tentatively stepped inside. He stopped. The chamber was full, every seat taken. They were all there — the Great Council, all twelve of them, muttering amongst themselves, the mood sombre, the air heavy with apprehension. Something had happened — something big. It was etched on their faces.

'Ah, he's arrived — finally.' Her words cut through the air like an icy blast. 'How gracious of you, Parseus. One would have thought a Time...'

'One would have *thought* we had more important things to consider, my Queen.' The king's voice boomed across the chamber, silencing the room. Everyone's eyes turned to Parseus. The king cleared his throat.

'There's been a Prophecy,' he announced, anger brimming under the surface.

Parseus was surprised. Prophecies happened all the time. Why would the king be so bothered? 'A prophecy Your Majesty? Concerning...?'

'Concerning *US*.' The king roared with rage though Parseus sensed the faintest hint of fear in his voice. A low, uneasy murmur ran round the room. No wonder, he thought. For Prophecies concerning the Great Council were rare indeed — almost unknown.

'*Us*, Your Majesty?'

The king nodded solemnly. 'There's a boy. He's...'

'A boy?' Parseus interrupted. All this for a boy?

'YES. A Boy. And something's been sent,' the king added. He beckoned Parseus with his finger.

Parseus stepped forward. The king lowered his voice. Parseus could hardly believe what he was hearing. It was the very worst news. Had they done that much damage? Had they brought them all to *this*?

The king pulled him closer. 'So you must leave at once,' he said before dismissing Parseus with a wave.

'I will leave this instant, Your Majesty.' Parseus bowed deeply.

'Are you sure he's up to the task?' the Queen spat, fixing Parseus with a cold, hard stare.

The king turned on her, fury filling his face. 'Be quiet. He's the best we have. He knows their ways. Who better? Only he can take him...'

'But...'

The king slammed his fist down on his throne. 'Enough. I will not be questioned.' He turned back to Parseus. 'Everything is prepared. You must go at once. We cannot allow...' His face contorted with fearful disbelief. 'The boy...' He paused. 'There's no time to lose.'

'There never is, Your Majesty.' Parseus was all too aware of that.

The king pointed towards the door. 'Then GO.'

Parseus nodded, turned to the assembled Council and bowed again. Then, gathering his robes about him, he left the chamber.

He pushed past the guards, his face grim and hurried back down the passage. His feet pounded across the stone floor, it sounded like a death knell. Perhaps it was, he thought. But Parseus knew there were far worse things than Death. Things that would make you pray for Death, beg for it. Welcome it with open arms. Death, however, was not an option.

The palace doors opened as he approached — nothing it seemed was to stand in his way. The urgency of his task preceded him. He pressed on down the avenue, his mind in turmoil. This Prophecy? What a Prophecy it was. There hadn't been one like this since... He shook his head as he watched the gates open. And now it was up to him to stop...He sighed heavily. Was that even possible? Whatever the truth, he couldn't think about that now. There really was no time to lose.

But as he raced out, the palace gates closing behind him, he glanced up: the sun was already starting to set. A cold chill ran through him. Time, it seemed, was *not* on their side...

1. IN THE SHADOWS

IT arrived, as Evil often does, without fanfare. There was no great clap of thunder nor bolt of lightning to announce its presence. It simply slipped in, unnoticed by all except a flock of birds which flew up into the sky squawking in fear and then fled west. Startled, Charlie looked up but as he watched the birds disappear towards the horizon he thought little of it. A moment later he stumbled in a muddy pool. He groaned silently as he felt the cold water seep into his socks. It was all Max's fault, he decided. He had dragged him across the moors for hours and Charlie was starting to wish he had never come.

'You realise it's a three-mile walk back to the village,' he said as he picked himself out of the mud, his feet squelching in his boots. 'And it'll be dark soon. My Mum'll ground us for sure this time.'

'I know, but...' Max scratched his head. 'Sorry, I just don't know how we strayed so far. I mean, I know these moors like the back of my hand.'

'Great. I could be at home by now with my feet up,' said Charlie.

'What, with one of your books?' teased Max.

'What's wrong with books?' replied Charlie. 'You could do with reading one once in a while.'

'Just don't know what you see in them.'

'Action, adventure, knowledge, you know — interesting stuff.'

Max waved his arm dramatically. 'This is adventure. Not those stupid stories you read.'

'No this isn't. We've just trekked across the moors for hours and the only things we've seen are some sheep, a few peat bogs — oh, and some birds. Hardly adventure,' replied Charlie.

'I'm sorry, what did you expect to see? Exotic animals roaming the grassland? Mystical warriors galloping across the plain?'

'No. But at least that would be interesting,' said Charlie.

'Interesting? These moors have hidden depths you know. There are peat bogs here that could take an elephant down,' said Max.

'An elephant? Yeah, because we're likely to see one of those on the moors.'

'You read too many fantasies, that's your problem. Of course if you want real adventure...' Max pointed to the wood which lay a hundred yards away. 'We could always go through the grounds of Hesper House.'

Charlie stiffened. Then he looked up. Although the light was fading and the sky turning violet, ahead, beyond the dense wood that surrounded it, he could just make out the turreted towers of Hesper House — forbidden territory to all the children in the village.

'But they're out of bounds,' he said, his voice catching in his throat.

'And what's more adventurous than exploring forbidden grounds, eh? We may even come across some of these ghouls and monsters everyone keeps talking about.'

'They're just stories, that's all,' said Charlie.

'So why is it out of bounds then?'

'Probably because the house is a death trap. Falling down by all accounts.'

'Yeah, well, whatever the truth, it's also a short-cut. We'd be home in thirty minutes. Problem solved,' said Max. 'Unless you want to stay on the moors, that is?'

Charlie didn't, and satisfied that the matter was agreed, Max strode on.

Maybe he was right, Charlie thought as he watched Max

march towards the trees. At least they would be home before dark. So he ran and caught up with him.

Moments later they reached the fence which bordered the wood. It was broken, twisted and leaning to one side. There was a sign loosely nailed to one of the trees. It read: TRESPASSERS WILL BE...' but the rest of the warning had long since worn off, though Charlie knew what it said.

He had heard far too many tales about what happened if you did trespass. And even though he knew they were just ghost stories he still shuddered.

They both peered uneasily into the gloom.

'So who's going first?' said Max, his earlier bravado now fading.

'It was your idea,' replied Charlie, bowing mockingly.

'Fine,' said Max and as if to prove the point he vaulted over the fence and disappeared into the trees.

Charlie hesitated. Neither he nor Max had ever set foot inside the wood before and they were breaking all the rules in doing so. If his parents found out, he could expect to be grounded for the rest of the week — and it was half-term. Yet if he didn't get home before dark, his mother might ground him anyway, at least for a day or so. He decided his mother was the greater risk. It was only a wood after all.

Taking a deep breath, he brushed the wet hair out of his eyes and clambered over the rickety fence. But the moment he did so he regretted it. Close up the trees appeared far more menacing. Looming up into the sky above, they blocked out most of the fading light so it made the wood feel cold and gloomy, and as Charlie crept forward he could hear strange whispers and faint cries. He told himself it was just the wind, but he wasn't entirely convinced.

'Where now?' asked Max.

'Straight across, I guess,' said Charlie.

But as they started across the wood the trees seemed to crowd in around them, like soldiers closing rank. Before long they were clawing their way through the thicket, the ferns so tall they were almost chest height. While underfoot, the gnarly roots, which were splayed out in all directions, seemed intent on tripping them up at every step. Even the branches appeared to have it in for them, flicking in their faces as they passed, as strange shrieks and howls filled the air.

'I'm starting to think this short-cut wasn't such a good idea,' said Max.

'Now you tell me,' groaned Charlie. 'Well, we can't go back. There isn't time. And anyway we're halfway through.'

A loud shriek rang out. Max spun around. 'What was that?'

Charlie glanced back briefly. 'Probably just a bird.'

'Didn't sound like a bird,' said Max.

'Not scared are you?'

Max shook his head, but Charlie knew that he was, just a little. They both were.

There was no other option though, so they pressed on. Before long the trees started thinning out, allowing a little more light to peek through. Charlie and Max quickened their pace. Soon enough they were making good progress. The worst, it seemed, was over. Not long after, they saw the edge of the wood up ahead. They both sighed with relief.

'Well we're nearly there,' said Charlie. 'Wasn't too bad, was it?'

'Guess not,' replied Max.

Just then Charlie spotted something through the trees. 'What's that?' he said, pointing.

Max squinted into the distance. 'What's what?'

'That black thing twenty yards away, through those trees.'

'Thing?' Max stared again. 'What do you mean?'

Then they both saw it. It was moving fast, slinking in and out of the trees.

Charlie suddenly felt the hairs on the back on his neck stand on end. For whatever it was it appeared to be moving with purpose, as if it had somewhere to go. It seemed to be heading towards the grounds, but then it turned back and disappeared into the gloom.

'What was that?' gasped Max. 'Some kind of animal?'

'No', said Charlie. 'Not an animal.' He stared again, but whatever it was, there was no sign of it now. 'Looked like some sort of shadow. But that's weird. How could it be?'

'Yeah — well, I don't like weird,' said Max.

'Nor do I, so come on, let's go — we're nearly out of here.'

Ahead of them Charlie could see the fence bordering the grounds of Hesper House, this one just as broken and twisted as the other. But, as they hurried towards it, the shrieks grew louder and more incessant, as if the wood itself were warning of their approach.

'I don't like this, Charlie,' said Max.

Charlie glanced over his shoulder. The wood was darkening fast. 'We can't go back now. We have to head on.'

'But what are we heading into?' asked Max.

Although Max had a point, Charlie knew they had little choice. 'It's only a house, isn't it?' he said.

'Suppose you're right,' replied Max.

'Then follow me.'

Charlie clambered over the fence. Beyond it a row of cypress trees rose up into the sky. Pushing through them he stumbled onto the lawn.

Then he looked up and his mouth fell open. For there, towering up into the sky — in all its gothic monstrosity — was Hesper House. He stood for a second, stupefied.

All these years he had grown up with the horror stories that abounded about the place, but he had never before seen it up close. Now that he was here, standing right in front of it, he was filled with a mixture of fear and awe.

The original house was centuries old but, long since abandoned, it had fallen into disrepair: half the windows were broken, and thick, dark green ivy crawled up the sides of the house.

At some point in its long history, four huge turreted towers had been added — though no one seemed to know by whom. It was an age-old mystery that only fuelled the rumours about the place. It was as if they had been built to protect the house itself. They sat on each corner like giant guards.

Yet it was the strange, stone gargoyles attached to almost every available corner and ledge which made Charlie's skin crawl. They looked so monstrous, so real, as if they, like the towers, were there to guard the place. Staring up, Charlie felt as if their ghastly glares were fixed on him, watching him.

'Bit spooky, isn't it?' said Max, his voice wavering.

'Certainly is. So the quicker we're out of here the better.' But as Charlie began to move, something caught his eye on the edge of the wood behind them. It was the black shadow. In the little light left he could see it quite clearly. It was weaving in and out of the trees, as if it were searching for something – as if it were hunting. Instinctively, Charlie realised that they shouldn't let themselves be seen by it. Grabbing Max he pulled him back behind one of the trees.

'Hey, what are you doing?' said Max.

Charlie put his finger to his lips and pointed to the edge of the wood. 'It's that thing, that black shadow.'

Max stared open-mouthed. 'What's it doing?'

'I don't know, Max, but I suggest we get down.'

They dropped to their knees, their eyes fixed on the shadow, dreading it might approach. Moments later, much to their relief, it turned and disappeared back into the wood.

'Let's get out of here,' said Charlie. 'We'll cross the lawn, slip round that end tower and head down the drive to the village road. Agreed?'

'Agreed,' said Max.

'How far do you think it is?' asked Charlie.

'Couple of hundred yards or so.'

'Shouldn't take too long. But don't stop until we are on the other side of that tower.'

The boys stood up, checked to make sure there was no sign of the black shadow behind them, and started running as fast as they could across the lawn. By the time they reached the far tower they were out of breath. They quickly tucked themselves out of sight and crouched down next to a couple of overgrown holly bushes that ran along the outer wall.

'Stay down. I'll make sure the coast is clear,' said Charlie.

He inched his way round the side of the tower and peered out across the lawn. Then he froze. The black shadow was now creeping towards the house, slithering over the ground, changing shape as it went. A moment later it stopped in the middle of the lawn and turned towards the house.

Charlie's blood ran cold. For even in the gathering gloom, there was no mistaking it. This shadow had eyes— huge, yellow *eyes*.

Charlie felt his knees buckle. Then the tales came flooding back, washing over him in waves. Tales he had thought had been told only to keep the children out of the grounds were no longer tales — and the terrifying proof of that was hovering on the lawn in front of him.

The shadow rose up, growing taller as it did so. Snaking up into the sky it started turning this way and that as if it had caught a scent on the wind. Charlie couldn't tear his eyes away. He was mesmerised. It was like nothing he had ever seen before, like some fearful shadowy spectre.

Then the shadow slowly turned in his direction, and Charlie immediately came to his senses. For in that moment something told him that The Shadow *had sensed him*.

2. STRANGERS IN THE NIGHT

COLD fear now turned to abject terror as Charlie watched The Shadow slither forward. Every instinct told him to run. But where? Keeping close to the wall he inched his way back to Max.

'What's going on, Charlie?' Max whispered.

'We need to hide.'

'I thought you said...'

'That's no shadow out there, Max.'

'What do you mean?'

'Not sure what it is but it — it had eyes,' said Charlie.

'Eyes? Yeah right. How could it have *eyes*?'

'Well, it does — and I think it's looking for us. Now be quiet. Can't let it know where we are.'

'Looking for us?' Max seemed incredulous. 'How can a shadow do that?'

'How do I know?'

'You're seeing things, that's what. Let me have a look,' said Max.

'Don't do that,' hissed Charlie. But it was too late. Max was already crawling towards the tower.

Seconds later he scrambled back behind the holly bushes, ashen-faced. 'You're right. It...it's got... eyes,' he stammered.

'Told you it did. So we need to go,' said Charlie.

'Where exactly?'

Charlie, desperately looking around for somewhere to hide, spotted a small set of steps, hidden behind one of the holly bushes. It led to a door. He nudged Max. 'How about there — looks like a cellar?'

'You want to go inside the house?' Max looked aghast.

But Charlie knew it was their only hope. They had nowhere else to go.

Keeping low to the ground they crawled towards the steps. Reaching the cellar door, Charlie turned the handle but it was stiff and wouldn't budge.

'Let me have a go,' said Max.

Charlie gladly stepped aside. Max was far bigger than he was. More brawn than brains, as Charlie's father put it, but there had been more than a few occasions when Max's might had come to good use — usually during a brawl with the other village boys.

Max gave the door a good kick. It opened. Thankful, the boys tumbled inside.

The cellar was dark and damp and they could barely see anything so they crouched down in the corner behind the door, praying that The Shadow wouldn't follow. There was a dank, nasty odour to the place and Charlie screwed up his face in disgust as he and Max huddled in the corner. It took a while for his eyes to grow accustomed to the dim light, but soon enough he could make out the piles of junk and broken furniture which were scattered about, covered under a thick layer of dust.

Charlie pointed to a large chest pushed up against the window, which gave a ground-level view of the lawn outside. 'We'll climb up there. Let's hope it doesn't know where we've gone. If we don't see it in the next ten minutes then we'll go, OK?'

Max agreed and they clambered up. Sitting in silence, they kept their eyes glued to the window, watching as the setting sun turned the sky blood red.   A little while later Max spoke. 'So that Shadow, do you think that's why this place is forbidden?'

'Don't know. I thought they were just ghost stories. But I never imagined anything like this. Did you?'

'No. But we've never been in the grounds before,' said Max.

'Maybe we shouldn't have come at all.'

'Bit late for that now,' Max grunted.

Then Charlie grabbed his arm and pointed. 'LOOK. It's here. I think it's found us.'

The Shadow had turned the corner of the house and was creeping towards them, twenty yards away, its eyes turning from side to side, searching the ground. They had shut the cellar door behind them, but Charlie had no idea if it could get inside. If so, they were trapped.

'We need to get out of here, Max,' he said, desperately looking around the cellar.

'But how — and where?'

Charlie pointed to the back of the room. 'We have to go into the house. There must be a door over there. Let's go.'

'You mean even further inside?' Max whispered.

'We don't have any other choice,' said Charlie.

Climbing down from the chest he and Max picked their way across the cellar to a short set of wooden stairs. At the top was a trapdoor. Charlie pushed hard. It was heavy, but with Max heaving as well, it began to open. Then, with a clash, it sprang back against the wall above. They scrambled inside the house and found themselves in the hall that looked out over the lawn they had just crossed.

A wide staircase ran up one side to a gallery above and two long corridors ran off to the left and right. There was a musty smell to the place and it was deathly cold — much colder than it was outside. Charlie shivered.

He pointed to the staircase. 'Why don't we go upstairs? We'll have a better view outside and we can hide there.'

They started up the stairs, but many of the steps were rotten and broken so they had to pick their way carefully, clinging tightly to the banister as they went, both terrified they might fall. They reached the landing. A long corridor ran to their right, lined with doors on each side.

'Should we hide in one of these rooms?' said Max.

Charlie looked down the gloomy corridor. 'No, let's just get down behind this chest. We can see the lawn from here and we need to keep an eye out for that Shadow in case it comes inside.'

'You think it might?' said Max.

Charlie could hear the fear in his voice. 'Perhaps.'

They crouched down behind the chest and peered through the gallery window, though with the day giving way to dusk it was growing harder to see. But they watched and waited anyway, neither one daring to ask the obvious.

It was Max who broke the silence. 'So what do you think it is?'

'Not sure, but it's no shadow, I know that. Reckon it's a ghost,' said Charlie.

'Ghost? No. Must be a monster.'

'Can't be a monster, it's not solid.' Charlie paused. 'It has to be a ghost. That would explain the eyes.'

'But...' Max was just about to argue that when they heard a sound from inside the house. A door banged in the distance, and a moment later the boys spotted a light in the passage that led from the west tower. Crawling back towards the stairs, they fell to the floor and lay as low as possible, hardly daring to breathe.

The light grew brighter and, peering through the banisters, Charlie saw a cloaked figure, carrying a flaming torch, appear in the hall. He couldn't believe his eyes. First The Shadow and now this? He tried to get a better look but the figure's hood hung so low that he couldn't make out its face. Then his heart leapt into his mouth. For this figure wasn't walking — it was *floating* across the stone floor. A moment later it glided out of the house through the French windows which faced the lawn.

Charlie and Max crawled back towards the gallery window. Sitting up, they stared down at the figure now standing on the terrace below.

'Do you think it's the witch?' Max whispered breathlessly. 'I didn't think she existed.'

Neither did Charlie. Like everyone else, he had heard stories of the infamous witch, Mrs Payne. She was legendary. Many a child had been kept in check by threats that she might come for them. It was said she'd been alive for centuries, but no one had ever seen her, though the fear of doing so kept everyone in the village out of the grounds. Some people even referred to her as the Gatekeeper although Charlie had always wondered what it was she was supposed to be guarding.

Then Charlie spotted The Shadow again, now illuminated in the flickering torchlight. It was slithering towards the cloaked figure, like a snake through grass. A moment later it stopped right in front of them and the figure raised an arm, as if in command. Charlie could just make out a bony hand protruding, the fingers long and unusually tapered, the skin bluish white. The figure beckoned The Shadow forward, turned and swept back inside the house. The Shadow obediently followed.

Charlie stared in horror. For no matter how terrifying The Shadow was, there was now something infinitely more frightening — the cloaked figure which commanded it.

He and Max inched back and crouched down, watching in disbelief as the figure disappeared back into the darkness, The Shadow in tow. A minute later they heard the sound of a door closing heavily in the distance.

'Let's get of here,' said Charlie.

'Right behind you,' said Max and getting to their feet they carefully crept back down the staircase and slipped through the French windows onto the lawn. Within seconds they were running towards the drive as if their lives depended on it.

The driveway was long and lined on either side by fir trees that stood like sentries, silent and still. It wound down steeply to the lane which led to the village a mile below so that Charlie and Max had to take care not to slip as they ran.

Charlie didn't dare look back. By the time they reached the rusty, iron gates that hung, broken and twisted at the entrance to Hesper House, their lungs were bursting. They stopped to catch their breath. Charlie's heart was beating so wildly he thought it might explode but neither he nor Max dared stop for long. Leaving the grounds, they turned down the lane. Charlie checked back to see if The Shadow might have followed. Thankfully, there was no sign of it.

Darkness had started to creep in but they weren't going to take any chances so they ran on as hard as they could. Five minutes later they passed Max's home — a pretty, stone-built cottage, with a climbing rose which crawled up the walls and tumbled over the door. They barely gave it a glance as they pounded down the lane towards the village square and the safety of Charlie's home, the *George & Dragon* inn. Another half-mile, and as the lane widened, they saw the lights of the village houses ahead. They were nearly home.

IN welcome contrast to the sinister mansion on the hill, the village of Hesper was a friendly little place. There was one main road in and out of the village, which was lined with stone-built cottages and a small, cobbled square sat in the village centre. On the corner, and set back from the road, behind an enormous and solitary oak tree, was an arched gateway leading to the church and the vicarage beyond it.

Charlie's parents owned the white-painted three-storied *George & Dragon,* stretched across one side of the square, its garden sloping down to the river Hesper. A humped bridge across the river gave the village its only access to the rest of the world — or rather to the market town of Ferrick, some twelve miles away. The moors bordered it on all other sides. In centuries past the village had been a vibrant little place but there had been a steady exodus over the years and few now called it home.

Panting heavily Charlie and Max passed the oak tree and raced across the square, where the lights of the inn spilled out, warm and welcoming. Moments later, he and Max fell through the side entrance in a heap, still gasping for air but grateful to be home.

They quickly got to their feet. Charlie was hoping he and

Max could sneak up the backstairs to his bedroom but just then his mother waddled out of the kitchen. She was wearing an apron and her curly red hair was piled up untidily on her head.

On seeing Charlie she planted her hands on her hips. 'Charlie Goodwin, where have you been? You were supposed to be back ages ago. You know you're not to be out in the dark.'

'Mum, I'm not a kid, you know,' said Charlie. 'And it's half-term,' he added as if that made a difference. His mother glared at him. 'That is hardly the point and you know it. But don't let it happen again — or else.'

Charlie looked down at his feet. 'Sorry, Mum, we just didn't realise the time — got a bit lost.'

Charlie felt bad. His mother was such a worrier, even at the best of times, but perhaps, given what they had just seen, she had good reason.

'Sorry, Mrs Goodwin, my fault really,' said Max.

'Well isn't that a surprise Max Harper.' Mrs Goodwin rolled her eyes. Then her face softened. 'Still no harm's done, I suppose. Supper won't be long. It's only shepherd's pie, mind. So go and wash up.' And with that she shuffled back into the kitchen.

'Thanks, Mum,' Charlie shouted after her. Then he and Max raced upstairs, washed up and went to his room.

Like most boys of his age, Charlie's room was untidy. He liked it that way. A few posters adorned the walls, though some were peeling off, their edges curled over. In the corner sat his old toy box, now a dumping ground for anything he no longer needed but couldn't bring himself to throw away. Beside it, a worn riding hat lay on the floor next to an old tennis racket.

A wooden bookshelf was pushed up against one wall, crammed full of Charlie's treasured stories, and an old armchair sat grumpily in the corner, as if in a sulk. There was also a chest of drawers, a bedside table with a small lamp and the curtains were open, giving a view of the square outside.

Max's suitcase was sitting next to the spare bed. It was

practically all Max owned. Charlie felt sorry for him. Max's mother had died when he was a small boy and after his father had gone away he had been brought to the village to live with his grandmother. But she had fallen ill and was in hospital, so he was staying at the inn. He did so a lot. Charlie's mother often teased that he might as well move in altogether since he spent so much time there, but Max liked to keep his options open.

Charlie sat down on his bed. The adrenalin had started to wear off and his hands were shaking. He leaned forward and struggled to untie his shoelaces. His boots were still soaking wet and it took some effort to get them off. He peeled off his sodden socks and tossed them into the corner of the room. Max plonked himself in the armchair.

It was a relief to be home. But Charlie couldn't stop thinking about what had happened — none of it made any sense.

Then the door burst open and Charlie's younger sister, Emily, stormed in. She stood in the middle of the room glowering at him. 'Where have you been?' she said, fixing Charlie with an angry stare.

Charlie knew she would be furious that he had gone off exploring without her. She hated being left out. She was always trying to follow him around and it bugged him. But now he was in no mood for her questions. 'None of your business. Just go away, Emily.'

Emily curled her lip. 'Just asking. Didn't realise it was such a big secret.'

'No secret. We've just been out. Like I said, it's none of your business where we've been or what we've seen,' said Charlie.

'What do you mean — what you've seen?' she said.

Charlie tried to backtrack. 'Don't mean nothing. Nothing at all.'

'What did you see?' Emily persisted, crossing her arms.

'Just tell her, Charlie. She'll find out soon enough anyway. You're bound to let it slip,' said Max.

Charlie reluctantly gave in. That was what annoyed him

most about his sister, she was always finding out everything. 'We were exploring Hesper House. That's all,' he said.

'You went into the grounds of Hesper House?' Emily seemed impressed.

'Not just the grounds.' Charlie grew boastful. 'The house too.'

'The house? What was it like?' Emily looked from one to the other. 'Did you see the witch?'

Charlie realised he might have said too much. 'No, didn't see anything, did we Max?' Charlie glared at his sister. 'Now leave us alone.'

'Suit yourself. Don't care anyway,' Emily replied, and without another word she flounced out of the room.

Charlie waited for a moment or two before speaking. 'Do you think it was the witch?'

'Don't know, but who else could it be?' said Max. 'And what was that shadow? Explain that,' he added.

Charlie couldn't.

'Do you think they heard us?' Max asked nervously.

But before Charlie could answer, his mother shouted up from downstairs. 'SUPPER'S READY.'

The boys leapt up. 'We'll talk about it later,' said Charlie. He and Max put on their slippers and headed out of the room. Stepping into the corridor, Charlie saw Emily hovering by her door a few feet away. He guessed she had been eavesdropping. But as he approached she just smiled innocently at him.

'By the way, not a word to Mum — is that clear?'

'Course, goes without saying,' Emily replied smugly.

But as they traipsed downstairs, Charlie had a feeling her silence would have a price. It usually did.

WHEN they entered the bar, their father was standing behind the counter, polishing glasses. He smiled cheerfully. Charlie felt better for seeing him. After everything that had happened, it was a comfort to see his shiny, bald head and jovial red face.

'Evening all,' he said.

'Evening, Mr Goodwin,' said Max politely.

'Had a good day?' Mr Goodwin asked.

Emily stuck out her tongue at Charlie. He shot her a warning look.

'It was OK, nothing out of the ordinary, Dad,' he said as he led the others to the back of the bar and pulled up a chair near the fire.

It was a Monday and still early evening so the bar was empty. Charlie assumed that Tom the boatman and Bill the butcher would pop in later for their usual pint, though they never stayed long. At the weekend the bar was busy enough but not on Monday. On a Monday the inn would usually be closed by ten.

Nevertheless, the George & Dragon was the focal point of the village. Charlie's dad, like his dad before him, was the innkeeper and one day Charlie supposed that it would be his turn to take over. That was how things worked in Hesper.

The bar was much like that in any village pub, or so Charlie assumed. There was a main entrance, which led onto the street, and two doors leading off from it: one to the hall and one to the kitchen. There was a long bar that ran down one side of the room, and lots of tables dotted about, while wooden beams ran along the low ceiling so that anyone much taller than six foot would have to stoop a little as they entered. A small, log fireplace sat at the back of the room, opposite the main entrance. Copper pots hung above the mantelpiece, while old swords, antique guns and pictures adorned the rest of the room.

Their father stopped polishing. 'Wouldn't help your mother would you, Emily?'

Emily huffed loudly.

'It's your turn,' said Charlie.

Sighing, Emily stood up and eyeing Charlie with thinly-veiled contempt she stomped into the kitchen, leaving the boys alone.

Their day out on the moors had given them a hefty appetite and they were both looking forward to supper. As the aroma drifted in from the kitchen, and they warmed themselves next to the roaring fire, it started to seem as if the dramas of the day were really nothing more than their imaginations running wild.

Charlie felt a bit silly now that they were back at home and everything was as normal as ever. Sitting back in the slightly frayed armchair and staring into the fire, he tried to persuade himself that somehow their minds had been playing tricks on them. A shadow with eyes? It just couldn't be true.

Just then the inn door flew open and a cold draught blew in causing the flames to flicker wildly. Startled, Charlie and Max turned towards the door. Their faces fell. For there, standing before them, framed in the doorway, was a tall, dark, cloaked figure.

3. CLOAKS AND DAGGERS

THE stranger now standing in the entrance, a large wooden trunk hoisted on his back, was a huge, heavily-built man, with a weathered face, and long, jet-black hair that hung past his shoulders. Charlie thought he looked rather old-fashioned, as if he belonged to another age.

He hovered in the doorway, his dark, deep-set eyes slowly surveying the bar, his gaze curious and cold. Lifting the trunk off his shoulders he dumped it on the floor. It landed with a thud. Then with a flurry he removed his cloak and swept into the room, stooping as he did so to avoid the beams.

The man had such an outlandish appearance that Charlie couldn't help staring. He wasn't so much tall as enormous and in the small bar he seemed to fill every inch of the room. His face was tanned and chiselled, but heavily lined and though Charlie thought he might be old, his long dark hair and broad physique suggested otherwise. His ears were odd too: narrow, pointed and pinned back against his head — Charlie thought they gave him an oddly elfin look — and his fingers were unusually long and narrowly tapered.

Mr Goodwin stopped polishing, put down his tea towel, wiped his hands on his apron and smiled warmly. 'Good evening, sir. What can I get you?'

The man folded up his cloak and sat down on a stool at the far end of the bar. 'A pint of your finest, thank you,' he replied, his voice deep and hoarse.

'Certainly, sir.' Mr Goodwin started pouring the pint. 'So what brings you to our little village?' Charlie knew that visitors, however odd, were always welcome in his father's book — they were few and far between at this time of the year. The stranger looked over at Charlie and Max. 'Just passing through,' he said.

Charlie stared wild-eyed at Max. His face said it all. No one just passed through Hesper. There was nothing beyond Hesper — nothing but the moors.

Max leaned forward to Charlie. 'Is that the person we saw up at the house?'

'Don't know. But how many cloaked people do you think there are in Hesper?'

'What's he doing here?' asked Max.

'How do I know?' said Charlie. Perhaps he and Max had been spotted in the house after all, he wondered. Perhaps they had been followed. But why? He looked across at the stranger, but just as he did so the man turned around and their eyes met. Charlie shuddered. It felt as if the man were staring straight through him. Charlie looked away but he could still feel the stranger's eyes boring into him.

Emily marched in with two steaming plates of food and slammed them down in front of the boys. 'There you go. Tuck in,' she snapped before storming back out of the room.

Charlie sat in silence staring at the food on his plate, far too unnerved by the stranger's presence to think about eating. But his father didn't seem bothered at all. Leaning across the bar, he was happily chatting away to the stranger. 'So just passing through?' Mr Goodwin asked.

The man nodded. 'Yes, and I'll be grateful for a room if you have one?'

Mr Goodwin's face lit up at the prospect. 'Indeed we do, sir. How long might you be staying?'

'At least for the night, if that is not too much trouble.'

'No problem, sir. I'll just pop out and tell the wife so she can make up the bed.' Mr Goodwin rushed into the kitchen to relay the good news.

Charlie, appalled, leaned across to Max. 'He's going to stay here? In my house?'

Max grimaced. 'Looks like it. Not much we can do about it though, is there?'

A moment later Mr Goodwin came back in, beaming. 'That's all settled, sir. The wife's just preparing the room. Now would you like any supper?' He picked up a slightly-worn menu, quickly wiped it down with a cloth, and handed it to the stranger. 'I'd recommend the lamb, sir.'

The man briefly perused the menu then put it down. 'I shall look forward to that.'

'You're on holiday, is it?' Mr. Goodwin asked as he picked up another glass and began polishing it.

'Not really. Just here to visit someone, that's all.' The stranger let the words hang in the air.

Charlie felt his stomach tighten. What did the man mean by that? He pushed away his uneaten supper. 'Let's get upstairs Max — don't want to hang around here.'

Max agreed and they started clearing the table.

'We're going upstairs, Dad. See you in the morning,' said Charlie.

'Alright son,' his father replied, barely looking up.

'Thanks, Mr Goodwin,' said Max.

The boys hurried into the kitchen, scraping their plates into a bin before dumping them on the sideboard, and racing upstairs

Once in his room, Charlie closed the door firmly behind them.

Max sat down glumly on the spare bed. 'What's he doing here, Charlie?'

'Don't know.' Charlie started pacing up and down the room. 'But we'll have to find out — somehow.'

'Find out? How?' asked Max.

Charlie stopped pacing. 'We've got to, Max. That shadow was weird — and so was that cloaked figure. That man downstairs…he could be the same...' Charlie paused. 'And I didn't like the way he was looking at me.'

Max was about to say something when they heard a sound outside the room. Charlie put his finger to his lips and tiptoed over to the door. He listened for a moment before turning the handle and peeking out. His dad was walking down the corridor, the stranger following behind, his trunk on his back.

'It's just here at the end, sir. The wife's put fresh sheets on the bed. Got a lovely view of the square outside,' said Mr Goodwin as he opened the door.

The stranger paused outside. 'Is this the only guest room you have?'

'No, we've another one down there on the right. Looks out over the river but it's a bit small,' Mr Goodwin replied.

'And these?' The man motioned to the other rooms in the corridor.

Mr Goodwin pointed down the hall. 'They're the children's rooms.' He waved at the door across the hall. 'And the guest bath's just here. The wife and I are upstairs.'

The man nodded, as if satisfied with the arrangements.

'Supper will be ready when you are,' said Mr Goodwin.

'I'll be down in five minutes,' said the stranger, ushering him out of the room. Smiling politely, Mr Goodwin backed into the corridor. Charlie quickly closed his door. Moments later his father walked past and retreated downstairs.

'He's going down for supper,' whispered Charlie.

'So?' said Max.

'So while he's downstairs, we can start investigating.'

'Investigating what?' asked Max doubtfully.

'We could take a look in his trunk for starters. Did you see that thing?'

'But your Mum'll go mad if she finds out,' said Max.

Charlie ignored him and went back to listen at the door. He could hear the stranger walking down the corridor. A second later he heard the man stop right outside his room. Charlie's heart started thumping but he didn't dare move and kept his ear pressed close to the door. It seemed like ages before the stranger walked on. Finally Charlie heard the sound of footsteps going downstairs.

He turned round. 'He was listening.'

'What?' Max grew nervous. 'Maybe we should forget it then.'

'Forget it? We need to find out who he is and what he's doing here,' said Charlie.

He went to the door.

Max leapt to his feet. 'OK, OK, hold on there for a minute. When I said you should be adventurous I didn't mean you should go nosing in other people's stuff.'

'Listen, after everything we've seen today, Max, I think we have a right to know who he is. He could be that cloaked...'

'So you keep saying,' said Max.

'Then you'll come?'

Max sighed. 'Alright. You're going to need someone to watch your back anyway.'

Charlie grinned. 'Knew you wouldn't let me down.'

Slipping out of his room they crept down the corridor, Max looking over his shoulder all the way, fearful they might be caught. When they reached the stranger's door, Charlie opened it and they went inside.

The stranger's trunk was sitting squarely in the middle of the room. It was clearly very old and bound with thick leather straps fastened with a bronze padlock, which now hung loose. Sitting there in the middle of the room it reminded Charlie of the treasure chests he had seen pictured in his books.

'Look, it's unlocked,' Charlie said. He bent down and tried to lift the lid, but it was heavy. 'Come on, give us a hand.'

Max bent down and with a little effort they managed to heave it open. Charlie peered inside. He had half-expected to find it full of gold coins and jewels. But although there was no treasure — or anything that looked like treasure — the trunk was full of strange objects. There were lots of little wooden boxes and odd little instruments, as well as pieces of parchment and scrolls, all yellowed and worn, tucked down the sides or lying on top.

He and Max started searching through the contents. Max picked up one of the small boxes and opened the lid. There was a green jar inside with a cork in it. He took it out, unstopped the cork and smelt it. 'Urgh. That's awful. Here, smell this.' He thrust the jar in Charlie's face.

Charlie recoiled in disgust. 'That's revolting. What is it?'

Max looked at the jar but it didn't have a label. 'No idea.' He put it back and picked up another one, which he also uncorked and smelt. 'Hmm, this one smells like strawberries.'

'Yeah, well I doubt it is,' said Charlie.

Max was about to replace the cork when he spilled some of the contents onto his hand.

'What are you doing?' said Charlie.

'It just spilled. It's not my fault,' said Max.

'Well put it back and clean yourself up.'

'But it's all sticky,' said Max. He looked around for something to wipe it away with but there was nothing to hand so he licked it off instead. 'Tastes like strawberries too,' he added.

Charlie grabbed the jar and put it back in its box. 'We're just looking, not licking,' he said, returning the box to the trunk. 'You have to admit though, he's got some weird stuff in here,' he added, picking up a piece of parchment stuffed down the side of the trunk. 'I mean — it's like ancient...'

Then Charlie spotted something at the bottom of the trunk. It was catching the light. Reaching down he tried to take it out but it was stuck. Pushing some of the other stuff aside, he reached down again and pulled it out.

'Hey, he's got a sword,' Charlie said, waving it in the air.

Max looked at it, astonished. 'Why?'

Charlie had no idea. He started inspecting it. It was very shiny but so incredibly light it felt as if he were holding it and not holding it. It seemed to be made from some strange metal, and the hilt was studded with what looked like jewels, though he had no idea whether they were real or not. There was also an inscription running down one side of the blade, written in some strange language that Charlie couldn't understand.

He swung the sword through the air. 'Hey, maybe it's a prop, like the ones they use in theatres,' he said. 'Or maybe he sells antiques. I mean this stuff looks pretty old.'

Charlie went back to his search. Then he spotted something else. It was a small, bronze instrument tucked down the side of the trunk, half hidden by some of the scrolls.

He took it out. It had three dials that seemed to swivel in different directions and there was a thin, metal bar with a pointed end like a clock hand, which ran halfway across its centre. There were also symbols carved around the edges, but Charlie didn't recognise any of them.

He held it up to Max. 'What do you think this is?' he said.

Max eyed it briefly. 'No idea. But I think we should go. He could come back any minute.'

'OK, maybe you're right.' Charlie pushed the bronze instrument back down the side of the trunk and tried to rearrange everything the way they had found it. He shut the lid and turned to Max. 'After you,' he said.

Back in his own room Max plonked himself in the armchair again and Charlie sat down on his bed.

'So what do you think that stuff was, Max? Like that brass thing. What was that?'

'How should I know? But I don't like it — any of it. I mean, why's he got a sword, eh? And what about those green jars?'

'Maybe they're full of potions — or poisons,' said Charlie.

Max sat up sharply. 'POISONS?'

Charlie shrugged. 'I don't know. Could be.'

'But I spilled some on my hand.' Max sounded worried.

'Stop harping. You didn't drink it,' said Charlie.

'No, but I did lick it off,' said Max, his voice rising.

'I told you not to touch it.'

'You don't think it was poison, do you?' Max was growing more anxious by the second.

'No, otherwise you'd be feeling it by now, wouldn't you?'

'I guess. But I still don't like it. I mean, who is this man?'

'I don't know — but he's no ordinary stranger,' said Charlie.

'You can say that again.' Max sat up. 'Do you know, I think I'll just go back to the cottage,' he announced as he started putting on his boots.

'Why? You're supposed to stay here while your gran's away.'

'I just feel uncomfortable with that man here, that's all. Think I'd prefer to be there tonight.'

'You can't leave me alone,' said Charlie.

'Come with me. We can slip out through the side entrance,' said Max.

'What about my parents?'

'They think we've gone to bed,' said Max.

'And Emily?'

'She won't be bothering you again 'til morning.'

Max did have a point, Charlie thought. The stranger was weird and his trunk was full of strange stuff. And after everything else that had happened, he didn't relish sleeping under the same roof. 'OK, let's do that.'

Max seemed relieved. Hauling his suitcase onto his bed, he rummaged around for a jumper.

Charlie was about to put on a clean, dry pair of boots when he heard footsteps in the corridor and a door closing. The stranger was back in his room. Charlie wondered if he would notice they had gone through his trunk. If so, the sooner they were gone, the better. But now he was worried his parents might spot them leaving.

'What's the time?'

Max glanced at his watch. 'Just after ten.'

'Mum and Dad will be off to bed soon. They always close the bar early on a Monday. Let's at least wait until they've gone.'

'Maybe you're right,' said Max.

Charlie sat down on his bed, put on his boots and tied his shoelaces. Standing up he went to his chest of drawers and searched for a sweater.

Shortly afterwards they heard his parents coming upstairs to their own room on the next floor, and then their door closing.

'Right, let's go. But keep quiet,' said Charlie. 'Don't want Emily hearing us.'

The boys tiptoed out of the room and along the corridor, then crept down the backstairs and silently slipped outside.

LEAVING the inn behind, they crossed the square. It was empty and dark. The inn's welcoming lights were now turned off and the villagers no doubt tucked up for the night. Charlie was thankful for that at least. They turned into the lane that led to Max's cottage, half a mile away. Five minutes later they rounded a bend in the lane — and then stopped dead. For there, hovering right in front of them, blocking their path, and clearly visible in the moonlight, was The Shadow.

Seeing the boys, it raised itself up to a great height and hissed loudly. Then it fixed Charlie and Max with its cold, yellow eyes. Charlie felt himself instantly gripped in a trance. Paralysed.

Now frozen to the spot, Charlie could only watch as The Shadow swiftly began to transform right in front of them: from shadow to form. Twisting and writhing on the ground, it looked as if there were some frightful monster inside it, which was now trying to escape. And even though it was still more shadow than form, Charlie could just make out the shape of its heads. There were three of them. They looked like giant serpents.

Then came a sudden roar and a bright, blinding light appeared on the brow of the hill. A moment later a huge lorry thundered noisily down the narrow lane towards them. On seeing the boys, the driver hooted his horn loudly. The Shadow, startled by the light and noise, turned around and the trance was immediately broken.

Jolted to their senses, the boys realised what was happening and leapt into the grass verge just in the nick of time. Seconds later the truck smashed into the half-formed monster. Crushing it under its wheels and trapping it in its undercarriage, the truck dragged it past them and into the darkness, its frightful hisses drowned out by the roar of the lorry as it headed towards the village and the main road beyond.

Scrambling to their feet, the boys staggered back into the lane.

'WHAT WAS THAT?' screamed Max.

'No idea,' said Charlie as he looked back down the road, the lights from the lorry disappearing into the distance. 'But it's definitely no ghost, Max, that's for sure.'

'Told you it was a monster,' said Max as he too stared down the lane towards the village. 'Do you think it's dead?' he added.

'Must be. It was crushed under the wheels. What could survive that?' said Charlie.

'But that truck? Where did that come from?'

The lane stopped at Dead Man's End, it went nowhere except the entrance to Hesper House and the moors beyond. 'Must have got lost and thought it was a short-cut or something,' said Charlie. 'Lucky it did though — it saved us.'

'Yeah, and that thing's probably dead now,' added Max.

But whether it was or not Charlie knew they had to get away. For a moment he had half-a-mind to head back to the inn but then, remembering the stranger, he dismissed the idea. If that creature had anything to do with him, there was no way he was going to sleep under the same roof.

'Come on, let's get to your cottage. We'll be safe there. It's not far.'

They hurried on, quickly covering the hundred yards or so to his home. Max opened the door, switching on the lamp as he entered. Charlie followed him inside.

Charlie rarely visited Max's cottage but he remembered the

sitting room as small and cosy. The walls were covered with pictures and there were lots of little china ornaments dotted about on side tables. A two-seater sofa sat in the middle of the room behind a small, antique coffee table. At the back of the room was the door to the kitchen.

Max walked through and Charlie followed.

The kitchen was about the same size as the sitting room. There was an old cooker, a large sink and sideboard, a solitary cupboard attached to one wall and a pine dresser, with cups hanging on it. In the middle of the room was a wooden table and four chairs.

Max went over to the sink. 'Tea?'

'Thanks,' said Charlie. He sat down at the table. His knees were shaking.

Max picked up the kettle and went to fill it. Then he stopped and turned to Charlie. 'But how could it have changed shape like that,' he said, his voice wavering. 'How could it do that?'

'I don't know, Max. But I'm starting to wish it was a ghost.'

'Yeah, well I don't like ghosts,' said Max as he started filling the kettle with water. 'Or monsters for that matter,' he added quietly.

'It must have something to do with Hesper House. That's where it came from,' said Charlie. They should never have gone there, he told himself. Perhaps they had disturbed something — something evil. Perhaps that was why it was forbidden to go there.

Charlie got up and went to the window to check that it was locked. He peered out briefly before closing the shutter. 'At least that man doesn't know where you live,' he said.

'Yeah, good thing too,' Max said.

While Charlie searched the cupboard for a tin of biscuits, Max finished making the tea and put the pot on the table. 'No milk, I'm afraid,' he said.

'That's OK,' said Charlie. 'Sugar?'

Max fetched the sugar and they sat down. Max poured them

both a cup of tea and Charlie handed him a biscuit. They sat for a while drinking in silence.

Charlie was the first to speak. 'At least it's gone,' he said, trying to sound positive. 'Can't have survived that lorry. Must have dragged it for miles by now. Glad he didn't stop. He can't have seen it in the dark because it was black.'

'Yeah, it's dead for sure.' Max replied, but he still sounded scared.

A second later they heard a noise at the kitchen door. They both stiffened. Charlie got up from the table, tiptoed across to the back window and peered out. Then he stepped back in horror. The stranger, his cloak hung low, was standing right outside. Charlie went to lock the door, but the key wasn't there.

'Come and help me bar the door,' he screamed at Max. 'It's the stranger. He followed us.'

'What?' said Max and leaping forward, he grabbed a chair and they wedged it under the knob.

'Let's get into the sitting room. We can go out the front,' shouted Charlie. It was his only thought now — to run.

But as he raced into the sitting room, closely followed by Max, he knew they were too late. For there, creeping under the door and seeping across the floor towards them, was The Shadow. It was not dead — and it had found them. They were trapped.

Then Charlie heard the sound of glass breaking in the kitchen and moments later the stranger burst into the sitting room. But as he did so he too stopped in his tracks, The Shadow now transforming into solid shape.

Before Charlie could cry out, the stranger leapt forward and pulled him back, shouting, 'GET IN THE KITCHEN.'

With Charlie already in his grip, the man grabbed Max by the arm and dragged him through the door just as The Shadow lunged forward. Stumbling into the kitchen, he let go of the boys.

Charlie turned and slammed the door shut behind them. Looking around he spotted the pine dresser. He tried to push it across the door but it was so heavy it wouldn't budge it all. 'HELP,' he called out.

Leaping forward Max put his shoulder against it and with one mighty push, tipped it over, the cups smashing all over the floor as he did so.

Charlie was astonished. The chest weighed a ton. But there was no time to wonder how Max had done it. 'Let's run for it,' he cried. He turned towards the back door — only to find the stranger standing in front of it, blocking their exit. '*We have to get out,*' Charlie shouted.

The stranger shook his head. 'It's too late for that, I'm afraid. You can't outrun the Dark One,' he announced calmly.

'What?' screamed Charlie.

'We'll have to escape another way.'

Charlie looked at him blankly. 'Escape?'

'Yes, so come here.'

The stranger reached into his cloak pocket and took something out. Charlie recognised it at once: the brass instrument he had spotted earlier in the man's trunk. The stranger began fiddling with the dials.

A moment later, they heard an almighty crash as the creature, now fully transformed, hurled itself at the barricaded door. The boys screamed and backed away.

The stranger held up the instrument and wrapped his cloak around him. 'There — all done,' he said. Then he looked up. 'I said — *COME HERE NOW,*' he ordered. 'It's our only chance of escape.'

Charlie was utterly bewildered. 'But how?'

Before the stranger could answer, the doorframe, and most of the wall, crumbled into pieces. Terrified, Charlie and Max staggered back towards the man — convinced they were doomed. There was a bright flashing light and Charlie felt a strange pulling sensation. Then everything went black.

4. FAR FROM HOME

CHARLIE felt himself spinning downwards. He dimly remembered flashing blue and white lights and a dull whirring sound. Then it all went black again.

He came to slowly and immediately wished he hadn't. His whole body ached mercilessly. He felt as if he had been hit by a truck. He tried to open his eyes but was blinded by a bright light. As his senses slowly returned he realised he was lying down on something soft. It felt like grass. Then the memories came flooding back. He sat bolt upright, wincing as he did so, and looked around for the monster. But there was no sign of it. There was also no sign of the cottage.

He glanced around. He was in a meadow, sandwiched between a cliff top and a small wood situated a few hundred yards away. The grass was brown and dry, which was odd because it had been raining for days in Hesper.

What's more, it was broad daylight. The sun was shining, the sky was blue and there was not a cloud in sight. It was also hot, as if it were the middle of summer. Charlie could feel the warm air gently lapping at his face and birds were singing in the distance. But he had no idea where he was, or how he had got there.

He heard Max shout his name.

'I'm HERE,' he shouted back. He tried to get up but he felt sick and dizzy and he had to take a few deep breaths to steady himself. Slowly straightening he scanned the meadow. Max was about twenty yards away, sitting up, rubbing his head.

Charlie ran over. 'Are you OK?'

'Think so.' But as Max got to his feet, the memories flooded back. 'Where's that monster?' He spun around.

'Don't worry,' said Charlie. 'It's not here.'

Max looked around confused. 'Where are we, Charlie?'

'Don't know.'

'And how did we get here?' asked Max.

'We must have blacked out. That man must have brought us here.'

'But how?' said Max. 'And where is he then?'

Max had a point but Charlie knew that wasn't the only one. He glanced up at the sun. 'What time is it?'

Max looked at his watch. 'Just after eleven...' Frowning, he tapped the glass and held it up to his ear. 'It's stopped.' He seemed surprised. 'That's weird. My watch never stops, even that time when I fell in the river.'

'Yeah, well I'd say it's more like eight, maybe nine. We must have blacked out for hours,' said Charlie.

'But that's breakfast time. Your Mum'll go crazy when we don't appear.'

'I think we have bigger problems than that, Max.'

'You're right,' Max said. 'So how do we get home?'

'No idea. But we need to find that man. He got us here, didn't he? Come on, let's go over there.' Charlie motioned towards the cliff.

They walked across and peered over the edge. Down below was a small cove. The sea was a deep blue, like a sapphire, and there was a white sand beach, the waves gently lapping at its shore. Above, on a small sand bank, a solitary goat was grazing on the long grass. But other than that, there was no sign of life.

'Where on earth are we?' said Max.

Charlie stared down at the sparkling sea. 'I don't know, but we're a long way from Hesper, that's for sure.'

Max pointed to the cove below. 'I can see that. But what are we going to do?'

'We just need to get back to the village, that's all,' said Charlie.

'Yeah, but how?' asked Max.

Charlie, squinting in the sunlight, looked around for any sign of a house or cottage, but there was none. Yet there had to be someone somewhere. 'Must be a village or town nearby. We can ask for help there,' he said. Fumbling in his pocket he brought out a few coins.

Max brightened. 'Hey, we could find a phone and call your dad. He could come fetch us. Barry'll lend him his car.'

'What, the mechanic?'

'Yeah, we can't be that far away, can we?' said Max.

Charlie didn't want to say so, but he had a feeling that they were very far away indeed.

'Well there's no way we can walk along the coast. It's far too treacherous,' he said. There was no path along the cliff, and on either side there were rock-strewn gullies barring their way. 'We'll have to head inland through that wood over there.' Charlie pointed across the meadow to the long line of trees which stretched on either side as far as the eye could see.

'So do you think we were unconscious?' asked Max as they set off towards the wood.

'We must have been, otherwise we'd have remembered getting here,' said Charlie.

'And what about that monster? Explain that,' said Max, his voice rising sharply.

'How exactly? I'm as clueless as you are.' Charlie stopped for a moment. 'I've never been so terrified. I thought it was going to kill us.'

'So did I,' said Max.

'Wish we hadn't gone to Hesper House now, that's for sure. No wonder it's forbidden,' Charlie added.

'But why did it come after us?' asked Max.

Charlie didn't know. But first things first, he told himself, they had to find out where they were, and how they were going to get home. And for that they needed to track down the stranger.

As they neared the wood, Charlie found himself struggling to keep up.

'Hold on, Max. What's got into you?' he said.

Max slowed down. 'Sorry, hadn't noticed. It's just that I feel so much fitter. Don't know why.'

They walked on, Max now keeping pace with Charlie.

'Still don't understand how we got here,' said Max.

Charlie had a vague memory of spinning but he couldn't make any sense of it. 'That man must have brought us by car,' he guessed.

'So where is he then — and where's the car?' Max looked around. 'I don't see any roads nearby.'

Max was right. There was no sign of civilisation anywhere. Even so, they must have come with the stranger, Charlie decided. So he had to be about — somewhere. 'Let's just find that man. He must know what's going on.' Charlie pointed to the wood. 'Maybe we'll find him in there.'

At that moment a figure emerged from the trees. There was no mistaking who it was, his long, dark hair was blowing in the wind, his cloak billowing behind him — it was the stranger. The boys stopped abruptly, suddenly unsure whether this man was friend or foe.

He waved as he approached them. 'Ah, you're awake, finally. Thought I would leave you to recover for a while. First time's always difficult for you people. I was just finding my bearings.'

Charlie, strangely relieved to see the man, looked at him blankly. 'What do you mean — first time?'

The stranger ignored the question and tapped the little bronze instrument in his hand. 'And we seem to have landed in the wrong place. Awfully annoying. But then we were in a hurry.'

'Landed?' said Charlie.

The stranger ignored him again.

Max slowly started backing away. 'What's he talking about, Charlie?'

'How should I know? But we're going to find out.' Charlie turned and addressed the stranger in his most defiant tone. 'We want to know what's going on — now.'

The stranger put the instrument back in his pocket. 'Of course you do. You must find all this very alarming.'

'You can say that again,' said Max.

The stranger started scanning the cloudless blue sky above, as if looking for something. Then gathering his robes about him, he turned and headed back towards the wood, shouting over his shoulder as he went. 'Now do hurry up, we have a long walk ahead of us.'

'A long walk where?' Charlie shouted after him but the stranger didn't answer.

'I don't like this, Charlie. I've got a funny feeling about it,' said Max.

'Me too, but we don't have much choice. We have to stick close to this man. He brought us here — wherever here is. Which means he's our only hope of getting home.'

'Some hope,' Max replied glumly.

Charlie smiled and slapped him on the back. 'Let's just look at it as an adventure, shall we?' he said as he set off after the man, now standing at the edge of the wood waiting for them.

'Adventure? Oh, that's rich. Throw that one in my face, why don't you,' Max called after him. Then reluctantly he followed.

As soon as they entered the wood Charlie grew uneasy. He could feel his skin tingle. It was as if there were a small electric current coursing through the air. Hesper Wood had been eerie enough but this wood was far stranger than that.

Below them the ground was covered with a blanket of blue flowers, dancing in the breeze, their aroma so strong it made him feel light-headed. The trees, most of which he didn't recognise, were of all shapes and sizes. He could also hear more birds, their strange song drifting on the wind, like music playing in the distance. It was all so exotic and yet strangely sinister at the same time.

Max looked around warily. 'What *is* this place, Charlie?'

'Search me.'

'Maybe we should go back to the meadow. I don't like this. There is something very wrong here.'

Charlie knew what Max meant. The wood seemed so alive — almost too alive. But going back was out of the question. 'I'm sure it's OK,' he said, trying to reassure him.

'What's OK exactly? The fact that we were attacked by some monster or that we suddenly find ourselves in this weird wood following some strange man, dressed in a cloak,' said Max.

'Point taken. But come on, it's not that bad, is it? At least we found the stranger. And we've got to face it — he did save us last night.'

Charlie looked at the man walking ahead of them. He was muttering loudly to himself and peering at his instrument. There was an absent-minded air about him. Maybe Max was right, thought Charlie. They had no idea where they were, where they were going, or who they were following.

Even so, he realised that they had no choice but to follow, so they continued along the winding path, keeping the man in sight up ahead. A hundred yards further on Charlie grew uneasy again — he sensed that they were being watched.

He tried to convince himself that it was just his imagination. Yet as he walked on he was certain that he could see faces appearing in some of the trees, though every time he turned to look, they vanished.

'Have you noticed anything odd about the trees, Max?'

'No. Why? Is something wrong?' said Max, peering warily into the thicket.

'Just keep walking and then look out of the corner of your eye,' said Charlie.

Max did as he asked. A moment later he pointed to one

of the trees. 'I think I just saw a face — in...in the bark,' he stammered.

'Me too. Not in every tree but just a few, now and again,' said Charlie.

Max started turning slowly in circles. 'Where are we, Charlie? This doesn't feel right. It's just not…'

'Natural?'

'Exactly,' said Max.

Charlie and Max had become so distracted by the trees that Charlie hadn't realised that they had fallen right back. With the path meandering through the wood the stranger was now out of sight. What was more, the trees seemed to have closed in and the wood had grown gloomy. Charlie shivered. It didn't augur well.

'Come on, we need to catch up with that man. Can't lose sight of him,' he said.

'Right behind you,' Max said, glancing round nervously.

Charlie led the way, eager to catch up with the stranger. Moments later he heard a strange shuffling sound. He turned around, his eyes widening in shock. For the trees appeared to be moving. Not just blowing in the wind, but actually moving forward — as if they were following them.

Charlie grabbed Max's arm. 'Hurry,' he whispered.

They quickened their pace. The shuffling grew louder. Charlie wondered whether it was just his mind playing tricks on him. It was very hot after all and he was thirsty. Perhaps he was hallucinating, he told himself. He hoped so.

Then he felt something touch his leg. Looking down he spotted a gnarly root slowly curling round his ankle. Horrified, he tried to pull his foot free but the root tightened and a second later he was jerked off his feet. The next thing he knew he was screaming as he felt himself being dragged along the ground towards the trees.

He heard Max shout his name and felt him grab his foot. He stopped moving. But now more roots started encircling his body and within seconds he was wrapped like a cocoon. Then the roots started pulling him towards the tree-line as Max, shouting all the while, pulled him back the other way. It was like being in a tug-of-war.

'Don't worry, Charlie, I won't let go,' screamed Max. Charlie, unable to see for all the dirt and leaves, could feel Max desperately struggling to keep hold of him. He felt as if he might be torn in two.

The branches of the trees now leaned down and began whipping at him, slapping his face and arms, stinging them. Charlie couldn't even put his arms up to protect his face, he was so tightly wrapped. He heard Max scream in terror. The trees were attacking him too. But as Max frantically tried to beat them off his grip loosened and he let go of Charlie's foot.

A cold dread engulfed Charlie as the roots started dragging him down. He wriggled desperately to try to free himself but it was no use. An instant later he disappeared into the ground and the soil started filling his mouth. He dimly heard a distant shout, and then, just as he had given up all hope, he felt the roots unfurl from his body and the ground spat him out.

Charlie landed back on the path with a bump. He sat up, coughing and spluttering, spitting leaves and soil out of his mouth, gasping for air.

Wiping dirt from his eyes he saw the stranger standing on the path, his arms outstretched, shouting.

Charlie couldn't understand what he was saying. It was no language he had ever heard before. Yet whatever it was, it seemed to be working because the line of trees began shuffling backwards, their branches bowed in submission, as the stranger's voice boomed through the wood.

Max rushed over, desperation on his face. 'Are you OK?'

Charlie coughed again. 'Think so.'

He shook his head, dislodging more twigs and leaves, and tried to get up. Max helped him to his feet. He stood weaving for a moment or two, still choking and gasping for air.

Straightening, he looked back at the trees, now stood silent and still, as if nothing had happened.

The stranger came over and briefly inspected Charlie. 'Hmm, no harm done. You'll live,' he said, patting him casually on the back.

He turned back to the trees and shouted something else. His voice echoed off the trunks and a strange murmur rippled through the wood, the trees now bowing so much they looked almost apologetic.

'What's going on?' said Charlie, spitting out more soil.

The stranger waved his arm dismissively. 'Don't worry. They'll behave themselves now, mark my words,' he said, wagging his finger.

'Behave themselves? But they're just trees. What on earth's going on?' Charlie looked around the wood. 'And where are we?' He turned to the stranger. 'And who are you?' he added, his voice trembling.

'Ah.' The stranger sighed heavily. 'I suppose I am going to have to explain,' he said, stroking his chin. 'But we'll walk and talk, if you don't mind. We do have a long way to go.'

He beckoned the boys forward. Charlie held Max back. Brushing the remaining leaves off his jumper he stood his ground. 'I'm sorry — but we're not going anywhere until you tell us what's going on.'

'Yeah, and what was that?' Max added, pointing at the trees.

The stranger looked up at the sky. 'Typical. This is what happens when you have to deal with mortals. Always want explanations,' he muttered as if to himself.

'Mortals?' Charlie and Max both said at once.

The stranger ignored them. 'I'm afraid when the Dark One started transforming, I had to act quickly,' he said.

'Dark One?' said Charlie.

'Yes, the monster which attacked you in your cottage, remember? I'm sure I mentioned it at the time.' The stranger's voice grew quiet. 'That's why we had to escape here. It was the only way to save you.'

'Escape? Here? But where is here?' Charlie was starting to dread the answer.

'Ah, I shall explain that later.' The stranger pointed ahead. 'For now we must hurry. You see I had meant to deliver us right outside the forge.'

'What's a forge?' asked Max.

'Like a blacksmith's. You know where they make horseshoes and stuff,' said Charlie.

'Why are we going to a forge?' Max was confused.

The stranger didn't explain and set off once more at a brisk pace, shouting over his shoulder. 'It's really not that far. A few hours' walk, a day maybe — no more.'

'A DAY?' shouted Max. 'How far from home are we?'

He was about to rush off after the man but Charlie stopped him. None of it added up. Even if they had been unconscious, they certainly hadn't been out for eight hours or so. And there was the searing heat to consider. After all, it was October in England – it couldn't be that hot.

'BUT WHERE EXACTLY ARE WE?' Charlie shouted after the man.

The stranger stopped and sighed in exasperation. 'Very well, if you insist.' He walked back to the boys. 'Although I rather think I should introduce myself first.'

He held out his hand. 'My name is Parseus.'

Parseus? It sounded foreign and yet the man spoke perfect English. 'But who are you — that's what we want to know?' said Charlie.

'That's simple. I am a Time God,' the stranger replied nonchalantly.

The boys reeled back. 'Time God? What do you mean, Time God?' Charlie stared at him as if he were mad.

Parseus paused, as if not entirely understanding the question. 'It means exactly what it says, Charlie Goodwin. I am a Time

God. I can travel through time.' He patted the instrument in his cloak pocket. 'That is why we were able to escape the Dark One. We travelled back in time.'

Stunned, it took the boys a minute or so to find their voices again.

'Travelled back in...That's...' Charlie looked around in disbelief. 'I don't understand. *Where are we?*

Parseus peered down at him. 'The answer is very simple.' He swept his arm around the now silent wood. 'We're in the Ancient World.'

5. ANYTHING IS POSSIBLE

CHARLIE's jaw dropped. Time God? Ancient World? He had heard what the stranger had said — this Parseus as he called himself — but his brain didn't seem to be able to process the information. Maybe he had misheard him.

'What did you just say?' asked Charlie.

'We've travelled back in time,' said Parseus. He reached into his pocket, took out the bronze instrument and waved it in the air. 'See this? It is a Time Compass. It opens portals. They're…'

Charlie interrupted. 'Hang on a minute. Let's just backtrack a little here. You say we've travelled back in time?'

'Oh yes,' replied Parseus.

'But th...that's ridiculous,' stammered Max.

'Not if you have a Time Compass it isn't,' said Parseus.

'What? Rubbish. Where are we?' said Max.

Parseus leaned forward. 'I told you. We're in the Ancient World.'

'How far is that from Hesper?' asked Max, clearly unable to make sense of it.

'Not as far as you'd think,' Parseus replied.

Charlie was bemused. 'But you said we've travelled through time.'

'Yes, using this.' Parseus held up his compass for the boys to see. He didn't seem to understand their disbelief.

Charlie shook his head. 'But that's impossible.'

'Actually, it's not. I have already told you, we travelled through a portal. It's really quite easy,' said Parseus.

'What's a portal?' asked Max.

'They're tunnels through time and space. We are now in the past — or rather a past dimension that is.' Parseus showed the boys the compass once more, pointing out the three dials on which he had plotted the co-ordinates. 'It was made by Hephaistos, he's very clever.'

'Who?' asked Max blankly.

'Hephaistos?' Charlie thought about it for a moment and then remembered the name. 'You're not talking about the Inventor God are you?'

'Indeed, the very same,' replied Parseus, nodding approvingly. 'At least I see you have some knowledge of this world.'

'Inventor what? How do you know that?' Max was confused.

'My Greek mythology book, I guess,' said Charlie. 'But I thought they were just stories — you know, myths. I mean, Gods don't really exist.'

'I can most certainly assure you, that they do,' said Parseus. He seemed almost offended that Charlie could doubt it.

Charlie began surveying the wood, as if searching for proof. Wherever they were, it was nothing like their own world. 'So we're in the past?' Even as he said it he could hardly believe it.

'In the Ancient World — yes. But we haven't just travelled back in time. We've also travelled to a different dimension. Think of it as another world, if you will.'

'Another world?' Max's voice rose sharply. 'OK, let's rein in the ponies here: Gods? Time travel? Another world? Do you think we're stupid? It's impossible.' He crossed his arms.

'I'm afraid you're quite wrong.' Parseus shook his head. 'Quite wrong. Anything is possible,' he said, waving his arm around. 'And can there be any other explanation? You are, after all, no longer in your cottage, and this is most definitely not Hesper.'

Charlie could hardly argue with that. 'But how do we get back there?'

Parseus smiled. 'Don't worry. You'll get home eventually. A few days, perhaps, but no more I would think.'

'A few days? We are not even allowed out after dark. My parents are going to come looking for us,' said Charlie.

'No, they won't,' said Parseus.

'Why not?' Charlie was worried that they might already have found him missing. His Mum would be furious.

'Because we'll return to Hesper at the exact time and place that we left. They won't even know you've been away.'

'How come?' Charlie knew that this strange man was their only chance of getting home, but he couldn't understand what he was telling them. 'And *how* do we get back to Hesper?'

'We'll use the compass. It got us here, didn't it? And it'll get us back. We shall only be here for a day or so,' replied Parseus, seemingly satisfied he had explained himself. 'And as I said, when we do return it will be to the very moment we left.'

'Why the very moment?' Charlie asked again.

'Because, Charlie Goodwin, humans are not permitted to time-travel in their own world. It would interfere far too much. There are time paradoxes to consider,' said Parseus.

'Time paradoxes?' Max sounded baffled.

'Yes. Have either of you heard of the Grandfather Paradox?'

Charlie and Max shook their heads.

'Let's say you went back in time in your own world and killed your grandfather, then that would prevent your own birth, which would mean that...'

Charlie interrupted. 'That you would never be born, and therefore couldn't go back in time to murder him?'

'Exactly. That's why only Time Gods can travel in time. We don't live in your world you see, so we're not a part of it,' replied Parseus. 'Though I go there quite often, as it happens.'

'Doing what?' asked Charlie.

'Fixing the past,' said Parseus.

'Fixing the past?' Max was more confused than ever. 'Like how?'

'Sometimes things don't go the way they're planned, that's all. And they have to be fixed.' He frowned. 'Everyone makes mistakes you know.'

'Fixed? I don't get it,' said Charlie.

'There is destiny to consider you know and when things don't work out as they should, it's my job to come back and put things right.' Parseus pointed ahead. 'Now we really must press on.'

Charlie wasn't ready to move. He had too many questions. 'But where are we going? And why do we have to be here for a few days? Why can't we go back to Hesper now?'

'You just can't — not yet, anyway.' A troubled look crossed Parseus' face. 'We need to find something first. Then you can go, but not until then. Trust me.'

Charlie, however, was not in a trusting mood. 'How do we know that you're telling the truth? How do we know this compass will work?'

He was trying to goad Parseus into proving it there and then. If they could just get back to Hesper, everything would be OK.

'Yeah, sounds like mumbo jumbo to me.' Max added. 'Time Travel? As if.'

But Parseus was not to be challenged. 'I'm afraid we cannot go back yet. The monster, remember? The one that crashed through your wall. The Dark One. It will be waiting for you.'

Charlie felt a cold chill run through him. He had almost forgotten about the monster. Being reminded of it, he didn't need any further convincing. He certainly didn't want to find himself facing that again. Yet the thought that they were in another world, somewhere in the ancient past, was almost as frightening.

'So why was this monster — this Dark One —after us?' he asked. 'Was it because we went into the grounds?' Charlie wondered whether they might have disturbed it. Perhaps they had been seen in the house. Perhaps it was their fault.

'Grounds?' said Parseus.

'Of Hesper House. That's where we first saw it,' said Charlie. 'There was a cloaked figure there too. We thought it might have been you but then...'

'Wasn't me,' said Parseus. 'A cloaked figure you say?'

'Probably the witch,' said Max.

'What witch?' asked Parseus curiously.

'Mrs Payne. They say she's the Gatekeeper of Hesper House,' said Charlie.

'Ah, I see.' Parseus walked on, but Charlie could tell from the look on his face that he knew something about her.

'Anyway we have to find something before we go back and I have a feeling Hephaistos might be able to help,' said Parseus.

Charlie was not reassured though he realised they had little choice but to trust Parseus. After all, he had saved them from the monster and the trees. Watching him disappear round a bend, he was keenly reminded of that threat. The sound of shuffling grew louder and the trees started crowding in around them once again, the faces fading in and out of the bark. They did not appear friendly.

'Max, I think we should stick as close to this strange Time God as possible.'

'Good idea,' Max said as the trees shuffled forward.

So without another word the boys hurried after Parseus. Charlie, for one, still had a million-and-one questions.

'I still don't understand this place? I mean why do the trees move? And why can we see faces in the bark?' asked Charlie, catching up with him.

Parseus frowned. 'I see I'm going to have to explain again. But I'll be brief if you don't mind.' He continued walking. 'As I said, we're in another world and it doesn't work the same way as yours.'

'Yes, I can see that — but why?' asked Charlie.

'Your world doesn't have Gods, for instance. I mean they don't walk in your world as they do in this one.' Parseus glanced down at the boys trudging beside him. 'You've heard of the Gods, of course?'

'You mean the Greek Gods?' asked Charlie.

'Yes, but they're everyone's Gods in truth, though I'm not one of the Olympian Gods. I'm just a minor God, I'm afraid.'

Charlie was still struggling with it all. 'Let me get this straight. You're telling us that we are in another world, in the past, which is inhabited by Gods?'

'Not exactly inhabited, Charlie. Most of them live in the immortal realm — it's another dimension to this one. But they mix freely with humans and they're always popping in and out. The entrance to the immortal realm lies in these parts, you see, on Mount Olympos.'

Charlie had heard of Mount Olympos. He remembered reading about it once in one of his books. 'But that's in Greece, isn't it? And you said we were in another world.'

'We are. But it's a parallel world. Th e Ancient World. Everything's the same — except that it's not. Your world doesn't have any magic for example,' explained Parseus.

'Magic?' said Charlie.

'Yes, this world is full of it.' Parseus took a deep breath. 'Can't you feel it?'

Charlie, remembering how he felt when he entered the wood, was in no doubt about that — though Max would have none of it.

'Magic?' he muttered, shaking his head. 'That's ridiculous if you ask me.'

Parseus ignored him and strode off once more, beckoning the boys to follow. 'Now do come along. We can't hang about here.'

The boys, so incredulous at everything that they had been told, trailed silently after him. It was Max who eventually broke the silence.

'What's with all these Gods? Do you believe him?'

'Not sure, Max. But what other explanation is there that

wouldn't be just as bizarre?' said Charlie. 'Anyway I guess we'll find out one way or another soon enough.'

'And what was that strange language he was speaking?'

'Don't know. Greek maybe?'

Parseus overheard them and stopped. 'Ah, almost forgot.' He fumbled in his cloak pocket and brought out a small silver tin. 'You'll need these while you're here. It's just easier.'

He opened the tin and took out a tiny bug. It wriggled between his fingers. He held it up. 'This is a translation bug. They're very useful little creatures. Enable you to understand and speak any language spoken. They really will help while you're here. You just pop it in your ear.'

Parseus handed one to Charlie. He looked at it. 'Translation bug? You've got to be kidding.'

'No, I'm not,' said Parseus.

Charlie inspected the tiny bug. 'It looks like an earwig.'

'Perhaps, but it isn't,' said Parseus.

Charlie held up the bug to Max. 'What do you think?'

Max backed away. 'I'm not putting no bug in my ear.'

Charlie looked at it again. Understand and speak any language spoken? It was a tempting thought.

Parseus grew impatient. 'Come along. Put it in.'

Charlie shrugged. After everything else that had happened, what harm could it do? So he stuffed it into his ear. He could feel it wriggling its way into his ear drum. It tickled but it didn't hurt. He shook his head a couple of times and looked up. 'That wasn't too bad — can't feel a thing now.'

Then Parseus said something to him. Charlie realised it was in a different language, but he understood it perfectly, and when he replied he found himself doing so in the same language. It was astonishing.

Max looked at him in disbelief. 'What were you saying, Charlie? Couldn't understand a word.'

Parseus took out one more bug. 'Just put this in your ear, Max Harper and you would soon know what he was saying.'

'Come on, Max,' said Charlie, now speaking English again. 'After all, being able to speak any language is pretty cool.'

Max gave in. 'OK. Just don't let me see you do it.'

He stood still, his face screwed up in disgust as Charlie stuffed the bug into his ear. He shuddered a little and shook his head.

'See, that didn't hurt, did it?' said Parseus.

'Guess so,' admitted Max.

Parseus put the tin back in his cloak pocket and walked on. Charlie caught up with him. 'You still haven't explained why that monster was after us?'

'Haven't I? Oh, that's simple. It's an assassin,' said Parseus.

'ASSASSIN?' said Charlie.

'Indeed. You see there's been a prophecy.'

'What?' said Charlie.

'And there's going to be a war,' Parseus added.

'Huh?' both boys said at once. 'What war?' asked Charlie.

Parseus sighed again. He seemed frustrated. 'I'll try to explain as we walk.'

'Thanks, that would be nice,' said Max.

'You see many, many eons ago, there was a great war between the Titans and the Gods,' said Parseus

'Titans?' said Max.

'I think they ruled the universe before the Gods did,' replied Charlie.

'Indeed Charlie. But the Gods defeated them and imprisoned them in Tartaros.'

'Tartaros?' said Charlie.

'The hell realm,' explained Parseus.

'The what?' said Max.

'Don't worry, Max. It's another dimension. An anvil would have to fall for nine days and nine nights before it could reach Tartaros,' said Parseus. 'The point, however, is that The Prophecy has foretold that the Titans will rise up and wage another war against the Gods.'

'But what's that got to do with us?' asked Charlie.

'Because it's your fault, Charlie,' said Parseus. 'Not yours specifically, of course,' he added. 'I mean it is the fault of all you humans.'

'But why?'

'Why? Because you've damaged your planet with all your pollution and your waste. You have poisoned it. And worst of all, you have damaged the very foundations of Tartaros. You have weakened them. Now the Titans might soon be able to escape. If they do —' Parseus' voice fell to a whisper — 'the war will be waged in your world.'

'Why?' asked Charlie again.

'Because your dimension — your world if you like — sits between the immortal realm and Tartaros. They are all linked.'

'So we're stuck between heaven and hell,' said Charlie.

'Yes. And a war won't be pretty. Take my word for it. The last time these two foes met, the earth burned for ten years,' said Parseus.

'Great. We're going to get barbecued,' groaned Max.

'But where do we fit in?' pressed Charlie.

'That's simple. The Prophecy has foretold that there is a hope of salvation. That's why the Titans sent the Dark One.'

'The assassin?' said Charlie.

'Yes, it is an Ancient, a creature that pre-dates even the Gods themselves. It comes from the depths of Tartaros and it can be both shadow and form. Worst of all, it's virtually indestructible.'

'Indestructible?' said Max. 'That doesn't sound good.'

'And what is this hope of salvation?' said Charlie.

'A Destined One. Someone who might be able to defeat the threat and save the universe — a saviour,' said Parseus.

'And who's that?' asked Charlie innocently.

'You,' Parseus replied casually.

'ME?' Charlie choked.

'Charlie?' snorted Max. 'You must be kidding.'

'No I am not. It was seen in the Font of all Knowledge. It holds all the secrets of the universe. Unfortunately not long after you were spotted, the Dark One arrived. So I had to come to your world immediately. It was all a bit rushed.'

'Font of all...' Charlie shook his head. 'But why me?' He was aghast.

'I don't know. The Fates would not reveal that.'

'The Fates?'

'They control the destinies of men, Charlie — decide them for the most part. It is they who handed down the Prophecy – though they do not control prophecies, you understand. But what we do know is that you are the Destined One — whatever the reason for that — and I am here to help you fulfil that destiny.' Parseus paused. 'If that's at all possible, of course,' he muttered.

Parseus seemed satisfied that he had explained himself but Charlie had just one more question. 'But if all that's true, then this Dark One has been sent to...'

'Kill you? Yes,' said Parseus.

6. DESTINY UNFOLDS

CHARLIE felt his stomach drop. After everything else, this last piece of news was the most frightening of all. The Dark One had been sent to kill him.

'But why me? And what am I destined to do?' he whispered breathlessly.

'Save the universe, of course.' Parseus paused. 'Though I have no idea how — yet.'

'Save the...the universe?' Charlie was wide-eyed in shock. 'But I — I'm just a boy.'

'That really isn't the point, Charlie.'

'But how?'

'I'm sure that will become clear in good time,' said Parseus. 'First though we must find something to protect you from the Dark One or you won't be saving anyone.'

Charlie was speechless.

Parseus walked on.

'That's just ridiculous,' said Max. 'Save the universe? It's madness.'

Charlie agreed. It was madness. Yet everything that had happened to them since they had wandered into Hesper House had been madness.

He hurried after Parseus. 'This prophecy — what else does it say?' he asked.

'Not much at the moment, I'm afraid. Prophecies tend to be vague. Some of them come in waves — though this one seems clear enough, at least so far as you're concerned.'

'What do you mean, as far as I'm concerned?'

'I told you, the Titans are going to rise up against the Gods and you, Charlie, are destined to stop them.'

Charlie stiffened. 'Me?' He couldn't get his head round it. 'And exactly how am I supposed to do that?'

'Not sure yet. But that, Charlie, is why I was given this compass. It wasn't just to let us escape — though that proved useful enough. No, there are answers here and this compass was specially designed to enable us to come here to search for a way of defeating the Titans. Otherwise we wouldn't be here at all. You see, this world has been off-limits for eons. Forbidden territory.'

'Why?' said Charlie.

'Because the Gods used to mix freely with humans in this world. They fell in love with them sometimes and even had children. They were called demi-Gods. But mortals and demi-Gods grew old and died and the Gods became disillusioned with mortals. Anyway Zeus...'

Charlie interrupted. 'Hang on a second. Do you mean the King of the Gods?'

'Indeed I do,' said Parseus. 'Anyway Zeus decreed that they should distance themselves and leave humans to their own devices. So they created a mortal world, your world.'

'Why did they do that?'

'Because this world is a magical world, Charlie. It's not suitable for mere mortals.'

Given their own experiences Charlie was not surprised by that. 'So we've come here to find out how to defeat the Titans?'

'Yes — but first we need to find something else,' said Parseus. 'Protection.'

Much as Charlie wanted to go back, remembering the Dark One waiting for him in Max's cottage, he had no wish to return without it. 'What kind of protection?' he asked.

'Not sure. That's why we're going to see Hephaistos. Of course it's a few thousand years in the past and he might not be quite as accomplished as he is these days but he's bound to have some idea. He is the Inventor God, after all. Which reminds me, don't mention the time compass.'

'But didn't Hephaistos invent it?'

'Yes, Charlie but not for a few thousand years yet,' replied Parseus. 'And I don't want you interfering with the past.'

Charlie still found it hard to get his head round the whole concept of time travel but at least that sounded encouraging. Thinking about Hesper though, Charlie remembered something else.

'This witch, the one who lives in Hesper House — you've heard of her, haven't you?' he asked.

'Of course. She is the gaoler of Tartaros. She once used to guard it, but being so close to so much evil for so long has turned her heart black. Now she is on their side.'

'The Titans?' said Charlie.

'Precisely,' said Parseus.

'But what's she doing in Hesper House?' asked Charlie. It was an important point, he thought. After all, he and Max lived in the village — his whole family did.

'Because Hesper House lies directly above the earthly entrance to Tartaros. It's the gateway to Hell.'

'Gateway to hell?' gasped Max.

Charlie gulped. No wonder the villagers hated the place — even though they couldn't know why. Could they?

Yet he was still confused. 'How come this Dark One came from Tartaros? You said the Titans couldn't escape yet.'

Parseus' voice hardened. 'As I said, you humans have damaged the foundations. They have been weakened enough to allow the Titans to send it to the surface. A crack here, a crack there, it is enough. Remember, unlike the Titans themselves, the Dark One can be both shadow and form.' Parseus wagged his finger in the air. 'And the foundations will continue to weaken.'

'How did they weaken?' asked Charlie.

Parseus' face darkened. 'You humans think you are so

creative, don't you? Yet the most powerful things you ever create are designed only to destroy.'

Charlie gulped and fell silent. Parseus seemed so angry.

Max didn't seem to notice. 'Point is, how long's it going to take to find this protection?' he said.

Parseus calmed down. 'Not long, I hope, Max. A couple of days, perhaps, and then we can go back.'   He gathered his cloak around him. 'But we have to hurry. We really mustn't be out here when it grows dark. We are in the wildlands — and anything can happen in the wildlands.'

Charlie's stomach tightened. They were clearly not out of the woods yet.

THE path soon wound up a hill and the trees started to thin out. The presence of Parseus had deterred even the most ardent from following. Even though Charlie still questioned what they had been told, Parseus had proved that he could protect them. Given the bizarre world they had found themselves in Charlie was thankful for that, at least.

They had been walking for several hours and Charlie was exhausted. The sun was now high in the sky and it had grown blisteringly hot. He'd already had to tie his jumper round his waist but now his shirt was sticking to his back and his feet were sweating. Yet Max didn't seem to have tired at all. 'Can we rest for a bit? I'm knackered,' he said.

Parseus stopped. 'Alright. I'll go on to find my bearings. I'll be back soon. Just don't wander off the path.'

The boys watched Parseus disappear over the crest of the hill. Charlie spotted a fallen tree trunk a few yards away. 'Let's go over there,' he said, pointing.

He carefully examined the tree trunk, then satisfied that it was not about to get up and move he sat down and untied his shoelaces. Grimacing, he kicked off his boots. His feet were sore. 'At least we can rest for a bit, eh?' he said.

'Yeah,' replied Max but he was clearly troubled. 'Wish I had never suggested we went into those grounds now,' he said.

'From what Parseus says, not sure it would have changed anything, Max,' said Charlie.

'I suppose.' Max joined him on the tree trunk. 'What do you make of it all?'

'Not sure. Some of it makes sense, and some of it doesn't. I guess we'll know more when we get to wherever he's taking us.' Charlie wiped his mouth. He could still taste the soil he had been buried under in the wood. 'Right now all I want is some water.'

He climbed up onto the tree trunk and started scanning the wood. He pointed down the hillside. 'Let's go and have a look, there might be a stream.'

They set off down the hill. Five minutes later they came across a bubbling brook, gurgling noisily as it flowed into a deep pool below, its clean, clear water sparkling in the dappled light.

The boys ran forward, the trees now providing welcome shade from the heat of the day, and knelt down beside the pool. Leaning forward they cupped some water in their hands and started to drink. It was crisp and cold and Charlie instantly felt better — he hadn't realised how thirsty he had been. But leaning forward again, he heard a voice.

'DO YOU MIND?'

Startled, he and Max sat up and looked around.

'Who was that, Charlie?' whispered Max.

Charlie searched the tree line. 'Don't know, can't see anyone. Maybe it was Parseus.'

He knelt back down to take another drink.

'I SAID — DO YOU MIND.' The voice grew louder, echoing off the trees.

Leaping back from the edge of the pool, the boys jumped to their feet and spun around in alarm, but there was no one there.

'This is getting weird again. I don't like it,' said Max.

'Neither do I,' said Charlie.

Just then a young woman started rising up out of the water and began hovering above the pool just a few feet in front of them. The boys staggered back, their mouths agape.

The woman was a vision. She had long golden hair that fell all the way down her back in tight coils. Her eyes were as deep as the pool below, her skin as white as marble and her whole body and even her strange robe shimmered and sparkled in the light.

Beautiful though she was, she was also angry. Peering down at them, her eyes narrowed, a shadow crossed her face and her dazzling demeanour darkened.

'Do you have permission to drink from *my* stream?' She leaned forward accusingly, her eyes interrogating them. 'Well, do you?'

'S-s-sorry, didn't realise this was your stream,' stammered Charlie.

'Didn't realise? I am a water nymph and this is my stream — it's sacred. Everybody knows that.'

She came down and hovered on the bank next to them, went up to Max and sniffed him.

'Hmm, human I see. Tell me, what are you doing out here? Not very clever what with all the dangers that lie in these parts, is it?' she said.

She leaned forward again and stared at each of the boys in turn. Then she began circling Charlie. 'Let me see — what should I do with you?' she said as she crept closer and ran her finger down Charlie's cheek. Her fingernail was long, like a talon. Charlie could feel she was starting to draw blood. It hurt.

'After all you have desecrated sacred ground,' she added, her face now so close to Charlie he could feel her cold breath.

Charlie started backing away but she grabbed his arm and started pulling him towards the pool.

'Why don't you come with me? There's something I'd like to show you,' she whispered.

Charlie tried to resist but the nymph was surprisingly strong. Her grip tightened as she dragged him towards the water's edge, her face now twisted with rage. He tried digging in his heels but it was no use.

'Oi,' Max said as he leapt forward. Grabbing Charlie's other arm he tried to pull him back the other way. Unfortunately the edge of the river bank was so muddy he couldn't get a grip. Helpless to stop themselves sliding, they were both swiftly dragged towards the edge.

The water nymph gave one last heave and pulled Charlie towards the pool. He slipped down the bank, certain he was going to drown.

'STOP THAT RIGHT NOW.' The voice came from behind the trees. It was Parseus.

The nymph immediately relaxed her grip and let go of Charlie. He fell into the pool and disappeared beneath the surface, emerging seconds later choking and spluttering. Clambering back onto the bank, soaking wet and coughing, he looked up and saw Parseus advancing. Relief swept over him.

The nymph leapt up into the air, hovered back over the pool and crossed her arms. 'Sorry, didn't realise they were with you, Parseus,' she said, smiling innocently.

Parseus stopped at the water's edge. He was furious. He appeared to grow in stature, his face thunderous as he rose up in front of the nymph. 'Leave these boys alone or you will feel my force,' he shouted menacingly.

'Just protecting my territory, that's all. It's my right, isn't it?' she replied, fixing Parseus with an icy stare. Then with a flick of her hair she exploded into a shower of gold and disappeared beneath the surface.

Charlie, his mouth open, peered down at the pool but there was no sign now of the nymph. He pointed to the water as the ripples dissipated. 'What was that?'

Parseus walked over to the pool and looked down. 'Ah, nymphs, feisty little creatures but they can be deadly. They have been known to take men to their watery deaths. You must be wary of them. Great shape-shifters though. Knew of a lovely one once...' Parseus' voice trailed off.

Charlie was lost for words. Parseus explained everything so matter-of-factly: trees picking up and following people, nymphs rising up from the water and changing shape, ancient assassins — it was all utterly fantastic and yet Parseus made it sound so normal.

'Of course, not everyone here is like that,' said Parseus. 'There are mortals in this world too and half-breeds and they can't change shape at all.'

'Are nymphs immortal?' Charlie hoped not.

'No, they just live for a very long time.' Parseus looked around cautiously. 'Now we really mustn't dawdle. I told you anything can happen here, you know.' He walked back up the hill and stood waiting for the boys by the tree trunk. They hurried after him.

Charlie sat down and struggled to put his boots back on, wincing as he did so, his feet swollen and aching. 'How far is this forge? I'm exhausted,' he said.

'Hmm, perhaps some Strength would do you both some good,' said Parseus. He reached into his cloak pocket. 'I should have thought of it earlier.'

Charlie groaned. 'I don't have any strength left, sorry.'

'No — I mean you could do with some,' said Parseus. And with that he took out one of the small green jars the boys had first seen in his trunk. Unstopping the cork, he passed it to Charlie. 'Just a sip though. No more. It's precious stuff.'

Charlie inspected it. 'What is it?'

'Strength,' said Parseus. 'It's a potion. It'll give you strength.'

Charlie sniffed it. 'Smells like strawberries.' He looked at Max. 'Wasn't this the one that...'

Max elbowed him in the ribs. 'Shush, don't tell on me.'

'Is something wrong?' asked Parseus.

Charlie and Max shook their heads. Charlie didn't want to admit that they had rifled through his trunk.

'Good, then have a sip and let's press on,' said Parseus.

Charlie took a long sip. Max was right. It did taste of strawberries. A few seconds later Charlie could feel it coursing through his veins. He felt himself growing stronger. Within seconds, the exhaustion had gone. 'Wow, this is amazing. I feel great.'

He handed the potion to Max. 'No wonder you walked so fast,' he whispered. 'And remember that chest in the kitchen? I wondered how you managed to push that over so easily — it weighed a ton.'

'Yeah, well at least we know what it was now. I was worried it might have been poison. But you're right — I did feel stronger.' Max took a sip and handed the jar to Parseus.

Parseus put it back in his pocket and marched up the path. Charlie quickly tied his shoelaces and he and Max followed.

'How long before we get to Hephaistos' forge?' Charlie asked.

'A few hours. Then you can rest.'

'And Hephaistos will have something to protect me?'

'I hope so, Charlie. Because the Dark One will be waiting and I'm afraid I don't know how to kill it yet,' said Parseus.

'Can it be killed?' said Charlie.

'Quite sure it can. Bound to be a mystical weapon somewhere around. Usually is.'

But there was something about the way that he said that which worried Charlie. Parseus didn't seem sure at all.

IT was late afternoon when they found themselves on a small cliff path overlooking a lush valley. Parseus pointed to the east where a small column of smoke could be seen rising up gently into the blue sky. 'That's where we're going, boys. Just a couple more hours, I'd say. And we'll be able to rest and eat.'

The boys cheered up at the prospect of food and water —

Max particularly, looking more cheerful now than he had been all day.

They started down the winding path that led to a rock face, which jutted out in front of them. Following the path round it they saw a cave entrance fifty yards up ahead. Parseus stopped and held out his arm. 'Careful,' he said.

'Of what?' asked Charlie.

'Dragons.'

'Dragons? You're joking, right?' said Max.

At that very moment there came a deafening roar from inside the cave. Charlie and Max froze. Parseus turned, a horrified look on his face, and barked just one word. *'RUN.'*

Charlie and Max immediately took to their heels but moments later Charlie tripped and fell sprawling across the ground. Ahead of him, and oblivious to his tumble, Max and Parseus ran on, diving behind a large rock on the other side of the entrance. It was only then that Parseus realised Charlie was not with them.

Unfortunately it was too late. Just as Charlie got to his feet, a dark shadow crossed the path. There was another great roar, this one so loud that Charlie had to clasp his hands to his ears, and a monstrous creature emerged from the cave, its head so huge it seemed to fill the whole entrance. It slowly crept out and blocked the path between him and the others.

It was obviously the dragon Parseus had warned them about but it looked like a giant lizard. It had dark green, scaly skin and sharp, spiky ridges all the way down its back. It was also far bigger than Charlie had first thought yet it moved with surprising agility because a second later it pounced forward, its long claws clattering onto the path, glinting like scythes in the afternoon sun. It reminded Charlie of the Dark One and it filled him with just as much dread.

He started backing up the path, hoping the dragon hadn't noticed him. The deafening roars turned to a high-pitched cackle as the dragon craned its long neck forward, jabbing at the air, snorting, its nostrils flared as if it were sniffing for prey. It was then that Charlie realised it was sniffing for *him*. As he stood transfixed the dragon's tail swished out of the cave like a lash, whipping him off his feet, and sending him crashing into the mountainside. He slammed into the rock face and landed on the ground in a heap. Crying out in pain, he crawled onto his knees and tried to take a breath but the wind had been knocked out of him. His ribs hurt so much he was certain they were broken.

The dragon crawled forward, its black, webbed wings grating noisily on the wind as they slowly unfurled and flapped free. They were so large they blocked out the sun, plunging the path into shadow.

The dragon started spitting, great globs of green goo spattering all over the path, the stench engulfing Charlie like a poisonous fog. He retched as the smell soaked into every pore. Then the dragon turned towards him, its cold, green eyes narrowed, and its nostrils flared once more.

Everything now seemed to go into slow motion as the dragon uttered a deep guttural roar, threw back its head and opened its mouth. Charlie, his heart pounding in his chest, every breath an effort, his body shaking in terror, prayed for some way of escape as the dragon exhaled loudly and sheets of green flame shot out of its mouth and headed straight at him.

Shocked into action and grabbing the only chance he had, Charlie pulled himself up and dived head first into the narrow ditch which bordered the path. He curled up in a ball in a desperate attempt to protect himself as the flames swept over it. He could hear the shrubs on either side exploding in all directions and he could feel the searing heat. It seemed to suck the oxygen out of the air. Then a ball of acrid smoke engulfed him, its poisonous cloud filling his lungs. He started suffocating.

Gasping for one more breath, Charlie feared it would be his last.

7. GODS GALORE

CHARLIE felt the darkness engulf him as his life flashed before his eyes: images of his Mum and Dad, trekking through the moors with Max, fishing by the river, arguing with his sister, Emily. And then they all vanished. He felt the pain in his ribs again. He opened his eyes, but the smoke made them sting and when he tried to breathe he felt a searing pain in his throat. The next thing he knew he was choking. Crawling onto his knees he retched violently and vomited.

With the smoke beginning to lift, Charlie realised he was still on the cliff path. He looked around fearfully but the dragon had now lumbered back into its cave, seemingly satisfied that it had defended its territory. For no one could have survived such an attack — yet somehow Charlie had done just that.

There was no time to wonder how though because moments later, Parseus came charging through the swirling smoke. When he saw Charlie sitting up, he stopped abruptly, astonished to see him still alive.

'Thank the Gods, thank the Gods,' he shouted. Rushing forward, he pulled Charlie to his feet and inspected him closely to check he was unhurt.

Max came running up, no less astonished to see Charlie standing there, his face blackened but otherwise unharmed. 'YOU'RE ALIVE. We thought you must be…' Max looked at Parseus. 'But how? We saw the flames.'

Parseus pulled a face. 'Don't look at me. I have no idea. It's quite unnatural.' He shook his head in relief and disbelief before adding, 'You should be dead.'

Charlie, back on his feet, started coughing and spluttering again.

'Take it easy. You've inhaled some very poisonous fumes there,' said Parseus.

'Poisonous?' Charlie started to panic. His throat was still burning. 'You mean I might die?'

'No. Believe me, you would have died instantly,' said Parseus. 'Dragon fumes are lethal — death is instantaneous. Even so, you should be dead.' He shook his head. 'It's hard to believe. Incredibly fortunate — but quite unnatural.' Parseus took Charlie's arm and pulled him forward. 'Never mind all that. We must get away from here. That dragon might come back out.'

With Charlie still unsteady on his feet Max took his other arm and he and Parseus helped him down the path. It was not until they were out of sight of the cave that they slowed down.

'I think I can walk by myself now,' said Charlie.

'Good. But may I suggest you take another sip of Strength,' said Parseus, handing Charlie the jar.

Charlie took a long sip and gave it back to Parseus.

'Lucky there was a ditch. For a moment I thought I was a goner.'

'It wasn't luck, Charlie. There's no such thing in this world. No, something very strange is going on. No mortal can cheat Death,' said Parseus. 'But then destiny does indeed weave a wondrous web,' he muttered before walking on.

Charlie coughed heavily. 'What's he talking about?'

'Who cares? You're alive — that's all that matters,' said Max as he brushed some ash from Charlie's back. 'How do you feel?'

'Remarkably good, considering.' Charlie peered back up the path. 'So that was a dragon, eh?'

'Yeah,' said Max. 'Hard to believe, isn't it?'

'So is everything else,' said Charlie, shaking his head. After all, they had been in the Ancient World for only a few hours and already he had survived three terrifying encounters. What else might he still have to face?

THE boys fell silent as they made their way down the path to the valley below. An hour later they found themselves in a meadow. There was a small river flowing through it. Parseus stopped. 'You can wash that soot off your face here, Charlie.'

Charlie hesitated, glancing at the water suspiciously.

Parseus laughed. 'Perfectly safe. No nymphs here. We're out of the wildlands now. And it's fine to drink.'

The boys knelt down gratefully, cupping their hands in the clear, cool water. They drank steadily. Then Charlie leaned forward, splashing his face clean and rubbing his head with water to get the soot out of his hair.

Refreshed they got back to their feet.

'Not far now, boys,' said Parseus. He set off once again. Charlie and Max trailed after him.

They followed the line of the river until they rounded a bend. Up ahead they spotted a waterfall, cascading into a deep pool beneath it.

'Good. We're here,' said Parseus.

'Where's here?' said Charlie.

'Hephaistos' forge. We're here.'

Charlie and Max looked around but there was no sign of any building. 'It's through there.' Parseus pointed at the waterfall.

'The waterfall?' said Charlie.

'Yes, it's the hidden entrance. Just follow me.' Parseus started making his way across the boulders bordering the edge of the pool. Charlie and Max followed, carefully picking their way across the moss-covered rocks. A few minutes later, they reached the waterfall.

'Just walk through it,' shouted Parseus as he disappeared into the wall of water.

Charlie stepped closer and peered through. He could just make out a small path behind it.

'How about it?' he said, turning to Max.

'After you,' replied Max, bowing mockingly.

Without another word, Charlie walked through the waterfall. It was cool and refreshing and a relief to feel it wash over him. He looked down at his soot covered clothes and scrubbed at them until he felt he was cleaner. Then he walked through to the other side.

Max rushed through next. 'Great. I'm soaked right through now,' he said.

'Stop moaning. We're about to meet the Inventor God.'

'Huh?'

'Hephaistos, remember? Parseus says he might have some kind of protection for me.'

Max shrugged. 'Oh yeah.'

The path led to a small grove, with a well standing in one corner. There were piles of twisted metal and wood scattered about. It looked like a junk yard. Beyond it lay an entrance, carved out of the rock face. It appeared to lead into the mountain itself.

Max looked around. 'So this is the forge then?'

'Looks like it,' replied Charlie.

Just then Parseus appeared from the entrance and beckoned the boys. 'Come on, Hephaistos is here.'

The boys followed. Once inside, they found themselves in a large chamber. It was hot and dimly lit. There were all manner of strange objects scattered around or stacked high against the walls. At the far end of the chamber stood a huge, round furnace with a chimney which rose up through the mountain. A large, heavy-set man, dressed in a dirty tunic was crouched over the furnace, busily banging something so hard that sparks were flying off it.

'That must be Hephaistos,' said Charlie.

The banging stopped and the God turned round to face

them. But as he stood up Charlie and Max stepped back in horror. For Hephaistos was not only a hunchback, he was hideously disfigured: his face was pitted and scarred, with a big lump sticking out over his left eye, his neck twisted slightly so that his head was at a tilt.

He was also lame, for as he shuffled towards them he dragged his right leg behind him. Yet despite his hunchback he was huge, and even though he stooped, he was still far bigger than Parseus. Then Charlie noticed his hands. They were long and narrow, delicate even, though the fingers tapered down to blackened nails. He might be a hunchback, Charlie thought but he certainly had the hands of a master craftsman.

Max, however, didn't seem impressed. 'This is the Inventor God?' he muttered sarcastically.

'Indeed I am, boy,' shouted Hephaistos, coming up to them.

Max stiffened, embarrassed that the God had overheard him. 'Sorry,' he mumbled.

Hephaistos waved his arm. 'No need, no need. Appearances can be deceiving,' he said, eyeing the boys with almost as much curiosity.

'So Parseus, what brings you here?' said Hephaistos as he shuffled past, flinging the metal object he had been banging into a trough which stood near the entrance. It hissed as it hit the cold water and a cloud of steam billowed out.

'Just passing through — thought I'd drop in.' Parseus replied. 'You look a bit glum. How's Aphrodite?'

Charlie remembered the name — Aphrodite. That's right, he said to himself. She was the Goddess of Love. And yes, she was married to him.

Hephaistos shrugged and looked up to the heavens. 'Who knows?' He walked over to a small marble table and grabbed a flagon. He put it to his lips and drank steadily. 'Ah, that's better.'

He put the flagon back down on the table. 'And who are

these...' he waved his arm at Charlie and Max. '...these strangely dressed boys?'

'They're with me. We're on a mission,' said Parseus.

'Mission?' Hephaistos looked intrigued. 'Interesting. What kind of mission?'

Parseus seemed reluctant to explain. 'Later perhaps, but these boys have been walking for hours and have suffered a number of ordeals. Perhaps we could trouble you for some food first?'

Hephaistos looked the boys up and down once again and then smiled broadly. 'As it happens, you're just in time. The girls are preparing something.' He clicked his fingers. 'Bring food and water,' he called out.

While they waited, Hephaistos went back to the trough. Taking out the metal object which had now cooled, he limped over to a marble bench and began flattening it out with a heavy hammer, the noise of it deafening.

'What's that?' asked Charlie politely when the banging stopped.

'A shield,' Hephaistos replied.

Charlie looked about him. 'Is that all you make? Weapons?'

'Of course not. I am an inventor. I make lots of things.'

Max picked up a strange object, sitting on one of the tables.

Hephaistos looked over. 'If you don't mind, try not to fiddle,' he said, shuffling over to Max.

Max put the object down. 'Sorry, was just looking.'

Hephaistos picked up the object and checked to see it was not damaged. 'Please try not to touch. This is a very precious instrument.'

'What is it?' asked Max.

'It's for counting,' said Hephaistos. 'It adds up numbers. It can do multiplication and division too,' he added proudly.

'Like a calculator?' said Max.

'A calculator? Don't know what you are talking about, boy. No, this lets you add up, subtract and multiply numbers.'

'Yeah, like a calculator. I've got one of those,' said Max.

Hephaistos' face fell. 'You can't have. I've just invented it.' He seemed upset. He walked over to another table. 'Do you know what this is?' He held up what looked like a crossbow.

Charlie shot Max a warning look but Max ignored him. 'Let me guess — it shoots arrows?'

Hephaistos looked down at the object with dismay. 'Yes, actually,' he replied quietly. He was clearly disappointed.

Charlie wished Max would shut up. They needed Hephaistos' help. Upsetting him would do them no good. Hoping to smooth things over, he picked up a piece of silvery metal. It had a strange sheen to it and felt incredibly light. It reminded him of the sword in Parseus' trunk.

'This is amazing — I've never seen anything like it before,' he said, admiring it. 'I bet you make lots of great things with it. Parseus said you're very clever.'

Hephaistos brightened. 'Indeed. That metal is called Adamantine. It's the strongest substance known to the Gods. It's ideal for all manner of weapons and instruments. And yes, I use it all the time.'

Two serving girls now appeared, laden with food, flagons of water and more wine for their master.

Hephaistos looked at the boys. 'You both look a little wet. Why not sit near the fire to dry off.' He motioned the boys to a table near the fire as the girls laid out the platters of food.

Max, spotting a chair nearby, sat down. 'NOT THAT ONE,' Hephaistos shouted. But it was too late.

There was a loud clash and two chains flew out from the sides of the chair, wrapping themselves tightly around it, trapping Max.

'Hey, what's going on?' Max shouted as he started wriggling furiously, trying to free himself.

'Sorry. I did try to warn you,' said Hephaistos. 'It's a special chair. I've made a few of them over the years. Can't remember where they all are though, but they're around somewhere.'

'Get me out,' screamed Max.

Hephaistos laughed and shuffled over. 'Don't worry, boy. I'll release you.'

He bent down and fiddled under the chair. The next moment the chains retracted, releasing Max. He leapt to his feet and looked down, eyeing the chair suspiciously.

'That's fantastic,' said Charlie, stepping forward to inspect the chair. 'I bet no one could escape from that,' he added, still anxious not to offend Hephaistos.

'Not unless you know its secret. There's a hidden catch,' said Hephaistos. 'Clever, isn't it?' He smiled.

'Yes it is.' Charlie was suitably impressed.

Hephaistos turned back to the table. 'Now enough of that, let's get some food into you. Pushing the chair to one side, he motioned the boys to sit down on a nearby bench.

Max, still smarting about the chair, inspected the bench carefully before tentatively sitting down. Nothing happened. Relieved, he turned his attention to the food. He pointed to a bowl of what looked like black cherries. 'What are they?'

'Olives. They're a fruit,' replied Parseus.

'Great,' said Max, putting one in his mouth. An instant later he spat it out. 'Urgh, that's no fruit. It's bitter.'

Parseus laughed. 'They are something of an acquired taste, Max. Delicious when you get used to them.'

'Doubt that,' muttered Max.

Charlie hadn't realised how hungry he was until he saw the food. 'Is this lamb?' he asked, pointing at a rack of char-grilled chops.

'No, it's goat,' said Parseus.

'Goat?' Charlie picked up one of the chops. 'Never had goat.'

'Then try it,' said Parseus. 'It can be very good.'

Charlie picked up a chop and took a nibble. 'It's great,' he said, passing a chop to Max. Between them they swiftly devoured the entire plate before munching their way through a bunch of grapes and a plate of figs.

When they had finished, Hephaistos looked at Parseus. 'You said you were on a mission. What is it, and why are you here?'

'We need to find something that would protect a mortal from…' Parseus leaned forward. 'From the Dark One.'

Hephaistos slowly put his flagon down on the table. 'The Dark One?' He sounded astonished. 'But it's imprisoned in Tartaros. It cannot escape, surely?'

'But let's say it did escape, what would protect a mortal from its attacks? Hypothetically,' said Parseus.

Hephaistos stiffened and then shook his head gravely. 'I don't know. I doubt there is anything,' he said as he took another swig.

Charlie glanced at Max. This was not good news. How were they going to return home now? Without any protection, he was doomed.

'But surely there must be something,' insisted Parseus.

Just at that moment a dark shadow crossed the threshold and a cold draught swept through the chamber. Charlie turned towards the door. His jaw dropped. For there, framed in the doorway, stood the most fearsome figure he had ever seen. He was enormous, at least seven foot tall, and as wide as the door itself. He had sharp, chiselled features, eyes as black as night, and long, black hair which fell wildly down his back. His red robe, trimmed with gold and jewels, billowed behind him as he entered, a strange icy mist swirling around his feet.

Charlie shivered. This surely had to be another God, he thought. But given the icy atmosphere that now filled the chamber he was obviously not a friendly one. Charlie saw his face was filled with fury, his brow furrowed with suspicion and rage.

The figure hovered in the doorway for a moment, his stony gaze penetrating the room.

Parseus leant across the table, his voice falling to a whisper. 'That is Hades, the king of the Underworld.'

'Underworld?' said Max.

'It means he rules over the dead,' said Charlie. He remembered reading something about Hades but until now he had just been a name in a book, a figure in a story. Seeing him here in the flesh, Charlie trembled.

'You're quite right, Charlie. He governs the death realms. He is one of the three great Gods and one of the most feared of all. So say and do nothing,' warned Parseus.

Spotting Hephaistos, Hades marched into the room, his feet thundering noisily across the stone flagstones, the icy blast following in his wake. Approaching, he clicked his fingers at one of the serving girls.

'A flagon and be quick about it,' he roared, his voice echoing off the walls.

Hephaistos smiled weakly. 'Hades, what are you doing here? What's wrong?'

'What's wrong? I'll tell you what's wrong? Death has been KIDNAPPED,' snarled Hades, spitting the last word out with such venomous fury that Charlie shuddered.

'What do you mean?' said Hephaistos.

Hades slammed the table. 'I mean exactly what I say. Death has been kidnapped by that wily Sisyphos.'

'But why?' asked Hephaistos.

'Sisyphos betrayed the secrets of the Gods. So Death was sent to take him down to Tartaros as punishment. But now he has escaped my clutches and kidnapped Death instead,' said Hades as he began pacing the flagstones.

Charlie leaned over to Parseus. 'Death isn't a person, is it?'

Parseus shook his head. 'No, more of a spirit really. He works for Hades.' He put a finger to his lips. 'Be quiet. I'll explain later. I now remember what happened here. Just hadn't realised we had come back to this particular time,' he said.

Hades came back to the table and stared at Parseus. 'And what brings you here?' he barked.

'Just passing through, your majesty.' Parseus bowed his head as reverently as possible. 'Very sorry to hear the news.'

'Not as sorry as I am, Parseus,' Hades replied coldly. He looked around for the serving girl. *'Where is my flagon?'* he demanded.

A petrified girl rushed forward, her eyes cast downwards and hurriedly placed a large flagon of wine on the table before trying to scurry away. Hades grabbed her by the wrist. She winced in agony as he squeezed it tightly. Then Hades pulled her close. 'Hurry up next time, slave,' he snarled. The terrified girl bobbed her head before fleeing the room.

Charlie and Max watched fearfully as Hades downed the flagon in one. Fortunately, it seemed to calm him a little and he lowered his voice, though it still cut through the air like a knife.

'You realise now that no one can die,' he said, flinging back his head. 'It's chaos. And I will not tolerate chaos.' He clenched his hand into a tight fist. 'I will crush Sisyphos like a grape. I will curse him with a punishment so severe they will talk of it for eternity,' he spat as his black eyes swept the room. 'And after I find him, no one will ever dare to betray the Gods again.'

Hades reached for his flagon, realised it was empty and smashed it on the floor. 'Another one — NOW.' He slammed his fist down on the table once more, so hard this time that one of the dishes flew up into the air before smashing into pieces on the ground. Distracted, his eyes fell on the boys. 'And who are you?'

Charlie and Max looked down at the floor. Charlie felt his heart quicken.

'They're with me, Hades. This is Charlie and this is Max,' said Parseus.

Hades' eyes narrowed and he pointed at Charlie. 'Why is your hair singed?'

Charlie opened his mouth, but the words wouldn't come out.

'Well?' shouted Hades.

'I...I...was attacked...' Charlie stuttered quickly, but before he could finish, Hades leapt to his feet, picked him up in one hand and sniffed him. 'Dragon fumes,' he muttered before dropping Charlie on the floor. He turned to Hephaistos. 'You see what I mean?'

Hephaistos stared at Charlie's singed hair. 'Hmm, yes.'

Charlie winced and picked himself up from the floor.

Hades looked around impatiently but just then the serving girl re-appeared with another flagon, placed it down on the table and scurried away. Hades downed it quickly and continued his rant. 'Remember when Asklepios, the God of Medicine became so good at it that he started bringing people back to life?'

Hephaistos waved a hand. 'Who could forget?' he said.

'I won't have another situation like that. You can imagine how angry Kerberus got when the dead started coming back to life.'

'Nice dog, that Kerberus of yours,' said Hephaistos.

'Nice dog? He's the guardian of the Underworld and the fiercest, three-headed hound ever to walk the face of hell,' thundered Hades. And with that, his thirst now quenched he slammed the empty flagon back on the table and wiped his mouth.

He glared around the table. 'If you see or hear anything, I want to know immediately or you will know my wrath. Do I make myself clear?'

Everyone nodded meekly, including Hephaistos. And without another word, Hades stormed out of the forge, the cold chill vanishing with him.

Relief swept through the chamber — even Hephaistos seemed pleased that he had gone.

'What's going on?' said Max, as if to himself. 'I mean Death kidnapped? A three-headed hound?'

'You mean Kerberus — the hound of hell. He's very fierce. He's a sort of reverse guard dog. He's there to make sure no one who enters the Underworld ever leaves,' replied Parseus.

'Wish I hadn't asked.' Max leaned across to Charlie. 'The

sooner we're out of here, the better. The more I see, the less I like.'

Charlie felt much the same. Sitting there with Hades looming over the table, his icy mist surrounding them, the Ancient World seemed a very inhospitable place indeed. But the problem was that they couldn't go home without something to protect them from the waiting Dark One. They had to find something, and fast. The Inventor God remained their only chance of that.

Hephaistos picked up his flagon. 'You know, Parseus, I feel quite sorry for Sisyphos. Hades will be quite merciless when he catches up with him.'

'Yes, Sisyphos is a very clever man isn't he?' said Parseus.

Hephaistos waved his hand around his forge. 'He has been a frequent visitor here, you know. Very interested in my work. Pity he betrayed us,' he said.

'Yes it is. But I really must press you again. I had asked, before we were interrupted, if you knew of anything that might protect a mortal from the Dark One? You really are our only hope,' said Parseus.

'Alright, let me think for a minute.' Hephaistos took another swig from his flagon and sat drumming his fingers on the table. A moment later, his face lit up. 'Ha, of course, the Helmet of Invisibility.' His eyes narrowed. 'And you know who has that?'

Parseus looked towards the door and shook his head. 'Hades. How stupid of me, I should have remembered.'

Hephaistos frowned and stood up. 'And he isn't going to give it up lightly — not in his present mood.'

'Quite, quite,' said Parseus.

Charlie was now in despair. Hades held their fate in his hands. And having met him, it wasn't likely that he would help them. But as Hephaistos limped away, he saw a smile cross Parseus' lips.

He leaned over and patted Charlie's arm. 'Don't worry, Charlie. I have a solution. Remember, I'm a Time God.' Parseus smiled again. 'And I now recall exactly what happened when Death was kidnapped. What's more I know how to get him back.'

'How?' interrupted Max.

'I know where Sisyphos is keeping Death,' said Parseus.

'So what good is that to us?' said Charlie.

'Because if we return Death to Hades, we can ask him for a favour in return — to let us borrow the Helmet.' Parseus paused. 'But we are going to need help.'

'From who?' Charlie gazed down the chamber at Hephaistos, bent over his worktable again. 'Him?'

'Good heavens — No. He won't be any use. We need Ares.'

Charlie blinked. 'You don't mean Ares — the God of War?'

'Exactly. Who better?' Parseus clapped his hands together. 'Think about it. No one has more of a vested interest in making sure people die than he does.'

He pointed to the far corner of the chamber. 'But that is quite enough for now. We have a busy day tomorrow so I suggest you go and lie down. Get some rest.'

'And then what?' said Charlie.

Parseus smiled. 'Then we find Death.'

8. BATTLING ON

CHARLIE woke with a start. He had been dreaming of dragons and nymphs and strange Gods in dark, deathly places, but as the memories of the previous night flooded back, he was no more thankful to be awake. He sat up and looked around the chamber. Max was still asleep, snoring quietly, curled up in a ball, his head resting on his jumper. Charlie tried to get up but he was stiff. They must have walked for twenty miles the day before but it felt more like fifty. He rolled onto his side and pushed himself up gently.

Parseus appeared. He seemed in a hurry. 'Ah, good, you're up. We must be on our way, there's much to do today.' He stopped and looked at Max, lying near the fire. 'Still asleep? Well that won't do.' Parseus went over and prodded him. 'Come along. Wake up. Time to leave.'

Max yawned and sat up slowly. 'Huh?' He looked around, startled. 'Where am I?'

'The Ancient World, remember?' said Parseus.

Max rubbed his eyes as he got to his feet. 'Oh yeah,' he groaned. 'Rather hoped it was all a dream.'

'But it isn't,' said Parseus briskly. 'Now come along. We must find Death.' He nodded at Charlie. 'Rather fortunate for you that he was kidnapped or you would have died at the hands of that dragon. Told you it was unnatural.'

Max winked at Charlie. 'Sounds like you were lucky, then.'

'Yeah, that's me — lucky,' said Charlie as he grabbed some grapes from a bowl. 'Let's hope I stay that way.'

They were about to leave when Hephaistos appeared and

beckoned Charlie. 'I thought you should have this. It might well prove useful on your mission,' he said, handing Charlie a small silver cylinder.

Charlie looked at it. 'Thanks. But what is it?'

'It's a whistle,' said Hephaistos. 'You may well need it soon enough.'

'When?' asked Charlie.

'Trust me, you'll know when,' Hephaistos replied. Charlie looked at him blankly. What was he going to do with a whistle? But he didn't want to appear rude so he thanked Hephaistos again and slipped it into his pocket.

THE boys left the grove, walked back through the waterfall and joined Parseus waiting on the other side.

'Great, we're all wet again,' grumbled Max.

'You'll soon dry off in this heat, young Harper,' said Parseus. 'Now do hurry up. We have to find transport,' he added impatiently.

Transport? Charlie wondered what he meant. A cart and horse perhaps? But Parseus had walked on without explaining so he and Max followed, retracing the line of the river until they passed the path which had brought them into the valley the day before. There were a few clouds dotted about but otherwise the sky was bright blue. It was going to be another hot day.

They began wending their way gently up into the hills, and ten minutes later, Parseus stopped beside a lone cypress tree and, shielding his eyes from the sun, started scanning the sky. 'We must wait next to this tree. They're like bus stops in your world. Should be one along in a minute.'

'Bus stops?' Charlie looked up, but all he could see were clouds.

A moment later, he got his answer. One of the clouds jumped up, turned and started towards them, moving at great speed. Then it stopped abruptly right in front of them and, still shrouded in a cloudy mist, began transforming itself into a chariot. Charlie and Max stood dumbfounded, scarcely able to believe what they were seeing.

Parseus rubbed his hands together excitedly. 'Excellent. Here it is.'

He looked at the boys, their mouths still agape. 'It's the only way to travel around here,' he said and without further explanation, he climbed inside, sat down and beckoned the boys.

Charlie and Max stepped back, shaking their heads.

'Do come along. We must fetch Ares,' said Parseus.

'In this?' said Charlie. 'But it's just a cloud.'

'Yes it is, Charlie Goodwin. In this world all immortals travel by cloud. They're very quick. We would have taken one yesterday, if there had been any around — alas not. Very annoying. Now get in,' Parseus ordered.

Max backed away, clearly appalled at the idea. Charlie hesitated and then stepped forward, gingerly putting out his foot. The cloudy mist engulfed it but, when he actually stepped inside, he found it surprisingly solid. He sat down next to Parseus, the mist swirling round his feet.

Max still hung back.

'Come on. It's fine.' Charlie waved him forward. 'Just try it. Don't let your eyes fool you.'

'Well, they're already fooled,' said Max, shaking his head. 'Guess I don't have much choice though do I?' he sighed as he slowly inched forward, testing the base carefully before stepping inside, tottering as he did so. Then, astonished to find that the cloud was in fact solid, he relaxed slightly and sat down next to Charlie.

Parseus leaned forward. 'Now hold on tight. Understood?'

The boys nodded.

'All settled?' asked Parseus.

'Yeah, real comfy, thanks,' replied Max sarcastically.

'Good, so let's go,' said Parseus. He raised his arm. 'To Thrace,' he shouted.

The cloud lifted up into the air and hovered briefly before shooting up into the sky. Charlie felt his stomach drop as it climbed ever more steeply upwards. Terrified that he was going to fall out, he closed his eyes tightly and held on for dear life.

After what seemed like an age, the chariot finally levelled out and began to slow down. Charlie's stomach returned and he opened his eyes. The cloud was now cruising through the sky. They were so high that Charlie could see for miles in every direction. The view was magnificent. He had never imagined seeing his own world from such a height, let alone this one.

Max opened one eye and peered out. 'Are we there yet?'

'No, but you have to see this, Max.' Charlie could hardly contain his excitement.

Max opened his other eye and sat up. 'WOW. I mean WOW,' he said, wide-eyed in disbelief and awe.

'I know. It's amazing,' said Charlie breathlessly.

A few hundred feet below them the terrain was mostly hilly. The grass was dry, interspersed with vast tracks of craggy rocks that snaked around the hills. Every now and then it levelled out and they came across a lush meadow or river lined with marshes. But it was all very different to their own world. It was all so wild.

'Not many people about,' shouted Charlie against the wind. Even here in the past, he had expected more 'civilisation'.

'We're still passing through the wildlands. The coastal areas are more populated. You'll see more shortly,' Parseus called back.

He was right. Another fifteen minutes and Charlie saw something in the distance. 'What's that, over there on top of that mountain?'

'The Temple of Delphi,' said Parseus.

Charlie had heard of that. He vaguely remembered seeing pictures of a ruin somewhere in Greece. But this was no ruin. The temple was round with a series of golden columns that encircled it and rose up into the sky. Just below the temple, there was another building — rectangular and made of white marble. Sprawled out below that at the foot of the mountain was a village, its houses and streets hugging the hillside around it.

'What's the Temple of Delphi?' asked Max.

'People go there to receive oracles,' said Parseus.

'Oracles?'

'Divine messages, Max. People ask questions and they receive oracles in return. Tend to be a little obscure though. The Gods do not like to reveal the whole truth, but they're very popular.'

They flew on, leaving Delphi behind. Some time later, Parseus pointed to the far north. 'And there's Mount Olympos, the entrance to the immortal realm. It's where the Gods live.'

Charlie and Max, their hands still gripping the sides of the chariot, sat up to get a better look. In the distance, partially obscured by a blanket of cloud, they could just make out the snow-capped tip of a huge mountain, rising far above them.

'How long till we reach Thrace?' asked Charlie.

'We'll be there soon,' replied Parseus.

The cloud started turning to the right. Max sat back in his seat. 'You've read about these Gods, Charlie. Do you know anything about Ares? Because if he's anything like Hades, I'll wait outside.'

'He's the God of War, Max, but that's all I know — except I doubt he's the friendly type. We'll just have to trust Parseus. There's not much else we can do.'

Max shook his head. 'Still wish it were it all a dream.'

'So do I,' said Charlie.

Half an hour later, Parseus pointed to the coastline in the distance. 'There we are — Thrace. Not long now,' he said.

Charlie leaned over to get a better look. Soon enough they were passing over the cliffs and heading inland. The landscape was mountainous and dry. Down below, he could just make out a small river as it meandered through the rocky terrain.

The cloud began to dive downwards. Charlie and Max

rammed their feet against the front of the chariot to stop themselves from falling out as it plunged towards the ground. Then the cloud levelled off and started cruising again.

Charlie peered over the side. They were flying just above the ground. He nudged Max, who still had his eyes closed. 'It's OK,' he said. 'I think we're nearly there.'

Max opened his eyes as the chariot began its final descent, this time more gently. There was a large walled palace on the plateau ahead of them. Moments later the chariot pulled up in front of it.

Parseus climbed down. 'Now comes the hard part, of course,' he said as he headed for the entrance.

Max sighed. 'He doesn't explain anything, Charlie. Have you noticed that?'

'Let's just go along with it, eh? Remember, he's our only hope of getting home.'

'Guess you're right, and if this helmet can protect you, well...' said Max.

The boys climbed down from the chariot and ran to catch up with Parseus. When they reached the gate, he leaned forward and whispered something. The gate groaned and slowly opened.

Charlie walked through and stopped dead. In front of him there was a magnificent garden: the grass was bright green and there were trees and flowers in almost every colour and shape.

It was vibrant and beautiful and in contrast to the dusty plateau outside, with its dried out shrubs and searing heat, it was cool and fresh.

Charlie closed his eyes and took a deep breath. It smelled of honey and freshly baked bread. It reminded him of his childhood when he would wait avidly for his mother's home-made buns then eat them warm, dripping in butter and honey. He felt a gentle breeze brush against his cheek, enveloping him like a soft hug.

He felt happy — even safe — for the first time since setting foot in this strange world.

The palace lay at the end of a wide avenue that stretched out before them, lined on either side by giant poplars. Carved out of the rock face the palace looked as if it had grown organically rather than been built. The steps leading up to the wooden entrance were flanked on both sides by four huge columns wrapped in gold leaf, sparkling in the sunlight. Statues painted in garish colours stood between each one.

'Blimey Charlie — this is nice,' said Max, as they walked down the avenue.

'Nice? This is Heaven.'

'You're quite right, of course, Charlie,' said Parseus. 'All the God's palaces are like this. Hephaistos designs them. He always adds a bit of paradise. It makes the Gods feel more at home. Lovely isn't it?'

'So why's his own place such a dump?' asked Max.

'That's because it's his workshop. And he's also far too busy working on everyone else's palaces to bother with his own.'

Max took a deep breath. 'Hmm, smells like lamb.'

'No it doesn't, smells like bread and honey,' said Charlie.

'You're both right actually. You see, heaven is different for everyone,' said Parseus. 'One man's poison and all that...' He pointed ahead. 'Now let's see if Ares is about.'

The boys followed, each lost in his own blissful wonder. But when they neared the palace steps, they heard an almighty crash and the doors flew open.

It was at that moment that Charlie first set eyes on Ares. His wonder now turned to terrified awe. Ares was huge, even by immortal standards. And as he thundered down the steps towards Charlie and Max, dressed from head to toe in bronze-plated armour, great sparks flew off his body exploding in every direction like fireworks. The sound of his feet on the flagstones was like a thousand horses galloping across a plain.

To Charlie it was like watching a storm sweep towards him. The tranquil effect of the heavenly gardens instantly vanished. For they were no match for the fury of the God of War.

Max's fears had been realised: Ares appeared even more fearsome than Hades.

Parseus held up his hand. 'Ares, I have grave...'

'I know — Death has been kidnapped,' shouted Ares, striding furiously past him. On seeing Max and Charlie, he stopped. Puffing out his chest, his eyes narrowed and he peered down at the two boys cowering in front of him. 'And who are YOU?'

'They're with me Ares. Now please listen to me,' said Parseus.

Ares sliced his sword through the air. 'LISTEN TO YOU?' Then his voice went quiet, though the menace was loud and clear. 'I've got a battle going on today — a battle. Do you know what happens in battles?'

'Yes, Yes, Ares, I am vaguely aware of what occurs.'

'People die, Parseus. And they can't die if Death has been kidnapped.'

'I understand. That's why we're here — to help.'

Ares fixed him with a cold stare. 'Help? You think the God of War needs help?' He raised his sword aloft, tightly gripping the gleaming shaft. 'Cold, hard Adamantine, that's all the help I need.'

He looked down contemptuously at Charlie and Max. 'And you think mere mortal boys can help me?' he sneered.

Charlie averted his gaze. He started to wonder whether Max had been right. Perhaps they should have stayed outside.

Parseus began backtracking. 'No, no, great Ares. Of course you don't need our help. We need yours. And we are here simply to beg you, humbly, to give it. You are our only hope. Only a God of your standing could possibly rescue Death.' He bowed deeply then looked up. 'It's just that we may know something of value to you.'

The appeal seemed to work. Ares calmed down and standing tall, he threw back his head, shook his long mane of jet black hair and squared his shoulders.

'Speak then, and make it quick,' he said.

Parseus bowed again. 'Thank you, great Ares. I was trying to tell you that I know where Sisyphos has taken Death.' Parseus paused. 'If that is any assistance to you at all?' he added.

Ares eyed him suspiciously. 'By all the Fates, how do you know?'

'I just do, great Ares.'

Parseus said it so confidently that Ares now seemed to accept it without question. He lowered his sword. 'So where is he?'

'His palace, near Corinth,' said Parseus.

'You are certain of that?'

'Absolutely.'

'Then what are we waiting for?' snapped Ares. 'Let's go. But first I must check on the battle. It's on the way,' he added.

Charlie forgot all about his fear for a moment. Check on a battle first? That was definitely worth seeing he thought, as he and Max quickly hurried after Ares.

THEY emerged into the dry, dusty heat of the plateau. Ares clicked his fingers. Then they heard a deafening noise. It sounded like a train. Moments later a tornado tore round the side of the mountain, stopped sharply right in front of them and span wildly, kicking up so much dust that it almost blinded them.

The tornado slowed and the dust settled. When Charlie opened his eyes he found it had transformed itself into a chariot. But unlike the one in which they had travelled, this one had four black stallions harnessed to its front. Hovering, they neighed and wrestled at the bit, tossing their heads wildly.

'I thought you told us Gods travelled in clouds?' whispered Charlie.

'Yeah, and we didn't have stallions,' added Max.

'Some Gods always have to be special — particularly Ares,' said Parseus.

'You don't like him much, do you?' said Charlie.

'It's not that. Of course he's belligerent, but as the God of

War that's only to be expected. It's just that he lacks a certain — let me put it this way — a certain finesse.'

The horses now calmed down and trotted round so that the chariot was right in front of them.

'Good. Let's go,' said Ares, leaping into the front. Charlie and Max approached cautiously, taking care to keep clear of the horses impatiently pawing the ground.

'For the Gods' sake,' huffed Ares and leaning over the side, he grabbed Charlie and Max by the scruff of their necks and hauled them in, dumping them on the seats behind him. Charlie landed with a thud, wincing in agony, though not daring to cry out in pain. Parseus, his face expressionless, climbed in and sat down next to them.

Ares stood up and took the reins. 'Everyone ready?' And without waiting for an answer he waved his sword. '*To the Battle of Eritrea,'* he shouted.

The chariot lifted into the air, the horses neighed loudly and broke into a gallop, shooting up into the sky before turning south-west and levelling out. Charlie waited for his stomach to settle before peering over the side at the sea sparkling beneath them. 'Where's Eritrea, Parseus?' he asked.

'Euboea, an island just off the coast of Attica to the north of Athens. It's not far,' said Parseus.

Charlie had heard of Athens. But that was in his world — yet it was also in this one. He still couldn't understand it.

Some two hours later, Parseus pointed below them. 'We've just flown over the coast. Not long now.'

Charlie sat up excitedly. 'Who's fighting this battle?'

'Just a tribal conflict. Two neighbouring armies are fighting for control of the city of Eritrea. These things happen all the time here,' said Parseus.

CHARLIE heard the battle long before he saw it — the distant sound of chanting and a rumbling like thunder. When they arrived, the chariot stopped and hovered immediately above it, giving them a clear view of what was happening. Charlie eagerly peered down.

On the plain below thousands of men were lined up in formation on either side: their swords, spears and bows at the ready, their armour gleaming in the sunlight. The men were chanting and banging their shields. Stomping their feet in unison, they were kicking up clouds of dust. The din was deafening as each side tried to out-chant the other.

On the left and right flanks, cavalry divisions stood poised. The horses were chomping at the bit, pawing the ground, neighing, as if desperate to charge headlong into battle, their riders struggling to rein them in. Alongside there were soldiers in small chariots, two men to each one, each armed with a bow and arrows.

To Charlie sitting high above them in the cloud, they all looked like toy soldiers in a board game — except that this was no game.

The sound of war cries grew louder as Charlie saw the infantry units begin moving into position, the charioteers trotting forward from both left and right, the archers at the rear readying themselves for the attack. The minutes ticked by until the final cry was heard and battle commenced.

As the soldiers on one side advanced, those on the other side crouched down using their shields to create a shell around them, while the archers behind began firing their arrows. Charlie heard a great whooshing sound and the sky darkened as a barrage flew up into the air and rained down on the advancing men. From above, Charlie watched in horror as the arrows pierced the chests of screaming soldiers. They fell like dominoes.

In response, the chariots of the attacking army charged from their flanks towards the bowmen, cutting down the archers with their arrows before they rounded and returned to their positions.

A great cry then went up and the defending infantry stood up as one, returned their shields to their chests, and began to advance before the charioteers had the chance to regroup. With that, the infantry on both sides fell upon each other in hand-to-hand combat. Charlie, torn between fascination and disgust at the slaughter, watched as the men below savagely sliced and stabbed at each other with their spears and short swords, throwing their whole bodies against one another as they battled their way through the tangled mass of limbs.

Charlie winced as he heard, even from high above, the sound of metal upon metal and then metal upon bone. Great spurts of blood flew up into the air as the screams of the wounded rang out, their limbs severed. The ground quickly became blood-soaked and the field filled up with bodies.

It was then that Charlie realised something extraordinary. The piles of soldiers were beginning to move again as those seemingly killed started wriggling out from the massive mounds below. Slowly struggling to their feet they looked around in confusion.

'Look, they're coming back to life,' shouted Max.

'They're not coming back to life. They never died,' spat Ares, his knuckles turning white as he gripped the reins with fury.

Charlie could hardly believe the scene below. Soldiers were stumbling around, at first still senselessly trying to fight one another until the two armies realised what was happening: that neither side was capable of killing the other.

With that, the battle simply petered out, both armies retreating to their respective camps, the seemingly dead hobbling along, some carrying their severed limbs, some still with spears and arrows in their chests.

Charlie and Max watched in shocked silence, while Ares stood up, shaking his fist.

'This is not how war WORKS,' he screamed at the soldiers below him, banging his sword against the side of the chariot. 'People have to die for war to work. Where is Victory without Death?' he shouted. Turning to Parseus, his eyes narrowed. 'I WANT SISYPHOS.' He spat the words out with such fury that, for a moment, Charlie almost felt sorry for the fate that awaited Death's captor: it was quite clear that Ares was not a God you should upset — ever.

Parseus raised his arm to calm Ares. 'I understand your frustration Ares, but we must make sure we don't fall into any traps. He's a clever one that Sisyphos. We must be careful.'

Ares, it seemed would have none of it. 'Careful, Parseus? Let me tell you, I'm going to drag Sisyphos back to the Underworld using as much force as I see fit. There is nothing more to be said.'

And with that Ares whipped the stallions and the horses broke into a gallop. Falling back in their seats, Charlie and Max clung on desperately as they left the battlefield behind and shot off across the sky.

9. FINDING DEATH

THE journey was surprisingly short. Ares drove the chariot at such speed that Charlie reckoned that it took them no more than thirty minutes or so before they had landed in front of another palace. It sat on a cliff top, overlooking the sea.

'That's the Gulf of Corinth,' said Parseus.

Unlike Ares' palace in Thrace, built by Hephaistos, the palace of Sisyphos appeared to lack such ostentatious magic. It was a small, simple building with two marble columns situated on either side of steps, which led up to the main entrance.

No one seemed to be about and it was clearly in disrepair: the shrubs were overgrown and unkempt and a mural painted long ago was cracked and faded. Ares pulled up the horses and the chariot landed in front of the palace.

'I'm not sure this is a good idea, Ares,' said Parseus.

Ares ignored him. 'Wait here, I'll be back soon.' Leaping out of the chariot, he stormed up the steps, kicked open the wooden door and entered the palace, leaving the others behind.

An hour later, as they waited with growing concern for his return, Charlie feared the worst — Parseus had obviously been right about the need for caution.

Realising that they could wait no longer, Parseus sighed heavily and climbed down from the chariot. 'Wait here, boys,' he ordered.

'But what could have happened to Ares? asked Charlie.

Parseus refused to speculate. 'Just stay where you are.' Then he too disappeared into the palace.

The long minutes ticked by, and Charlie and Max began to

grow desperate. They were now alone in the Ancient World, and without Parseus they were lost.

'What if they don't come back, Charlie? We'll never get home,' said Max.

Max was right. 'I'm going to find out,' said Charlie. 'You stay here.'

'Are you insane? If two people go into a building and don't come back out, you don't follow them in. And you certainly don't split up.'

'Let's both go, then,' said Charlie. 'Safety in numbers, eh?'

'Safety in numbers? Two Gods have vanished. There is no safety,' replied Max.

'You can stay here if you like,' Charlie said as he climbed down from the chariot.

'Stay here? Not on your life.' Max quickly climbed down and followed Charlie inside.

CREEPING through the main entrance they found themselves in a small courtyard. A set of steps on the left-hand side led to an upstairs gallery that ran around it. The flagstones were dusty and there was little sign of habitation. It was deserted.

'Let's try up there,' he said, dragging a still reluctant Max behind him.

'I don't like this, Charlie,' muttered Max as he followed.

Charlie ignored him. Without Parseus they had no chance of getting home and without Ares they had no chance of borrowing the helmet. Reaching the top, Charlie was relieved to see Parseus, peeking through one of the doors that led off from the gallery. He turned around, saw the boys and beckoned them over. They tiptoed across.

'What happened?' whispered Charlie. He knelt down and Parseus leaned back so that Charlie could peer through the gap. He gasped. For there, sitting chained to a chair, was Ares.

Charlie watched him wriggling furiously, his face red with rage, his body arching against the chair as he struggled to free himself.

Then Charlie felt a cold chill run through him like a knife. For sitting next to Ares was the most terrifying sight he had yet seen — it had to be Death itself.

Parseus had been right. It was some kind of spirit. There was a ghostly air about it and a strange luminescent light surrounded it like a halo. While its mouth — if that was what it was — was a dark cavernous hole with a swirling mass inside it. Its eyes were soulless, black and empty.

Death was also tied to a chair, though its bonds were different: they looked like barbed wire and they crackled with blue light. But unlike the struggling Ares, Death was still and silent.

Max knelt down and pushed Charlie out of the way. 'What's going on in there?' he said, peering inside. Then he sat back, shaking his head. 'What the....?'

Parseus stood up grim-faced. 'I did warn Ares. Sisyphos was bound to have a few tricks up his sleeve.'

'Is that...Death?' asked Max, his face as white as a sheet.

Parseus nodded.

'He looks like...'

'Death?' Parseus interrupted him.

'I was going to go for terrifying ghostly entity, but...' Max paused. 'Are you sure we should we rescue it?'

'Yes, we must if we're to get you home again,' said Parseus.

'So who's going to do that?' asked Charlie nervously.

'It's down to us, I'm afraid,' said Parseus. 'But don't worry. I'll go. You two stay here.'

'Good idea. We'll do just that,' said Max, visibly relieved.

Parseus slowly opened the door and slipped inside, closing it behind him.

'So that's Death?' said Charlie.

'Yeah, and I don't like the look of it,' said Max.

'I don't think we're supposed to like the look of it, Max.'

Charlie peered back through the gap. Ares was still wriggling wildly and shouting. 'Get me out of these chains, Parseus. That Sisyphos — when I get my hands on him…'

'What happened?' asked Parseus.

Ares stopped wriggling. 'I came in, found Death and was about to release him when Sisyphos appeared. I told him exactly what I intended to do to him, but he apologised, said it was all a mistake and told me he could explain everything. Then he offered me a seat.'

Ares lowered his eyes and coughed. 'The next thing I knew I was chained to this chair. Now get me out of it.'

Charlie, peering through the gap, watched Parseus step forward. Then he heard a strange whooshing sound and a net fell from the ceiling, sweeping Parseus up into it. He was now dangling upside down above the floor, trapped.

'Oh NO,' cried Charlie.

'What is it?' Max pushed him out of the way again and looked inside. 'What? How did that happen?'

'Don't know, but we're going to have to do something.'

'Like what? Two Gods and the spirit of Death have been tricked — what hope is there for us?'

Charlie peered back into the room.

Ares was shouting at Parseus. 'Well done. That's marvellous, Parseus. I thought you were supposed to be wise to his tricks.'

Parseus was trying to claw his way up the netting to right himself, while below, Ares writhed more furiously than ever.

'You mustn't struggle,' shouted Parseus. 'It only makes the chains tighter.'

Charlie was racking his brain wondering what to do when he saw one of the walls on the other side of the room slide open to reveal a secret entrance. A man dressed in a simple brown tunic appeared. It had to be Sisyphos, he thought as he watched the man walk into the middle of the room, stooping as he did so.

Sisyphos was old with grey hair that hung limply against his face and he had a pallid complexion: his cheeks slightly sunken, his eyes glassy. But he also had a smug look about him. Walking forward he stroked his straggly beard and began to speak, his voice raspy and high-pitched.

'Parseus is right, of course, Ares. The harder you struggle the tighter they grow.' Sisyphos looked up at Parseus. 'Sorry, Parseus, but if you will interfere, what do you expect?'

Sisyphos turned and walked over to a torch holder on the wall near the door. He pulled it down sharply and a strange, creaking sound reverberated around the room.

'The game is still afoot, I'm afraid,' he cackled before disappearing back through the secret door, which closed silently behind him.

Max, unable to see or hear anything, feared the worst. 'What's going on, Charlie?'

Charlie sat back on his heels. 'It's not looking good, Max.' He peered back into the room, his mind racing.

Ares, still shouting threats at the now vanished Sisyphos, gave up and shouted instead at Parseus who was swaying above him.

'What was Sisyphos on about — the game is still afoot?'

'I think he may have laid more than one trap, Ares,' said Parseus.

'Now what do we do?' shouted Ares.

Parseus stared down at the floor. 'I'm thinking about it.'

'Thinking?' Ares strained against his chains. 'Is that the best you can do?'

Parseus looked towards the door. 'We have no choice — we must summon the boys.'

'Boys? You're putting our rescue in the hands of those boys?' Ares gritted his teeth. 'Fine, then get them in here at once.'

'CHARLIE, MAX,' shouted Parseus.

Charlie, listening on the other side of the door, gulped. He stood up. 'It's down to us now, Max.'

'Us? Are you joking? How can we save the day?'

'Don't know.' Charlie could feel his knees wobbling.

'We're done for then,' groaned Max.

'Maybe, but we can't give up without trying. Are you in?'

Max took a deep breath. 'Not like we've got any choice is there?' he huffed. 'So yeah, I guess.'

CHARLIE opened the door and they crept into the room. 'What happened?' he said, looking up at Parseus dangling from the ceiling.

'Sisyphos laid a trap. Silly of me really, should have known. So we need your help,' said Parseus staring down. He seemed embarrassed.

'But what can we do?' asked Max helplessly.

'Just do as I say. It's a puzzle and the answer lies in the flagstones. Some have symbols, the others have numbers.'

'So how do we get across?' asked Charlie.

'I think I've worked it out. It's an equation. Just follow my instructions. Be careful though, some of the flagstones are traps,' Parseus called out. 'Don't step on the wrong ones.'

'Yes, but does he know how to free my chains? That is the point,' bellowed Ares as he continued to struggle.

'I'm sure that can be done,' Parseus shouted down. 'Looks to me like that chair was made by Hephaistos. There's bound to be some secret catch somewhere.'

Hephaistos? Charlie looked at Ares' chair and smiled to himself. Parseus was right — it had been made by Hephaistos. He recognised it. It was exactly like the one which had trapped Max in the forge. Somehow Sisyphos must have got his hands on one of them.

'Why are you smiling?' asked Max. 'What's to smile about?'

'This is the same chair that you sat on. Remember?' Hephaistos made it. I think I know how to release the chains. '

'Really?' said the others at once.

'Yes. There's a hidden catch somewhere under the chair. I am sure I can find it.'

The mood changed. Ares and Parseus now looked at Charlie with respect, though in Ares' case it was grudging respect. 'Then get on with it,' he ordered. 'Sisyphos could be back at any moment.'

Parseus began shouting instructions from high above to guide Charlie across.

Charlie did as he was told. Stepping forward he skipped across the first squares with ease. Halfway across, however, the squares became smaller and he had to step twice to the right. But just as he did so he briefly stepped out of the square. An instant later, two arrows shot out from the side wall, aimed directly at Charlie.

'GET DOWN,' Ares screamed, seeing them a split-second before anyone else.

Charlie ducked — but in doing so lost his balance and stepped back. The flagstone behind crumbled beneath him. Falling, he grabbed hold of the edge of the floor. Desperately clinging on by his fingers, his grip loosening, he looked down. Below him was a pit filled with sharp spikes just waiting to tear his flesh to pieces.

'MAX,' he screamed.

Forgetting his own fears, Max darted forward and following Charlie's lead, skipped across the squares in order. Dropping down, he grabbed hold of Charlie's wrists and dragged him up enough so that Charlie could heave himself to safety.

Charlie slowly stood up. He was shaking. 'Thanks Max — thought I was a goner there.'

Max wiped his brow. 'Me too.'

But Charlie knew it was not over yet. He took another deep breath and, with Parseus shouting instructions, stepped forward, testing the flagstone as he did so. The first was solid. So was the next one. He trod carefully across the others until he was right in front of Ares.

'What now, boy?' he said.

'I think all I need to do is reach under the chair. There should be a catch somewhere.' Charlie knelt down and fumbled under the chair until he felt something. 'I've got it,' he shouted.

'Good boy,' Parseus called out.

Charlie had found a small lever and he pulled it. He heard a click and the chains, which had bound Ares so tightly, instantly came free and retracted into the chair.

'Excellent work, boy,' said Ares leaping out of his seat. He looked up at Parseus. 'What now?'

Parseus peered down. 'Release Death, of course — and only you can do that. No one else has your strength. You have to break his bonds.'

Ares tested the flagstones before stepping forward. Reaching Death's chair, he took the bonds in his hands and with one mighty heave broke them. Death at last was free.

Ares unsheathed his sword, retraced his steps and sliced through the adamantine chains from which the net was suspended. Parseus crashed to the floor.

Clambering out of the netting, he dusted himself down and looked at the boys. 'We owe you our thanks. You saved us all.'

'Yeah, but we could have died you know,' said Max.

Parseus patted him on the back and smiled. 'Actually, Max, you couldn't have died while Death was still tied up — but we're grateful none the less. Aren't we Ares?'

'I suppose,' grunted Ares, clearly irked that he should have to be grateful to anyone.

'That's a relief. Glad it's all over...' Just as Max said that he turned around and found himself staring directly at Death. Their eyes met — and he fainted.

Parseus rushed forward. 'Sorry, I meant to warn both of you about that. Mortals mustn't look directly at him.'

'Why?' said Charlie as he knelt down and gently shook Max to bring him round.

'Because you faint for one thing, that's why,' said Parseus.

Max came to slowly and Charlie and Parseus helped him to his feet.

'Are you OK?' asked Charlie.

Max shook off his arm. 'OK? Are you kidding? I just looked Death in the face.' He shuddered. 'It was horrific.'

'You'll be fine,' said Parseus. 'Just don't do it again.'

Ares, now back in full voice, interrupted him, 'Enough of that. We have work to do. We must find Sisyphos. I'm going to make him pay for this.'

Parseus pointed to the secret door through which Sisyphos had disappeared a few minutes earlier.

'Follow me then,' said Ares. 'He can't have gone far.'

THE door led into a small passageway which wound downwards. It was dark but there was only one way to go so they felt their way using the narrow tunnel walls to guide them. Not long after it grew slippery, the dark, dank atmosphere providing perfect conditions for the moss that covered the passage walls. They slowed down, picking their way carefully.

Shortly afterwards, Charlie heard the sound of waves crashing onto rocks and saw a small circle of light appear up ahead. Emerging from the tunnel, they found themselves in a cove. A small jetty had been crudely carved from the rocks. And there, desperately struggling to untie the ropes of a small fishing boat was Sisyphos.

Spying the trickster, Ares leapt forward, sparks flying off his bronze armour, his face twisted with rage. He grabbed Sisyphos by the scruff of his neck, pulled him out of the boat and threw him up against the wall, pinning him by his throat. 'Sisyphos, you thief,' he snarled as he started squeezing the very life out of him.

Sisyphos' face turned red, his eyes almost bulging out of their sockets.

'Perhaps it would be best to let Hades...' Parseus suggested.

Ares stopped squeezing. 'You're right. A simple death is too good for Sisyphos. He deserves a more suitable retribution.' Releasing Sisyphos' throat he grabbed him by the arm and began to drag him back up the tunnel. The sobbing Sisyphos seemed doomed to a dreadful fate.

'What will they do to him, Parseus?' Charlie asked as they trailed after them.

Parseus hung back, not wishing Ares to hear. 'The story is well known, even in your world. His punishment is what you mortals call a Sisyphean Task. He's sent to Tartaros where he's forced to push a boulder up a hill but just as it reaches the top, the boulder rolls back down again and he must start all over. It's a punishment for all eternity,' he said. 'An impossible task.'

Rather like mine, thought Charlie glumly.

Reaching the chariot, Ares threw Sisyphos into the back and Charlie and Max climbed in beside him. Although Charlie had every reason to hate him for nearly killing him, knowing his fate as he did Charlie felt only pity for the weeping old man.

Parseus sat down opposite them with Death climbing in last, though neither Charlie nor Max dared look at him. The cold chill that emanated from him was bad enough.

Ares turned to Parseus. 'I don't think I need to stress this, but what happened back there, never happened, is that clear?' he said.

'Don't worry, Ares. No one will ever know of this. I'll make sure of that,' said Parseus. 'I promise.'

'Good, I shall depend on it,' said Ares, seemingly relieved that his reputation, such that it was, would remain intact.

'But there is one small favour I have to ask before we go.'

'What's that?' asked Ares.

'I would like you to help us secure the Helmet of Invisibility.'

Ares rolled his eyes. 'I doubt Hades will give that up.'

'Not to me maybe, but to you he would,' said Parseus.

Ares thought about it for a moment, and then pointed to the boys. 'For them?'

Parseus nodded.

'I suppose I owe them that,' said Ares as he picked up the

reins. 'But remember, not a word about any of this.' He whipped the stallions and the chariot rose up into the sky before setting off once again, this time to the west.

'Where now, Parseus?' said Charlie.

'We're taking Sisyphos and Death back to Hades.'

Charlie sat up. 'Where is Hades?'

'At the end of the world, in the far west,' said Parseus.

'Where?' asked Max.

'The Death Realms,' said Parseus. 'The Underworld.'

Charlie and Max exchanged a worried glance. That didn't sound good at all. And as the chariot flew away from the Gulf of Corinth, which sparkled below in the late afternoon light, any confidence Charlie had found in saving Ares vanished. He shrank back in his seat and a sense of dread crept over him once more.

After all, they were on their way to the world of the Dead.

10. DOWN BELOW

THE sky darkened as they sped towards the Underworld and a thick belt of cloud gathered ominously on the horizon. Not long afterwards the turbulence began: black clouds swirled round and gale-force winds battered the chariot, tossing it about as if it were nothing more than a leaf blowing in the autumn wind. Terrified, Charlie and Max clung desperately to the sides as Ares reined in the horses, struggling to maintain their course.

The air soon turned deathly cold and icicles started forming on the sides of the chariot. Parseus passed the shivering boys a fur rug and they huddled under it, grateful for any shelter from the freezing winds which now blasted them relentlessly.

A little while later they peeked out from under the rug.

'Are we nearly there yet?' said Max.

'I don't think so,' said Charlie, rather hoping that they weren't.

For the closer they came to the Underworld, and the more desperate the groans of Sisyphos, the more worried Charlie became. Sitting next to Death was bad enough. Its icy chill seemed to creep into every bone and sinew. But how much more dreadful would it be when they got to the world of the Dead, he wondered? He shrank back under the fur rug.

Shortly afterwards the winds eased, the stallions gathered pace and the chariot descended sharply before levelling out. Parseus pulled back the rug. 'Almost there,' he shouted. 'You can come out now.'

The boys lifted their heads and sat up. They were skimming

across a swamp. The dark clouds had given way to a pea-green fog, which hovered over the weed-infested waters. And as they sped across the surface, strange sounds filled the air — cries of despair and misery. It was all very different to the dry mountainous terrain they had left behind.

Charlie spotted something slithering silently through the dank, fetid waters behind them, as if in pursuit. It had a long snout and bulbous, green eyes. It looked like a giant crocodile. Other creatures, unseen, howled and hissed in the shadows.

Minutes later they left the swamp behind them and began flying across a barren landscape devoid of vegetation or life. The fearful sounds of the swamp now replaced with a stony silence.

A river appeared in the distance. Parseus stood up and pointed. 'That's the river Styx, boys, the river that dead souls must cross to enter the Underworld. We should see Charon soon.'

Charlie sat up. 'Charon?' He vaguely remembered reading about him.

'The ferryman,' said Parseus. 'He transports the dead across the river. That's why they're buried with an Obol.'

'What's an Obol?' asked Charlie.

'A coin. They place it in the mouth. It's Charon's payment.'

Max sat up. 'Ferryman? He's not another spirit is he?' he said, groaning. It was clear he was not eager to meet any more of them.

The fog cleared a little and a small jetty came into view. Charlie spotted a tall, cloaked figure standing up in a boat. It was the ferryman.

Ares pulled in the reins and the chariot stopped next to him.

Charon had a long grey beard that hung down almost to his waist and a wild mop of grey hair that looked as if it were trying to escape from his head, springing out as it did in all directions. His skin was also translucent as if drained of blood long ago, while his face was drawn: his cheeks sunken, his eyes hollow.

Charon eyed them suspiciously. 'What's going on?' he said, pointing to his empty boat. 'I've had nobody for at least two days.' He glowered at Death. 'What have you been up to?'

'He got himself kidnapped, that's what,' said Ares. He picked up Sisyphos by the ear and dangled him in the air. 'By this reprobate.'

'Did he indeed?' Charon leaned on his oar, clearly disgruntled. 'Thanks for telling me. Nice to know I'm being kept informed,' he said.

Ares was in no mood to placate him. 'Look, we're not here to chatter. We're here to see Hades.' And without another word, he whipped the stallions and the chariot set off once again.

'Don't worry,' Ares shouted back at him. 'You'll soon be kept busy enough.' Charon, almost knocked out of his boat by the rising chariot, shook his fist in anger as they disappeared into the fog.

Charlie, remembering his own brush with Death, grew uneasy. 'So what exactly happens to all the people who didn't die, Parseus?'

'Death'll catch up with them,' he said.

Charlie froze. 'What?'

'Don't worry. We'll secure you a reprieve, won't we Ares?' said Parseus.

'I give you my word as a God,' said Ares. 'Of course, it depends how charitable Hades is feeling,' he added, laughing.

Charlie gulped. He felt the blood drain from his face. What if he didn't get a reprieve? Would he die?

THE fog soon lifted and they found themselves flying across a flat, dusty plain that stretched out as far as the eye could see. A dull light emanated from the clouds which hung heavily in the sky, while a chill wind kicked up the black dust into great swirls. They swept across the plain like a herd of wild animals.

Then the shadows came — seemingly out of nowhere. Flitting about the chariot like flies, the strange apparitions ducked and weaved around them, wailing miserably, their shadowy faces twisted in despair.

'What are they, Parseus?' asked Charlie fearfully as he looked about him, the shadows diving in and out of the chariot, buzzing around his head, as if taunting him.

'They're the Dead, Charlie. We're in the valley of the Dead. This is where souls come before they're judged,' said Parseus.

'Judged?'

'Yes, all dead souls must be judged, Charlie. They go before the three kings: Minos, Rhadamanthys and Aeacus: it is they, who determine their fate,' Parseus replied in his usual casual manner.

'So what happens then?' asked Charlie. He had never read about this in any of his books.

Parseus tried to explain. 'Depends on the life they've lived. If it has been an exemplary life, then they will go to the Elysian Fields, which is paradise. If they've been evil, they go to Tartaros, the hell realm. Otherwise, if they have been neither virtuous nor evil, like most ordinary mortals, they will go to the Asphodel Fields. There they are made to drink from the river of Lethe — of forgetfulness — after which they no longer remember their former lives.'

'Nothing?' said Charlie.

'Nothing. They are simply shadows, trapped in an eternal limbo,' replied Parseus.

It sounded like a dreadful fate, Charlie thought. 'So where are these three kings?' he said.

Parseus pointed across the plain that stretched towards a ridge of black rocks which jutted up like knives in the distance. Charlie could just make out a large cave up ahead.

'They're in there. The dead must pass through the cavern of souls. It is here where they are judged,' Parseus said.

'We're not going inside are we?' asked Charlie. After all, what if he didn't get a reprieve from death? He might end up being judged too.

'Don't worry, Charlie. You're not dead — not yet anyway. And I'm sure we can secure a reprieve.'

But Parseus didn't seem very sure at all and as they neared the ridge of rock Charlie grew more worried.

The chariot ascended rapidly to clear the tips of the rocks. Parseus clapped his hands delightedly. 'We're here boys, Erebos, the home of Hades,' he said, pointing to a sinister-looking palace situated in the valley below.

Like the palace of Ares, Erebos had been carved out of the rock surrounding it. But unlike Ares' heavenly home, this looked more like a fortress. It seemed so impenetrable. Its walls were sheer black rock and there were no windows at all. Two towers stood on either side rising up into the darkness, sharp spikes jutting out of them like spears.

The valley below was littered with jagged rocks. As they grew closer, howls and hisses echoed through it.

'We're going there?' said Max, his voice quivering.

'Afraid so,' said Charlie.

Max put his head in his hands.

The chariot descended, coming to a stop outside an enormous wooden gate. Ares jumped down, dragging Sisyphos behind him and headed towards it, closely followed by Death.

A huge metal bar ran across the middle of the gate and as Charlie looked up at the towers he spotted strange, shadowy creatures perched on top.

'What are they, Parseus?'

'The eagles of Erebos,' he replied.

'Don't look like eagles?' said Max.

Parseus smiled. 'True. They are nothing like the ones in your world but they are useful enough. They're messengers of a sort — they keep an eye on the death realms and report to Hades.'

Parseus climbed down from the chariot. 'Now I'm sure we won't be here too long. All we need to do is borrow the helmet and you can return to your world.'

But as Charlie cast his eyes around he wondered how sure

Parseus could be. They were in the world of the Dead and further from home than ever. What if Hades refused their request? They would never get home. So as he clambered out and followed the others, it was with a heavy heart.

Ares waited for them before stepping up to the gate. He knocked and stood back. A moment later, Charlie and Max heard it. Barking. It sounded like a pack of wild dogs. Charlie turned instinctively to head back to the chariot, while Max was already setting off towards it.

Parseus grabbed Max by the arm and pulled him back. 'Don't worry. It's only Kerberus. He's harmless,' he said.

'Harmless?' said Charlie. He remembered Hades' description of him in the inn: the three-headed Hound of Hell didn't sound harmless.

The horizontal bar started screeching against the wood and slowly slid apart. Then the gate creaked open and an icy blast hit them squarely in the face. Charlie and Max tried to back off again but Parseus grabbed Charlie and pushed him inside, pulling Max in after him.

They entered the grounds, and both boys stopped in their tracks. For there, standing right in front of them, was Kerberus and it was a far more terrifying sight than anything Charlie had imagined.

It was enormous, more like a lion than a hound, its jet-black body covered in slime, its muscles tensed and rippling, as if ready to leap upon them at any second. And it did indeed have three heads, each of them snapping ferociously, their yellow teeth bared as a strange, green drool dripped from their mouths. Their red eyes, all six of them were filled with fury — and now firmly fixed on the two boys standing petrified before them.

Kerberus turned slightly and Charlie spotted its tail. It was made of snakes — hundreds of them, all writhing and hissing. The boys were transfixed. Nothing they had heard had prepared them for the actual sight of this hellish hound.

Yet neither Ares nor Parseus seemed the slightest bit

119

concerned. Ares, dragging the wailing Sisyphos behind him with Death trailing in his wake, calmly walked past the hound, barely giving it a glance. Kerberus obediently moved aside.

Parseus waved the boys forward. 'See, it's harmless. You're in no danger now. I told you, its job is to stop people leaving. So take no notice of it.'

The boys still held back but as Parseus walked on they saw Kerberus move aside once more. Realising they had no choice but to follow, they crept forward, Charlie's heart pounding as they did so. But Parseus had been right: Kerberus simply stepped aside, growling.

Once clear, they broke into a run and quickly caught up with the others. Neither one wanted to be left behind. Not in the Underworld.

Close up, the palace seemed even more sinister, surrounded as it was by huge, black marble columns, illuminated against the dark night by the strange, green glow. In the shadows Charlie could hear whispering and hissing, but he couldn't see anything.

Ares climbed the palace steps and rapped on the door, the sound echoing throughout the valley. A minute later, it creaked open and they walked inside.

They found themselves in a huge, black marble hall populated with strange ghoulish statues, dotted about in all manner of petrified poses. They all looked so life-like, as if frozen to the spot, and there was a strange mix of human and half-human sculptures, though each shared the same horrified expression.

Ares clearly knew where he was going and strode off down a dark passage to the left. And even though he had to drag a kicking and screaming Sisyphos along with him, the boys struggled to keep up with him. But as they followed, Charlie noticed something out of the corner of his eye. The statues were moving. As if they were turning to look at him as he passed.

He grabbed Max's arm. 'Check out the statues, I think they're alive,' he whispered.

'Alive?' Max glanced sideways. 'But I thought we were in the world of the Dead.'

'Maybe they're the un-dead?' said Charlie.

'Oh, that's alright then,' replied Max sarcastically.

'Stop worrying, Max. We're with the God of War, for crying out loud, what could possibly happen?'

'Anything — that's what,' said Max.

Max was probably right, Charlie thought as he walked on. Anything could happen here.

Ahead of them Charlie saw Ares stop outside a door, guarded on either side by shadowy spirits. 'I'm here to see Hades,' he said, dragging Sisyphos forward.

The spirits bowed deeply and moved aside. The door opened and Ares entered.

Parseus held the boys back. 'You're about to see the King of the Underworld, Hades, the one you met in the forge. Just keep quiet and say nothing. Is that clear?'

The boys nodded and nervously followed him inside.

The chamber was warm and surprisingly inviting. The walls and the floor were both in the same black marble, but richly coloured drapes adorned the room and jewel-encrusted divans and statues were scattered about casually. At the other end of the room, a large roaring fire was blazing in the hearth. In front of it, sat on a golden throne, was Hades himself, dressed in the same deep red robe he had worn in the forge.

He looked up as they entered. At the sight of Sisyphos, he leapt to his feet and stormed towards him. 'WHY YOU LITTLE THIEF,' he shouted.

Sisyphos slumped to the floor, whimpering.

'Whimper all you like. You have no idea what I have in store for you,' said Hades, picking him up in one arm and dangling him above the floor. He turned to Death, his face filled with contempt. 'Glad to see you back. But I want order restored quickly. Do you hear?'

Death bowed.

'With your permission, there is one exception, your majesty,' said Parseus, pointing at Charlie. 'The boy?'

Hades looked down at Charlie. 'Have I met you before?'

Charlie gulped. He wasn't sure whether he should say anything.

Parseus quickly stepped forward. 'Yes, your majesty, at the forge last night.'

Hades snapped a finger. 'Ah, yes. Dragon fumes. I remember. But what's he done to get a reprieve?'

Charlie felt his knees give way. Was this the end of him?

Ares stepped forward. 'He did help me rescue Death, Hades,' he said, shuffling awkwardly. 'In a small way,' he added.

Hades glowered at Death. 'Is that true?'

Death nodded.

Hades turned to Ares. 'You needed the help of a mortal boy?'

'We all needed his help, Hades,' replied Ares stiffly. 'He has earned a reprieve. I gave my word.'

Hades clenched his fist. 'The dead belong to me, Ares. It is my word which must be sought.'

'And I delivered Death to you. So you owe me a favour in return,' snapped Ares. 'I gave my word. Now give me yours.'

Hades' face twisted in fury and he began to change shape. Huge black horns sprouted from his head as his body transformed into a monstrous dragon-like creature, all sinews and veins and huge, black, webbed wings. Flapping them free, he flew up into the air and loomed over Ares.

'I am King of the Underworld. I do NOT take orders from you,' his voice was so loud it shook the whole room.

Charlie and Max backed into the shadows, certain they were now both doomed.

But Ares stood his ground, seemingly unfazed by Hades. 'What is one mortal boy to you? I give you more than enough souls. How many would you have if there were no wars?' he said.

Hades stopped flapping and flew back down to the floor, slowly transforming into his former self, though his face was still contorted with fury.

'Everyone dies eventually,' he muttered angrily. He stared down at Charlie as he fought back his rage. 'So be it,' he said finally through gritted teeth. 'He can have his reprieve. But he will be the sole exception.' He turned to Death. 'Mark my words — he is to be the only one. Now get back to your duties.'

Death bowed again, and turning, glided out of the room.

Charlie's heart had been beating so fast he thought it might explode but now relief washed over him. His life had been spared. He took a deep breath and tried to calm down, not daring to look at Hades, in case he changed his mind.

Hades, however, seemed to have lost interest in Charlie. Returning to his throne he angrily planted himself back down. 'That will be all then. You may leave now,' he said, waving a hand in dismissal.

'Actually Hades, I do have another favour to ask,' said Ares.

'Another one?' hissed Hades. 'What do you want? Jewels? Gold?'

'I said a favour, not a reward.' Ares stepped closer. 'I merely want to borrow the Helmet of Invisibility — that's all, nothing more.'

Hades leapt from his throne. 'The Helmet? But it is MINE. It cannot be so easily given. It was forged for me by the Cyclopes themselves. It was a gift for ME.'

'And I rescued Death, Hades and brought you Sisyphos,' Ares replied curtly. 'That is two favours, not one. You have repaid the first, but not yet the second. And I am not asking you to give me the Helmet, only to lend it. You'll get it back. I promise you that. You have my word.'

Hades fell silent as he considered the request. After what seemed like an age his rage subsided and he calmed down.

'Two favours?' He sighed heavily. 'If that is the price of Sisyphos then very well, you may borrow — borrow — my

Helmet. It's in the treasure chamber. Come, follow me and I will show you.'

Leading the way he swept out of the room and marched down a long, dark corridor before stopping outside an imposing gold door. Reaching into his robe, he brought out a large set of keys, found the right one and unlocked it.

Parseus pulled the boys to one side. 'You're about to see something truly amazing,' he said. 'Hades owns anything that comes from deep within the ground. All the jewels and gold in the Ancient World belong to him.'

'Wow — he must be rich,' said Max.

'Believe me, there's no one richer than Hades.' Parseus walked towards the open door. 'And in here is his treasure trove.'

The boys excitedly followed him inside and gasped in wonder. For it was indeed the treasure trove of the Gods. Piled high from floor to ceiling there was a dazzling array of the most beautiful jewels Charlie could ever have imagined. There were mounds of emeralds and sapphires, some the size of eggs, open chests brimming over with gold coins, huge and intricately carved swords and shields encrusted with jewels — all of them carelessly scattered about. The whole room sparkled so brightly that Charlie and Max had to shield their eyes from the glare.

Hades picked his way amongst the piles of treasure that filled every inch of the floor. He pointed to some armour hanging on the wall in the far corner. 'There it is, one of the finest pieces ever to have been forged,' he announced proudly.

It was a huge helmet, with a long strip that ran down the middle to cover the nose and two small slits for the eyes. It seemed to be made from a strange metal. It shone like a mirror making it sparkle in the jewelled light.

'Who made it again, Parseus?' whispered Charlie.

'It was forged for Hades by the three one-eyed Cyclopes. He used it in the ten-year war against the Titans to slip unseen into the palace of Atlas, the Titan. It played a vital role in the Gods' victory. It's a piece of immortal history,' said Parseus.

Even Ares seemed impressed. 'Tell me how it works?' he asked curiously. It was clear that he too had never seen it before.

Hades held up the Helmet and showed Ares a small catch on the underside. He clicked it and the Helmet instantly disappeared from view. His fingers clicked it back and it reappeared. 'See, it's quite simple.'

'Remarkable,' said Ares. He held out his hands for it.

Hades hesitated, as if unable to bear parting with it.

'You have my word it will be returned as soon as possible,' said Ares.

'I shall hold you to that. Remember, you have to be wearing it to be invisible but it will also hide anyone else holding onto the wearer. Do you understand?' replied Hades.

'Yes, yes, sounds straightforward enough. Believe me, I shall take very good care of it,' said Ares.

'Good. Then my debt to you is paid.' With that Hades threw the Helmet to Ares. 'Just make sure I get my souls,' he added.

'Trust me, I will give you them with pleasure,' replied Ares. 'And now that Death is back, that will no longer be a problem. But we can't afford to lose him again, can we?' he sniped.

And with that parting jibe, Ares bowed to Hades and turned to leave, beckoning Parseus and the boys to follow.

He stopped outside the door. 'My debt to you is also paid. Now I must get back to the chariot. I do have wars to wage.' He tucked the helmet under his arm and marched off down a small passage that branched off to the left.

'That's not the way we came in,' Parseus shouted after him.

'It's a short-cut,' Ares called back as he disappeared into the shadows.

PARSEUS sighed. 'Typical. Come boys, we must not lose sight of him,' he said.

They quickly set off in pursuit and a few minutes later reached a crossroads. Parseus stopped. 'Oh dear,' he said.

'What is it?' asked Max anxiously.

Parseus peered down each gloomy tunnel in turn. 'Not sure which one to take.'

'Don't tell me we're lost,' groaned Max.

Parseus hesitated. 'In a manner of speaking, yes.' He peered again. 'Although I think it's the middle one,' he added.

'Are you sure?' They all looked exactly the same to Charlie.

'No, but it's worth a try.' And without another word Parseus set off once more, the boys having no choice but to follow.

They had gone about a hundred yards when Charlie stopped and stared back down the passage. 'Did you hear that? Sounded like barking.'

Parseus listened. At first there was silence, and then the sound came again, much louder this time. 'It's Kerberus.' Parseus frowned. 'I'd hoped we could avoid an encounter. We will need to hurry.'

'I thought you said it was harmless,' Max edged forward nervously.

'Yes — when you arrive. Not quite so friendly when you try to leave, I'm afraid. I had assumed we'd be safe with Ares you see but...' Fumbling in his cloak pocket he pulled out a green jar. Charlie recognised it at once. It was the Strength.

Parseus uncorked the jar and handed it to Charlie. 'Take a good slug this time and then give it to Max — but be quick about it.'

Charlie did as he was told, the potion instantly coursing through him. He handed it to Max and he glugged it back before handing the jar back to Parseus. Then they heard something else. Growling. The hound was closer than they had thought. A moment later Kerberus appeared, creeping down the passage some fifty yards behind them, its teeth bared, its poisonous drool dripping to the floor.

'What do we do now, Parseus?' Charlie asked desperately.

Parseus briefly looked down the long, dark passage and then shouted, 'WE RUN.'

Charlie and Max took to their heels, neither one daring to

look back as Kerberus, barking furiously, began chasing them down the passage.

Racing after Max, Charlie felt his lungs bursting but as the Strength worked its magic his feet flew across the flagstones, barely touching them at all.

The barking grew louder. Kerberus was gaining ground. Fuelled as much by fear as Strength, Charlie pressed on, though neither he nor Max knew if they were even in the right passage. As he began to despair, the tunnel veered to the left and he saw lights up ahead. Seconds later he spied the open gate and beyond it, hovering expectantly, the chariot with Ares waiting impatiently, his horses chomping at the bit. For once Charlie was relieved to see him.

'Only a few more yards, boys,' Parseus shouted over his shoulder as Kerberus continued to gain on them. 'Come on,' he screamed.

Max reached the chariot first and leapt in, but as he did so Charlie, keeping up the rear a few paces behind, stumbled to his knees. Something fell from his pocket onto the ground beside him. It was the whistle Hephaistos had given him in the forge. His words flashed into his mind: You will know when to use it. With the fearful spectre of Kerberus bearing down on him, its heads snapping ferociously, its hot poisonous breath threatening to engulf him, Charlie reached for the whistle, put it to his lips and blew.

Kerberus, ready to pounce, suddenly stopped in its tracks.

Charlie blew the whistle again.

This time Kerberus dropped to the floor, whining like a sheep dog. Charlie could hardly believe it — it was a miracle. Seconds from certain death and he had been saved yet again. Staring at the now helpless hound, with the whistle still in his mouth, he got up and backed slowly away, keeping Kerberus firmly in his sights.

When he reached the chariot, Ares leapt down, and grabbed Charlie by the scruff of his neck. 'Come along, boy. This is no time to play with dogs,' he declared impatiently. 'You are holding us up.'

Hauling Charlie inside he picked up the reins and the chariot lifted off the ground. Whipping the stallions, the horses broke into a gallop and they flew over the wooden gate, back towards the ridge of black rock.

Parseus dusted himself down, sat back in his seat and smiled at Charlie. 'Didn't know Hephaistos had given you that whistle. Rather useful,' he said. 'If we ever meet him again, remember to thank him for it — saved your life.'

'What is it, Charlie?' said Max.

'Oh it's a will whistle,' interrupted Parseus.

'Will whistle?' said Max.

'Yes. Wonderful tool. Excellent for controlling behaviour. Only works on some creatures however,' said Parseus.

Max shook his head. 'Wonders never cease...'

Charlie laughed. 'You're not wrong there,' he said as he put the whistle back in his pocket.

'You're lucky. You know that, don't you?' added Max.

'I told you there's no such thing as luck, Max. Not here. There's only Destiny,' interrupted Parseus once again. He patted Charlie on the shoulder. 'And Destiny seems to like you,' he added.

Charlie smiled quietly to himself. That was something at least.

THE chariot cleared the ridge of rock and the dark shadows came again, flitting around them, wailing in misery. Down below, the boys saw a long line of people — still definable as such, but now just shadows of their former selves —queuing up in front of the cavern of souls.

Charlie leaned over. 'What's happening, Parseus?'

'We're back in the valley of the Dead again. It's getting busy with Death back in business.' He pointed towards the figures. 'They're waiting to be judged.'

Ares grunted. 'Think yourself fortunate, boy, that Hades agreed to your reprieve, or you'd be lining up there with them.'

Charlie's stomach tightened. 'Thanks,' he said weakly.

The chariot dived down and hovered above the ground outside the cave. 'Just want to make sure everything's getting back to normal. I won't be long,' said Ares jumping down and disappearing inside.

Charlie and Max watched the souls queuing patiently only a few feet below them, chattering amongst themselves. Some were soldiers, still dressed in armour. Charlie pointed at them. 'I think they're from that battle we saw — you know when they couldn't die.'

'You're right,' said Max.

Leaning over, Charlie was close enough to hear two of them talking.

'So what do you reckon: Asphodel or Elysian Fields?' said the first soldier.

'Not sure. I mean you've got to be pretty brave and true to get into the Elysian Fields. It's a tough one,' replied his friend.

'Think I'm probably headed for the Asphodel Fields myself. Never really been that heroic,' he said.

'Me neither. Still, at least you don't remember your former life. That's something, eh?'

'Considering what it was like, that's probably no bad thing,' replied the first soldier. Both men laughed and shuffled forward as the queue started moving.

Charlie was eager to see more. 'Can we go in and have a look?'

'If you wish,' said Parseus. 'But stay close, is that clear?'

Charlie promised and he and Max climbed down from the chariot and crept inside. Parseus followed.

The cavern of souls was huge, dark and deathly cold. There were torches hanging on the walls, but they gave off very little light, though Charlie could just make out three smaller passages at the back of the cave. In the foreground, sat upon jewel-encrusted thrones behind a large, marble table and surrounded by a host of efficient-looking spirits, all armed with scrolls, were the three kings.

Parseus pointed them out. 'The one in the centre is Minos — he's the most important — the one on the left is Rhadamanthys and the other is Aeacus,' said Parseus.

Charlie didn't like the look of any of these grim-faced kings.

Ares was standing to one side watching the proceedings, so they went and stood next to him. A strange spirit with a scroll started calling the deathly shadows forward one by one. The soldier the boys thought they recognised from the battle stepped up.

The spirit looked him up and down. 'Name?'

'Arestaeus,' the soldier replied.

The spirit ran his finger down the scroll, beckoned him forward and turned to the three kings. 'This is Arestaeus, soldier by trade, married with two children.'

Minos looked down at the table and began leafing through some parchment. 'Says here that you're guilty of pillaging,' he said.

Arestaeus shuffled awkwardly. 'Yes, your majesty, but to be fair, thieving goes with the territory. It's the spoils of war, ain't it? I mean there's got to be some reward, surely? Have you seen what we get paid?' he added hopefully.

The three kings huddled together, whispering. Then Aeacus looked up and raising his arm stamped the scroll. 'Asphodel Fields.'

Arestaeus grunted miserably but before he could object, another spirit rushed forward, grabbed him by the arm and dragged him down the middle passage.

'So he's been judged, Parseus?' asked Charlie.

'Oh yes. Judged, and found wanting,' Parseus said, tapping the side of his nose.

Charlie felt a twinge of pity for the poor soldier. He didn't seem to be that bad, but then he remembered what Parseus had said — 'neither virtuous nor evil,' those were the criteria for the Asphodel Fields.

The next soldier stepped up and stuttered a little as he said his name. He too was then judged. But he was luckier. It seemed he had lived an exemplary life and as Aeacus handed down the judgement, he clasped his hands in relief.

'There you go. That one's going to the Elysian Fields,' said Parseus.

Charlie and Max watched as a beautiful nymph-like spirit floated forward and gently took the man by the hand before guiding him down the passage on the right.

The next man stepped up. He was a mean-looking brute with a battered face, which was covered in scars. The three kings leaned forward and whispered conspiratorially. Minos looked up and fixed the man with a cold stare.

'You have murdered many men, stolen from even more and brought nothing but misery and pain to those you have encountered along the way,' said Minos. He turned to Aeacus who raised his arm and stamped the scroll with a loud thud.

'TARTAROS,' he shouted.

The whole cavern fell silent.

Charlie looked at Parseus. 'Tartaros? But that means he's going to...'

'Hell, yes,' said Parseus nodding his head gravely.

Then they heard it: a deep rumbling sound from far below. It grew louder, like thunder rolling in and the ground started to shake. The next moment they heard shrieking — a sound so terrible that everyone clasped their hands over their ears to try to shut it out. But they couldn't. It bored into their very souls, filling each one of them with dread.

Charlie felt the hairs on the back of his neck stand on end as the dark spirits emerged from the shadows. They almost defied description. If he had thought Death a terrifying sight, it was no match for these hellish ghouls.

They looked as if they had rotten flesh falling off them. They smelled like rancid meat and they moved sideways on all fours like crabs, their faces contorted in fury as their claws scraped along the ground. Charlie could hardly bear to look as they scurried towards the hapless man.

'What are they, Parseus?' he gasped.

'The spirits of hell.'

Charlie shrank back. Whatever fate awaited him in the future, he prayed it wasn't this.

The soldier, his fate sealed, sank screaming to the floor, begging for mercy. But there was none to give — only retribution to face.

The spirits swiftly engulfed him in their fearful stench and dragged him down the passage, his cries slowly dying out as he disappeared into the darkness and the depths of Tartaros.

Charlie had seen more than enough and thankfully Ares was growing bored. Satisfied that everything was back to normal he turned to leave. 'Come on. I haven't got all day, you know.' And with that he strode out of the cave. Parseus and the boys quickly followed. None of them wanted to be left behind — not in the valley of the Dead.

They climbed back into the chariot, Charlie and Max both too shocked to speak. Ares whipped the stallions and they shot off into the sky. When they came to the river, Charlie spotted Charon below, but this time he was too busy ferrying souls to notice them. A few hours later, they were back in the land of the living.

THE sun had just risen, bathing the landscape in a warm light. Charlie took a deep breath, the fresh mountain air dispelling the deathly odour of the Underworld. He was relieved to be back, even this dangerous Ancient World was preferable to the dank depths of Hades' realm. And he was alive — a debt admittedly he owed to Ares, who now seemed anxious to be rid of them.

'It's time to say goodbye, Parseus,' he said.

'Then drop us anywhere here,' Parseus replied.

Ares whistled and pulled in the reins. The chariot dived down and came to land on a grassy plain. Parseus and the boys climbed out. Ares handed Parseus the helmet.

'Thanks, Ares,' he said.

'Just remember, not a word, do you understand?' warned Ares.

Parseus clasped his hand over his chest. 'On my honour, Ares. I will say nothing.'

'You'd better not,' shouted Ares as the chariot took off once again. Charlie watched it shrink to nothing more than a black dot on the horizon.

'Where next?' he asked. Having escaped the Underworld, Charlie was in no mood to explore any more of this Ancient World.

Parseus took out the bronze compass. 'Home. That's where,' he said.

Max's face lit up. 'Really?'

'Yes, Max. And not before time. Your essences are fading,' said Parseus.

'Essences?' said Charlie.

'Indeed. Didn't mention them before. Thought it best not to worry you. You see, you belong to another dimension and when you leave your dimension it tends to notice your absence. Without your physical body your essence starts to fade,' said Parseus.

'What happens if our essences fade?' asked Charlie.

'You won't be able to return to your world,' said Parseus.

'What?' said Max. 'You mean we'd be stuck here forever?'

Yes, if we stay too long. That's why we need to go back. Give your essences a little recharge. Of course, I've no idea how long it actually takes them to fade. Could be weeks,' said Parseus. 'Or days,' he added casually.

'You mean we may not be able to go home at all,' said Charlie.

Max rolled his eyes. 'That's marvellous — we've become time-travelling guinea pigs.'

'Quite, so let's put it to the test, shall we?' said Parseus.

He checked the compass and handed Charlie the helmet. 'Now put this on.'

Charlie hesitated. 'But it's so huge. It will never fit me?'

Parseus grew impatient. 'Just put it on.'

Charlie lifted the helmet and tried to place it over his head. He had expected it to engulf him but to his surprise it started to shrink until it fitted him perfectly.

Parseus smiled knowingly before pulling Max forward. 'Now let's link arms, then you flick the switch, Charlie,' he ordered.

Charlie did as he was told, and the next moment they were engulfed in a strange mist. Yet he could still see the others clearly.

'It hasn't worked,' he said, despairingly.

'Oh it has. We're invisible to anyone else,' replied Parseus.

He finished fiddling with the dials. 'Now it's time to leave, so hold tight,' he announced calmly.

A swirling mass of light opened up in the ground in front of them. Charlie and Max stepped back, astonished.

Parseus pulled them closer. 'I said stay together.'

'But what is that?' said Charlie.

'It's a portal. That's how we got here, remember?' said Parseus.

'No, we don't,' said Charlie. Both he and Max had blacked out the first time and neither had remembered anything. Looking down at the whirring mass of cosmic energy spiralling into the ground, like water down a plughole, it was hard to imagine that this was how they had got here or how they would get back home.

'Remember, the Dark One will be waiting for us, so whatever happens, don't break the chain,' Parseus said.

Charlie felt a moment of panic. The relief at escaping the Underworld and the snapping jaws of Kerberus was short-lived.

For so much had happened in this world that he hadn't had much time to think of the Dark One. Being reminded of it now filled him with renewed dread. After all, he was the assassin's target.

But he had no choice. He could feel the portal draw him in, its force magnetic, the blue black lights almost hypnotic. An instant later, he was sucked into the abyss and it all went black — again.

11. BACK TO REALITY

THEY landed with a thud. Disoriented from spinning and feeling sick Charlie found it hard to steady himself but, helped by Parseus, he remained on his feet. He could feel Max's grip loosen so he grabbed his hand more tightly. The portal imploded and vanished into thin air.

Charlie opened his eyes and tried to focus, but the bright lights had sent a shower of black spots across his retinas, and it took a few seconds for them to dissipate. He shook his head and blinked. They were back in Max's kitchen, huddled near the back door exactly as before. Then he looked up and shrank back in horror. For there, looming in the doorway, was the Dark One, shaking its heads from side to side, startled by the flashing lights.

Charlie felt Max's grip now tighten in fear as they both held their breath praying that the helmet would protect them. Neither had quite believed that it would. For a moment the world seemed to stop as Charlie watched the Dark One hiss in fury, its eyes searching the room.

Now fully transformed, Charlie could see it had three black serpent heads, which were shaking wildly, their blood-red tongues lashing out in venomous fury. Its body was like that of a giant scorpion, its shiny black shell reflecting in the dim light gave it an almost metallic appearance and its barbed tail cracked like a whip through the air. It was an alien — there was no other word for it. More terrifyingly, it was an alien which had been sent to kill him.

Thankfully Charlie soon realised it couldn't see them — the helmet had worked. But any relief at that quickly vanished as the Dark One started creeping towards them, its heads sweeping across the floor, scouring it inch by inch. Although they were invisible, Charlie knew if it bumped into them, it would surely strike out and they would surely die.

He felt Parseus pull them back into the corner of the room but as he did so, the middle head lunged forward — stopping inches from Charlie's face. Closing his eyes tightly he could feel its cold breath, its sickly stench so overpowering that he hardly dared breathe. The head hovered for a moment but sensing nothing it slowly withdrew.

By the time Charlie dared open his eyes, the Dark One was back in the crumbled door frame, hissing.

It thrashed about for a few seconds more and then with a final hiss gave up its hunt and transforming itself back into shadow turned and disappeared into the sitting room.

Parseus waited for a minute then letting go of the boys he crept towards the kitchen door and peered into the sitting room. 'Good, it's gone — for the moment at least.' Smiling he put the compass back in his pocket. 'Glad the helmet worked. I wasn't entirely sure it would work against an Ancient,' he added, more to himself than anyone. 'But we should be safe now.'

Charlie and Max were too shocked to speak. They just stood there horrified. It had been their first proper sight of the fully-formed Dark One. And although they had escaped this time, Charlie knew if they were cornered like that again they might not be so lucky, helmet or no helmet.

'We must try and get back to the inn. It knew you were here so it's bound to come back and look for you again,' said Parseus. 'Grab hold of my arm, Charlie. Best if you remain invisible for the rest of the night.'

'Is it after all of us?' asked Max fearfully.

'No, but it is evil and if you get in its way it won't spare you just because you're not its target,' replied Parseus.

'Thanks. I feel so much better now,' groaned Max.

'And when we get back to the inn, remember to keep very quiet — I don't want your parents hearing us.'

'I wouldn't worry. They'll be fast asleep,' said Charlie.

'Good,' said Parseus. 'At least that won't be a problem.'

The boys joined Parseus and clambered into the sitting room. It was carnage. Tables were up-ended, ornaments smashed on the floor and broken chairs scattered about in pieces.

'My grandma's not going to be happy about this,' said Max as he surveyed the damage.

'She's the least of our problems, Max,' said Charlie.

'I suppose you're right,' replied Max as he looked around the room.

The boys followed Parseus out of the cottage, crept into the lane and turned right towards to the village.

The wind was whistling gently through the trees, an owl was hooting in the distance and Rufus, Tom the Boatman's dog, was barking. Nothing here had changed, yet after everything they had been through it felt so different. So much had happened since — as if a lifetime had passed, and Charlie knew it could never be the same again.

He looked up at the church. 'We're back at the same time that we left. Look.' Charlie pointed to the familiar clock through the trees ahead, its round face illuminated in the moonlight. It was just after eleven. No time had passed here at all.

'Hey, and my watch is working again.' Max put his wrist to his ear.

'I don't believe it,' Charlie said.

'But it is. It's ticking.'

'I'm not talking about your watch,' said Charlie.

'What is it?' Max looked up.

'There.' Creeping down the lane towards them was his sister, Emily. Charlie groaned. She should have been safely tucked up in bed, not creeping about in the dead of night.

'What's she doing out here?' said Max.

'Nosing, that's what,' said Charlie. 'Stupid girl...'

He was about to shout to her when he saw a frightened look cross Emily's face. Turning, he looked back up the lane. He gasped. The Dark One, still in shadow form, was heading towards them, searching the ground as it went.

Charlie's only thought now was for his sister. '*EMILY — LOOK OUT.*'

'Keep quiet,' hissed Parseus, pulling at his arm. But it was too late. The Dark One had heard him. Rising up, it turned this way and that, its eyes searching the lane but it couldn't see Charlie. Unfortunately it was Emily it now had in its sights. And as if sensing some new target, it fixed her with its cold yellow eyes and began to transform.

Transfixed in the Dark One's trance, Emily was paralysed. Charlie knew he had no choice but to get to her. Letting go of the others he leapt towards his sister. Parseus and Max immediately came back into view.

Grabbing Emily's arm Charlie enveloped her in the invisible mist, instantly breaking the trance.

Startled, Emily pulled back in surprise. 'Charlie? What's going on?'

'Shush,' he whispered.

'But what is that?' she said, pointing at the Dark One, which distracted by her sudden disappearance and the equally sudden appearance of Max and Parseus, hissed again, reared up, and finished its hideous transformation.

Emily gasped loudly.

'I said shush,' said Charlie, clasping his hand over his sister's mouth and pulling her back by the hedge which bordered the lane. They stood stock still, holding their breath while Max and Parseus remained stuck in the middle of the lane, in plain sight of the Dark One.

'Where's Charlie?' shouted Max.

'He's here somewhere,' said Parseus. 'But we can't risk him. We must draw the Dark One away.'

'Draw it away? You mean like bait?' said Max.

'Exactly. So start running.' Max needed no further encouragement and they both set off. 'We'll meet at the inn,' Parseus shouted back at Charlie.

With a trembling Emily clasped in his arms, Charlie could only watch as Max and Parseus raced down the lane. There was nothing he could do. The slightest sound and the Dark One would know where he was, even if it couldn't see him. So he held Emily tight instead, keeping his hand firmly over her mouth, praying the others would escape.

The Dark One hissed once more, and began chasing Max and Parseus. When it reached the point where Charlie had grabbed Emily, it stopped for a moment, looking around for its vanished prey. Charlie, hidden from view only a few feet away, held his breath.

The Dark One hovered a moment more and then, the scent lost, moved off down the lane in pursuit of the others, now disappearing down the village road towards the bridge, drawing the Dark One away from the square.

Charlie, trembling, waited until it had gone before taking his hand away from Emily's mouth and releasing his grip. She fainted. Charlie could hardly blame her but there was no time to lose. Max and Parseus had saved them. Now they had to do the same. He slapped Emily firmly across the face to bring her round.

Emily came to in his arms. 'What happened?' she groaned. Then remembering what she had seen she stood up and straightened sharply. 'What was that, Charlie? I mean it was... it was a monster,' she stammered.

'I'll explain later. We must get home and quickly.'

'But what's going on? And what's this mist?'

'We're invisible, Emily,' said Charlie.

'What?'

'Never mind now, we've got to go. Just do as I tell you.'

Taking her hand he pulled her into the lane and they started running — Emily was still dazed with shock but she ran for her life nonetheless.

At the oak tree beside the village church they paused. Charlie guessed Max and Parseus had drawn the Dark One towards the river, hoping to lose it by backtracking along the river bank. They could then slip up the lane to the inn's side entrance before it realised where they had gone. If they could only get back under the protection of the helmet they would be safe.

But that meant that Charlie and Emily had to get to the inn first.

Charlie dragged Emily forward. 'Come on — run.'

Emily stumbled for a moment but Charlie pulled her to her feet. Racing across the square, they headed for the inn's side entrance. Once there, Charlie threw open the door and they tumbled inside, breathless and desperate.

Moments later Charlie heard Max and Parseus racing around the corner and then they too tumbled through the door. Charlie reached out and grabbed Max's arm. Max in turn grabbed Parseus. He pulled the door closed behind them.

They huddled together under the helmet in a corner of the hallway and waited, no one daring to speak, hardly daring to breathe, their hearts pounding in their chests like drums.

Parseus inched them over to the window. Charlie peered out. The Dark One had raced past the inn but then stopped. Max and Parseus were nowhere to be seen and it was clear it had lost the scent. Its heads were darting from side to side, confused. It hovered for a moment more then transformed back to shadow.

A second later they heard Rufus barking again in the distance. Distracted by the sound, The Shadow stopped and then started slithering away from the inn.

Parseus who had kept his eyes fixed on the square turned back to the others. 'I think we're all right now. It's heading back towards the lane,' he said, visibly relieved. 'Probably thinks that's where we went. We've lost it for now.'

Max gasped loudly and bent double, taking huge deep

breaths as the shock and effort of the chase caught up with him. Shaking from top to toe it took some time for him to calm down. Then straightening he looked at Charlie. 'You know, if I could run like that in the school race I'd always win.'

Charlie burst out laughing. 'I always said all you needed was a bug up your bottom,' he replied.

'Some bug,' Max said, shaking his head.

Emily, still terrified and utterly confused, burst into tears. 'What's going on? I don't understand it. I mean, what was that?'

'Don't worry Sis. You're safe now and I'll explain everything, I promise,' said Charlie.

Emily wiped a tear from her cheek and then, clearly angry that she had been seen crying, she punched Charlie in the shoulder. 'Well, you'd better.'

Parseus raised his arm. 'Explanations can wait. For now I want you all upstairs. And keep that helmet on until dawn. Do not break the chain. You must all remain protected tonight — it might well return. We're not taking any chances. Just remember the Dark One can only attack at night. Do you understand?' he said.

They all nodded. 'But what about you?' Charlie asked.

'Don't worry. I'll be fine. I'm a Time God.'

'Time God?' said Emily. 'What's a...'

'Later, Emily,' said Charlie. And whispering goodnight to Parseus, he hushed the others before they crept upstairs to his room, anxious not to wake his parents on the top floor.

'I want to know what's going on?' said Emily, sniffing back the last remaining tears as Charlie quietly closed the door behind them.

Charlie knew he had little choice but to tell her exactly what had happened. She deserved to know. He tried to make it as simple as he could, but as the story unfolded, he could see Emily veer from fear to open-eyed amazement as he recounted the events of the last few days.

Incredible though it sounded, Emily accepted it without the slightest hesitation — the terrifying sight of the Dark One was proof enough that it was the truth, though she remained silent for a while after Charlie finished.

'So you're this — this Destined One. Is that right?'

'Yes, it is,' interrupted Max. 'Probably because Charlie's super-clever. He's always reading books,' he added as if that were reason enough.

'Don't be stupid, Max.' But his mention of books did give Charlie an idea. 'Come on, shift over here, will you,' he said dragging the others over to the bookshelf. He started rummaging through his collection.

'What are you looking for?' asked Max.

'A book on Greek mythology. I've got it somewhere, I know I do,' said Charlie, more to himself than anyone else.

He kept searching and then pulled out a dog-eared book. Kneeling down he started leafing through it but many of the pages had been lost and the rest were stuffed in haphazardly, but it was better than nothing, Charlie thought.

'So what's it say?' asked Max.

Charlie flicked through the pages. 'There's lots of stuff about the Gods, and some of the myths but I can't find anything about the Dark One,' he said. 'Parseus did say it pre-dated the Gods. So maybe there won't be anything. I don't remember reading about it.'

He turned over a page. There was a picture of Kerberus on it. He held it up.

'Remind you of anything, Max?'

'What? That looks nothing like it,' said Max.

'Then what does it look like?' said Emily, her curiosity now returning.

'A lot fiercer, I can tell you,' said Charlie.

'And it's got this poisonous, green drool which drips from its mouths,' added Max.

'Poisonous?' Emily whispered.

Max was starting to enjoy himself. He put a hand across his throat. 'One drop and you're dead.'

Charlie went back to the book but he still couldn't find any mention of the Dark One. He was about to close it when he spotted something. He froze. The Shadow was back and *it was creeping under his door.*

12. HEAVENS ABOVE

CHARLIE carefully closed the book and, putting his finger to his lips, pointed to the shadow now creeping into the room. Emily gasped silently as the room darkened and the shadow started crawling up the walls. Charlie grabbed her arm and pulling her close they crouched down by the armchair, holding their breath as they watched The Shadow creep across the ceiling, down the walls and over the beds. Charlie knew they couldn't afford to make a sound.

The Shadow slithered across the floor towards them. Charlie wondered what would happen when it reached them. Would it be able to penetrate their cloak of invisibility? It was still only shadow, after all.

Fortunately, with no scent or sound to pick up, The Shadow stopped, turned, and crept back under the door, disappearing into the corridor. Charlie motioned Max and Emily to remain silent. It was a minute or two before anyone even dared move.

Charlie leaned forward. He was relieved to see the light from the corridor was again visible under the door. The Shadow had gone.

'Are we OK?' choked Emily.

'I think so,' said Charlie.

He was just about to get up when the light vanished once more. His heart sank. Was The Shadow back?

Then the door flew open and Parseus burst into the room.

'We've been summoned,' he announced loudly.

'What's going on?' said Max. 'Where's The Shadow?'

Parseus stopped. 'The Shadow was here?' he asked.

'Yes — just before you came in,' replied Charlie.

'Wait here,' and with that Parseus disappeared back into the corridor. He quickly returned. 'It's gone. I caught sight of it through the window — heading back up the lane again. I doubt it will be back tonight. There's no scent to pick up here.'

Charlie stood up. 'Good, now maybe we can get some sleep —I'm exhausted.'

'Not possible, I'm afraid. You and I must go,' said Parseus urgently.

'Go where?'

'To see Zeus.'

'Zeus? The king of the Gods?' said Charlie. 'But why?'

'Not sure. We've been summoned, that's all,' said Parseus. 'They don't come with explanations.'

'Summoned where?' said Charlie.

'The Heavens,' replied Parseus.

'Heavens?' said Max.

'Yes, the immortal dimension.'

'Another one? How many dimensions are there?' said Max.

'Never you mind. Just come along. Charlie. Zeus doesn't like to be kept waiting.' Parseus turned back to the door.

'So what do we do while you're gone?' said Max. 'What if it comes back?'

'You'll be perfectly safe under the helmet. Charlie won't need it where he's going. You and Emily can stay under its protection until sunrise,' said Parseus. 'We'll be back by then.'

Charlie protested. 'But can't we go tomorrow? I told you, I'm exhausted. I can't remember when I last slept properly.'

Parseus shook his head. 'Zeus is not to be kept waiting, believe me.' He took the jar of Strength from his cloak pocket. 'Here, a sip of that will see you through — but just a sip, no more. We won't be long.'

Charlie groaned, but did as he was told.

Parseus turned to leave. 'We'll go from my room. We can't risk taking the others with us.'

'OK,' said Charlie wearily. He followed Parseus into the corridor, glancing back briefly as he was shutting his bedroom door but Max and Emily had both safely disappeared from sight.

Charlie hurried along the corridor, still fearful that somehow The Shadow might return. Without the helmet he was completely exposed. It was not a comfortable feeling. When they reached Parseus' room, Parseus fumbled in his trunk and brought out what looked like a bracelet. He fixed it to his wrist.

'What's that?' asked Charlie.

'This works much like the compass, so hold on tight.' Parseus grabbed Charlie's arm and flicked a switch on the bracelet.

A portal opened up. Charlie felt the now familiar pull and everything went black.

OPENING his eyes, Charlie recovered his composure more easily than before. There wasn't the nausea which he had felt when he had travelled to the Ancient World.

'I'm starting to get used to this portal travelling,' he said as he straightened. 'Don't feel sick.'

'That's because you haven't travelled back in time. It's time-travel that causes the nausea. We've just travelled to a different dimension that's all,' said Parseus. 'The immortal realm exists in the same time as your world.'

Charlie looked around. Like Hesper it was the middle of the night. But he could tell he was in a very different dimension. The sky was filled with an array of stars arranged in all manner of weird and wonderful constellations but these ones actually looked real. Charlie spotted a scorpion and a hunter.

Looking around it felt to Charlie as if he were in a world of giants. They had landed in front of a huge, golden gate which led to an enormous palace beyond. It reached so far up into the sky that it seemed to go on forever. Leading up to the palace there was an avenue, laid with bronze flagstones, bordered on either side by huge trees. A set of steps stretched up to the palace itself, surrounded on either side by four columns, cased in gleaming gold.

It reminded Charlie of the palace of Ares, though it was far larger and far more magnificent. 'Where are we exactly? he asked.

'Zeus' palace,' said Parseus. 'And, as I said, he does not like to be kept waiting. So come along.'

They set off towards the palace, and a few minutes later reached the entrance. The door was made of bronze and intricately carved with figures and symbols. It slowly swung open as they approached.

Parseus pushed Charlie inside. 'Remember, speak only when spoken to — is that clear?'

Charlie nodded though he was so dumbstruck he wasn't sure he would be able to speak at all.

Once inside, he found himself in a white marble hall, its walls covered with murals: men in armour fighting monsters, women dancing with all manner of strange creatures.

A figure appeared out of the shadows and drifted towards them, as if walking on air.

'Ah, here's Hermes,' Parseus said. 'It must be urgent.'

'Hermes? Isn't he the Messenger of the Gods?'

'Yes, that's right. He'll be taking us to see Zeus.'

Hermes stopped in front of them. Very handsome and young he was dressed in a simple short, white robe, his blonde hair hugging his hair in tight curls.

He eyed Charlie with disdain. Charlie, with his torn trousers and ripped shirt, had forgotten how dishevelled he looked. For a moment he wondered if Zeus might be bothered by that. But there was nothing he could do about it now.

Hermes beckoned them and led them down a passage to the left. A few minutes later he stopped outside a golden door and knocked. The door opened. 'Zeus will see you now,' he said.

Charlie followed Parseus inside, but as he entered the chamber he stepped back in shock. For there, sitting on a huge throne and surrounded by a halo of light was what he assumed must be Zeus himself.

He was another giant of a God, with white blonde hair that flowed past his shoulders and a short, well-manicured beard. His face was deeply tanned but there were no lines or wrinkles, though he didn't seem young — just ageless, while his white robes shone with such brilliance it gave him an ethereal air.

He was also throwing what looked like thunderbolts at the wall. They were exploding in great balls of light as they hit it. Seeing Charlie, he stopped and stared at him.

Charlie didn't dare move. He could feel the God's eyes sear him into like a hot poker, his power exuding from him like a scent.

'So this is The Boy, is it?' Zeus declared. His voice was deep and ominous and echoed round the chamber, bouncing off the gold covered columns.

Hermes stepped forward and bowed. 'Yes, great Zeus.'

'Bring him here,' Zeus ordered.

Parseus pushed Charlie forward. 'This is Charlie Goodwin, your majesty. The Destined One.'

'I know who he is, Parseus,' said Zeus. He rose from his throne, picked up Charlie in one hand and began inspecting him, as if he were an artefact of some sort. 'Hmm, bit small isn't he?' Zeus said to no one in particular.

'Yes, your majesty but he has great spirit,' said Parseus, almost by way of apology.

'He's going to need more than just spirit,' snapped Zeus. And seemingly satisfied with his inspection, he dropped Charlie onto the floor and sat back down in his throne. He started tossing a thunderbolt up and down in his hand.

'As you know, the Dark One was an unexpected and unwelcome development,' he said. He looked at Charlie, who was slowly getting back to his feet. His tone grew icy. 'To think the Titans have been contained for millennia and it takes humans a mere two hundred years to weaken the foundations of Tartaros.' He threw another thunderbolt at the wall. 'I've half a mind to wipe them from the face of the earth,' he roared.

Charlie shuddered. Was he serious?

Parseus patted Charlie reassuringly on the shoulder and stepped forward. 'Your majesty I understand your rage but The Prophecy...'

'Yes, I know,' Zeus snarled, raising his hand. 'The Fates have made my position quite clear, thank you. The humans must be spared.' Zeus eyed Charlie critically. 'At least you got to The Boy in time.'

'Indeed, your majesty. The Dark One was already there.'

'No thanks to the Fates. You'd think they would have seen the Dark One coming.' Zeus drummed his fingers on his throne.

Hermes intervened. 'No one could have known that, your majesty. Even the Fates cannot see everything, especially in the depths of Tartaros.'

Zeus glared at him and Hermes backed away. Charlie detected the slightest of trembles. He was almost glad that even a God felt the same trepidation that he did.

'Speaking of the Fates, we must pay them a visit. There is much we still need to know, Parseus. That is why I summoned you. Come, we will go now,' said Zeus.

Rising from his throne he grabbed Charlie's hand. 'Here Boy, it's time to see what trials and tribulations destiny has in store for you.'

Charlie winced as Zeus' grip tightened, the blood draining from his veins as the great God pulled him forward.

A moment later a bright light appeared in front of them. By the time Charlie stopped blinking he realised that they were no longer in Zeus' chamber but standing in a courtyard in front of a small, round building, surrounded by columns that rose up into the night sky. However, unlike the sumptuousness of Zeus' palace, this place was dark and derelict.

Zeus let go of Charlie's hand and swept into the building.

'Where are we?' Charlie whispered.

'The Temple of the Fates,' replied Parseus.

'Not much to look at, is it?' said Charlie, trying to sound braver than he felt.

'That's not really the point. Now come,' said Parseus.

Once inside the temple Charlie was no more impressed. Inside its circle of columns and centred on the chamber floor sat a small, moss-covered marble font. A strong breeze wafted in and out of the columns and a strange, blue mist swirled round their feet. It was cold and eerie — and there was no one about.

Charlie tugged Parseus' sleeve. 'Where are the Fates?'

'Believe me, they'll be here soon. You'll see,' said Parseus.

Zeus stepped into the middle of the chamber and clicked his fingers. 'Come NOW,' he ordered.

An instant later three wizened women emerged from the shadows. Charlie was taken aback. They were ancient: bent double and haggard, their pallid skin hanging loosely from their faces in great folds, their straggly grey hair so long it trailed along the floor behind them, their eyes bulging so much they looked as if they might pop out at any moment.

'That's them?' said Charlie.

'Yes. And they're very powerful indeed.'

'But they're so ugly,' whispered Charlie.

One of the women now leapt forward, startlingly quickly, grabbed Charlie by the shoulders and looked him straight in the eye. Charlie leaned back and tried to avoid her gaze.

'Looks aren't everything, boy,' she snarled through blackened teeth, her voice deep and hoarse.

He pulled back. 'So-so-sorry, didn't mean to offend you.'

The old woman threw back her head and cackled. 'Offended? You couldn't offend me, boy.' Her face softened a little and her mouth cracked open in what appeared to be a smile. Then the other two crept over, pushing each other out of the way as they did so.

'Let me have a look — let me see him in the flesh,' said the smallest of the three as she crawled towards him, her arms outstretched, her face flushed with excitement. The other one punched her in the arm. 'You've always got to be first, haven't you?' she snarled.

Zeus clicked his fingers again. 'Enough. Come. Tell us why are we here? What news? Speak,' he said.

The Fates shuffled over to the marble font.

Parseus leaned over and whispered in Charlie's ear. 'That's the Font of All Knowledge. Remember I told you? That's how we know about the Prophecy.'

The Fates leaned over the font and dipped their fingers into the water. The blue mist that had been swirling round their feet now drifted towards the marble font, enveloping it and the Fates in a cloud. The swirling grew more violent as it spun faster and faster and then the Fates appeared to slip into a trance, their arms outstretched they started mumbling incoherently.

Zeus watched them intently. He seemed impatient.

A plume of blue mist spiralled up out of the font like a funnel of light, reaching up into the dark expanse of night — and then just as quickly vanished. The mist dissipated and the Fates turned around.

'So what have you learnt?' demanded Zeus.

The three Fates approached him and bowed reverently.

'The Boy must return to the Ancient World, your majesty,' said one. 'He is to be trained by Cheiron.'

'Who?' whispered Charlie.

'Cheiron, the centaur. He has trained some of the finest heroes in the Ancient World. A good choice I would say,' replied Parseus.

Charlie blinked. 'But trained to do what?'

'Shush, I will tell you later.'

Zeus stepped up to the font. 'But what of the Dark One? Do we know how to defeat that?'

The Fates exchanged a troubled look.

'And how did the Titans find out about The Boy?' Zeus added. He was clearly angered by that.

'We cannot know it all. The Font of All Knowledge does not show us everything. Especially not in Tartaros, great Zeus,' said one. 'You know that. The Dark One could not be foreseen.'

'So you say. Yet we've had no time to prepare and the Dark One poses a grave threat.' Zeus glared accusingly at the Fates.

One of the Fates shuffled forward. 'It is not our fault, great Zeus. The Titans have knowledge of the Prophecy too. The Boy will just have to find a way, your majesty. It is his destiny.' Her face darkened. 'But be clear, only he can do it.'

'How wonderfully cryptic,' sneered Zeus. 'But can The Boy defeat the Dark One?'

Charlie gulped. Defeat the Dark One? ME?

Another of the Fates approached Charlie and ran her long, bony finger down his cheek. 'Perhaps Zeus. Time will tell.'

'Typical,' sighed Zeus. 'But how is he to save the universe if he cannot even defeat the Dark One?'

'The Prophecy did not say that he would. It said only that he could. That he is the only hope. Many obstacles stand in his way, great Zeus,' she replied.

'Indeed they do,' said Zeus. He clicked his fingers once more and the temple was filled with a ball of bright, white light. Gathering his robes about him, he took one last look at Charlie. 'Fulfil your destiny Boy, or we are all doomed,' he warned. A second later he vanished.

Charlie shook his head. It was all so utterly confusing and so hopeless. Did they realise what the Dark One was? Did they realise he was just a boy?

'You'll just have to find a way. You're the only one who can,' said one of the Fates.

Charlie looked up. 'Did you just read my mind?' he asked.

The old woman laughed. 'Humans, you are so ignorant,' she said. 'Anyway you're not just *a boy*. You are the Destined One.'

'Destined to save the universe?' Charlie could hardly believe he was saying it.

'Perhaps yes, but first you must defeat the Dark One,' she said.

'But how?' said Charlie. He was feeling sick again and his head had started spinning.

'You must protect your sister, for without her all is lost,' said another of the three Fates.

'My sister?' Astonished, Charlie looked at each of them in turn but they wouldn't elaborate.

Then one of them grabbed him by the wrist. 'Destiny is not easy Boy. But it always works for the good. Remember that. So let Destiny unfold and play your part,' she added unhelpfully.

'But why am I the Destined One?' asked Charlie.

The Fates exchanged a knowing look, but refused to say more. And with that they disappeared.

Left alone in the eerie and now empty temple, Charlie's mind was racing — but now all he wanted to do was get out of the temple as quickly as possible.

'Can we go home, Parseus?'

'No, not quite yet. We still have a few hours until daylight — and I think we should pay Hephaistos a visit. We have much to thank him for. His workshop's not far away.'

ALTHOUGH Zeus had brought them to the temple instantaneously, they now left it on foot, making their own way down the mountain path to the immortal realm below. They reached the main square an hour or so later. Hurrying across it, they made their way down a small side street which led to a cobbled courtyard.

Charlie saw a slightly haphazardly-constructed house on the other side. A marble trough sat outside along with piles of metal and broken bits of wood. It had to be Hephaistos' workshop, he thought. Almost on cue the God appeared, muttering to himself as he started searching through a stack of twisted metal.

Hephaistos looked up, surprised.

'Ah, Parseus — back so soon?'

'Zeus summoned us,' replied Parseus. Hephaistos smiled knowingly. 'I hear there have been developments.'

'You could say that. Lucky we had your Time Compass,' said Parseus. 'You have no idea how useful it has been. Thank you.'

'Really, so it works as I said it would?'

'I'll say. We used it to escape the Dark One. We've been back to the Ancient World. We even met you there.'

'Me? How fascinating. When was that precisely?'

'When we visited you at your forge in the Ancient World,' Parseus reminded him.

He pulled Charlie forward. 'You remember the boy? He was with me. It was just after Death was kidnapped.'

Charlie wondered for a moment why Hephaistos might have forgotten him after only a few days, then remembered that for him many thousands of years had passed since then.

Hephaistos stared at Charlie for a while and then snapped his fingers. 'Of course. Who could forget that? Ares still goes on about it: Of course when I rescued Death...' Hephaistos imitated Ares' booming voice.

Charlie couldn't help giggling. 'Yes but we helped him rescue Death too,' he piped up.

'Did you?' asked Hephaistos. 'How very interesting. Ares never mentioned that.'

Parseus shot Charlie a warning look. 'Yes, but we promised that our small part in it would remain a secret. It was the only way he would help us secure the Helmet of Invisibility,' said Parseus. 'No need to say more. I am sure you understand.'

Hephaistos put a finger to his lips. 'Quite. But it does make more sense. Ares rescue Death? I never quite believed he did it on his own.' He glanced at Charlie. 'So the helmet's proved successful?'

'Oh yes, just as you said. It's proved to be the perfect protection from The Dark One,' replied Parseus.

'No trouble in getting it then?' Hephaistos asked.

'Thanks to you, no,' said Charlie. 'Kerberus would have got

me, otherwise. That whistle you gave me really saved my life. I'd have been lost without it.'

'Ah, thought it might prove useful,' said Hephaistos.

Charlie glanced curiously around. 'Any more inventions?'

Hephaistos playfully cuffed his ear. 'Of course there are, boy. What do you think I've been doing for the last few thousand years — twiddling my thumbs?'

'Sorry, forgot. For me, it's only been a few days.'

'I know. I did invent the Time Compass,' said Hephaistos. 'It's my finest work, you know.'

'Indeed it is,' replied Parseus.

'Tell me, what do you want now?' asked Hephaistos.

'Nothing,' said Parseus. 'I thought we'd come and thank you for all you have done, that's all.'

'Glad to have been of help. Very interesting, very interesting indeed.' Hephaistos eyed Charlie. 'But enough of that. Are you hungry?'

'Tired more like,' said Charlie.

'Mortals? Always wanting to sleep and eat. Of course, if you had ambrosia and nectar...'

Parseus coughed loudly. 'You know the rules Hephaistos. That is the food of the Gods. It is not for mortal mouths.'

'Yes, yes I know. Can't have a mortal tasting the fruits of immortality.' Hephaistos wagged his finger mockingly and then beckoned Charlie. 'Come boy, you can sleep over there.' He pointed to a pile of furs laid out on a bed.

In all the excitement Charlie had forgotten how tired he was. The strength had worn off now. Climbing onto the bed, he lay down and almost immediately fell fast asleep.

PARSEUS woke him a couple of hours later. 'It'll be daylight soon and safe to return,' he said.

Charlie yawned and sat up. He had quite forgotten where he was for a moment but the memories soon flooded back. Getting up he followed Parseus back through the chamber.

Hephaistos approached.

'Are you leaving?' he asked.

'Yes, time to go.'

Charlie said goodbye. 'Thanks again Hephaistos.'

'No need for thanks. Just take care boy. It seems Destiny has great plans for you. Any time you need my help just ask. I am working on a few gadgets that might prove useful in the future. So keep in touch,' Hephaistos replied.

And with that they bade goodbye and left the workshop. Parseus fixed the bracelet to his wrist. 'Time to get back to your world,' he said.

But as Charlie looked around the immortal realm he didn't really feel like going back. He wasn't looking forward to his Destiny at all.

13. BRIEF RESPITE

CHARLIE and Parseus arrived back in the inn just as the sun was rising. Charlie was relieved to see it. The threat from the Dark One was over — for the moment.

'Why can't we just stay in the heavens every night until we find out how to defeat the Dark One?' he asked.

'Same problem, Charlie — essences.' Parseus replied. He took off his cloak. 'Besides, mortals are not allowed in the immortal realm except by special dispensation — we can go only if summoned by Zeus.'

'Pity,' replied Charlie. 'I liked it there.' After the wonders of the immortal realm — the temple of the Fates notwithstanding —Hesper seemed dark and cold, drab even. Charlie didn't think he would ever see his own world in the same light again.

Parseus started rummaging around in his trunk, muttering to himself as he picked out various objects and placed them on the bed.

Charlie watched him curiously. 'What are you doing?'

'We have our instructions. We must return to the Ancient World so you can be trained. I'm just making sure we're properly equipped, that's all.'

'But how long will that take?' Charlie asked. 'We came back after only two days because you said our essences were fading.'

'Yes, but they didn't fade as much as I had feared. I think you could probably last a few weeks in the Ancient World, which is good news, isn't it?'

Charlie groaned silently. He wasn't sure he could last a few days in the Ancient World. He'd already had enough adventure to last a lifetime. It was a lot more fun when he read about it, he decided.

'We'll be leaving in a few hours,' said Parseus. 'We must do so while it is still light so we can avoid the Dark One.'

The mere mention of the Dark One sent a cold chill down Charlie's spine. The Fates had said he had to defeat it, but how on earth was he going to do that?

He returned to his own room. He couldn't see Max or Emily but feeling his way across the bed, he found Max's leg and immediately entered the invisible shroud. Max and Emily, lying head to toe, were both sound asleep so Charlie shook Max to wake him.

'What's going on?' Max mumbled before looking nervously round the room.

'It's alright. It's daylight. You're safe,' said Charlie.

Max removed the helmet and he and Emily came back into view.

Charlie looked down at his sister, curled up in his duvet, asleep on his bed and remembered what the Fates had said about her: protect your sister, without her all is lost. But why he wondered? Why hadn't they explained it? Zeus was right, he decided, the Fates were very cryptic.

'Well, how was it?' said Max, rubbing his eyes.

'Quite amazing, actually. But I'll tell you later. Why don't you go back to sleep.'

Max yawned and lay back down. Charlie went and sat in the armchair, his mind racing with everything he had seen and had been told.

'CHARLIE, IT'S NEARLY NINE,' his Mum yelled. Charlie sat up slowly. He had fallen asleep in the armchair, too tired to crawl into bed. Max and Emily were just stirring. When Emily woke up she immediately started pestering Charlie with questions.

'So what was whatever you call it — the immortal realm

— like?' she asked. 'Is it very different to our world? What does it look like?

'Difficult to describe but it was, well, I suppose it was perfect,' said Charlie.

Max yawned and stretched. 'Did you meet this king of the Gods?'

'Zeus. Yes.' But Charlie was in no mood to say more. 'You should go back to your room, Emily. We'll see you at breakfast,' he said.

'But I want to know what...?'

Their Mum shouted again, this time for Emily.

'Later, Emily,' said Charlie. 'Now go.'

Sighing, Emily leapt off the bed and skipped across the room. 'Fine. I'll see you downstairs. But I want to hear all about it. You're not leaving me out any more,' she said.

As she left the room, Charlie sensed the vaguest hint of a threat. Would she tell their parents if he did leave her out?

He clambered to his feet and caught sight of himself in the mirror. His face was slightly tanned, his hair singed, and his arms were covered in cuts and bruises. The last few days had certainly taken their toll, he thought. He also seemed a little thinner. He wondered if his Mum would notice.

'One thing's for sure, I'm starving,' said Max, climbing out of bed.

'Me too,' said Charlie. 'But I want a bath first.'

'Good idea. I'll go next,' said Max, inspecting his face in the mirror.

CHARLIE was still scrubbing himself from top-to-toe in the bathroom when his Mum screamed up the stairs, 'I said GET OUT OF BED—IT'S HALF PAST NINE.'

The bathroom door flew open, steam pouring into the corridor and a towel-clad Charlie emerged from the mist. 'I'M COMING,' he shouted back before walking into his room. 'Better?' he asked.

Max looked him up and down. 'You'll do,' he said.

Charlie started getting dressed, while Max went off to the bathroom.

Charlie looked out of the window. The village square looked the same as ever, bathed in the morning sun, but now the Prophecy loomed over him like a black cloud. He sat down glumly on his bed and reached for his boots.

His Mum interrupted his thoughts, 'CHARLIE, MAX,' she shouted.

'WE'RE COMING,' Charlie screamed back, as he struggled to put on his boots, his feet still sore. He tied his shoelaces and straightened.

Max returned to the room. 'I could eat a horse,' he said, as he started getting dressed.

'You and me both,' Charlie replied. He waited for Max to finish dressing and they left his room. Walking into the corridor, the smell of bacon and sausage came wafting up the stairs. It did much to lift Charlie's spirits.

Emily was already sitting down when Charlie and Max walked into the bar. Their Mum bustled out of the kitchen.

'Finally — was starting to think it would be easier to wake the dead,' she said as she laid the table. 'Full breakfast...?' She stopped. She seemed surprised. 'What happened to you, Charlie?'

'Nothing,' he said. 'Why?'

'Don't know, you just look — different,' said his mother.

'Come on, Mum? Don't be daft. What could have happened to me since last night?'

His mother frowned, and shook her head, bemused. She looked at him again, but said no more.

Emily pulled a face at Charlie, as if to suggest she might let the cat out of the bag.

Max quickly stepped in. 'Full breakfast — sounds great. Thanks, Mrs Goodwin,' he said, trying to change the subject.

'Coming right up,' said Mrs Goodwin.

Emily waited until she disappeared back into the kitchen. Charlie knew she was desperate to badger him about his trip to the Heavens. She was bouncing up and down in her chair. 'Go on, what did you do in this immortal realm?'

'*Shush.* Keep it down,' said Charlie.

'Sorry, forgot. But I still want to know.'

Max was just as eager to find out and as he and Charlie sat down, Charlie began to explain what the Fates had said.

'What's a centaur?' asked Max.

Charlie shrugged. 'Not sure. I think it's some kind of half man, half horse.'

'Half man, half what?' said Max. 'You're joking.'

Charlie knew it sounded ridiculous.

'What kind of training?' said Emily, pressing him further.

'I don't know,' said Charlie.

Their Mum came back in with the boys' breakfasts, just as Parseus walked into the bar.

'Morning, Mr Parseus? Sleep well?' she asked.

'Very well, thank you,' said Parseus sitting down at a nearby table.

'Full English?' asked Mrs Goodwin. 'You know, bacon, sausage, eggs...'

Parseus peered at the boys' breakfast plates. 'Thank you. That sounds splendid.'

Five minutes later, she returned with his breakfast and a large pot of tea before disappearing once again. Parseus ate quickly, then came over to their table.

'About your training, I think we should start as soon as possible,' said Parseus.

'What kind of training is Charlie going to do?' Max asked.

'The usual, I would imagine,' replied Parseus.

'Like what?' asked Max.

Parseus ignored him. 'Now finish up, Charlie. We must go.'

'Can't we leave it for today?' Charlie yawned. He was still tired. He'd had only a few hours' sleep.

'No. The danger is too grave. We must go back now. Cheiron has to train you to become a hero.'

'Cheiron? Who's he?' asked Max.

'The centaur. He is renowned throughout the Ancient World.'

'What exactly does he look like?' asked Emily.

'He has the front torso of a man but the body of a horse. But Cheiron is no ordinary centaur. He's immortal and the son of Kronos, the Titan.'

'Titan? I thought they were the threat,' said Max.

'Not all of them. Some are on our side,' said Parseus.

'So you're saying that Charlie's going to be trained by some half-breed.' Max did not sound impressed.

Parseus straightened. 'I wouldn't refer to Cheiron as such within earshot, if I were you — but yes. And he's the best there is. He has trained some of the finest heroes in the Ancient World.'

'Like who?' said Charlie.

'Herakles, Jason, Achilles,' replied Parseus.

Charlie's face lit up. He had heard of all those heroes. Was he really about to join their ranks?

'Herakles?' said Max. 'Who's he?'

'You might know him better as Hercules, his Roman name,' said Parseus.

'Hey even I've heard of him,' replied Max, his face brightening.

'Anyway, we're leaving soon,' said Parseus. 'I just need to gather some things.' He looked at Max. 'We'll see you on our return. You can ask questions then.'

Max stood up. 'No way. You're not leaving me behind. Where Charlie goes, I go. Anyway you might need me. I came in pretty useful when we were rescuing Ares.'

Max was right, Charlie thought. And he was glad Max wanted to come. He didn't want to do it alone.

'I want to come too,' insisted Emily.

'NO,' Charlie and Max both shouted at once.

Emily crossed her arms. 'If you don't...'

'Forget it, Emily. It's too dangerous,' said Charlie. 'It's no place for a girl, believe me.'

Emily huffed loudly and stormed out of the room.

It was not a good sign, Charlie thought. It usually meant she was plotting something.

Parseus got up. 'Very well, young Harper. Come by all means. But we leave in an hour.'

'From where?' said Charlie.

'My room, as before,' said Parseus.

'Maybe we should choose somewhere else? I don't trust my sister. I don't want her sneaking along,' said Charlie. 'She will if she can.'

'Yes, you're right. We must keep her safe.'

'Why?' said Max, oblivious to the Fates' warning. Charlie had left that bit out earlier. Now he explained what they'd said.

'But why?' Max asked again.

'We don't know,' said Charlie. 'Not yet.'

'And you have to defeat the Dark One?' said Max.

Charlie sighed. 'Apparently.'

'So where should we go from?' said Max, changing the subject.

'Your cottage seems a suitable spot,' said Parseus. 'You two go first. I will meet you there.' He got up and left the room.

'Don't know about you, but I'm going to finish breakfast first. Who knows when we'll get a decent meal again,' said Max, buttering another piece of toast.

Breakfast over, Max wrapped the left-over toast in a napkin and they returned to Charlie's room to get their jumpers. Max stuffed the toast in his trouser pocket.

'Ready?' said Charlie.

Max took a deep breath. 'Guess so.'

'Let's just make sure Emily doesn't see us leave, OK?'

Charlie and Max slipped out of his room, crept down the

back stairs, and headed across the square to the lane that led to Max's cottage. Once there, Max opened the door and they slipped inside to wait for Parseus.

He joined them a few minutes later. 'This time we're going back prepared,' Parseus said, pulling a sword out of his cloak.

Charlie recognised it at once. 'Isn't that Ares' sword?' he asked. He had remembered seeing it when they had first met the God of War but now he realised it was the same one he had spotted in Parseus' trunk when he and Max had been investigating.

'Indeed it is,' said Parseus. 'In fact, Ares gave it to me himself before I came on this mission.'

Parseus handed it to Charlie. He took the sword and inspected it once again. It still surprised him how light it was. 'Didn't Ares say it's made from Adamantine?'

'Yes, the strongest substance known to the Gods. It can slice through anything,' said Parseus. Then he pulled out a shield. Charlie recognised this too. It was also from his trunk. Parseus held it up. 'And this shield is impenetrable, even against the sword.'

The shield was shiny and round, with symbols carved around its edges and a picture of a strange creature embossed in the middle. Parseus handed it to Max. 'Here, you can hold on to this.'

'Hey — it's really light,' said Max.

'It's made from the same metal,' said Parseus.

Charlie and Max started play-fighting: Charlie diving forward with the sword, thrusting and parrying, while Max deflected the blows with the shield.

Parseus finished plotting the course. 'Come here, and link arms,' he said.

Max and Charlie stopped fighting and did as they were told. But just as a portal opened up in the floor, the door opened and Emily burst into the room.

'EMILY, I SAID...' shouted Charlie.

The next instant he felt himself being sucked into the abyss.

14. THREE'S A CROWD

CHARLIE sat up and looked around. They had landed in another meadow, at the base of a large mountain. It was early evening and the sun was just starting to dip, clothing the meadow in a warm pink hue and cloaking the mountain in shadow. On the western slope, Charlie could just make out a small path winding up the mountain.

Parseus was already standing up a few feet away, dusting himself down, muttering. Max was sitting on the grass, his head between his knees, breathing deeply. Charlie waited for the nausea to abate before he got to his feet. Then he spotted Emily lying on the grass a hundred yards away. 'Oh no,' he cried out. He rushed over and shook her gently to bring her round. She opened her eyes and tried to focus.

'What happened?' she said as she sat up.

'You were too close to the portal. You ended up coming with us,' said Charlie, helping her to her feet. 'I told you to stay away.'

She staggered as she straightened.

'Don't worry, it's just nausea — it will pass,' said Charlie. But it didn't seem to bother Emily. She steadied herself and took her first glimpse of the Ancient World. She was clearly delighted that she had managed to tag along — she had probably planned it that way, thought Charlie.

Parseus approached. 'I see you decided to come along anyway,' he admonished her.

Emily smiled smugly.

'So where are we exactly?' asked Charlie.

'Mount Pelion, where Cheiron lives, the centaur who's going to train you,' said Parseus.

Max staggered to his feet, rubbed the back of his head and approached.

'How did she...?' he said, pointing at Emily.

'She did what she always does. Sneaked in,' said Charlie, glowering at his sister.

'I said I didn't want to be left out again. That's all. And why should I?' said Emily defiantly.

'Because this world's dangerous,' said Charlie. 'And we need to protect you or...' he quickly stopped himself. Emily didn't need to know what the Fates had said.

He pulled his sister close. 'Just remember, we're in a very different world — a very dangerous one. So no games — understood? Do exactly as you're told.'

Emily shook off his arm. 'OK, OK, I promise, I'll be good.'

'Yeah, that's what bothers me — I've heard that before,' said Charlie.

Parseus pointed up at the mountain. 'Come along. Let's go and find Cheiron,' he said, setting off towards the path.

Charlie looked up at the mountain. He could just make out a cave entrance. 'Guess it's time to meet a centaur then,' he said.

'This is going to be interesting,' replied Max.

'Exciting, more like,' said Emily.

Charlie groaned. He hoped his sister wasn't going to be a liability. They set off after Parseus, reaching the path a minute later. Parseus was still some way ahead.

'What kind of training do you think it'll be,' asked Max.

'Not sure. I'll probably learn to fight or something.'

Max brightened. 'Sounds fun. I hope I can join in?'

'Me too,' said Emily.

'I don't think so, Sis,' said Charlie. 'You're just a girl.'

'Yes, and you're just a boy,' replied Emily angrily. 'Which makes us even, so there.'

The path levelled out a little, widening just in front of a

cave entrance. From a distance it had looked a little like the dragon cave they had encountered on their first visit but as they neared it Charlie saw that it was clearly inhabited by something civilised. A big pot, like a cauldron, sat outside and a small pile of logs were stacked up against the cave wall. Just inside the entrance were more pots and an assorted collection of jars, as well as spears and arrows piled up in one corner.

Parseus shouted, 'CHEIRON.' There was no reply. At the entrance he spotted a piece of parchment nailed to one of the walls. It was a note. Parseus ripped it off the wall and threw it on the ground. 'Typical,' he snorted.

Charlie peered at the note. 'What does it say, Parseus?'

'It says, Gone to the Inn — If anyone's interested.' Parseus frowned. 'It means Cheiron's at the *Satyr and Sickle*. And that's not good news.'

Max brightened. 'Sounds like a pub.'

'It's not just a pub, Max, it's the finest watering hole in the whole of the Ancient World,' said Parseus. 'It's run by the God of Wine, Dionysos.'

'There's a God of Wine?' said Max incredulously.

'Of course there is,' said Parseus heading for the path. 'Come on, there's no time to lose. I spotted a cypress tree on our way up. We can be at the inn in an hour,' he called out over his shoulder.

'What's this about a tree?' asked Emily.

Max winked at Charlie. 'Let her find out for herself.'

Charlie smiled. It was about time Emily got taken down a peg or two. A chariot ride in a cloud would teach her a lesson she needed to learn, he decided.

Charlie and Max led Emily back down the dusty path. Parseus was already waiting for them by the cypress tree.

A cloud quickly arrived. Emily watched in stunned silence as it transformed itself into a chariot. Unable to believe her eyes, she backed away.

Max grinned. 'It's OK, Emily. There's nothing to worry

about.' To prove the point he and Parseus climbed in and sat down. It made no difference. Emily stood fixed to the spot.

Charlie grabbed her arm. 'Come on, we've got to get on. You're holding us up.'

Emily still refused to budge. 'What is that?' she gasped.

'It's a flying chariot. It's how they travel in this world, Emily.'

'Well I...I'm not going in it,' she stuttered.

'I did tell you not to come, you know. But honestly, it's quite safe. I promise. Now come on,' said Charlie. He climbed in, and sat down. 'See, it's perfectly OK.'

Emily backed away again. Exasperated, Parseus stood up, stepped out and picked her up. Carrying her into the chariot, he dumped her on the seat next to Max.

'Since you insisted on coming here, there'll be no more complaints from now on. Is that clear?' he said.

Emily was too shocked to argue. The chariot lifted off the ground and shot into the sky, her terrified screams ringing out as it did so.

A little while later, with Emily realising that there was no need to be scared, and now rather enjoying the experience, they reached the outskirts of a village. Although the sun had set, Charlie could still make out the little houses that lined the winding streets.

They landed in a square in front of a large building. Charlie assumed it was the inn. Lights were spilling out onto the cobbled square and he could hear singing from inside. The *Satyr and Sickle* was obviously busy.

Parseus climbed out and waited for the others to follow. He took Charlie to one side. He seemed annoyed.

'You're about to meet Cheiron and I had hoped your initial meeting would take place in better circumstances but unfortunately that is not to be,' he said. 'Try not to judge him on first impressions. They won't be good.'

Just then the door flew open and a large drunken man

stumbled out, singing loudly. 'What kind of inn is this, Charlie?' asked Emily.

'Don't worry. It's probably like ours at home. I'm sure it will be fine,' Charlie reassured her, though he wasn't sure himself. 'But stay close, do you hear?'

Emily promised and cautiously followed the others inside. Then she stopped, her mouth agape. 'It's nothing like home,' she said quietly.

THE *Satyr and Sickle,* at first glance, seemed like a quaint little inn. There were wooden beams running along the ceiling with vines entwined around them and in the far corner a large hearth, with a roaring fire blazing as a wild boar turned on a spit. There were wooden tables dotted all around. Charlie surveyed the dimly-lit room: it was full of soldiers and what he assumed to be farmers, singing and laughing loudly.

Then Emily tugged his sleeve and pointed to the group dancing in the corner near the fire. Charlie had not noticed them at first, but staring at them now he realised they were not quite human.

Max spotted them too. 'What are they?' he asked.

'Oh, they're Satyrs — as in *Satyr and Sickle,*' Parseus replied casually.

'But what are they? I mean, they've got horses' ears and...' Charlie looked down. They had also hooves for feet.

'They're what you call half-breeds. They live mostly in the wildlands but they follow Dionysos, and they like to party,' Parseus explained. 'Oh, and you see those' — he pointed to the women dancing with them. 'Be wary of them. They're Maenads. Harmless here in the inn, but out in the wildlands they're to be avoided. If they get into a frenzy they can rip a man to pieces.'

'And you say this is what's going to train Charlie,' said Max.

Parseus laughed. 'Good heavens, No. Different kind of half-breed. Charlie will be trained by a centaur. They're skilled in the arts of hunting, swordplay, medicine and mathematics. Cheiron is one of the greats — a centaur of huge renown, a legend...'

At that moment the group parted and there, in full voice and full swing — and clearly very drunk indeed — was another strange half-breed: this one half man, half horse.

'Like that?' said Charlie, pointing.

Parseus' face fell. 'Yes, just like that. In fact, that is Cheiron.'

Cheiron was dancing with one of the serving wenches, spinning her round in circles before throwing her onto his back, the girl giggling all the way. With the body of a horse, the front torso of a man and his long, black hair falling down his body like a horse's mane, he was a bizarre sight indeed.

Cheiron was also singing loudly, a large flagon of wine in his hand, its contents spilling all over the floor as he twirled.

Parseus was not amused. He pointed to a small table in the corner. 'Go and sit down over there,' he said sharply.

Emily and the boys shuffled over and sat down quietly, fascinated but half-horrified by the scene before them.

'This is the Ancient World?' Emily looked shocked.

'I did tell you to stay at home,' Charlie reminded her.

'I thought you said it was a world of Gods.' Emily surveyed the room. 'I didn't expect this.'

'There are more than just Gods here, Emily,' said Charlie.

'Yeah, there are half-breeds too,' added Max

They all looked over at Cheiron, now staggering drunkenly round the inn crashing into tables as he went. Charlie watched him with dismay. How was he ever going to fulfil anything — let alone his destiny — if his training lay in the hands of this drunken half-breed?

Parseus seemed to share his concern and as he came over and sat down with them he watched Cheiron's antics with increasing anger. Moments later, mistiming a twirl, Cheiron careered towards them and crashed into another table, landing in a heap in front of Parseus.

Rubbing his head, Cheiron looked up and squinted. 'Parseussss?' he stammered. 'Didn't we meet at Peleusss' wedding?'

Parseus nodded glumly. 'Yes, Cheiron. I well remember the incident. I had to fish you out of the lake.'

'Ah yes-ss, I remember now,' said Cheiron, burping loudly. He tried to sit up. 'S-s-so what brings you here?' he said. And with that his head rolled from side to side, his eyes drooped and he slowly fell back — dead drunk.

Parseus sighed and stood up. 'Help me get him out of here, boys. I'll take his shoulders, you two grab his back legs and we'll drag him out into the courtyard. It's time to start sobering him up. It may take a while.' He turned back to the table. 'You stay here, Emily.'

Parseus and the boys slowly pulled the unconscious Cheiron across the inn floor until finally they got him outside. A marble trough sat to one side of the courtyard and Parseus walked over to it and picked up a wooden bucket before filling it from the pump. He brought it back and handed it to Charlie.

'Perhaps you would like to do the honours,' he said. Charlie hesitated. 'Go on,' Parseus insisted.

'Right,' said Charlie. He lifted up the bucket and poured it over Cheiron.

There was a loud screech, a cross between a cry of pain and a neigh and a second later, Cheiron sat up, wide-eyed and gasping. He blinked and looked around.

'Where am I?' he said, rubbing his head. 'Ow. Did I fall over?' He tried to get to his hooves but he couldn't manage it, so Charlie and Max stepped forward to help him. He stood weaving for a moment. Charlie held his breath, hoping he wouldn't fall down again but fortunately he managed to stay upright.

He shook his long mane and looked about him. 'What's going on?' he demanded. He pointed at the boys. 'And who are you?'

'They're with me, Cheiron,' said Parseus, 'We've been sent by Zeus.'

At the sound of the great God's name, Cheiron staggered back. 'Zeus?' He wiped his brow as if worried that he had somehow offended him. 'What does he want, Parseus?'

'All in good time, Cheiron. Perhaps a drink of water and some food would help first,' he suggested firmly.

Cheiron looked apologetic. 'Perhaps you are right, Parseus. May have overdone things slightly.' He burped. 'Sorry.'

'Then let's all go back inside.' Parseus ushered the boys in front of him. The Satyrs and their womenfolk had now departed and the inn had quietened down. The party, it seemed, was over.

Emily was sitting contentedly at the table. Some food had been laid out and she was happily sampling the delights.

'Hey, I like these,' she said. 'What are they?'

'Olives,' said Max. 'They're disgusting.'

'No they aren't — anyway, I like them,' she said as she stuffed one in her mouth. 'By the way, what's everyone saying around here? I can't understand a word. How come you two can?'

'Translation bugs,' said Max.

'Translation what?'

'Ask Parseus for one. They let you understand and speak any language spoken,' said Charlie.

'Really? What do they look like? How do they work?' asked Emily.

'Oh, they look like earwigs and you have to push them in your ear,' said Max, smirking, as if he had taken his bug without a second's thought. 'We all have them, but…'

Emily tried to put on a brave face. 'I'm not scared,' she said. 'I want one.'

Parseus reached for his silver tin. 'Good idea. Can't have you running around unable to speak the language, now can we?' He took out a bug and held it up.

Emily took a deep breath. Charlie knew she didn't want anyone seeing her being squeamish.

'So what do I do?' she said boldly.

'Stuff it in your ear,' declared Max.

Emily took the bug and, closing her eyes tightly, pushed it inside her ear. Grimacing, she shook her head and then looked up smiling. 'There, all done.'

Cheiron sat down cross-legged at the end of the table. He was still swaying slightly. Parseus pushed the platter of fruit towards him. 'As I was saying, we have been sent by Zeus.'

'So?' said Cheiron, picking up an apple and taking a bite. 'What's any of this got to do with me?'

Parseus pointed at Charlie. 'He wants you to train this boy.'

Charlie glanced nervously at the floor, now worried that the centaur might not think him good enough. Would he measure up? Was he capable of fulfilling his destiny — whatever that was?

Cheiron took another bite of apple. 'Train him to do what?' he said, eying Charlie up and down.

'Train him to defeat the Dark One,' replied Parseus.

The apple fell from Cheiron's hand and he looked fearfully over his shoulder before leaning forward. 'The Dark One?' Bewildered, he shook his head. 'But it's in Tartaros.'

'No longer, I'm afraid. But let's leave it at that. I just need you to train him to face it,' said Parseus. 'Remember, it is the will of Zeus.'

Cheiron blanched before clambering noisily to his hooves. Refusing to look Parseus in the eye he shook his head.

'It cannot be done,' he replied and without another word he staggered out of the inn.

15. MAKING A HERO

CHARLIE watched Cheiron leave. The look on his face had spoken volumes — defeating the Dark One was clearly impossible. Charlie felt his hands tremble.

Parseus leapt off his stool. 'Wait here. I'll be back,' he said, before he too raced out of the inn, leaving them alone.

'That was encouraging,' sighed Charlie.

'Cheer up. You're not the Destined One for nothing,' said Max. 'And he doesn't know that yet, does he? He thinks you're just a boy.'

'I am just a boy,' said Charlie.

'Never mind, I didn't think much of him anyway. He's a drunk,' declared Emily as she put another olive in her mouth and glanced back towards the door.

Charlie picked up a grape and rolled it between his fingers before squashing it on the table. 'You're right. He is just a drunk.'

Several minutes later, Parseus returned, looking relieved. 'That's done. I've persuaded Cheiron to help. He's waiting in the cloud. We're leaving now.'

Surprised at the turn-around, Charlie and the others followed Parseus out of the inn. In the square they found an unhappy-looking Cheiron waiting in the chariot. But as Charlie and the others climbed in and set off back towards Mount Pelion, Charlie was still worried about this centaur and his training. Was this drunken half-breed up to it? Even if he was, was *he* up to it?

They reached Cheiron's cave an hour later. Cheiron had slept for most of the journey, but woke up as they landed. Mumbling incoherently, he stumbled inside. Within minutes he had passed out again.

'Best leave him to sleep it off. There's little we can do until morning,' said Parseus. 'Meanwhile let's build a fire. The evenings grow cold around here.'

Charlie and Max fetched some logs from the pile near the entrance while Parseus went off to get some fruit and bread. Before long they were huddled round a roaring fire.

'What's his story?' asked Charlie, glancing towards the cave.

'Ah, centaurs, they're a strange breed. There's a wildness about them. They're human but not human, animal but not animal. They're something of a contradiction,' said Parseus.

'You can say that again,' said Max.

'Unfortunately, their fondness for drink and women can sometimes prove a problem,' Parseus added.

'I think we got that part,' said Max.

'Quite. But Cheiron is a troubled sort. His wife keeps leaving him — tends to send him a bit crazy,' said Parseus.

'And he's the one who's supposed to train me to face my destiny?' Charlie was not impressed.

'Let him sober up and give him a chance,' said Parseus. 'You'll be surprised. There is no finer teacher than Cheiron, not in the art of the sword or archery. Now I know you've not been up for long but I suggest you get some more sleep. Tomorrow is going to be a long day.'

Charlie groaned silently. He was not looking forward to it.

CHARLIE woke early the following morning. He was anxious about his training. The fire had long since died out but Max and Emily were still asleep. Parseus had found some fur rugs the evening before and they were happily snuggled under them. Charlie decided to leave them be and take a look inside the cave. It stretched quite far back, opening out into a large chamber, full of shelves stacked high with little pots and jars. In the middle was a marble table. Behind it and leaning awkwardly against the wall, his head tilted to one side, was Cheiron. He was snoring loudly.

Charlie accidentally knocked a flagon over and Cheiron sat up sharply.

'Where am I?' he said, looking around, confused. His eyes fell on Charlie. 'And who are you?' he said, squinting.

'We met last night,' said Charlie. 'Sorry to wake you.'

'SHUSH, don't talk so loudly,' said Cheiron. 'My head hurts. By the way, what happened? Last thing I remember was being in the...'

'You got drunk,' said Charlie.

'I know that,' said Cheiron. 'But how did I get home?'

'We came by cloud.'

'Ah, yes,' said Cheiron as he rubbed his head. 'It's all coming back now.' Using the wall to support him, Cheiron got to his hooves, teetered for a few seconds, then steadied himself.

Parseus appeared. 'Come along Cheiron, we have work to do.'

'Huh?' said Cheiron.

'Remember last night? I told you about the Dark One.'

The mere mention of the Dark One seemed to shock Cheiron out of his stupor.

'Yes, I remember.' He shook his head. 'But I think I need some water first,' he said, stumbling out of the cave.

Max and Emily were just waking up as Cheiron staggered past, though he took no notice of them. He went straight for the water trough and ducked his head in. Then he grabbed a wooden jug, scooped some water from the trough and drank thirstily. He wiped his mouth.

'I really don't feel well,' he said, leaning against the trough.

'I suggest you start pulling yourself together,' said Parseus curtly.

Cheiron burped loudly, rubbed his head and turned around. 'So you want me to train this boy,' he said, pointing at Charlie.

'It is the will of Zeus,' said Parseus.

Cheiron stared at Charlie. 'And you think he can face the Dark One?'

'Yes, Cheiron. That is why he needs to be trained,' said Parseus. 'By you.'

Cheiron inspected Charlie. He didn't seem impressed. 'Alright,' he sighed.

Then he straightened, shook his long mane and cleared his throat. 'But if I am to train him, I will have to work him to the ground. There'll be no slacking. Is that clear?' he said, wagging his finger at Charlie.

Charlie nodded meekly. But being worked to the ground didn't sound much fun.

'Glad I'm not the Destined One,' Max whispered.

Cheiron overheard him. 'That goes for you too. If you're here, you're here to train.' He glanced at Emily. 'A girl? Excellent. We need someone to cook.'

'Cook?' Emily's voice rose sharply.

'Yes — cook. You can start by making breakfast. You'll find food inside.'

Emily huffed loudly. 'But that's not fair. How come I've got to...' she looked to Charlie and Max for support. There was none.

'This is what happens when you insist on tagging along, Sis,' said Charlie.

Cheiron waved at the boys. 'And you two, you'll find a couple of axes just inside the cave. Go down to the meadow and start chopping some wood,' he ordered.

'Chop wood?' protested Charlie. 'I thought I was supposed to train.'

'Just go,' said Cheiron.

Charlie muttered angrily as he and Max grabbed the axes before starting down the mountain path.

'Wood chopping, Charlie? What kind of training is that?' grumbled Max.

'How would I know,' said Charlie. 'But it's not what I was expecting.'

FOR the rest of the day all Charlie and Max were made to do was to chop logs. Charlie wondered if Cheiron just wanted to keep them out of the way so that he could nurse his hangover. However, over the following few days all they seemed to do was traipse up and down the mountain, chopping down trees or carrying pails of water from the river below.

To make matters worse when their own clothes became dirty Cheiron had given them tunics and sandals to wear. Both boys had complained bitterly.

'These tunics itch like mad you know,' moaned Max but Cheiron had no sympathy and the training continued apace.

To the boys, this 'training' seemed to consist only of hard labour. Yet the now very sober Cheiron would not let up. Charlie began to think he preferred him as a drunk.

Emily, allowed only to cook and clean, fared no better. Eventually she confronted Cheiron.

'I didn't come to the Ancient World to peel vegetables and skin chickens,' she said.

'But you're a girl, so you must do girls' work,' he replied.

Emily, crossing her arms, would have none of it. 'Let me tell you, in our world, girls are treated equally. They can do anything a man can do. Not just cook.'

'How ridiculous. Females are far inferior to males. Everyone knows that. You really ought to know your place,' chided Cheiron.

'My place?' said Emily, her voice rising, 'Let me tell you something, my place is right up there with any boy.'

'In that case you can swap with me,' said Max dumping yet another pile of wood on the ground. 'Because if I have to chop another log — I'm going on strike.'

Charlie also felt on the verge of mutiny. They had been 'training' for almost a week and all they had done was chop wood and carry water. What outraged him now was that after carrying two pails of water all the way up the mountain path, Cheiron had just poured them out on the ground in front of him.

Charlie snapped, kicking over the pails in fury. 'This is stupid,' he said. 'When do I start my training?'

Cheiron crossed his arms. 'You have started your training. We had to build up your strength first. There's little point in wielding a sword if you can't put any power behind it, boy. But I see we have enough logs for the winter now and you are getting stronger. Maybe we'll start with some light swordplay this afternoon. I think you're almost ready for that,' he said.

Charlie felt a bit foolish. That actually made some sense. He pointed at the pails lying on the ground. 'Sorry about that,' he said.

'No need for apologies. But don't waste your energy on anger. Save it for the fight,' replied Cheiron. He looked at Max. 'The same goes for you too, boy.'

'So long as it doesn't involve going up and down that mountain, I don't care,' said Max, dusting himself down.

Emily pressed Cheiron again. 'Can I train too?'

'I don't think so, Sis,' said Charlie.

'I see. I'll just get back in the cave then and make lunch for you all?'

'Excellent idea,' said Cheiron, rubbing his hands in glee.

'No wonder your wife left you,' muttered Emily angrily.

Charlie saw Cheiron' eyes narrow. Emily had clearly hit a nerve.

Parseus tried to smooth things over. 'You know, Emily, there are many arts a woman can learn that are equally important.'

'Like what?' snapped Emily.

'The art of medicine, for one. It's a most valuable skill. Perhaps Cheiron could teach you?'

Cheiron glared at Parseus. He obviously saw no reason to teach a mere girl anything.

'Medicine?' said Emily, brightening.

'More like magic, really,' said Parseus.

'Magic?'

'Yes. Would you like that?' Parseus said.

'Yes, I would,' she replied eagerly.

Cheiron held up a hand. 'First things first, Parseus. Let's start with the sword,' he said. 'We must focus on the boy. He's the Destined One, isn't he?'

'Indeed he is,' said Parseus. He disappeared inside the cave to fetch the sword. Returning, he unsheathed it and handed it to Charlie.

Cheiron was impressed. 'It's magnificent, isn't it? They don't make them like that anymore.'

Charlie had held the sword before but this time he could really feel its power coursing through him like a current. It felt as if it belonged to him.

'What kind of training am I going to do?' asked Max.

'You can use the shield. We'll need you later to help Charlie practice. You can block his attacks,' said Cheiron.

'I get the shield? Is that all?' Max grumbled.

Cheiron then began to show Charlie a simple sequence of moves, which he made him repeat time and time again. But it was hard. He kept forgetting to move his feet properly or he would thrust forward with the sword too early and Cheiron would scream at him. It was exhausting.

'You have to learn to be as swift as foot as you are of hand, Charlie,' said Cheiron, making him practise again and again.

Max and Emily spent most of the day just watching, both relieved not to be doing chores. Then Cheiron called on Max, handed him the shield, and showed him how best to use it to block Charlie's attacks. By the end of the day, they were both exhausted yet thrilled that they had started to learn to fight — Charlie now realising how good Cheiron was.

That evening Emily started pestering Cheiron to show her some of the potions. Reluctantly he led Emily into the back of the cave to have a look. Charlie smiled to himself. Cheiron certainly had his work cut out with Emily.

CHEIRON woke Charlie early the next day and they started practising archery in the meadow below. Charlie spent hours shooting static targets and towards the end of the day he was getting quite good.

'This isn't so bad, once you get the hang of it,' he said.

'Sure — if you get the hang of it,' said Max, who had spent most of the day just trying to string his bow.

'Now, the next step,' Cheiron said to Charlie. 'Let's see if you can hit the target while moving.'

'Moving?'

'Hop on my back and try it while we're riding around,' said Cheiron.

Charlie climbed up but at first he found he failed to hit any of the targets, his arrows flying off wildly however hard he tried to concentrate his aim.

Cheiron would not let up though and the training was relentless. Eventually Charlie began to strike the targets, or at least most of them. But with the sun setting, Cheiron finally called it a day. He seemed pleased. 'You've shown promise,' he said. 'We will start again tomorrow.'

Charlie's arms ached so much he could hardly lift them, but at least he had done better than he thought he might. Wandering back into the torch-lit cave, he found Emily and Max poking around in the back of the chamber.

'What are you two up to?' he asked as he joined them.

'Just studying that's all,' Emily said. 'There are potions here that cure the funniest things.'

Max held up a jar. 'Hey, this one cures baldness. Maybe we should take it back for your Dad.'

Emily laughed. 'I know, there are cures for the strangest

things. I found one that sends a person into a living death,' she said.

'A living what?' said Charlie.

'Sends you into stasis or something. Anyway, that's what Cheiron said. I think it means it stops you getting any worse, though I suppose that's not really a cure, is it.'

'No idea. Never heard of it,' said Charlie. 'But at least you seem to be getting on with Cheiron at last.'

'Apart from the fact that he's a complete chauvinist? OK, I guess. But I'm putting him right. I said he should apologise to his wife and he's promised to lay off the drink. I told him it's not good for him. To be honest, I guess people here just aren't used to the idea of equality,' she said.

Just then Cheiron appeared, looking a little sheepish. 'I've started supper,' he said. 'It won't be long.'

Emily winked at Charlie. 'See?'

Cheiron it seemed had warmed to Emily. 'You know Emily you would make a good witch. Hecate would be proud of you.'

'Who's Hecate?' said Emily.

'The Witch Goddess. Very powerful indeed. In fact, there are many goddesses with great powers. Like Athene, the Goddess of Wisdom.'

Charlie smiled to himself. He had no idea how she had managed it, but somehow Emily had the gruff Cheiron exactly where she wanted him — under her thumb.

THE training continued for two more weeks with Charlie and Max spending hours switching from sword play to archery. It was exhausting but Charlie was growing more confident each day. He started to feel stronger, more powerful. Max too grew in strength and though his skill with the sword was no match for Charlie's he soon became proficient enough and he had finally managed to learn to string a bow. Emily had even managed to wash their own clothes and the boys were relieved to be back in jeans and T-shirts.

The following morning, Charlie woke earlier than usual. He went outside to watch the sun rise. Parseus was already awake. He seemed pensive.

'We must leave Charlie. We have been here long enough. Your essences are fading fast. They need re-charging,' he said.

Charlie felt almost sorry to leave. In the last few weeks he had grown used to this strange world. He had even started to enjoy it. It had also been a relief not to worry about the Prophecy or the Dark One, although he was also very aware that they were no nearer to finding an answer to the threat.

Parseus seemed to sense his mood. 'We'll be back soon. Have no fear. Your training must continue.'

'How am I doing?'

'Extremely well, Cheiron tells me. He's very pleased with you,' Parseus assured him.

Max stumbled out of the cave, rubbing the sleep from his eyes, yawning. 'Morning all.'

'Good, you're up. I was just telling Charlie, we need to go,' Parseus said, slinging the shield over his back and strapping the sword to his side.

'Go where?' said Max.

'Home.'

'Really?' Max greeted the news with relief.

'Yes, but we'll be back soon,' said Parseus. 'Now go and wake Emily. Time we were off.'

Just then they felt it — a strange, deep rumbling in the ground. A moment later the earth started to shake and the rock which Charlie was standing on split in two, tipping him off his feet. A deep rift appeared and rocks and boulders, upended by the force beneath them, and shaken from above, began tumbling down into the newly-formed crevice. Charlie desperately tried to keep a grip but the rock tipped up even more sharply and he started slipping down.

Max leapt forward, grabbing Charlie's hand just in time. Parseus dived after him and grabbed Max's leg. Another tremor struck and the rock Charlie had been standing on plunged into the crevice leaving him dangling above the gaping hole.

A cloud of dust engulfed them and they all started slipping into the abyss.

Woken by the earthquake, Emily rushed out of the cave. Spotting Charlie disappearing into the crevice she screamed and dived forward, grabbing hold of Parseus' foot. But it made no difference, they continued to slide down.

Then Cheiron appeared, and he too leapt forward, grabbing Emily just as another tremor sent the chain even deeper into the hole. Max was trying desperately to cling onto Charlie with one hand but it was a losing battle. With his hand beginning to slip, Charlie knew he could not hold on. The very next moment Max let go and Charlie felt himself fall.

16. THE ACCIDENTAL TOURIST

CHARLIE opened his eyes. They were back in Max's sitting room. Parseus must have used the compass just in time. But while the memories flooded back, his stomach took a little longer to return. Glancing around he saw that Max and Emily were still coming to. He got up, then stepped back in surprise. For there, sitting in a heap in the corner was Cheiron, his head darting from side to side.

'What's he doing here?' Charlie asked Parseus.

Cheiron was asking himself the same question as he scrambled to his hooves. 'Where are we?' he shouted.

'Calm down, Cheiron. I'll explain in a minute,' said Parseus.

'Are we back home?' asked Emily as Charlie helped her stand up.

'Yes we are,' he said.

'Thank goodness. I thought we were all going to die,' she said, clearly shaken.

'You and me both,' said Max, dusting himself down. 'Lucky you used that compass Parseus,' he added.

'We were lucky on more than one count, Max. I realised when we got back that your essences had almost faded completely. We can ill-afford to make that mistake again. You'll need to stay here for at least eight hours to recharge them.'

'But the sun...'

'Will have set, yes, Charlie. But we can't risk going back until your essences are restored. So you must rely on the helmet. We'll spend tonight in the inn.'

'But what about Cheiron?' said Max. 'Can't exactly take him to the inn.'

'No. We shall have to keep him out of the way. Can't risk anyone seeing him, can we?' said Parseus.

Emily tapped his arm. 'In that case, Parseus, you might want to go after him.' She gestured towards the door. 'Because he just left.'

Turning, Charlie saw that the cottage door was wide open. Emily was right. Cheiron had gone.

'Get after him,' screamed Parseus.

Charlie and Max raced outside, only to see Cheiron trotting steadily down the lane towards the village square. It was a disaster. There was no way they could explain away a centaur.

'STOP,' Charlie shouted.

Cheiron had almost reached the oak tree at the edge of the village. Any closer and he was bound to be seen. Hearing the shouting behind him, Cheiron stopped and turned to see Charlie and Max, waving furiously, racing towards him.

'You mustn't go any further, Cheiron,' said Charlie as he reached him.

'Why? I'm just having a look. By the way, where are we? Don't recognise this place at all. Thought we might be in the Underworld. And what was that all that spinning about? I didn't like that much,' said Cheiron.

Charlie tried to catch his breath. 'You can't be seen here.'

'Why?'

Charlie was struggling to think of an answer when Parseus appeared. 'For the Gods' sakes Cheiron, you really mustn't wander off.'

'Why not? Where are we?' said Cheiron.

'Just come here and keep out of sight. I'll explain in a minute,' replied Parseus.

Cheiron didn't like being given orders. 'I want to know where I am first.'

'All in good time,' said Parseus.

Just then they heard the hoot of a horn and there, driving along the road towards the village square, was a car. Cheiron's jaw fell open. 'What's that? Some kind of monster?'

Charlie groaned, worried they had been spotted. Fortunately the car turned into the square. They hadn't been seen.

Parseus dragged Cheiron back behind the oak tree.

'I'm afraid we need to get you out of sight,' he said.

Cheiron pulled back. 'Why? What's wrong with me?'

'We can't risk anyone seeing you,' said Parseus.

'Why?'

Charlie could tell that Parseus was losing his patience. 'Look, we're in another world where half-breeds like you don't exist. So we have to hide you. Do you understand?' he said.

'I'm no half-breed,' spat Cheiron, his back bristling with indignation.

'For the love of the Gods, we don't have time for this,' said Parseus.

'Hang on a moment. Did you say another world?' Cheiron looked around curiously.

'Yes. It's another dimension. A mortal world. Immortals don't exist here.'

'Don't exist? What kind of a world doesn't have immortals?'

'This one, Cheiron. Now please come back to the cottage. We can't risk you being spotted,' said Parseus.

Cheiron was so confused he just nodded. 'Alright,' he agreed.

'Good,' said Parseus. Removing his cloak he threw it over Cheiron's shoulders. 'We need to hide your front end.'

'My front end?'

'Yes. Anyone who sees you from your back-end will just think you're a horse,' Parseus added. 'Now do be quiet.' And without another word, he pulled the cloak over Cheiron's head and started guiding him back up the lane towards Max's cottage.

Charlie followed behind, hoping that to anyone who might glance up from the square it would look as if they were just leading a horse up the lane — and in Hesper there was nothing odd in that.

But just as they passed the field on the right, Charlie spotted movement near one of the trees. He stopped to take a closer look but whatever it was, there was no sign of it now. Dismissing it he continued up the lane.

When they reached the cottage, Emily and Max were trying to tidy up. It was chaos. Cheiron trotted in and Parseus removed the cloak from his head.

Cheiron shook his long mane. 'That's better,' he said. He looked around the room. 'So this is a mortal world, is it?' He started inspecting everything, as clearly astonished by their world as Charlie and Max had been by his.

'Once we finish tidying up, you three can go back to the inn,' said Parseus. 'I'll stay here with Cheiron.'

'Tidy up how exactly?' said Charlie. The kitchen door frame lay shattered, smashed furniture and broken ornaments were scattered all over the floor. The place needed more than just a tidy up.

Cheiron appeared from the kitchen, happily munching through a packet of biscuits. 'Don't know where we are, but these are fantastic. What do you call them?' he asked.

'Chocolate digestives,' said Charlie.

'They're really good,' said Cheiron, taking another one.

They spent the next few hours trying to tidy up the cottage but made very little headway. Cheiron spent most of the time snooping through drawers, asking incessant questions about how their world worked. When Max showed him the radio and switched it on, he took the whole thing apart in a desperate attempt to free the muse of music, which he claimed had to be trapped inside. No amount of explanation persuaded him otherwise. Before long, everyone was exasperated.

Parseus took the boys to one side. 'I have to get to back to the inn. I have a potion called the potion of Lethe. It makes people forget.'

'Like the river of Lethe in the Underworld?' said Charlie.

'Quite. The potion comes from that river. Very useful too. Anyway we really can't allow Cheiron to return to the Ancient World without giving it to him — not after what he has seen. So stay here and keep an eye on him. Do not let him near any alcohol. Understood?'

'Don't worry,' said Max. 'My grandma doesn't keep any drink in the cottage.'

'Good. I'll be back soon,' said Parseus. And with that he left for the inn.

HALF an hour later, Parseus had still not returned. Emily was becoming anxious. 'I should really go. Mum'll be expecting me.'

'Yes, you're right. Go on, we'll follow in a bit,' said Charlie.

Emily headed off. Charlie and Max continued to clear up, but as the minutes ticked by Charlie grew nervous. Parseus should have been back by now. Shortly afterwards the front door flew open. Charlie was relieved to see it was Parseus.

'I was starting to wonder where you were,' he said.

'Sorry, I got caught up in conversation with your father,' said Parseus. He looked round the room. 'Where's Emily?'

'Didn't you see her? She left ten minutes ago. You should have bumped into her on the way,' said Charlie.

'I didn't see her. She wasn't in the lane, and she didn't come into the inn — she certainly wasn't there when I left.'

Charlie and Max exchanged a worried glance.

'If she isn't at home, where is she then?' said Max. 'She wouldn't have gone anywhere else.'

Charlie now remembered the movement he had spotted in the field. He had shrugged it off as a bird or a fox perhaps. But what if it was something else? He told the others about it. 'What do you think?'

'Given our situation, I suggest we think the worst,' said Parseus.

'Mrs Payne?' said Charlie desperately.

'My thoughts exactly,' said Parseus.

Charlie's heart sank. For in that case Emily must have been kidnapped. And that meant there was only one place she could be — Hesper House.

His only thought now was to save her. 'We have to get to Hesper House,' he said, rushing towards the door.

'Where is this place?' asked Cheiron.

'The end of the village,' said Charlie. 'If I get on your back we'll get there far quicker.'

'Then let's go,' said Cheiron, following Charlie out of the cottage.

'WAIT,' screamed Parseus. 'It's a trap.'

But Charlie and Cheiron were already out of the door, with Charlie climbing onto his back.

'Where now?' said Cheiron as they reached the lane.

'Turn left,' said Charlie.

Cheiron set off at a brisk pace but by the time they reached the drive and passed through the gate the afternoon sun had dipped behind the trees and the air had grown cold.

'I don't like this place,' Cheiron said as he slowed to a trot.

'Join the club,' said Charlie. 'Nobody likes it. But Emily's here and we've got to find her.'

A couple of minutes later they reached the house.

'Where now?' asked Cheiron.

'Go round to the right,' said Charlie.

Cheiron trotted around the side of the west wing to the lawn. Charlie pointed to the open French windows and they slipped inside. Glancing down the passage that led to the west wing Charlie thought he spotted the edge of a cloak disappearing into the shadows. Then he heard the unmistakable sound of Emily's voice.

'Let go of me, you witch,' she shouted, her voice echoing along the corridor. A moment later Charlie heard a door slam.

'Hurry Cheiron — head down the passage,' he said.

Cheiron quickened his pace. When they reached the door at the end of the corridor Charlie climbed down.

'Where does this lead?' asked Cheiron.

'Not sure. I've never been this far before, but Parseus says this house lies directly above the earthly entrance to Tartaros.'

'What?' Cheiron started backing away. 'No one told me that — why didn't you say something?'

'I didn't realise it was a problem,' said Charlie.

'Problem?' said Cheiron. 'Do you know what Tartaros is?'

'Yes,' said Charlie.

'Hell — that's what. I have to get out of here. I have to get out of this world. What kind of place is this?' he said. He turned on his hooves and trotted back down the passage.

'You can't just leave me...' Charlie shouted after him but it was too late, Cheiron was already disappearing into the shadows.

Charlie could hardly blame him. He was no less terrified. But Emily was inside that room and he had to do something. Very slowly he opened the door.

He looked inside. It was a library. Bookshelves ran from floor to ceiling and there were no windows. But unlike the rest of the house, it seemed as if someone did live there. There were no dust covers on the furniture and there was a lighted torch hanging on the wall, its flame flickering wildly. The room itself, however, was empty.

Charlie opened the door wider and slipped inside. A cold draught blasted him in the face. Turning to see where it was coming from he spotted it, just as it was closing — a secret door hidden in one of the bookshelves. He ran over and started fumbling behind the books. There had to be a lever somewhere. That was how they worked, wasn't it? A moment later he felt it: cold hard metal. He was about to pull it towards him when he hesitated. What lay beyond it? Was Parseus right? Was he walking into a trap?

Charlie's mind was now full of the stories that he had heard about the witch. It was said she could cast spells that would turn people into rats and strike a person dead with one withering look. While her voice could compel a person to do anything she wanted. Whatever the truth, Charlie had no choice. Mrs Payne had kidnapped Emily and he had to save her.

He pulled the lever towards him and the door swung open. Peering inside he saw a narrow passage. The walls were smooth like a pebble, as if eroded over time. There were also cobwebs everywhere and it was bitterly cold. Charlie shivered, though more from fear than cold. A burning torch was hanging on the wall giving off a strange eerie glow, but there was no sign of Mrs Payne or Emily.

Charlie stepped inside. He heard the faint sound of cries in the distance. It had to be his sister. He was tempted to grab the torch but realised it would alert Mrs Payne to his presence, so he followed the sound of Emily's cries instead.

A hundred yards further on there were smaller passages branching off to the right and left. It was like a large rabbit warren. But he didn't deviate from the main path, which continued meandering downwards.

A minute later he heard Emily's voice again. 'Get off me, you witch. My brother's going to come looking for me, you know.'

'That was the point of kidnapping you, silly little girl. To lure him here.'

'Then it's a trap,' moaned Emily.

'Of course,' said Mrs Payne.

Charlie, listening some way back, could feel the power of her voice. It was deep and raspy, echoing through the passage. But he couldn't turn back. A few yards further on, he spotted a light up ahead. He slowed his pace. Keeping close to the tunnel wall, he inched his way forward.

Rounding a bend the passage opened up. There were two doors on the left, with a flaming torch hanging on the wall, but there was no sign of Emily or the witch. They had to be in one of the two chambers, Charlie reckoned.

But now that he was there he wasn't sure what to do. How was he going to save Emily? He was alone. He had no weapons – he didn't even have the helmet. He berated himself. He had acted in haste.

Then he heard a noise. Looking around desperately for somewhere to hide, he dived down the main passage, braced himself against the wall and held his breath.

He spotted Mrs Payne emerge. The hood of her cloak was pulled down so her face was clearly visible. Charlie grimaced. Her skin was deathly white, her eyes black, her lips blood red, thin and tightly pursed. Her nose was narrow and pointed and with her black hair pulled back tightly in a bun, she reminded Charlie of a raven.

She closed the door behind her and floated back down the passage.

Charlie waited until she faded into the darkness before creeping forward. Reaching the door he turned the handle and opened it. Emily was sitting tied to a chair. She looked up as he entered. But instead of being relieved to see him, she just shouted.

'IDIOT. This is what she wants.'

'Why?' asked Charlie as he went to free her.

A moment later he heard a noise behind him. Turning, he saw Mrs Payne standing in the doorway, a grim smile on her face.

'Welcome. So glad you could make it,' she sneered.

Her voice was strangely compelling. Charlie felt his will sapping away. He tried to move but couldn't. He was no longer in control of his body — she was. He felt a tightening around his neck as if someone had their hands around it, squeezing the life out of him. Yet Mrs Payne was still standing by the door.

'What do you want with us?' Charlie asked, choking.

'I want you to stay here until sunset. The Dark One has no power in daylight — you know that now. But soon it will come,' she said, before closing and locking the door behind her.

Charlie felt the grip on his neck loosen and he gasped for breath.

'What are we going to do, Charlie?' said Emily, struggling against the ropes.

'Escape,' he said.

'But how?' You don't understand. She has powers, Charlie. I tried to resist but she made me come.'

'I know, Emily. I felt it too. But we have to get out of here before sunset.'

'Maybe Parseus will save us,' said Emily hopefully.

Charlie shook his head. 'Afraid not, Sis.' He knew Parseus had no idea about the secret door, so there was no chance that he could rescue them. They were going to have to do it themselves.

He looked around the chamber. Apart from the chair to which Emily was tied, there was nothing else in the room.

'What time is it?' he asked.

'I don't know. I'm not wearing a watch,' said Emily. 'But you could at least untie me,' she added.

'Sorry.' Charlie undid the ropes and then went to the door. It was made of solid oak. There was no way of breaking it down.

'Have you got a hair grip?' he asked.

'Yes — but what for?' said Emily.

'Maybe we can open the door with it,' said Charlie. He knelt down and peered through the keyhole. But it was no good. 'The key is still in the lock.'

'So?' said Emily.

'I can't open the door if it's still in the lock,' said Charlie.

Emily peered through the keyhole. 'See what you mean,' she said.

Charlie got down and looked under the door. There was quite a large gap between it and the floor. It gave him an idea.

'Got a piece of paper?' he asked.

'Paper? Yeah, I always carry paper around,' replied Emily sarcastically.

'No need to be...'

'Hang on,' Emily interrupted. 'I do have something. Mum gave me a shopping list earlier.' She reached into her coat and pulled out a folded piece of notepaper.

'Great,' said Charlie, grabbing it from her. He unfolded it and flattened it out. 'This should do.'

'What good's that?' she asked.

'Just watch,' said Charlie. He slipped the paper halfway under the door. Then he took Emily's hair grip and pushed it into the lock, wiggling it around until he loosened the key. A second later it fell out and landed on the paper. Very slowly Charlie slid it back towards him. Grinning, he held up the key.

'Brilliant, Charlie, brilliant. How did you know what to do?' she asked, hugging him tightly.

'One of my books,' Charlie replied proudly.

'Let's get out of here then,' said Emily.

'OK. Keep close though, whatever you do,' said Charlie.

He listened at the door. He couldn't hear anything. So he slowly inserted the key and unlocked it. 'Remember — be careful. We have no idea where Mrs Payne is,' he whispered.

Opening the door Charlie peered out, but there was no sign of the witch. He waited for a moment to make sure, then he and Emily stepped into the passage. 'What now?' she said.

'Let's get back to the others. I expect Parseus is searching for us.' Charlie led Emily up the passage which wound back towards the library. However they had gone only a few yards when Charlie heard a noise behind them. He froze. Turning slightly, his heart sank. Mrs Payne was behind them.

Grabbing Emily's hand he pulled her forward. 'RUN, NOW,' he shouted, but as they started to do so he felt the tightening around his throat.

Emily felt it too. 'Charlie I can't breathe properly,' she said, gasping.

'You have to fight it, Emily, just try,' he said.

But the further they went, the slower their pace.

'I can't go on, Charlie. I can't fight it,' said Emily.

Charlie glanced over his shoulder. Mrs Payne was floating along the passage towards them, her arms outstretched, her force growing stronger as she neared. It felt as if she were literally pulling them back.

Desperately struggling to push on, he dragged Emily up the passage until, rounding a bend, he saw the library door only a few paces away. He grabbed the handle, swung it open, and with what seemed his last effort, threw Emily into the library beyond. At that moment he felt the ice cold grip of Mrs Payne's hand on his neck.

17. ALL IS LOST

THE last thing Charlie remembered before falling unconscious was the sound of Emily calling his name. When he came to, it was Mrs Payne who was lying on the floor beside him, unconscious — and Emily was slapping his face to bring him round. He shook his head and slowly got to his feet. Blinking, he realised that everyone was fussing around him: Max, Parseus, and even Cheiron, whom he had last seen fleeing the house.

'What happened?' he asked groggily. 'How did you get here?'

'Simple,' said Parseus. 'We knew where you had gone. Then we met Cheiron — owes you an apology by the way — and followed him here. We heard Emily shout and rushed in. Just in time as it happens.'

'What about her?' Charlie pointed at the prone figure of Mrs Payne. 'How did you knock her out?'

'I threw a sleep potion at her,' said Parseus, waving a small green jar in the air before putting it back in his cloak pocket. 'Very effective you know. She should be out for hours.' He stared down at Mrs Payne. 'I told you it was a trap. You really must listen, you know. The witch's power is still limited but here she is far stronger. Here she can feed off the evil energy.'

Parseus began leafing through a book. 'Fascinating place though, isn't it?' he said, waving his arm around the room. 'Glad you found the secret door. We would never have found it ourselves, would we?' he added, casting Cheiron an admonishing glance.

Cheiron shuffled awkwardly on his hooves. 'Sorry I abandoned you. It's just that being immortal, there's only one thing you fear — and that's Tartaros.' He stepped forward and took Charlie's hand. 'I promise I will never do so again. You have my word,' he said, bowing in apology.

'Thank you,' Charlie mumbled. He looked around the library. He had hardly noticed it the first time. There was a large mahogany desk in the middle, piled high with books and odd scraps of parchment. Dotted around the room were a number of side tables, while an old leather armchair, studded with brass tacks, sat in one corner. In many ways it looked so normal, so civilised. But it wasn't. It was cold and dank and there was a strange humming. It seemed to come from the books.

Cheiron shuffled awkwardly again. He was clearly spooked. 'We really must go,' he kept saying. 'I don't like this place. It's the gateway to Hell.'

'Indeed we should. But this is such a fascinating place. There are some powerful books in here,' said Parseus.

Charlie started inspecting the shelves. Most books were in the ancient language but the translation bugs were proving useful in this world too. He read some of the titles: *Potions and Poisons for All Occasions, How to Kill an Ithacan Dragon, Aphrodite: A Study in Love.*

'Where did these books come from?' he asked. They all seemed to relate to the Ancient World.

He picked up a large, leather-bound book, its pages yellowed and worn. He opened it and ran his finger down the page. He was just about to read out some of the text when Parseus leapt across and slammed the book shut. 'NO,' he shouted.

Charlie stepped back, shocked at the fury in Parseus' voice.

'Never read a book like this out loud. Do you understand?' barked Parseus.

'But why?' asked Charlie.

'Because you might wake them,' said Parseus.

'Wake them?'

'Yes. This library sits on top of the earthly entrance to Tartaros. Some of these books are infused with evil incantations. You must be careful — these ones especially,' said Parseus, pointing to the book that Charlie had opened. 'This one contains incantations that can wake the dead,' he said. 'And I don't mean the good dead.'

Charlie glanced back at the shelves. 'All of them?'

'Not all of them, some of them could prove useful to us but you can't always tell.'

'What about this one?' Charlie picked up another book and was about to read out the title when he hesitated. Should he even do that?

Parseus looked at the book. It was one of the ones Charlie had spotted earlier: *Potions and Poisons for all Occasions.*

'Ah, this one, of course, could prove very useful indeed,' said Parseus. He took it from Charlie and began slowly leafing through it.

Max coughed. 'Um, excuse me, but now that we're all safe, shouldn't we be leaving? It'll be dark soon.'

Parseus snapped the book shut. 'Sorry. You're right. It's just that...well it's this library. I had heard of such a place but I didn't believe it existed.'

'Existed?' said Charlie. It sounded ominous.

'There have been rumours for years amongst the Time Gods of a place such as this.'

'There's more than one Time God?' said Max.

'Indeed there are,' replied Parseus. 'It is said that when this world was created much of the ancient knowledge was stored somewhere here on earth, though I have no idea how it ended up here. Most of us thought that knowledge had long been lost.'

'What kind of knowledge?' asked Charlie.

'The powerful kind,' said Parseus. 'And there is more than just ancient knowledge in these shelves. There is evil too: books that can kill.'

'Books that can kill? That's exactly why I don't read much,' said Max, crossing his arms.

'Don't you think we should leave then?' said Emily.

'I'm with the filly on this. Let's go. The sooner I get back to my world the better,' said Cheiron.

They headed for the door. Opening it they started back down the passage but on reaching the French windows they realised it was much later than they had thought. It was almost dark.

'Huh,' said Max. 'I hadn't realised we'd been here that long.'

'My fault,' said Parseus. 'I was so fascinated by those books that I forgot all about the time. We must hurry.'

'Too late,' said Charlie, pointing towards the library door. The Shadow was now seeping into the corridor.

'What about the compass?' said Max. 'We can escape with that, can't we?'

Parseus shook his head. 'We can't risk using it here. This is the very gateway to hell. We might end up in Tartaros ourselves.'

'Tartaros?' said Cheiron.

'There's only one thing to do. RUN,' shouted Parseus, and without another word they fled the house. As they did so they heard a scream. The sleep potion expected to keep Mrs Payne out for hours had worn off — she was awake again.

Parseus grabbed Charlie by the shoulders. 'Protect your sister. Remember? She's vital to the mission. You must both leave now. Get on Cheiron's back. Get back to the inn and put on that helmet. We'll meet there later.'

Charlie leapt onto Cheiron's back, leaned down and pulled Emily up behind him. 'Hold on tight Sis, you hear?' he said.

Cheiron broke into a gallop and raced towards the drive. Charlie heard the Dark One crash through the French windows. The monster had already started its chase. They would never reach the inn in time. Charlie made up his mind in a flash. There was only one place they could go — the moors. Reaching the drive he shouted to Cheiron, 'Turn left NOW.'

Cheiron did as ordered.

'You'll need to clear that fence up ahead but we can lose it on the moorland. Just do as I say, OK?' said Charlie.

'Hang on tightly then,' Cheiron shouted. He launched into the air. Clearing the fence with only inches to spare he landed solidly on the other side, with Charlie's arms wrapped around his neck to stop himself and Emily falling off.

The Dark One was still on their tail, its red eyes flashing, its serpent heads darting forward reaching out to strike.

But Charlie knew the moors — Max had dragged him across them often enough. There were treacherous bogs littered everywhere and many a moorland pony had sunk without trace. It could be a death-trap if you didn't know where you were going.

The only problem was that it was growing darker with every passing minute. Charlie urged Cheiron on. Once on the moor, he screamed instructions to veer left and right to avoid the bogs. Yet the Dark One seemed to grow ever closer.

'He's gaining ground,' screamed Emily, gripping Charlie even more tightly.

'Faster Cheiron, faster,' shouted Charlie.

After a mile, Cheiron started to tire. Charlie could feel him falter. He knew Cheiron was drawing on every ounce of strength he had but with two passengers and treacherous ground underfoot, the strain was taking its toll.

Charlie desperately scoured the moorland, searching for a way out — a trap for the Dark One. The moor was full of hidden traps, but which one and where?

Then he saw it, up ahead to the right. There was just enough light for him to recognise the sign, haphazardly displayed, the wood rotten but the skull warning still visible even in the gathering gloom. It was The Devil's Playground, one of the most treacherous bogs on the moor.

Charlie leaned forward. 'Veer right NOW and when I tell you, take a sharp left — *and I mean sharp.*'

Cheiron did as he was told. Charlie looked over his shoulder. It was now or never. Holding his breath he waited for the right moment. The Dark One was catching up fast. Then Emily screamed and Charlie knew it was almost upon them.

A second later they reached the bog. 'Turn left NOW,' he shouted.

Cheiron did so, just in time, and they missed the bog by inches. An instant later they heard a deadly hiss. The Dark One had fallen into the trap. Glancing back Charlie saw it flailing about in the sticky peat bog, its eyes flashing with fury as it struggled to free itself.

He breathed a huge sigh of relief and patted Cheiron's neck. 'We did it, WE DID IT,' he screamed.

Cheiron slowed to a canter, but Charlie knew they couldn't afford to stop. The Devil's Playground would not contain the Dark One forever.

'We mustn't let up,' he shouted.

Cheiron pressed on, Charlie directing him as they worked their way back to the lane. Passing the cottage they saw Parseus and Max ahead of them, hurrying along on their way to the inn.

'We're here,' Charlie called out. Cheiron trotted on and caught up with them.

'Where is it?' asked Max.

'Floundering in The Devil's Playground,' said Charlie, beaming with delight. 'We escaped.' He patted Cheiron. 'Thanks to you.'

Parseus rushed forward and reached out to help Emily get down. But she didn't move. Charlie felt her head fall limply onto his shoulder.

'EMILY,' he shouted.

Parseus and Max pulled her off Cheiron's back and laid her down on the ground. Charlie jumped down and knelt next to her.

'What's wrong with her, Parseus?'

'She's been wounded.'

'Wounded?' Charlie didn't want to believe it — then he saw the blood. The Dark One must have struck her. It had got too close.

Cheiron bent over Emily and felt her head.

'She has been more than wounded, Parseus — she has been poisoned. A fever has already started to take hold.'

Charlie began to panic. 'What can we do? We have to help her.'

Parseus turned to Cheiron, but he just shook his head.

'We have to do something,' said Charlie. 'There must be a cure.' He looked pleadingly at Cheiron. 'You know about this stuff — all those potions in your cave — there has to be something.'

'This is a wound from an Ancient. I know of no cure for this,' said Cheiron.

'What are you saying?'

Cheiron shook his head once more. 'I'm sorry, Charlie. But your sister is going to die.'

18. CASUALTIES OF WAR

CHARLIE heard the words but didn't want to believe them. Emily couldn't die. She just couldn't. The Dark One was not going to kill his sister.

'We must try to do something, Cheiron,' insisted Parseus. 'The girl is essential to the fulfilment of The Prophecy. The Fates have decreed it.'

'I don't care about The Prophecy, Parseus,' said Charlie. 'I care about Emily.'

Cheiron inspected the wound more closely. It had started to go green.

'I might be able to stem the flow, slow the poison down but...' Cheiron paused.

'But what?' said Charlie.

'We would still need to find a cure,' said Cheiron.

Charlie grabbed him by the arm. 'So there is a cure?'

'I told you, I don't know,' he said. 'But maybe, somewhere...'

'Where?' asked Charlie.

Cheiron looked at Parseus. 'I must return home. The first thing we need to do is to stop the flow of the poison.'

'Do you have anything that can do that?' asked Parseus.

'Perhaps,' said Cheiron. 'If we could put her into some kind of stasis...if we could stop it spreading...'

'Stasis?' said Charlie. 'Emily found a potion that can do that. She told me about it. Sends people into a living death.'

'Of course. The potion of Thanatos: the spirit of Death. Yes, that would do it,' said Cheiron.

'Well?' said Charlie looking at Parseus.

'Your sister is too ill to travel. Don't worry, Charlie. I'll go back with Cheiron and return with the potion. You won't even notice I've gone.'

Parseus took Cheiron well away from the boys and Emily and plotted a course on the compass. The boys watched as the portal opened. A blink of an eye later, and Parseus was standing there alone. Cheiron was nowhere to be seen.

'We found it. I have the potion,' he said, holding it up. 'Now let's get Emily to the inn.'

'But what are Charlie's parents going to say?' said Max. 'They're going to kill us.'

'I doubt that very much,' said Parseus. 'Now come — there's no time to lose. No peat bog, treacherous or not, can contain the Dark One for long.'

Charlie and Max lifted Emily up between them, and slowly made their way towards the village square. Charlie nervously checked the lane behind them. He wondered how long it would take the Dark One to free itself from the bog. He knew it wouldn't be long.

THEY reached the inn ten minutes later. They had seen only one villager as they turned into the square, but he was heading the other way to the cottages beyond and didn't notice them as he turned down the road to his house. Charlie was thankful for that at least. The last thing they needed were villagers crowding around asking questions. But as they reached the inn's side entrance he grew more anxious. What were they going to say to his parents? What was his mother going to say when she saw Emily?

'I think it best if I do the explaining, boys,' said Parseus. He opened the door and Charlie and Max carried Emily inside. Just as they did so Charlie's father walked into the hall.

'EMILY? What happened?' Shocked, he looked to Charlie for an explanation.

Parseus held up his hand. 'Mr Goodwin, I think it is for me to explain,' he said. 'But let's get her upstairs first.'

Charlie's father was too shaken to argue and stumbled after them as Charlie and Max carried a now unconscious Emily into her room and laid her down on her bed.

'Get the helmet, Max,' Parseus ordered. Max hurried off to Charlie's room.

'We need a doctor,' said his father. 'I'll get a doctor.'

'No, Dad — it won't help,' said Charlie.

'Charlie's right, Mr Goodwin. No doctor can help. She's been wounded,' said Parseus.

'Wounded? How? We must get a doctor then,' insisted Mr Goodwin.

'We can't, Dad,' said Charlie.

'But she's injured.' His father looked at Charlie but he avoided his gaze. 'What's going on, son?' he said.

'*DAD* — you have to listen. We can explain,' said Charlie.

'I think you'd better — and quickly,' said his father.

'In a minute,' said Parseus as he took out the potion. 'We must stem the poison's flow before it gets into her bloodstream.'

'Poison?' Charlie's father grew desperate.

Parseus handed the potion to Charlie. 'She needs all of it, but do it gently,' he said.

Charlie knelt down and uncorked the jar. Parseus lifted Emily's head and held it up while Charlie poured the potion down her throat. Emily groaned as the last drops went down, but Charlie was relieved to see her body start to relax.

'Lay her back gently. She'll feel no pain now,' said Parseus. 'It has stemmed the flow.'

'Stemmed the what? What's going on Charlie?' his father pressed him again.

Charlie ignored him. 'That's all we can do, Parseus?'

'Until we find a cure, yes. The potion will only keep the poison at bay. But it might just buy us enough time,' said Parseus.

'Cure?' Charlie's father was almost beside himself.

Max returned with the helmet. 'Got it,' he said, holding it up.

'Good. Now put it on, Charlie,' ordered Parseus. Charlie and Max sat down next to Emily. Charlie put on the helmet and they all vanished from sight.

His father reeled back in disbelief. 'Charlie? Where are you?'

'I'm still here, Dad. Just invisible that's all.'

'Invisible? Hang on a minute.' His father's face turned red. 'I demand to know what's going on.'

'Quite, quite, Mr Goodwin. Sorry. You deserve to know. Let me explain,' said Parseus.

Parseus then told him everything he needed to know. When he finished, Charlie's father sat for a moment or two shaking his head. Yet his face showed no real sign of surprise. It was a minute or so before he spoke.

'I didn't think it would happen so soon. I mean nothing has happened for centuries. And I thought we had years yet. I hoped it would never happen. I...I...' He paused.

'Didn't think what would happen?' said Charlie. 'What are you talking about, Dad?'

'I think it's now time for you to explain,' said Parseus.

Mr Goodwin looked up. 'You see son...' His voice broke and he slumped into Emily's armchair. 'The fact is that I am...' He hesitated. 'I'm a Guardian.'

'A Guardian?' Charlie repeated blankly. 'What's a Guardian?'

'I come from a very long line of Guardians, Charlie. We watch over Hesper House, keep an eye on the place, make sure the evil is contained. But as I said nothing has happened for centuries. I mean the house has been dormant. Of course no one goes near it nowadays — and I didn't think anything would happen, at least until you were grown up, anyway.'

Charlie was shocked.

'I'm sorry, Charlie. I know this is hard for you. I hoped it would be years before you would need to find out,' said his father.

'But why didn't you say anything?' asked Charlie.

'I was going to warn you. Prepare you one day. I just never thought that time would come so soon.'

Parseus interrupted him. 'Yes, yes. But the point is — it has. Now we must deal with the immediate issue — your daughter.'

'Can I do anything?' Mr Goodwin asked.

'No, Mr Goodwin. Best if you get back to the bar. Just act as if nothing has happened. You can leave this to us.'

'What about my wife? She knows nothing about this.'

'Where is Mum?' Charlie realised he hadn't seen her.

'She's spending the night at old Mrs Bennetts — she's not well, and your mother's gone to look after her.'

'Good.' said Parseus. 'Then you don't need to trouble her yet. Let's see if we can cure Emily first.'

'Can you?' asked Mr Goodwin.

'We're not sure yet,' replied Parseus.

'Do whatever you can then. But be careful. I don't want you putting Charlie or Max in unnecessary danger. Is that clear?'

'I will do all I can to protect them. You have my word, Mr Goodwin.'

'And you two boys do as Parseus says, do you hear?'

'We will Dad. Don't worry.'

'Not much chance of that son,' said his father. And with that, a worried Mr Goodwin left the room.

Parseus waited until the door closed. 'Cheiron says that to find a cure, we must go to the Oracle at the Temple of Delphi.'

'Temple of Delphi? Didn't we see that when we were in the cloud?' said Charlie.

'You did indeed,' said Parseus.

'What about Emily?' asked Max.

'She will be all right until we return. Remember, we'll be

back in an instant. She must stay under the protection of the helmet of course. But the sooner we go, the sooner we're back.' Parseus turned to the door. 'We will leave from my room — cannot risk Emily coming with us again. So let's hurry,' he said. 'The Dark One will be free of that bog soon.'

Charlie took off the helmet and placed it over Emily's head. It shrank to fit. Then he squeezed her hand and let go. Coming back into view he and Max hurried after Parseus.

'Where now?' asked Charlie as Parseus plotted a course.

'First we must see Cheiron. Then we'll go to Delphi,' he said.

THEY arrived back on Mount Pelion, landing just outside Cheiron's cave. It was late morning. Rocks and boulders from the earthquake, which they had narrowly escaped the last time, were scattered all over the hillside. Charlie had quite forgotten about that.

Cheiron came trotting out. 'Good, you're back,' he said. 'I trust the potion worked.'

'Yes, thanks for that,' said Parseus. 'The girl's stable for now.'

'I assume you are on your way to Delphi?'

'Yes, but we need some more suitable clothes for the boys before we go,' said Parseus. 'It's not the kind of place they should be dressed as they are. We don't want to attract attention.'

'Agreed. Come then. Time to get back in the tunics,' said Cheiron.

Ten minutes later, they were dressed once again in tunics and sandals.

'Forgotten how much they itch,' said Max, squirming.

'Sorry, but you must wear them. Delphi is very busy and you need to blend in with the crowd,' said Parseus. 'Now let's go and find a cloud.'

'You'll need money in Delphi,' said Cheiron. 'Wait here.' Slipping back into the cave, he returned moments later and handed Parseus a small bag of coins.

Parseus put it in his pocket. 'Thank you. We'll certainly need these.'

Having said goodbye to Cheiron, they disappeared down the mountain path and stopped by the cypress tree. A cloud swiftly appeared.

'Where exactly is this Temple of Delphi?' said Charlie as they climbed into the chariot.

'Mount Parnassos. We should be there in about an hour,' said Parseus.

The chariot shot up into the sky and headed south. Charlie and Max settled down for the ride but this time neither was interested in the scenery below them.

'What's this temple like?' asked Charlie as they flew on.

'It's one of the most sacred places in the Ancient World. It was founded by the God of Prophecy, Apollo,' said Parseus.

'And this is where mortals go to seek oracles,' said Charlie. He remembered Parseus mentioning it when they first passed by it.

'Oracles?' said Max.

'Divine messages,' said Parseus.

'About what?' asked Max.

'Anything.' said Parseus. 'It's quite simple.'

'No it isn't,' muttered Max.

HALF an hour later they spied Delphi ahead. The temple's golden columns were sparkling in the sunlight, while below was a large village, hugging the hillside around it. The cloud came to rest in a field on the outskirts and they climbed out.

'Follow me — and stay close,' said Parseus as they set off.

In contrast to the quiet streets around the *Satyr and Sickle,* the village was teeming with activity. The main square was huge and filled with a variety of stalls, selling everything from statues of Gods and novelty jars to toy pythons, though Charlie had no idea what relevance any of them had.

Following Parseus through the crowded streets, they

passed people busy haggling with the stallholders as they tried to purchase their own special mementos. One stall further on seemed to be very popular. Charlie noticed a long queue stretching right back. 'What's that selling, Parseus?'

'Marble tablets with the logo of the Temple of Delphi. People have their oracle inscribed on them. They're very popular.'

Amongst the souvenir stalls, Charlie spotted others selling kebabs and pots of olives and the smell of lamb was wafting across the square. He had forgotten how hungry he was. But there was no time to stop for food, Parseus was already marching on ahead.

Charlie and Max tried to keep up but were harried at every step with offers of souvenirs, snacks and divination. People kept shoving things in their faces. Then an elderly man, with thin straggly grey hair and a brown tunic, shuffled in front of them. He had a slight stoop and a lop-sided face with one eye that looked the other way. He grabbed Charlie by the arm and grinned toothlessly. Charlie leant back in disgust, the man's breath smelt so bad.

'You look like you could do with some divination,' the man said, his voice hoarse. 'Can I interest you in my services? I charge a reasonable rate,' he added, looking at them expectantly.

'Divination?' asked Max.

'Shush,' said Charlie. He turned back to the man, trying to shake his arm free. 'Sorry, we haven't been to the temple yet.'

Smiling, the man reached into his belt and pulled a marble pebble out of his pouch. 'Then when you're done, and you need some interpretation, you'll find none better than I. The name's Sibilus. Sibilus the soothsayer,' he said, pressing the pebble into Charlie's hand.

Charlie tried to pull his hand free. 'Thank you very much, sir. If we need your services we'll ask,' he said.

Satisfied, Sibilus let go of Charlie and waved him on.

The boys caught up with Parseus. 'A man just said he can help us divine our oracle. What does he mean?' asked Charlie.

'Oracles tend to be obscure and need interpretation. But be careful of these people. They are charlatans, mostly.'

Parseus was probably right, thought Charlie but he decided to keep his pebble anyway, just in case.

Further on, the smell of manure wafted across the square from some livestock stalls on the other side of the street. Cages full of hens were stacked one on top of another while lambs and goats bleated and brayed anxiously in overcrowded pens. They reminded Charlie of the lambing season, the bleats of terror just the same.

A large, burly man, his face like leather, was shouting out to passing customers: *Get your sacrificial lambs here: goats, lambs and hens, perfect for sacrifice. Hens: two obols, lambs and goats: four obols. Guaranteed, top-quality sacrificial lambs and goats. Get yours here.*

'What's all this about sacrificial?' asked Max. 'Sounds gruesome.'

'That's how people honour the Gods. Sacrifice is a vital part of the religion. You can't seek an oracle without offering a sacrifice,' said Parseus. 'That reminds me. We need one.'

Parseus approached the stallholder and after some heated haggling, the man agreed on the price and handed him a hen. It squawked and struggled violently in his hands, as if fully aware of its impending fate.

It took Parseus a while to get it under control. 'Now we've got our sacrifice — let's go,' he said, walking off impatiently.

Armed with their hen, they meandered through the crowded village, jostling with people who appeared to have come from all corners of the Ancient World. Some were in garish, colourful robes, others in simple tunics. But they were all seeking the same thing: to have their prayers answered. And amongst them all, were the traders and interpreters, circling like predators, preying on the weak and needy.

'How far is it to the temple?' asked Charlie.

'Not far. I know a short-cut,' said Parseus.

The street widened a little, and they found themselves in another large square populated with a number of inns and boarding houses, all bearing suitably apt names — The Temple, Apollo's Den and The Parnassos. The last one seemed far grander than the others, boasting marble columns and its very own doormen.

Charlie was impressed. 'I bet that's expensive.'

'Indeed. Only the very rich are allowed to grace its doors,' said Parseus.

They continued across the square until Parseus stopped and looked around. 'I'm sure it's here somewhere,' he muttered. 'Ah, there it is.' He pointed to a narrow alley between two of the boarding houses. 'It's down there,' he said.

'How do these oracles work?' asked Charlie.

'It's quite simple: you ask your question, the priests then ask the oracle and the answer is handed down,' said Parseus. 'But only after you hand over your sacrifice.'

'Who gives the answers?' asked Charlie.

'Apollo, of course,' said Parseus, marching on.

The boys fell back a little. 'Do you think we're going to find out about a cure, Max?' Charlie was growing uneasy.

'Course we are. This is a magical world, Charlie — there's bound to be a cure of some kind. Emily will be fine,' he said.

They rounded a corner and found themselves in a dusty clearing situated at the base of Mount Parnassos. Halfway up was a small building with marble columns on either side and beyond that, situated high above, the temple itself.

Looming ahead of them was a large wooden gate, guarded by an officious-looking man, dressed in a short, grubby tunic with a scowl etched on his face. He stood still, his arms crossed defiantly. Next to him, attached to the wooden gate, was a sign. It read: 5 obols per person.

Charlie saw a queue of some 50 people already waiting patiently in line. At the rate they were moving forward, it looked to Charlie as if they were going to be there for hours.

Parseus eyed the queue then tapped his nose. 'Leave this to me,' he said, handing Charlie the hen before walking off to speak to the official.

The hen began squawking madly as Charlie struggled to keep it under control. He had never liked hens ever since he had spent part of the summer holidays earning a little extra money by cleaning out the chicken coops. This one was no exception.

It was still trying to break his grip when Parseus returned some minutes later. 'We're next in line,' he said. 'Come along.'

Just then a man bearing a tray of snacks walked down the line, shouting, 'KEBABS. Anyone for kebabs? OLIVES. Anyone for olives?'

'Can we get something to eat, Parseus?' Max pleaded.

'But we're next,' said Parseus. Then he relented. 'Alright, but we will have to be very quick about it.' He beckoned the man forward.

Parseus purchased two kebabs, took the hen off Charlie and then bought three tickets. The official waved them through, the boys devouring their kebabs as they started up the winding path.

'That's where we ask for our oracle,' said Parseus, pointing ahead to the building below the temple. We're not allowed in the temple itself, only priests and priestesses are allowed in there.'

It was a long, hot climb under the noonday sun, and the boys were sweating by the time they reached the steps of the building. Two guards stood at the entrance, directing people inside.

The guard inspected their tickets and directed them to a chamber on the left, with a row of wooden hatches embedded in the walls. At each of them people were handing over their sacrifices, or eagerly asking their questions. As one of the hatches closed, and an old man and his daughter turned to leave, one of the guards inside the chamber silently motioned to Parseus and the boys to move forward and take their place.

Parseus did so. He rapped firmly on the hatch door. Nothing happened. He rapped again. A moment later it opened and a face appeared. It was a wizened old man with a wild mop of white hair and a startled look on his face. He was eating a chicken leg and seemed annoyed at the interruption.

'YES. What is it? I'm on my lunch,' he said.

'Sorry, but we were next and we were told to come here,' replied Parseus firmly. 'And we have a question to ask, if that is not too much trouble.'

The old man peered out of the hatch and grunted. Tossing the half-eaten chicken leg aside, he wiped his mouth. 'Very well, but where's my sacrifice?' he asked.

Parseus handed over the struggling hen.

'A hen, how lovely. I like hens,' the priest said before closing the hatch. A few minutes later it re-opened and the old man stuck his head out again.

'What's your question?' he asked, his mouth full.

'A girl has been wounded by ...' Parseus paused, looked around to make sure that no one else was listening and whispered, 'by an Ancient. We are seeking a cure.'

'Hmm,' said the old man, his eyes narrowing. Then he shut the hatch once more.

'Where's he gone, Parseus?' asked Charlie.

'Don't worry. We'll get our answer soon.'

'Does it take long?'

'No, but we must be patient,' Parseus replied.

Ten minutes later the hatch re-opened and the old man reappeared. 'You must join Jason and the Argonauts on their quest. The cure you seek lies somewhere along the way,' he announced and without further explanation, he pulled the hatch and slammed it shut.

'So there is a cure, Parseus,' said Charlie, smiling. 'That means we can save Emily,' he added excitedly.

Parseus sighed. 'Yes, but only by joining the most perilous quest of the age.'

19. THE QUEST BEGINS

THEY started back down the mountain. Charlie and Max pestered Parseus with questions all the way, but they didn't get any answers. Back in the village they were swamped by interpreters, all desperate to ply their services. Parseus dismissed them with ease but Charlie and Max had to fight their way through the throng. By the time they had managed to push past them, Parseus was almost out of the village.

'Where now, Parseus?' said Charlie as he caught up with him.

'Mount Pelion,' he said. 'We need Cheiron's help.'

'What for?' asked Charlie.

'Because Cheiron trained Jason to be a hero and he saw the Argonauts off on their voyage from the port of Pegasai, in Thessaly.'

'You mean he could help us join them?' said Charlie.

'Let's hope so, because only the finest heroes in all of Greece were allowed to do so,' replied Parseus.

'But we're not heroes,' said Charlie.

Parseus stopped walking. 'Precisely. That is why we need Cheiron's help.'

'Didn't Jason hold games to see who could join the voyage?' said Charlie. He remembered reading about it in his book.

'Indeed he did. They were the first Olympic Games, in fact. And only the finest heroes in all Greece were accepted. That's what worries me. However, Jason holds Cheiron in great respect and he may just be able to persuade him to let us join them,' said Parseus. 'I cannot guarantee he will. But it's our best chance.' He paused. 'Our only chance.'

'If he does — problem over,' said Max. 'Right?'

Parseus turned and grabbed Max by the shoulders. 'Whatever you think you know about Jason and the Argonauts — which in your case is probably nothing— think again. This is one of the most perilous quests of the age in which many great heroes perished. Even if we are allowed to join we will be facing the gravest dangers. So no, Max, the problem will not be over.'

Max gulped. 'Sorry.'

'How dangerous is it, Parseus?' asked Charlie, almost wishing Parseus wouldn't tell him.

'The Argonauts journeyed to the edge of the civilised world, Charlie. They faced multiple threats from monsters, even nature herself. Forget anything you've already faced. It's nothing compared with this. Do you understand?' he said.

Charlie felt his stomach tighten, but he was determined to do whatever was necessary. 'If it means we find a cure for Emily, I will face anything,' he said.

'You may have to — and you could well die trying,' Parseus said. 'That's what really worries me.'

'But remember what the Fates said. Without her all is lost, so we have to find this cure, even if it means risking our lives,' said Charlie. 'Isn't that right, Max?'

Max gulped again. 'Course,' he whispered, but Charlie noticed that he had gone quite pale.

'Very well. But first we must find out if we can join Jason. So let's get back to Mount Pelion. Cheiron will know the best way to do that,' said Parseus.

THEY found a cloud, and not long after they reached Cheiron's cave. He was already waiting outside. Charlie and Max leapt out and immediately started bombarding him with questions.

'HOLD ON. One at a time — and slowly,' said Cheiron.

Charlie let Parseus relay the details of the oracle, but as he did so Cheiron's expression grew grave.

'You see our predicament?' said Parseus.

'I most certainly do,' said Cheiron. 'But it is not impossible.'

Charlie brightened. 'You think we could join then?'

'Perhaps,' said Cheiron. 'But it won't be easy.'

'Where are the Argonauts now?' asked Charlie.

'Not sure. They left months ago. Who knows where they might be,' said Cheiron.

'I doubt they'll have gone far,' said Parseus.

'How do you know?' asked Cheiron.

'You forget I know something about what happened on their voyage. Take it from me, they've not travelled far. We just need to follow their route,' he said.

'I'll have to come too,' said Cheiron. 'You will need me to convince Jason to let you join the quest,'

'Of course. But first let's find the Argo,' Parseus said.

'The Argo?' said Max.

'Yes, it's the name of the ship they sail in. It was named after the shipbuilder, Argo. It's why they're called Argonauts. And as I recall their first stop was the island of Lemnos. We should start there. But it's growing late, so I suggest we leave first thing in the morning,' said Parseus.

'What's Lemnos?' asked Charlie.

'The isle of women. There are no men there.'

'How come?' asked Charlie.

'Because the women murdered them all,' replied Parseus.

'Why?'

'They were cursed by the Goddess of Love, Aphrodite,' said Parseus. 'She made their husbands reject them. So the women killed them all.'

'And we're going there?' said Max. 'Is that a good idea?'

'Don't worry. I doubt we'll be stopping there, Max. I'm sure the Argonauts will have moved on by now,' said Parseus. 'Now let's eat and then rest. We leave at daybreak, and we have a long day ahead of us.'

Cheiron prepared food and they ate around the fire in silence. Afterwards, Charlie and Max settled down for the night, though Charlie found it hard to sleep. His mind was racing too much. Who knew what tomorrow was going to bring — or the next few weeks for that matter? And would they even live long enough to find a cure?

CHEIRON woke them early. 'Time to get up. We have no idea where the Argo is and it could take hours to reach them,' he said as he fussed round the cave.

Charlie yawned and stretched. He had slept fitfully. Max, stirring, looked around confused, momentarily forgetting where they were. He groaned as he remembered.

Charlie got to his feet. 'Are we off now, Cheiron?'

'Yes. We've been blessed with clouds, which is auspicious,' he said.

'What's that mean — auspicious?' asked Max, getting to his feet.

'A good sign, Max. It's a good sign,' said Cheiron, before disappearing into the depths of the cave.

Parseus appeared a few minutes later with some fruit and bread and sat down with the boys. 'Eat while you can. It may be some time before we get the chance again,' he said.

The boys tucked in before pocketing some figs and apples for later.

Charlie had been trying to remember what he had read about Jason. 'This quest — wasn't it to secure the Golden Fleece?'

'Yes. It's a sacred fleece, said to bring prosperity, and it lies in the land of Colchis,' said Parseus.

'Colchis? Where's that?' said Charlie.

'A long way away, at the very edge of the civilised world. I can only hope that we find the cure long before we reach it.'

'Who's on this quest?'

'I told you, Charlie, the greatest heroes of the age, named

after the ship itself — the Argo.' Parseus paused. 'The Goddess Athene herself helped with its construction.'

'How big is it?' asked Max.

Parseus looked up. 'The ship?' Huge. It was the first of its kind — they called it a long boat. Magnificent it was, too. A marvel of craftsmanship, worthy of the Goddess herself.'

'The Goddess of what, Parseus?' asked Max, stuffing a piece of bread into his mouth.

'Of Wisdom, War and Crafts.'

'I thought Ares is the God of War?' said Max.

'Of course, but only the nasty parts of it. Athene governs the more honourable aspects of war. She usually comes into play towards the end of a war, helps sort out the spoils and treaties. That's where the wisdom comes in,' said Parseus.

'But you said crafts as well. I thought that was Hephaistos?' said Charlie.

'Different kind of crafts. Hephaistos is good with metal, weapons, inventions, that sort of thing. Athene's good with wood, weaving and pottery.'

'Girl stuff,' laughed Max.

Parseus smiled. 'If you say so, Max. Yes.'

'This quest — what's it going to be like? You do know, don't you?' asked Charlie.

'Yes — but I think it best if you know as little as possible. I've already told you too much.'

'Too much — why?' asked Charlie.

'Because we must be careful not to interfere. The less you know of what happens, the better. Trust me.'

'OK, but why did Jason get sent on the quest? Surely you can tell us that?' asked Charlie.

'Because Jason, you see, was the rightful heir to the throne of Iolkus — it's a state in Thessaly. His uncle Pelias was the king. But when Jason turned up Pelias saw him as a threat. So he sent Jason on this quest. It was filled with danger and Pelias was certain Jason would perish. Indeed not everyone survived.'

Charlie saw Max baulk a little so he quickly changed the subject. 'Will it take long to get to this island — Lemnos, you say. That was their first stop, wasn't it?'

'In a cloud, maybe a couple of hours. If they've moved on, we'll follow their route until we find the Argo.'

'After that, how long until we get the cure?'

'I don't know, Charlie. But the oracle has spoken. We only know that it is to be found somewhere along the way.'

'But how will we know when we reach the right place? Will it just appear? How big is it? What if we miss it?' said Charlie.

'Be patient, Charlie. If we join the voyage, the cure's location will be revealed to us,' said Parseus. 'Just trust in that.'

Cheiron now appeared. 'Let's go,' he said.

The boys followed Cheiron down the mountain. They reached a cypress tree and waited. Charlie watched a cloud race towards them and come to hover next to them on the path. They clambered in and sat down.

Parseus shouted, 'LEMNOS,' and the cloud instantly took off. Charlie and Max, now used to such travel, clung on tightly to the sides waiting for it to level out and begin cruising through the sky.

Charlie sat back in his seat. What were these heroes going to be like, he wondered? What dangers would they face? Was anything they thought they knew about Jason actually true? All he had were questions, and no answers.

THEY had been travelling for some time before they saw land again. Parseus stood up in his seat. 'There it is, boys: the island of Lemnos,' he said, pointing ahead.

Charlie leaned over the front of the chariot. 'Do you think the Argo will still be there?' he asked.

Cheiron sat up. 'I doubt it. They should have passed by weeks ago. The Argo must be long gone,' he said. 'But don't worry, we can still find her, wherever she is.'

They neared the island and flying round a large headland they came in sight of the island's small harbour, a city sprawled out above it. And there, moored in the tranquil waters, was a large ship.

Cheiron was astonished. 'I don't believe it. They're still here,' he said. 'I don't understand what could have kept them here.'

'I told you they spent far longer here than they'd planned,' said Parseus. He frowned. 'Even so, they really should have left by now.'

The cloud dipped down as it neared the harbour. Charlie peered over the side. The Argo was huge, at least 90 feet long, with a large prow which rose up much higher than the rest of the ship and with what looked like a ram fitted at the front. There was a narrow plank running down the middle of the ship with benches on either side — for the oarsmen, he guessed. Sitting there in the water, gleaming in the sunlight, its oars raised and its white sails neatly tucked away, it reminded Charlie of pictures he had seen of ancient galleys. But this was the real thing.

The chariot grew closer. There was no sign of anyone on board. The harbour seemed empty too, deserted except for the ship itself. Parseus directed the cloud to land on a headland just above the bay. Climbing out, they made their way down the cliff path to the harbour below.

'Where is everyone, Parseus?' asked Charlie.

'Not sure,' he said.

'Look,' Max suddenly cried out, pointing to the sky.

Charlie glanced up and his jaw dropped. For there, high above him, two men were flying through the air, heading towards the Argo. They had two huge black wings flecked with gold attached to their backs, and each carried two large bronze pitchers in their hands. Moments later they landed on the ship.

Then they heard shouting. Turning, Charlie saw a large group of men appear on the hill above them. They were running towards the harbour screaming, *'Get to the ship.'*

As the men raced past, hurling themselves headlong into the water, and swimming desperately towards the Argo, Parseus grabbed the two boys and shouted the same order. *'Get to the ship.'*

Charlie heard a whooshing sound. Moments later, arrows began falling down around them. He knew there was nothing else for it. So he and Max jumped into the sea and started swimming for their lives.

20. ALL ABOARD

'GET under the water,' Parseus screamed as a couple of arrows narrowly missed the boys by inches. Taking a deep breath, Charlie dived under the surface and kept swimming downwards as the arrows struck the sea around him. Finally forced to surface, his lungs bursting, he was relieved to see he was now right next to the ship, and out of the arrows' range. Gasping for breath he felt someone's arm drag him out of the water and haul him on board. He landed next to a soaking wet Max, coughing up salt water and seaweed in equal measure.

Charlie scrambled on to all fours and did the same. Sitting up, he saw men clambering on board, pushing past him, shouting orders to each other. Arrows continued raining down. Fortunately, they too fell uselessly in the water.

Parseus and Cheiron now climbed on board. 'Get over there and stay down.' Parseus said, pointing to the stern. The boys did as they were told. Stumbling over the deck they planted themselves on a pile of cloaks and rugs stored there.

Then they heard a voice, booming from the beach. 'Raise the anchor and get to the oars.'

Peering over the stern Charlie saw two men, one draped in a sumptuous cloak and another, the largest man he had ever seen, running down the hill towards them. Pursued by another gang of women armed with swords and spears, the two men jumped into the sea.

Urged on by their crewmates, they started swimming furiously to the ship as the pursuing mob stopped at the harbour's edge, their archers again taking aim, but to no greater effect. The two Argonauts emerged from the depths and clambered on board.

With the anchor raised, the crew took to their oars and started rowing out of the bay.

One of the two men removed his sodden cloak and tossed it aside. Then he spotted Cheiron, standing near the stern. 'By all the Gods, what are you doing here?' he asked.

'Just dropped in, Jason. Thought we'd pay you a visit. See you're having a spot of bother,' replied Cheiron.

'Something like that,' said Jason grimly. 'Someone thought it would be a good idea to leave our weapons on board, in case it frightened the women...' His voice trailed off. 'Anyway, must see to the crew,' he added.

Turning, he noticed the boys. He eyed them briefly before making his way down the deck. Cheiron followed him.

Parseus sat down with the boys. 'Are you two all right?'

Charlie coughed. 'Yeah, just glad to be out of there.'

'Quite. I knew they were a murderous bunch,' said Parseus. 'But to make heroes such as these flee for their lives, well...'

'Not very heroic is it?' muttered Charlie.

'Watch what you say, Charlie,' warned Parseus.

'Sorry.'

Cheiron, picking his way carefully down the narrow plank, rejoined them on the stern.

'I've had a quick word with Jason. We can stay on board for the moment. And I've found out what happened. The women of Lemnos were persuasive in all manner of ways and wanted the Argonauts to stay, but when Herakles threatened to abandon the quest unless the ship left, the women turned ugly. There was nothing for it but to flee,' he said.

Just then they heard more shouting from the headland behind them. 'WAIT FOR ME.' The cry came from an Argonaut who had been left behind.

'Poor guy. What's he going to do?' said Charlie. The Argo was already heading out to sea.

'Don't worry,' said Parseus. 'That's Euphemos the Runner, the fastest man on earth. He's the son of Poseidon, the God of the Sea. They say he can run so fast that he can skip across the swell of the sea and only his toes will get wet.'

That was exactly what the Argonaut now did. Euphemos pushed past the women and leapt onto the water, skipping like a stone towards the Argo, his feet so fast they could barely see them flying across the waves. Reaching the ship, he clambered aboard.

Charlie looked down at the Argonaut's feet. They were massive, his toes slightly webbed, his legs and arms exceptionally long. No wonder he could run so fast, he thought.

'That was close,' Euphemos said, catching his breath. 'Could have told me you were leaving,' he complained to the others before making his way to his bench and taking his seat.

They started rowing round a headland and Charlie took one final glance back at the island. The women were still standing on the harbour side, wailing and beating their chests in fury. But as the Argonauts pulled away and the island disappeared from view, they breathed a collective sigh of relief. They knew they had only just escaped with their lives. However, leaving Lemnos far behind, the drama of their departure seemed to give way to embarrassment. For they had fled a mob of women — hardly the stuff of legend, regardless of how murderous they had been. An awkward silence descended on the ship.

The Argo now cut a swathe through the tranquil sea, the smell of sea-water wafting over the boat, a gentle breeze taking the edge off the heat of the sun. Charlie and Max tried to make themselves comfortable on the pile of cloaks and rugs and settled back for the next stage of the journey.

Charlie had never been in anything larger than a rowing boat — and that only on a river — but this ship was enormous. Not only was it long but it was deep too. The crew sat very low, their oars stuck through holes in the hull, the sound of them swishing through the water strangely hypnotic.

Sat as they were in the stern, Charlie was able to study the crew in detail: some were dressed in leather-armoured breastplates worn over simple tunics, others rowed bare-chested, wearing nothing more than loincloths, their sweat glistening in the sun. Most of them stored their weapons by their side: for many it was a sword, spear or axe, for others a bow and arrow.

And they all looked battle-hardened. Even the more friendly-looking ones appeared as if they had been in their fair share of fights. Many of them bore scars on their chests and faces.

However, watching them now pull their weight, Charlie wondered how he was ever going to do the same. How could he ever compare to these men? How on earth was he ever going to be as heroic as they were? How could he and Max ever be considered worthy to join them? It was a depressing prospect.

Charlie's attention turned to the huge man sitting in the middle, one of the last two to get on board.

'Who's that, Parseus?' he asked.

'The great Herakles himself,' Parseus replied.

Charlie had heard of Herakles. His adventures were legendary and looking at him now he certainly lived up to his image, even amongst these muscle-bound heroes. It was also clear that he had the respect of his fellow Argonauts. Urging them on at their oars, they seemed to hang on his every word.

'What about the others, Parseus?' asked Charlie.

'Some of them are of immortal parentage. For example, Herakles is the son of Zeus, as is Polydeuces,' said Parseus, pointing out a giant of a man with huge biceps, sitting a few rows in front of Herakles.

'The man sitting next to him is Kastor, his brother. They have the same mother but different fathers. Kastor is no demi-God, which is why he is smaller. You can always tell,' said Parseus.

'And who are they?' said Max, pointing at the strange men with huge black-feathered wings on their backs — the men they had seen flying over their heads at Lemnos.

'Ah, the winged sons of Boreas, the North Wind,' replied Parseus casually.

'North Wind?' said Max. 'How can a wind have sons?'

'They just can in this world. The one on the left is called Kalais, the other one is Zetes,' said Parseus. 'They're twins,' he added. 'And they can fly.'

'I did notice that,' said Max.

'And that's Jason is it, standing by the prow?' asked Charlie. He recognised him as the man who had climbed on board last with Herakles. He was staring out to sea.

'Indeed it is. He's the leader of the Argonauts.'

'Why is he talking to himself?' asked Max.

Parseus pointed to a wooden beam that formed part of the prow. 'He's seeking an oracle.'

'What?' Max pulled a face.

'The prow contains an oracular beam. It was a gift from Athene. It comes from the sacred oak tree at Dodona. It's prophetic.'

'A piece of wood is prophetic?' Charlie was incredulous.

'This one is.'

'What's he asking?' said Charlie.

'What to do next, I should imagine,' said Parseus.

Jason stepped back from the prow and made his way down the ship towards them. He ignored the boys and climbing up in front of them, cleared his throat and started addressing the crew.

'I realise that our departure from Lemnos was rather abrupt,' he announced.

A ripple of laughter swept through the ship as the crew temporarily banked their oars.

Jason raised his arm. 'But — and I don't think I need to reiterate this,' he said, pointing in the direction of the island —'that never happened. Is that clear?'

The Argonauts looked at each other and mumbled in agreement. No one would be telling the story as it stood.

Parseus leaned over to Charlie. 'History won't mention it. The Argonauts would be ridiculed if it became known they had fled a bunch of women. Even I didn't know they had.'

Jason continued. 'We will reach the land of the Doliones in two or three days and stop there to fetch food and water. But we have very little for now. What we have will be rationed and we must thank Kalais and Zetes for that,' he said, pointing to the two bronze pitchers of water and a handful of loaves. 'There are also some dried fruits and unsweetened wine which is all we had left when we got to Lemnos. It will have to do.' He raised his arm again. 'Until then, we row.'

A roar of approval rang out and the crew picked up their oars once more.

Cheiron, who had positioned himself near the prow, tentatively picked his way down the ship to join Jason on the stern.

'Ah, Cheiron, tell me — what brings you here?' asked Jason. 'And who are they?' he added, pointing at the boys and Parseus. 'We can ill-afford dead weight.'

Cheiron let Parseus answer. 'My apologies, Jason, we had hoped to speak to you earlier, but there was no time. We are here because an oracle told us to join your voyage. We are on a quest for a cure. It lies somewhere on the way to Colchis.'

'Join the voyage?' said Jason. 'Can't you see the ship is full? If we hadn't been in such a rush I would never have let you set foot on board. There's no room for passengers. Besides, we are on a dangerous quest — hardly the place for two boys.'

Charlie's heart sank.

Parseus nodded. 'I quite understand.'

Charlie was confused. Had Parseus given up so easily? Was this the end of it?

Cheiron intervened. 'I beg you to reconsider, Jason. They can be put to work. The boys are strong and they are willing and able.' He paused. 'If you will take them, I would consider it a great personal favour.'

Jason hesitated. 'Much as I would like to grant that, as I said there's no room. But they can remain until we reach land, provided they make themselves useful.'

He turned to the boys. 'Get up and start handing out water and food to the men. And I want no complaints or I will throw you both overboard. Is that clear?'

Charlie and Max nodded meekly. Then Jason turned and made his way back down the ship, stopping here and there to speak to the crew.

'What does he mean — until we reach land?' said Charlie. 'I thought we were going to join the voyage.'

'Be patient, Charlie. Jason has let us stay for now. We'll be fine,' said Parseus. 'Trust me.'

Charlie was not reassured but there was nothing he could do about it. So for the next few hours he and Max traipsed up and down the ship, handing out water and fruit. It was hard work and the Argonauts seemed to delight in barking orders at them. If it wasn't water they wanted, they shouted for brine to toughen their hands.

Charlie and Max spent the whole day serving their needs. But when the sea grew choppy, the narrow plank became so slippery that it was virtually impossible for them to stay on their feet.

'This is fun, isn't it?' sniped Max sarcastically as he passed Charlie on the plank. 'We're slaves. That's what we are now, slaves.'

'Stop moaning,' Charlie snapped back. While Max had a point they could hardly complain. If they were to have any chance of staying, they had to be seen to work hard.

Charlie quickly came to know some of the Argonauts, though some were less friendly than others. When Charlie accidentally spilled brine on an Argonaut known as Idas, it earned him a swift punch to his legs. The blow knocked him off his feet and he landed with a bump on his back. There were ripples of laughter through the crew, though Charlie didn't dare cry out.

'Not very sea-worthy are you boy?' jeered Idas.

The Argonaut sitting opposite Idas picked up Charlie with one arm and put him back on his feet. He pulled him close. 'Be careful of Idas, they call him the violent one. Take care or he'll throw you overboard,' he warned.

Charlie glanced fearfully at Idas. 'Thanks,' he said.

'My name's Perikylemenos by the way.' The Argonaut held out his hand. It was the first friendly gesture from the crew since the boys had come aboard.

Perikylemenos was an odd-looking man: he had a very large, red knobbly nose, a slightly cross-eyed look and short blonde hair that sprang out like candyfloss. Charlie shook his hand. 'Glad to meet you.' There was a kindness about this Argonaut, and he was grateful for that.

He made his way back down the ship.

'Enjoying the adventure?' Max asked bitterly as they passed each other on the plank.

Charlie shook his head miserably. 'It's certainly not like this in my books.'

Jason shouted from the prow. 'Lynkeus, come here. I need your eyes.'

Charlie and Max watched Lynkeus make his way down the ship. He was tall and slim with a thin face and a narrow nose, but his eyes were huge and piercing blue.

'Who's he?' asked Max.

'Apparently they call him the sharp-sighted one. According to Parseus, he can even see underground,' replied Charlie.

'You mean he's got x-ray vision?' said Max.

Despite his aches and pains, Charlie couldn't help giggling. He sounded like a comic-book hero but then they all did.

His eye fell on Herakles again. Sitting in the middle and still urging on the crew, he cut a magnificent figure. There was no disguising his power. He looked as if he could have rowed the whole ship by himself, such was his strength. Of all the crew, he was the one who impressed Charlie the most.

THE Argonauts continued rowing throughout the day, keeping the coast of Thrace on their left. When the winds picked up they lowered the sails but they did not rest and sailed on through the night. On the second night, they passed through the Hellespont, the waves crashing against the ship as it forced its way through the narrow channel.

Charlie and Max went on as before, carrying whatever was demanded of them, though by the third day there was no food left and very little water. Jason had ordered the boys to ration it, but that only made the crew more hostile towards them. Tempers began to fray.

'I blame those boys. They've been spilling our supplies and I bet they've been pilfering on the side,' Idas shouted, trying to stir up trouble. Arguments broke out and with the Argonauts exhausted and thirsty, Charlie and Max bore the brunt of their fury.

'I'm not sure we're going to make it, Charlie. This lot look ready to throw us overboard,' said Max. He sounded frightened.

Charlie was no less scared. Even the friendly Argonauts had stopped smiling at them, and most growled at them as they passed. The sea had also grown choppy again and it was proving much harder to manoeuvre along the water-drenched deck.

Fortunately Herakles now came to their aid. 'Enough,' he shouted. 'It is not their fault and any man here who raises an arm against them will have me to answer to. Is that clear?'

His words quickly silenced the threats. Although Idas still snarled at Charlie as he sat back down, the mood amongst the rest of the crew soon calmed. Charlie could only hope they reached land soon or it would not remain so. He had a feeling Max and he would be the first casualties if it didn't.

However, just before dawn on the fourth morning, Lynkeus shouted from the prow. He had spotted an island sloping down into the sea, joined to the mainland by a narrow peninsula.

Nearing the shore, Charlie saw the waves crashing over it. 'Where's that, Parseus?' he said, stumbling down the plank, his hands rubbed raw, his legs about to buckle from exhaustion.

'The land of the Doliones,' said Parseus.

'Are they friendly?' asked Charlie, but he was so tired he didn't really care. He just wanted to put his feet on dry land.

'Yes, and they will give us all the supplies that we need,' said Parseus. He paused. 'But it is also the home of the Earth-born.'

'Earth-born?'

'Violent and savage monsters, Charlie. Each one has six arms — three on each side from their shoulders downward. They can be very dangerous,' said Parseus. 'Only the Doliones are safe from their attacks.'

Max crossed his arms. 'In that case, I'm not leaving the ship. That's final.'

'Good — I'm sure Jason will be delighted to leave you in sole charge,' said Parseus.

Max glowered at him and nudged Charlie. 'He's really starting to annoy me.'

WITHIN the hour the Argo dropped anchor in a small harbour. Waiting for them on the beach was a detachment of soldiers. Jason sent Euphemos as a herald to shore: he returned to confirm that they were there only to welcome them.

'King Kyzikos has sent orders that we are to sail around to the next harbour. They have prepared a great feast for us. It seems a prophecy has foretold of our arrival. We are to be shown their finest hospitality, or they will risk the Gods' fury,' Euphemos declared.

A great cheer erupted from the crew and they happily took to their oars again. Not long after they reached the city harbour. Sailing in, Charlie saw fires being lit on the nearby beach and soon enough they were safely moored. The crew disembarked, and on reaching the beach made sacrifices to Apollo.

Charlie and Max waited impatiently. They were starving and the tantalising aroma of lamb and the promise of fresh fruit and water was hard to resist.

I don't get all these sacrifices. It's not as if these Gods eat any of them, is it?' said Max.

'I'm not sure that's what they're for. I think it's just a ritual,' said Charlie.

A makeshift camp had been erected, so they settled down to feast. Servants hurried around bringing roasted lamb and fruits. Charlie and Max were now treated like crew and, relieved to be included in the feast, they sat down beside the others and tucked into the food.

The crew fell silent while they gorged themselves but, their tongues loosened by wine, it wasn't long before they were happily swapping stories with King Kyzikos and his men.

Kyzikos seemed like a kindly king. Tall and muscular, he was dressed in fine robes and had a friendly face. There was a civilised air about him and his men, who in comparison to the hardened Argonauts, looked as if they might never have seen battle. Not that Charlie had any complaints. They seemed very eager to please.

A little while later Parseus beckoned Charlie to one side. 'We must keep an eye on Cheiron. I've no wish to see his tongue loosened by wine. Can't have him talking out of turn,' he said.

Charlie agreed but there was little he or Max could do about it. Before long, fuelled by drink, Cheiron was dancing round the fire to the music of a lyre. But since he wasn't yet behaving too badly, Parseus let him be.

Then another Argonaut approached. 'Parseus, surprised to see you here.'

'Peleus, haven't seen you since your wedding,' replied Parseus.

'Yes, you had to fish Cheiron out of the lake as I recall.'

'Indeed. How's your beautiful wife?'

'Thetis? Still shifting shape,' Peleus replied.

'Well, if you will marry a sea nymph...' said Parseus, smiling. 'And your son, Achilles?'

'Achilles?' Charlie blurted out. 'I've heard of him.'

Peleus was taken aback. 'How can you know anything of my son?'

Parseus shot Charlie a warning look before covering up for him. 'Cheiron mentioned him. His wife is charged with his care, is she not? Cheiron told the boys he has been asked to train the boy when he's older that's all.'

'Indeed. He has,' said Peleus. Then he wandered off to fetch more food, thinking no more of it.

Parseus bent over Charlie. 'That was not clever. I told you to be careful. Achilles is just a baby at the moment. Try to remember you're from the future, and things you know may not have happened yet. It could cause trouble.'

The feasting continued and the boys soon relaxed. 'This isn't too bad, is it?' said Charlie, gnawing on a lamb chop as he warmed himself next to the fire.

'Guess so. But that Idas is a nasty piece of work. I thought we were going to end up walking the plank,' said Max. 'Not very friendly bunch are they?' he whispered. 'At least not on board ship.'

But remembering Jason's words Charlie wondered if they were ever going to be allowed back on board ship. Dreadful though their experience had been he hoped they would. For the moment, however, Charlie put all thoughts of that out of his mind as he and Max listened to the Argonauts regaling King Kyzikos and his men with tales of their adventure. Although none of them seemed to have managed to agree their version of events on Lemnos. Depending on which Argonaut they were sitting next to, the Doliones heard a number of different versions. The boys listened with amusement.

Exhaustion soon overcame them and they settled down near the fire to sleep. But Charlie's thoughts turned once again to their quest. Would they be allowed to stay on the Argo, and if not, what then? He tried not to think of it, but he knew the answer: without the cure his sister would die.

PARSEUS woke Charlie early the next morning. 'Some of the Argonauts are going to climb the nearby mountain to get a better view of our on-going route. Jason has ordered Herakles and some of the younger heroes to sail the ship around to another harbour, called the Closed Harbour. It is far more secluded and will provide better protection from errant storms. I suggest you help him,' said Parseus.

'What are you going to do?' asked Charlie.

'Cheiron and I will go with Jason. It may take some time for us to persuade him to let you stay. At the moment he is still refusing,' said Parseus.

'Refusing?' said Charlie.

'Have no fear. At worst we will have to go home and return later when the Argo reaches the land of the Mysians. He will not refuse us then, I promise you,' Parseus assured him. Then without another word he left the boys alone.

'What was he on about?' asked Max.

'Who knows,' said Charlie. 'Let's just do as we're told, eh? If we are to have any chance of staying we can't give Jason any excuses. Understood?'

Max agreed and they climbed back on board the Argo. An hour later they helped moor it next to a rock in the nearby harbour.

Herakles approached Charlie. 'I hear you've done some training with Cheiron. He speaks highly of you. Would you like me to take you ashore to practise archery?' he said. 'My squire Hylas and I will help you.'

Charlie, still in awe of the great hero, nodded eagerly. Training with the great Herakles himself? What an honour, he thought. They disembarked and Herakles and Hylas led the boys down the beach to find somewhere quiet to train.

Herakles soon found a suitable spot and Hylas laid out an array of weapons on the sand in front of them. 'Of course I like to use my trusted club but you need strength to wield a weapon like that, and it's of little use when your enemy is far away. So we will practise with the bow and arrow instead. It is a weapon of finesse, of skill,' said Herakles as Hylas handed him his bow.

For the next few hours, Charlie practised hard. Herakles proved a stern taskmaster and it was exhausting work. Max too was shattered after hours toiling up and down the beach to retrieve the arrows, while Hylas just sat and watched him.

Max soon grew disgruntled. 'Hey, I'm not just a sidekick, you know,' he said after carrying yet another pile back to Herakles. 'Why can't I train too?'

'Of course you can. Why don't you and Hylas practise with the sword instead,' said Herakles. 'But I suggest you rest for a bit. You two look worn out.'

Grateful for any respite, Charlie and Max sat down on the beach and took turns sharing a goatskin of water.

It was a perfect day: there was a bright blue sky, not a cloud in sight and a gentle breeze wafted across the headland, bringing the sweet scent of flowers with it. Charlie felt so relaxed he started to wonder why this journey was considered to be so perilous.

Then he felt a rumbling. At first, he feared it was another earthquake and he leapt to his feet. However, he soon realised that this rumbling wasn't coming from down below. Rubble was rolling down the mountainside towards them, boulders and rocks were crashing down and a huge ball of dust filled the air, obscuring everything in sight. Then the dust cloud settled and there, standing high on a headland above him, were the Earthborn.

And they were far more terrifying than Parseus' description — they were huge, wild-eyed figures with mangled faces, bodies covered in brown mangy fur, and thick grey hair falling down around their shoulders. Their arms, all six of them, sprouted out like branches, their legs like tree trunks. And in their hands they held huge boulders, which they now began hurling down at the beach.

Herakles turned to the boys. 'RUN. *Run for your lives.*'

So they did.

21. NO SAFE HARBOUR

CHARLIE didn't dare look back as he and Max raced down the beach. Holding their hands over their heads, they ducked and weaved out of the way as the Earth-borns' rocks crashed down around them.

Herakles swiftly caught up with them, bent down and picked them up, one under each arm. He waded into the water, rocks crashing down all around them, some of them hitting Herakles on the head and shoulders, yet he shrugged them off as if they were nothing more than pebbles.

By the time they reached the Argo, the Earth-Born were hurling huge boulders into the harbour, whipping up the waves, making the ship tip and weave in their wake. Charlie had no idea what the monsters were trying to do, but Herakles did.

'They're trying to block up the harbour so we can't leave,' he shouted. 'Quick boys, gather as many arrows as you can find, and arm the other men,' he ordered. Leaping onto the prow, he bent his bow, and began unleashing a barrage of arrows at the Earth-Born.

Charlie and Max stumbled up and down the ship, as it lurched from side to side, gathering arrows and spears for Herakles and the other Argonauts who had remained on board. The Earth-born, now finding themselves under attack, changed their tactics and went for the ship itself.

Rocks crashed down, one falling near the prow, others smashing into the hull, sending great splinters flying into the air.

'Now's the time to test you, boy,' Herakles shouted. 'Grab that bow over there. Pull it back gently and keep your aim straight.'

Leaping forward, Charlie grabbed the bow, strung it quickly and taking aim, pulled back gently. He let fly and held his breath, but his arrow hit his target.

'Again, boy,' shouted Herakles.

Charlie strung his bow and began firing arrow after arrow at the same monster, hitting it with each strike. The monster tottered but although it didn't fall, it did stop throwing boulders.

'Good boy. Now do it again. Aim for the arms,' said Herakles.

Charlie kept on firing. He was about to re-stock his quiver when he saw a huge rock sail over the ship. Max, collecting arrows nearby, failed to see it. Screaming a warning, Charlie leapt forward, grabbed a shield and held it up to deflect it. The force of the blow pushed him to his knees, but the rock bounced off and landed in the water.

'Thanks, Charlie. Didn't see that one coming,' Max shouted.

'Don't worry.' He passed Max the shield. 'But you might want to keep this handy, they're coming down fast now,' he said before returning to the prow.

The Earth-born continued their relentless attack. Nothing, it seemed, could defeat them.

'It's no good, Herakles. We're never going to stop them. The arrows can't take them down,' shouted Charlie as he tried to make himself heard over the din.

'Your arrows can't, but mine can. The heads have been dipped in poison,' Herakles shouted back. 'Just keep distracting them. We have to stop them blocking up the harbour and destroying the ship. I'll finish them off,' he said.

Shortly afterwards Parseus, Cheiron and the other Argonauts returned to the beach. Seeing the attack they joined the battle, using anything they could find to stop the violent assault from above.

Eventually, and largely due to Herakles' efforts, the Earth-born were slain, the beach piled high with their fallen bodies. Parseus waded back to the ship and, clambering on board, went over to the boys. 'Are you two all right?'

Charlie, exhausted by the fight, nodded. Max, worn out by running up and down the ship and deflecting rocks with the shield, was beyond reply.

Herakles came up and slapped Charlie on the back. 'The boy did well. Stopped at least one of them all by himself,' he said.

Parseus seemed pleased, yet relieved. 'At least the boy is learning,' he replied.

'He most certainly is,' said Herakles, before wandering off to speak to some of the crew.

Charlie turned to Parseus. 'Did you know they were going to attack?' he said. 'You could have warned us.'

'We could have been killed, you know,' added Max.

'Apologies,' replied Parseus. 'I thought the attack came much later when we would have been safely beyond their range. I'd no idea you'd be in danger. My recollection is obviously a little shaky.' He rubbed his hands together. 'Still, no harm done. And I did warn you that this journey was perilous.'

'Oh, that's OK then,' muttered Max.

THE boys watched from the ship as the Argonauts lined up the monsters on the beach. They looked like sardines in a tin, Charlie thought, all neatly arranged from head to toe. They were so large that their bodies stretched from the top of the beach right into the water, boulders and rocks scattered around them.

'Why did they attack us, Parseus?' asked Charlie.

'And how come the Doliones have never been attacked?' asked Max. 'You'd think...'

'They're protected by Poseidon. We are not,' replied Parseus.

Euphemos and Lynkeus approached and greeted the boys warmly. 'We hear you helped defeat the attack,' said Lynkeus.

'We may yet make heroes of you both,' laughed Euphemos.

Charlie blushed with pride. For the first time since they had joined the Argo he started to feel accepted. Though not all the Argonauts were as welcoming — Jason in particular — but at least they had started to prove themselves. Charlie had even earned the respect of Herakles and that counted with the crew.

The Doliones, hearing the news of the attack, now appeared, apologising profusely. Soon enough their servants were rushing about, fetching more food and water. An hour later the Argonauts were celebrating once more, sitting around a hastily-built fire, while another sacrifice was made — this time to appease Poseidon.

Settling down to feast, the Doliones listened intently as the boys excitedly retold their part in the battle. They all seemed suitably impressed.

It was strange, Charlie thought. Only a few weeks ago he would never have imagined that he could fight anything, let alone giant monsters. But every encounter made him stronger. What's more, it seemed there was no better place to train than here with the Argonauts. Perhaps one day he might even be able to face the Dark One, he thought — perhaps even defeat it.

FOR the next ten days the Argonauts made repairs to the ship and waited for fair winds, while Charlie and Max trained under the watchful eye of Cheiron, who after his drunken antics was sticking to water. He seemed to inspire the array of heroes, many of whom he had trained himself, and it was clear that, regardless of the odd drunken escapade, he was highly regarded amongst the crew. Herakles was more helpful than most to the boys but many of the Argonauts were now willing to take the time to encourage them in their training.

The boys had formed firm friendships with Lynkeus — they never ceased to be amazed at what he could see, even from miles away — and Euphemos, though however hard they tried there was never any chance of beating him in a race.

Kalais and Zetes had also taken the boys under their wings — literally, in their case — and when the boys weren't training they were always offering to take them for a ride. The twins would soar into the air and dive down, ducking and weaving through the sky with the boys tied securely to their backs. Charlie and Max were constantly pestering them for another go.

Polydeuces, too, had developed a soft spot for the boys and offered to teach them the art of boxing. Max, in particular, was desperate to learn it.

'You're lucky to have such a fine teacher, Max,' said Parseus. 'There's no greater boxer in the whole of the Ancient World. Polydeuces has never been beaten.'

But the hero that was always close by was Herakles. Charlie felt an affinity with him that he didn't feel for anyone else, and Herakles surpassed everyone in skill, whatever weapon he used.

Back in Hesper it was Max who had always excelled at physical pursuits, here in the Ancient World, with Herakles as tutor, it was Charlie who began to do so, gaining steadily both in skill and strength. And although Max did too, it was Charlie who came to prove himself the better of the two.

However, while so many of the Argonauts had grown fond of the boys, Jason was still refusing to let them continue the voyage. It was clear that in his eyes they were no longer welcome.

Charlie overheard Parseus arguing with him on the beach.

'There is just not enough room, Parseus. I told Cheiron they could remain until we reached land. I've decided they go no further.' With that, Jason departed for the ship.

Charlie was crestfallen. He approached Parseus. 'I heard what he said. He's not going to take us, is he? Despite everything we've done.'

Parseus seemed untroubled. 'Have no fear, Charlie. We'll rejoin the voyage later. Trust me there will soon be room enough.'

'What about the cure? We still don't know where it is,' said Charlie. 'What if it's here?'

'Don't worry, I've spoken to Idmon. He's an Argonaut, but he's also a Seer.'

'What's a Seer?' asked Charlie.

'They have the gift of foresight,' said Parseus.

'So does he know where the cure lies?' asked Charlie hopefully.

'No, but he tells me it does not lie here. That being so, it is best if we return home for now. Your essences need recharging anyway. We can rejoin the Argonauts when they reach the land of the Mysians. The cure still lies some way beyond it,' said Parseus.

'Where exactly?'

'That he did not know, Charlie. However, he tells me there is a Seer who may,' added Parseus. 'We'll meet him soon enough.'

'Who's that?' asked Charlie.

Parseus dismissed the question. 'Let's just find Cheiron. Now we are leaving he may want to return home.'

They met Cheiron on the beach and said their farewells.

'I'm sorry I could not convince Jason to let you remain,' said Cheiron.

'Don't worry, we will find another way,' said Parseus.

Parseus took out one of his small jars. 'Before you go, there's something I want you to take. I'm afraid you cannot be allowed to remember anything of the future or the mortal world. I am sure you understand.'

'Ah, a sip of forgetfulness you mean?' Cheiron grinned as Parseus handed him the jar. 'Pity, mind you no one would have believed me anyway.' Cheiron twisted the cork out of the jar and took a slug before handing the potion back. Then he took the boys aside. 'I wish you both the blessings of the Gods. Your training is best left in the hands of the Argonauts now. You've done well. But destiny has plans of its own for me,' he said. 'So I too must return home.'

The boys and Parseus now accompanied Cheiron up the mountainside: Cheiron to find a cloud, Parseus and the boys to find a quiet spot to return home. A minute later a cloud appeared. Charlie and Max went to say goodbye then Charlie saw a puzzled look cross Cheiron's face. He rubbed his head. 'Hang on, where am I?' he said, turning in circles. He looked at Parseus. 'Parseus? Didn't we meet at Peleus' wedding?' Then he glanced down at Charlie and Max. 'Who are you? Have we met?'

Puzzled, Charlie glanced at Parseus — who just smiled and tapped the jar in his hand. Of course, thought Charlie, the potion of Lethe. It had now taken effect.

'Where am I?' Cheiron asked. 'Last thing I remember I was in the Satyr...'

'Quite, quite. Perhaps you should return home and get some rest,' said Parseus as he ushered Cheiron into the cloud.

Cheiron sat down, confused and shook his head. 'Perhaps I shouldn't drink so much,' he muttered as he gave the cloud its order and it lifted up and shot off into the sky.

Charlie watched the cloud disappear. He felt sad to see Cheiron go. He had grown fond of him — even when he was drunk. He felt a little lost now that he was gone. But since they were heading home, his thoughts turned once again to Hesper. It was night-time there so The Dark One would still be lurking. Watching Parseus fiddle with the compass, he felt the dread creep back into his stomach.

Then a portal opened up and he was sucked once again into the abyss.

THEY arrived back in Parseus' room. Charlie steadied himself and waited for the nausea to pass. Parseus went over to the window and peered out. 'How long do you think it will take the Dark One to free itself from that peat bog of yours?' he asked Charlie.

'How should I know? Anything else would have sunk without trace.'

'This isn't anything else, Charlie. So I suggest you get back to Emily's room and get under the protection of the helmet. If it even picks up a whiff of your scent it could trigger a transformation. We can't afford to have your cornered, not somewhere like this. Remember the cottage?'

Charlie didn't need reminding of that. Whatever protection the helmet did afford, it was not infallible.

'So should we go somewhere else?'

'If you're under the helmet before it comes looking, you'll be fine. It won't change unless it thinks it has reason. So go NOW.'

Charlie opened the door to find his father standing outside. 'Sorry, Dad, didn't realise you were there.'

'I just popped up to ask if...' His father stepped back surprised. 'Have you been away? And what are you wearing?'

Charlie looked down at his clothes. He was still in the tunic Cheiron had given him. He and Max had left their own clothes in his cave. 'This is what they wear in the Ancient World, Dad — and yes, we've been gone for weeks.'

'Weeks? But you only just...' His father scratched his head. 'I can't get my head round this time travel business.' He put his arm around Charlie. 'At least you're all right. That's something, eh? But you do look very different.'

'Feel pretty different too, I can tell you,' said Charlie.

Max came into the corridor. 'Any chance of a snack, Mr Goodwin?'

'Nothing ever curbs your appetite does it, Max? Go on help yourself,' Mr Goodwin said, smiling.

'The Helmet,' said Parseus, approaching the open door. 'NOW,' he insisted.

'Actually Dad, could you make us something? Sandwiches would do. We've all got to go invisible again,' said Charlie, stepping past him.

He and Max headed for Emily's room and had just reached her door when they heard a loud hiss. It came from downstairs, near the front door. *It's already here,* Charlie shouted.

Parseus raced into the corridor, his face grim. 'It's too late then, Charlie. You'll have to get out. It knows you're here. It will transform. You'll be trapped. Grab Emily and flee.' He pulled Mr Goodwin back into his room.

Charlie threw open Emily's door and he and Max rushed inside. Charlie fumbled across the bed for his sister. 'Quick, grab hold of her, Max.'

A moment later, enveloped in the invisible shroud, the boys lifted up Emily, Max taking her legs, and Charlie her shoulders.

'Where now?' said Max.

'Down the backstairs and through the side entrance. We've got to get clear of the inn,' said Charlie.

Carrying Emily between them the boys shuffled into the corridor. Making their way to the stairs, Charlie glanced back. The Shadow was already moving towards Emily's open door, its yellow eyes flashing with fury. Charlie heard another hiss — it was about to transform.

The boys carefully took Emily down the stairs and into the square outside. They had escaped just in time.

Max stopped. 'Where can we hide? We can't go round the village all night, hoping it won't bump into us.'

'Down the lane to the river,' said Charlie.

'And then what?' said Max. 'Go swimming?'

'No, we can hide in the boat-house. It's only five minutes away.'

They turned left and hurried down the moonlit lane towards the river. Charlie looked back, but the Dark One was nowhere to be seen. There was still no sign of it when they reached the boat-house. Thankfully the door was unlocked and they went inside.

Charlie switched on the overhead light. The boat-house was neatly arranged: fishing rods and tackle adorned every wall and a pair of waders hung on a hook. There were a couple of wooden chests pushed up against the wall and in a corner, a small rocking chair with some blankets draped over it. A paraffin lamp sat on a table next to it.

Now that they were there Charlie wasn't sure whether it was the best place to hide. It was far too small for all three of them. Then he spotted Tom the boatman's rowing boat, *Nelly*, tied up, bobbing gently up and down in the water. Her hull was dark blue, the inside white and on one side her name was boldly emblazoned in red.

It gave Charlie an idea. 'Get in the boat, Max. We can untie *Nelly* and let her drift onto the river. I bet the Dark One can't swim,' he said. 'Well, let's hope so.'

He held onto Emily while Max clambered into the boat to steady it. Then between the two of them they lowered Emily into it. Charlie stepped back to the boat-house and grabbed the blankets from the chair. It would be cold on the river.

Charlie slid open the backdoor of the boat-house, untied the rope, climbed back into the boat and pushed *Nelly* off from the jetty. Very slowly, with all of them back under the protection of the helmet, the boat drifted out into the river and began to move downstream.

They had gone about a hundred yards when Charlie spotted movement behind them on the river bank below the inn. It was The Shadow, its yellow eyes glinting in the moonlight, and it was heading towards the boat-house. He wondered if it would sense them there. If so would it follow them onto the river?

Charlie held his breath as *Nelly* drifted downstream. He hoped that her dark blue hull would make it impossible for the Dark One to spot her. And after all, they were invisible again. There was no need to panic, he told himself.

Ten minutes later they were out of sight of the boat-house and there was no sign of the Dark One on the opposite bank. It had not followed them.

'How long are we going to stay on the river?' asked Max.

'All night,' said Charlie.

'We can't just drift until dawn.'

'No. We'll row to the other river bank and tie her up somewhere. We can wait there until morning,' said Charlie.

Twenty minutes later, with Charlie satisfied that they were far enough away, they picked up the oars, rowed across to the bank and tied up *Nelly* next to a tree which overhung the river. Charlie tucked a blanket over Emily, and tried to make her as comfortable as possible.

'What now?' said Max.

'Let's try to get some rest,' said Charlie.

'Great. I was looking forward to a snack, a cup of tea and a warm bed,' grumbled Max. 'Not much of a homecoming, is it?' he added.

'At least we're safe,' said Charlie.

The boys eventually dozed off, too tired to do otherwise. Waking up, Charlie was relieved to see the first signs of daylight. He sat up and looked around. They had come much further than he had first thought.

Max woke up soon after. 'Where are we?' he asked.

'We must have drifted for at least a mile before we moored the boat. It's going to take a good hour or two to head back up river,' said Charlie.

'At least it's daylight,' said Max.

'Just think about breakfast. By the time we get back, Dad'll be frying up a couple of bacon sandwiches. How does that sound?' said Charlie.

'Sounds like a plan,' said Max, his mood improving. 'I'm starving.'

Charlie and Max now took to the oars and rowed back up river. By the time they arrived at the boat-house the sun had risen and the birds were singing in the trees. They tied up the boat, shut the rear door, and set off for the inn.

'Better wear the helmet until we get back inside. People might ask questions if they see us carrying Emily down the lane,' said Charlie.

'Probably best,' said Max. 'Can't wait for that bacon sandwich,' he added, licking his lips.

Five minutes later they slipped into the inn and entered the bar. Parseus and Charlie's father were anxiously pacing the room, waiting for them. Placing Emily on the floor, Charlie removed the helmet.

'You've been gone for hours,' said Parseus. 'I'd almost given up hope.'

'I know, we had to hide on the river all night,' explained Charlie.

'Never thought of that. Good idea,' said Parseus.

'What happened to the Dark One?' asked Charlie.

'Didn't stay long and never fully transformed. We heard no more.'

'It came down to the river. We saw it,' said Charlie. 'But that was all.'

Parseus knelt down next to Emily, pulled off her blanket, and inspected her wound. He shook his head gravely.

'What's the matter, Parseus?'

'The potion has started to wear off.'

'How long have we got?' asked Charlie, his voice catching in his throat.

Parseus looked up. 'She has hours, not days.'

22. FIGHTING FIT

CHARLIE knelt down beside Emily. 'What do you mean, hours? We still don't have the cure. That could take weeks.'

'Yes, but not in this world, remember. However that said we should return to the Argo,' said Parseus.

Charlie agreed. What mattered was finding the cure, and they had no idea how long that would take in the Ancient World. That was the problem.

'There's something else,' said Parseus.

'What now?' said Charlie.

Mrs Payne's power is growing,' he said. 'I can feel it.'

'I don't understand,' said Charlie.

'I'm afraid in our journeys we've brought back some of the magic of the Ancient World.'

'How?' said Charlie.

'It seeped in through the portals. You see, magic is like a bacteria. It spreads.'

'But what's that got to do with Mrs Payne's power?'

'Magic is a force, Charlie, an energy that can be used for good or ill. It was a risk we had to take. But now the magic has come, the force has taken hold. Mrs Payne's strength has grown,' said Parseus.

Max threw his arms up in despair. 'That's all we need. A more powerful witch.'

'There's still more,' said Parseus.

'What now?' Max seemed just as shocked as Charlie by Parseus' revelations.

Parseus paused. 'Let's get Emily settled first, shall we?'

Charlie and Max carried Emily back upstairs to her room and laid her down on her bed. Looking at her lying there Charlie was shocked at how pale she was. Parseus was right. It didn't seem as if she had much time left. He could only pray that the next time they returned it would be with the cure. Or his sister was doomed. And if the Fates were right — they all were.

They made Emily comfortable and left the room.

'I don't get it, Charlie,' said Max as they made their way downstairs. 'What's all this about magic coming into the world? I don't like it.'

'I know, Max. I don't like it either. And I'm getting sick of people hiding things from me,' he said.

They returned to the bar. 'Listen, Parseus, it's time you told us what else you know,' Charlie said as they entered.

'Maybe your father should show you,' said Parseus.

'Show me what, Dad?' said Charlie.

His father went behind the bar. Lifting up the hatch in the floor he beckoned Charlie and Max to follow him down the stone steps.

The cellar was dusty and filled with beer barrels, wine racks and broken bits of furniture that Mr Goodwin had always meant to get fixed but had never quite got around to doing so. A dull light dangled from the ceiling, and at the back of the room were shelves stacked high with all manner of odds and ends.

Charlie looked around. 'And?'

'It's over here.' His father started climbing over some boxes. 'You two could give me a hand with this,' he said, motioning to a set of shelves pushed up against the back wall. 'We need to move this forward a few feet.'

Charlie and Max stood at each end, lifted them up and shifted the shelves forward. Charlie peered behind, but all he could see was a wall. 'There's nothing here,' he said.

'Yes, there is,' said his father. He waved Charlie out of the way and slid behind the shelves, feeling along the wall. 'It's here somewhere. I know it.'

Charlie heard a clicking sound and a cold draught blasted through the cellar. 'There, that's it,' his father said. 'There's a secret chamber here.'

'What's in it?' asked Charlie.

'Have a look.' His father picked up a small paraffin lamp from the shelf and lit it. Charlie and Max followed him inside.

The chamber was full of weapons piled high from floor to ceiling. There were a vast array of spears and swords, shields and old muskets, many of them centuries old, if not older. 'Where did all this come from?' he asked.

'Remember, I'm a Guardian. But there are — were others, throughout the centuries, people who have guarded this place even before Hesper House or this inn were built. My Dad and his father before him...'

Looking more closely, Charlie realised that some of the weapons in this secret chamber were not from this world. Some were made from Adamantine, which meant that someone in the immortal realm had put them there. But when? And why? Parseus had not mentioned it, nor the towers at Hesper House. In fact, there was a great deal he hadn't mentioned. Perhaps he didn't know, Charlie thought. But someone did and Charlie intended to find out.

'What are these weapons for?' asked Max.

'I'm not sure but I expect they'll come in useful one day,' said Parseus. 'We'll have to investigate later, though. We must return to the Argo now. Your essences are fully recharged and Emily is running out of time.'

'Can I please have something to eat first,' said Max. 'I'm starving. We haven't eaten for a whole day.'

Charlie had quite forgotten about food but the mere mention of it made his stomach grumble. They had been given nothing to eat since leaving the Ancient World.

'I can make some sandwiches. You can eat before you go. I'm sure Parseus can wait ten minutes,' said Mr. Goodwin.

'Yes, but no longer,' insisted Parseus.

They made their way back up to the bar. Helpless to do anything else, Charlie's father shuffled off to the kitchen.

'Is my sister really going to be OK?' asked Charlie.

'For now — yes,' said Parseus.

But Charlie was hardly reassured. Parseus' casual attitude was frustrating. He was so impersonal about everything. Perhaps it was because he was immortal, Charlie wondered. He couldn't die, or get hurt and he didn't have family, people that he loved — people he could lose. But Charlie did.

His father came back into the bar with a plate piled high with ham and chicken sandwiches. Charlie and Max forgot all else, rushed forward, and swiftly devoured them all.

'I need to stock up before we go,' said Parseus. 'I won't be long.'

'Why don't we take the sword with us this time?' said Charlie. Given what they had already faced, it would probably be useful, he thought.

'Good heavens, no. We cannot risk losing it and it would invite far too many questions if anyone on the Argo discovered we had it in our possession.' And with that Parseus disappeared upstairs. When he returned, he motioned the boys to link arms once again.

'See you later, Dad,' said Charlie cheerfully.

'You will take care, son, won't you?'

'I'll try, Dad.'

'Now Mr Goodwin, get down behind the bar, keep your eyes closed, and don't move until I tell you to stand up again,' said Parseus.

Confused, Mr Goodwin hovered for a moment, then did as he had been told and ducked down behind the bar. The room filled with a ball of light.

IT was early morning when they reached the land of the Mysians. The portal had delivered them onto a small cliff which overlooked the bay in which the Argo was moored. They headed down to the beach. Argonauts were running backwards and forwards, loading the ship with supplies.

Parseus held the boys back. 'If they ask where you've been, just say we took another route here. I'll fend off any tricky questions,' he said.

Charlie and Max agreed and followed in silence.

Approaching Jason, his face darkened. 'What are you doing here? I told you we don't have room for you,' he snapped, storming off towards the ship.

Shocked, Charlie watched him go. 'I thought you said we would be able to join now, Parseus?'

'Patience, Charlie, you'll see,' he replied.

Lynkeus was standing nearby. He seemed gloomy. Charlie sensed that the mood in the camp had changed. 'What happened?' he asked.

'Tragedy befell us, a great tragedy. We left the land of the Doliones and set sail, but unknown to us during the night the winds turned and we found ourselves back there, but we didn't know that. And the Doliones, not knowing it was us, attacked. There was a great battle,' he said.

A sad expression crossed his face. 'We killed many, many men — men with whom we had broken bread and shared wine only the day before.' Lynkeus shook his head. 'The Gods can be cruel, Charlie. Cruel indeed.'

He set off towards the Argo where many of the crew were already aboard. Jason ordered the others to join them. 'We leave soon. There are favourable winds and we must take advantage of them,' he announced.

Charlie looked around for Herakles but he was nowhere to be seen. It was another hour before he finally appeared — he seemed worried. 'I cannot find Hylas,' he said.

'Shall we help search for him?' Charlie asked Parseus.

'No, Charlie this is our chance. I told you to be patient.'

'What chance?'

Parseus lowered his voice. 'Say nothing, but Hylas has been

taken by a water nymph. Remember your own brush with one?'

Charlie could hardly forget.

'He will never be seen again,' added Parseus.

'That's dreadful,' replied Charlie. He had liked Hylas. 'But why is that our chance?'

'Wait and see,' said Parseus.

Jason picked up his shield. 'We really must leave Herakles. I'm sorry, but we can't wait any longer — or we lose the winds.'

Herakles folded his arms. 'Then I go no further. I will not leave without Hylas.'

Jason tried to reason with him, but his pleadings made no difference. In the end he gave up. 'So be it. The ship has to sail, Herakles — we go without you.' He turned away, then abruptly turned back. 'Where is Polyphemus?' he barked.

No one seemed to know. The Argonaut was not on the ship and there was no sign of him ashore.

'By all the Gods, we'll lose the wind if we don't go now,' said Jason.

Parseus pushed Charlie in front of him. 'There are the boys, Jason…'

'The boys?' Jason grimaced. 'Anyone would think you'd engineered this situation, Parseus.' He sighed in resignation. 'Yet it seems that there is now room for you. Perhaps that is your good fortune, perhaps not. But destiny appears to be on your side and I can hardly argue with that, can I?'

'Then, we can join?' asked Parseus.

'Yes, you can join. But the boys must row.'

Charlie was relieved that Jason had changed his mind. However, when he and Max clambered back on board, the crew was far less welcoming than he had hoped. Many of the Argonauts were angry. Some accused Jason of leaving Herakles on purpose out of jealousy, others jeered at Charlie and Max.

'The great Herakles has been replaced by mere boys? Have the Gods abandoned us altogether?' said Idas. A mutinous murmur ran through the ship, and as Charlie and Max took their seats they were greeted with snarls and spitting.

'They're not exactly glad to see us back, are they?' said Charlie as he sat down behind Max.

'Yeah, I can really feel the love,' replied Max.

At the same time, Charlie could not blame them — he and Max were hardly substitutes for someone as great as Herakles.

Parseus stood up and raised a commanding arm. He had not addressed the Argonauts before, yet there was an air of authority about him which silenced the crew.

'Listen to me. It is the will of the Queen of the Gods, Hera, the patron of this quest, not Jason that has engineered Herakles' departure. He has labours to complete and his destiny lies elsewhere. The Gods have decreed it. Trust me. I know of their plans.' He walked down between the oarsmen before turning to face them all. 'I warn you now. Any dissent will only anger Hera.'

The crew stopped muttering and fell silent. They seemed to sense that Parseus had knowledge of the Gods' intent, so they sat back down on their benches and took to their oars once again.

Charlie was relieved. 'I think we get to stay, Max.'

'Great. But we're going to have to row.'

Charlie looked down at his huge oar. How on earth he was going to handle it, he wondered.

Jason walked down the deck and stopped next to the boys. He jabbed his finger at them. 'Mark my words, boys. I will have no slacking. You'd better pull your weight or I will throw you overboard. That's a promise. I don't care who protects you,' he growled.

Charlie had no doubt Jason meant what he said. He took a deep breath and prodded Max in front of him. 'I don't think we're going to enjoy this, Max.'

'You reckon?'

The rest of the crew silently took to their oars. They keenly felt the departure of Herakles and a gloom descended upon them. It was not surprising: the greatest hero of them all had left the quest — and destiny or not, that didn't augur well for anyone.

CHARLIE had been put beside Perikylemenos. 'Now rowing is hard but as long as you keep rhythm you'll have no trouble. You'll soon get the hang of it,' Perikylemenos said, smiling. 'Just watch what I'm doing and follow my lead.'

Charlie was glad he was sitting next to him. He was also relieved to see that Max was sitting alongside Polydeuces. They needed all the friends they could find. However, as he stared around the rest of the ship, many of the other Argonauts were still muttering malevolently. Any respect the boys had earned before had long been lost and he knew that if they had any chance of remaining they were going to have to do more than just pull their weight.

A moment later Jason gave the order and everyone leaned forward.

Charlie grabbed his oar. It felt even heavier than he had expected and his spirits sank. He realised the next few hours were going to be very hard indeed.

The sheer force required to pull the oar back and then force it through the water was immense, and keeping in rhythm near impossible at first. Even Perikylemenos, calling out the timing with every stroke, began to lose patience with him. Charlie persevered and at last he seemed to get it right. Perikylemenos stopped complaining.

Charlie kept his own concerns to himself, even though his hands were being ripped raw and every muscle in his body ached. He almost didn't dare look at Max who was sitting right in front of him and struggling just as much as he was.

It was at least two hours before they finally got a break. By then Charlie could barely let go of the oar. He had grown so used to holding it his hands were numb.

He released his grip. A sharp stinging pain ran through them and he winced. Perikylemenos gave him some brine but it only made his hands feel worse.

When the water came he drank desperately, trying to rid his mouth of the sea water that constantly sprayed across the ship as they rowed. Max turned briefly, he looked as bad as Charlie felt. Charlie forced a smile. Max though was beyond expression.

They had rowed for at least four hours, though it felt much longer, when Lynkeus the sharp-sighted one shouted *'LAND AHEAD.'*

An hour or so later they rowed the Argo into a bay and banked their oars. Charlie slowly released his hands. He tried to stretch them out, but the pain seared through them like a knife. It was agony even to straighten his back.

Max turned around, his face contorted with a mixture of pain and relief, his hands as blistered and raw as Charlie's. 'We've been press-ganged. That's what this is — press-ganged,' he grumbled. 'It's like in the old days when they used to take drunk people and frogmarch them to the nearest ship,' he said.

'Except that we did volunteer, Max,' said Charlie.

'More fool us. Preferred it when we were just serving water,' Max snorted.

Charlie sympathised with that. The fact that they had wanted to join this madness didn't make it any easier to bear. He tried to stand up but his legs wouldn't work. It took a while for the feeling to return. It was the same problem for Max and it took some time before they were able to stagger down the ship to where the other Argonauts were now disembarking.

They climbed down into the shallow waters and waded to shore. Charlie reached the beach first. Beyond it, the cliffs rose up sharply on either side of a small headland, which jutted out just above the sand. A path wound up from the beach but there was no sign of civilisation anywhere. Hopefully they would just rest for a while before continuing their journey. Charlie was not looking forward to any more surprises.

Then Lynkeus shouted and pointed to the headland. A band of armed men had appeared, their swords unsheathed, their bows ready, their cloaks billowing behind them in the breeze.

Polydeuces unsheathed his sword. 'What should we do, Jason?' he said.

'Patience, Polydeuces. Let's not act in haste,' Jason replied.

The armed men made their way down the cliff path, stopping in front of Jason. He bowed politely. 'My apologies for any intrusion. My name is Jason and these are my Argonauts. We journey to Colchis. We stop only to rest and fetch fresh water.'

The tallest of the group, wearing a tight-fitting leather tunic under a red cloak, and clearly their leader, put away his sword and stepped forward, his shield slung loosely over his back. His hair was short and he had a long black beard, which narrowed to a point, making his face seem longer than it was.

A handful of the Argonauts moved in to circle Jason, their hands hovering over the hilts of their swords. Jason put out his arm and motioned them to step back.

The leader cleared his throat and addressed him, his voice deep and gravelly. 'I am King Amykos. We saw your ship approach. Welcome to the land of the Bebrykes,' he said.

Jason bowed again. 'Thank you, your majesty. As I said, we come in peace. We stopped only to rest and fetch water.'

'Yet you are armed?' said Amykos.

'But only for our own protection. We mean you no harm.'

Amykos seemed satisfied by that. He held up a hand in greeting. 'Then you are welcome indeed. I take it you know little of the customs here in our land?'

'No, your majesty,' replied Jason. 'But we are eager to honour them all the same, whatever they may be.'

A smile crossed Amykos' face. 'Good. Then know that it is our custom to challenge visitors to a boxing match. You put forward your best man and I will fight him,' he said.

Max nudged Charlie. 'Big mistake. Bet he doesn't realise how good Polydeuces is.'

'We would be honoured to take part, your majesty,' said Jason, smiling. 'If that is your custom, we accept the challenge.' He called Polydeuces forward. 'This is our best man.'

Amykos seemed pleased by his opponent. 'I must warn you — I've never been beaten.' He flung off his cloak. 'You should also know that there is a price to pay if this man of yours loses.' He looked back at his heavily-armed soldiers.

'And the price?' asked Jason politely.

'You all die.'

The Argonauts looked at each other, bemused.

'I don't understand — we all die?' said Jason.

'Exactly as I say. If your man loses — his eyes swept the line of Argonauts — then you all forfeit your lives.' Amykos smiled. 'That is our custom.'

The soldiers who had accompanied their king now closed ranks as more soldiers appeared on the headland above them, swarming in from all sides, surrounding the Argonauts.

Jason looked at Amykos. 'And if you lose — what then?'

The king opened his arms. 'I promise that you may then have whatever you ask of me.'

Max ducked behind Parseus. 'Any idea how good this king is?' he asked breathlessly.

'No, but Polydeuces is unbeaten. Remember he's a son of Zeus.'

'That's good, then,' said Max.

'On the other hand, Amykos is the son of Poseidon,' Parseus added.

'The God of the Sea?' said Charlie.

'So not so good then,' gulped Max.

'Now let me explain the rules,' said Amykos briskly. 'There will be 12 rounds, one sand-timer per round and the Bebrykian rules apply.' His face twisted in devilish delight. 'Which means *there are no rules*.'

A ripple of laughter ran out from Amykos' soldiers.

Charlie mouthed silently to Parseus, 'No rules?'

Parseus seemed unconcerned. 'Polydeuces won't care.'

Amykos and Polydeuces moved forward to face each other on the ground between the Argonauts and the ranks of soldiers. Amykos summoned one of his men who came forward with a sand-timer. He held it up and then, on a signal from the king, turned it upside down. The match had begun.

Amykos charged straight at Polydeuces, who stood his ground. Amykos threw a wild punch but Polydeuces was too quick and easily darted out of the way. Amykos tried once more, and again Polydeuces was too nimble for him — as he proved to be every time Amykos tried to hit him.

After the first round Amykos was puce with rage, his soldiers muttering uneasily.

'Looks like a walkover. Never been beaten? Ha,' said Max excitedly as he and Charlie watched the spectacle — both sure that Polydeuces would win.

The next round went much the same way with Amykos throwing wilder and wilder punches and Polydeuces avoiding each and every one. Soon enough Polydeuces grew bored.

'Enough,' he bellowed. 'You are not worth my trouble.'

Amykos moved in for another attack, and Polydeuces threw a single punch — a furious right hook. Amykos fell like a stone. The Argonauts roared with delight as his body hit the ground. The king's soldiers stood in stunned silence.

'Typical,' grinned Max. 'You get all excited about a boxing match and it's over in a couple of rounds.'

'I don't think it's over,' said Charlie, looking at the prone king. One of Amykos' men had rushed forward, put his ear to the king's chest and turned, shaking his head.

'He hasn't been knocked-out,' said Charlie. 'He's dead.'

'You're right. That punch must have killed him. I smell trouble,' said Max

The Bebrykians, reeling from the shock of seeing their king die, unsheathed their swords.

'Oh dear,' said Parseus. 'We're in for a fight.'

Jason and the other Argonauts prepared themselves for battle. Parseus pulled the boys back behind their line. The king's soldiers charged forward. The fighting became so fierce however that the boys were soon caught up in the fray. The soldiers were now on all sides, and there was nowhere to run.

'What are we going do?' said Max fearfully. 'We've nothing to fight with.'

'We'd better get something,' said Charlie as the two sides slashed at each other with their swords.

Then Charlie spotted one of Amykos' soldiers fall right in front of him, dropping his sword and shield. Leaping forward he picked up the sword just as another soldier ran at him, raising his sword to strike. Charlie blocked his attack and fought back while Max grabbed the shield and fended off a blow.

Max knocked out another attacker with his shield, picked up his sword and then stood back to back with Charlie. For the next half an hour, they fought alongside the Argonauts, deflecting attacks and fighting close combat.

Although vastly outnumbered, the Argonauts' superior skill proved decisive in the end. The Bebrykians, though well-armed, were no more a match for the Argonauts than their king had been for Polydeuces. Ill-trained and leaderless, they began to desert the field.

It was then that one of their soldiers, cut off from his companions, rushed forward. Coming from behind Idas he raised his sword above his head. Charlie spotted him and diving forward, blocked the strike with his own sword. Idas turned and knocked out the soldier with a single blow.

Sheathing his sword, Idas put his arm around Charlie. 'Thanks boy, you saved my life.'

'That's OK,' replied Charlie.

Defeated, the remaining Bebrykians flung down their swords. The battle was over. A great cheer erupted from the Argonauts and they sank to their knees in thanks and relief. Then Jason ordered the Argonauts to round up and disarm the remaining soldiers. With that done, he addressed them.'We want no further trouble. We need food and water and then we will be on our way. Provide these and we will fight you no longer. Resist and you will all die. Is that clear?'

The beaten Bebrykians readily agreed and, leaving hostages behind, they sent men to do as Jason ordered. Soon enough the Argonauts were laden with enough provisions to keep them for weeks.

Marching the remaining soldiers back to the bay where the Argo lay moored, Jason forced them to build a fire before sending them on their way, disgraced and defeated — but alive.

The victorious Argonauts celebrated with a feast on the beach. Having settled round the fire, Idas stood up.

'I would like to propose a toast to the boys. I know many of us did not welcome them back but I think it right to say that they've pulled more than just their weight and as far as I'm concerned they've earned their place on this voyage and my heartfelt respect and thanks. So let us drink to the newest recruits to the Argo — to Charlie and Max, the Argonauts.'

Another great cheer erupted as the rest of the crew surrounded the boys, clapping them on the back and shaking their hands. Both boys beamed with pride.

Parseus came over. 'Congratulations, boys. You have certainly proved yourselves here,' he said. 'That training with Cheiron has been rather useful — not only on the Argo, but for our own mission.'

He was right, thought Charlie. They had earned the place on the voyage and the respect of the crew, which meant they were now better placed to pursue their own quest — to save his sister. 'So where now, Parseus?' he asked.

Parseus pointed across the moonlit bay. 'Thrace, to see Phineus, the Seer. Only he can tell us how the ship can pass through the Clashing Rocks.'

'Clashing Rocks?'

'The Symplegades, Charlie. They are at the end of the

Bosphorus, and it is the only way through to Colchis on the far side of the Black Sea. No ship has ever passed through before — well, not successfully.'

'Define successfully?' said Max.

'No one has ever tried to pass through and lived. But don't worry, I remember this bit.'

'And?' asked Charlie.

'I remember what happened. I mean, I remember the story. I wasn't there of course. I don't have all the details. Don't worry, though, we should be fine. We just need to get rid of the Harpies first and then Phineus will tell us how to get through.'

'Harpies?' said Max. 'Don't tell me — more trouble ahead.'

'Yes, the Harpies are monstrous creatures. They have the front torsos of haggard old women and the bodies of giant birds.' Parseus paused. 'So I suggest you get some sleep. We've got a busy day tomorrow and you'll need all your strength, believe me.'

'But I thought you said we'd be OK,' said Max.

'And you will be, at least with the Harpies. That's not what worries me.'

'Then what does?' said Charlie.

'The Clashing Rocks.'

23. SIGHT UNSEEN

CHARLIE woke with a start. Dawn had only just broken and it was still chilly. The sand felt cold beneath his feet. He sat up. The remnants of the previous night's feast were scattered all over the beach though the fire had long since died out. He thought back to the day before: Polydeuces' victory, defeating the soldiers, the ensuing feast. And while Amykos and his boxing challenge had been overcome, now it seemed they faced even graver threats: the Harpies and the Clashing Rocks. Neither sounded good.

He stood up. Many of the Argonauts were already awake, loading the ship with supplies. Max was still asleep, covered with a cloak, snoring. Charlie decided to leave him be and went to help. He spotted Periklymenos carrying pitchers of water to the ship. On seeing Charlie he stopped. 'Ah, the warrior himself. Sleep well?' he asked.

'Yeah, OK,' said Charlie.

'Good,' said Perikylemnos. He gestured to one of the pitchers. 'Give me a hand.'

Charlie picked it up and followed him to the ship.

'You fought bravely yesterday, boy. Herakles and Cheiron taught you well. A bit more practice and you'll be a great hero one day.'

Charlie was about to congratulate him on his efforts but he couldn't remember seeing Perikylemenos in the battle. 'Were you there?' he asked.

'Oh yes. But I've...' Perikylemnos paused. 'I suppose you'd call it a skill, a trick perhaps. It was a gift from the God of the Sea, Poseidon and it's proved useful I can tell you.'

'What skill?' asked Charlie.

'I can become whatever I pray to become,' said Perikylemenos. 'I can transform into anything I want when I'm in danger — animate or inanimate.'

'Like what?'

'Tree, bush, statue, animal, cloud of dust. Anything really. Though I don't much take to dust, plays havoc with my allergies. Usually I try to blend in by becoming a tree or a rock. Depends how grave the danger is,' said Perikylemenos, laughing.

'And last night — what did you become last night?'

'A rock,' said Perikylemenos, looking embarrassed.

Charlie remembered seeing a rock appear, though at the time he had been too distracted to wonder about it. At one point he had even thought of hiding behind it. He smiled at the thought.

'Anyway, that's my skill, for what it's worth,' said Perikylemnos.

'Does that mean you're immortal?'

Perikylemenos shook his head. 'No, unfortunately. That's why the skill's so useful. It's saved me from destruction many times.' He climbed on board the Argo and stored the pitcher of water. Charlie passed him the other one. 'You'd better go and wake Max. We'll be leaving soon,' said Perikylemenos.

Charlie returned to the beach. Max was just stirring. He rubbed his eyes.

'Are we leaving?'

'Soon. Parseus says we have to go and see that old man called Phineus. He lives in Thrace.'

'What for?'

'He's a Seer, a bit like Idmon, you know, one of the Argonauts. He can foretell the future or something like that.'

Parseus appeared. 'Good, you're both awake. Come along,' he said. They all set off to the ship.

'Do you really think this Phineus might know about the cure?' asked Charlie.

'Let's hope he does. If so, we might avoid the Clashing Rocks altogether — for otherwise, we face a perilous passage.'

'Perilous?' said Max. 'Let me guess. Very dangerous, and we could die.'

'Quite possibly,' said Parseus. 'But we have to face the Harpies first.' He climbed on board ship.

'Thought you said we'd be OK?' Max called out after him.

Parseus took no notice. Charlie and Max clambered aboard and took to their benches along with the other Argonauts. The day had started brightly and blessed with favourable winds, they lowered the sails and set off, this time heading north.

SOME hours later they reached Thrace and moored the Argo in a secluded bay. 'That's where we're headed. Phineus lives up there,' said Parseus, pointing to a cliff above.

Jason selected a small band of Argonauts to accompany him and agreed that Parseus and the boys could join them. Kalais and Zetes also volunteered. 'Jason, we must come too. For we received a prophecy foretelling us that we would help free Phineus from his tormentors,' said Kalais. Jason, no stranger to prophecies, agreed.

Leaving the other Argonauts on board, the detachment set off towards a small path, which ran up the eastern side towards the cliff. Parseus and the boys kept up the rear. 'Now do watch out, boys. The Harpies are never far away,' said Parseus.

It was a tough climb and the boys were panting by the time they reached the top. Charlie and Max had kept their eyes peeled for the Harpies but there had been no sign of them.

Ahead, was a small stone building, which Charlie presumed to be Phineus' house. It was the only one in sight. The door was slightly ajar, hanging off its hinges. A marble trough sat outside and nearby was a table on which some food had been laid out. It was the only sign that anyone lived there. The house otherwise looked as if it had been abandoned long ago.

Jason motioned the Argonauts to stay back and approached

the house alone. When he neared, the door opened wider and a figure emerged, stooping. It was Phineus.

Charlie watched him hobble out. He was a wretched figure: his clothes nothing more than rags, his face ravaged, his cheeks hollow and what was left of his thinning grey hair hung limply against his face. Bent double he held onto the door frame to steady himself.

'Who goes there?' Phineus cried out.

'My name is Jason. I've come to ask your advice.'

Phineus' face lit up. 'Jason — of the Argonauts?' he asked.

'Yes, you've heard of us?'

'I am a Seer. I do not need to have heard of you,' said Phineus. 'But yes — I know of your quest.' He beckoned him closer. 'I know why you've come.'

'Sounds as if he's been waiting for us, Parseus,' said Charlie.

'Indeed he has. He knows that Jason's arrival means his own salvation is finally at hand: for it has long been foretold that Jason and his Argonauts would deliver him from his torment.'

'Which is?' asked Charlie.

'The Harpies, of course,' said Parseus. 'They make his life unbearable.'

'Some food, quick,' Phineus called out as he stumbled forward.

'Is he blind?' asked Charlie.

'Yes,' said Parseus.

'A blind Seer? Isn't that...?'

'Ironic? Yes,' replied Parseus.

Jason was helping Phineus to the table when they heard screeching. Phineus cried out in despair, 'Too late — they're here.' Feeling for the table, Phineus scrambled under it to take cover.

Shielding his eyes, Charlie saw two dark spots appear on the horizon. 'The Harpies?'

'Yes, Charlie, so I suggest you hide. This is not our fight,' said Parseus. 'Leave this to the others.'

'What are they going to do?' asked Charlie.

'Just watch and wait.' Parseus pointed to a nearby tree. 'Hide behind there and don't come out until it's over.'

Charlie didn't argue and he and a much relieved Max scurried off and crouched behind the tree. Jason ordered the Argonauts to hide themselves, while the twins, Kalais and Zetes took up position behind Phineus' house.

They heard another terrible screech, and two Harpies descended from the sky. Their front torsos were of haggard old women, completely bald, with bright-green bulbous eyes. The rest of them were like birds, black as night, their huge wings, totally bereft of feathers, flapping wildly through the air. Parseus was right, thought Charlie. They were truly monstrous.

Swooping down to land, their talons glinting in the afternoon sun, they clattered noisily onto the stone courtyard.

Phineus was curled up in a ball under the table. Hissing and spitting, the Harpies darted forward and lashed out at him but they couldn't quite reach him. Keeping up the attack, they took it in turns to gorge themselves on the food.

'What are they doing, Parseus?' Charlie asked.

'Whenever the villagers bring Phineus food — in exchange for his advice — the Harpies descend. He barely has time to get to the table before they appear. As you can see they then attack him and steal his food. What they don't eat, they spoil. The ritual has differed little over the years,' replied Parseus. 'They persecute him like that every day.'

Charlie knew that this day, however, would be different. For as the Harpies began to foul what food they had left, Jason gave the order to attack. The hidden Argonauts sprang out immediately, swords unsheathed, banging their shields noisily. Startled, the Harpies screeched and flew up into the sky.

The Argonauts reached for their bows. Showered with arrows, the furious Harpies flew back down, lashing out with their talons at the attacking Argonauts, but the men were too quick on their feet to fall victim.

Charlie was itching to get involved. Taking his own bow off his back he stepped out from behind the tree, and fired an arrow. It struck one of the Harpies in the leg. Shrieking in agony she spun around and spotted Charlie reloading his bow. Hissing with fury she flew straight at him.

Charlie ducked out of the way behind the tree and the screaming Harpy flew back up into the air. Preparing to fire again, he failed to notice the other Harpy creeping up behind him. She took a swipe, trapping him in her claw, and flew up into the sky — with Charlie in her grasp.

'Cease fire,' Jason shouted to the Argonauts. They immediately stopped for no one wanted to hit Charlie. Jason then called for the twins. 'Get him back,' he yelled.

Upside down a hundred feet off the ground and petrified, Charlie watched the flying twins move out of their position. The Harpy, still holding him in her grasp, threw back her head and shrieked. Then she relaxed her grip and dropped him.

Screaming, Charlie plummeted to the ground below, certain he was about to die. Yet a second later he felt himself being lifted back up into the air. Opening his eyes, Charlie realised he was in the arms of Kalais. He had been saved.

One of the Harpies then flew straight at them, striking so hard at Kalais with her claw that he began spiralling downwards, Charlie spinning with him. Fortunately, Kalais somehow managed to straighten out, and climb back up into the sky, before coming down to land amongst the Argonauts.

Charlie crawled onto his knees. He was shaking from top to toe — but he was alive.

With Charlie safe, the Argonauts began another attack, sending a shower of arrows into the air, while Kalais, joined now by his twin Zetes, shot back into the sky, ready to attack either Harpy which came within range.

With the arrows beginning to strike home, the screeching Harpies turned and fled — the twins in pursuit, now harrying them in turn.

Max and Parseus raced over. 'You stupid fool. I told you not to get involved. You could have died,' said Parseus angrily.

'Sorry,' Charlie replied sheepishly.

'Are you OK?' Max asked, helping him to his feet. 'Thought you were a goner — again.'

'So did I.' Charlie winced in pain. 'My fault, I suppose. I should have kept out of it.'

With the Harpies gone, Jason helped Phineus clamber out from under the table. The Argonauts started fussing round him, eager to discover what he had to say. Jason ordered his men to clean up the mess left by the Harpies and guided Phineus to a seat.

'Thank you Jason. I knew that one day you would save me,' replied Phineus breathlessly.

'You can be sure they won't come back again.' Jason waved his arm at the empty sky. 'But I've…'

'A request?' said Phineus.

'Of course. I forgot. You know why we're here.'

'Yes, but if you don't mind, I'd like some food first,' said Phineus.

Jason dispatched Euphemos to the nearby village to gather food. Shortly afterwards, villagers appeared, laden with platters, delighted to hear of Phineus' salvation. On hearing them, Phineus waved them forward. 'Here, quickly,' he said.

Charlie, still trying to forget his own brush with the Harpies, joined the Argonauts watching Phineus stuffing food into his mouth — patiently waiting for him to reveal the secret to safe passage through the Clashing Rocks.

'What exactly are these Clashing Rocks, Parseus?'

'They are two narrow ridges of rock that stand between us and the entrance to the Black Sea. But they move, and whenever a ship tries to pass through them, they clash together. As I say, no ship has ever successfully passed through before,' said Parseus.

'How will the Argo manage?' asked Charlie.

'Patience, Charlie. Phineus has the answer.'

Phineus, now sated from his feast, summoned the Argonauts to gather round. Charlie and Max were as eager as anyone else to hear what he had to say.

'You want to know how to pass through the Clashing Rocks,' said Phineus, stuffing a fig into his mouth.

'Yes,' said Jason.

'You must send a dove through first. If it passes through without perishing, it will be safe to follow,' he said.

'That's it. Send a dove first?' Max whispered to Charlie. 'How's that going to stop the Clashing Rocks?'

Phineus overheard him. 'If the dove survives, then you have the Gods' blessing,' he said. 'And you will pass through safely. That is all I have to say.' And without another word Phineus dismissed them all.

The Argonauts drifted off, some less encouraged by his words than others. Charlie hung back. 'What about us, Parseus? Can we ask him about the cure?'

'Perhaps. Go and help that man,' he said, pointing towards a villager carrying a platter of meat. 'Take that dish, and offer it to Phineus.'

Charlie went to the villager, and thanking him took the platter to Phineus. 'There's some meat here for you, sir,' he said, putting the platter down beside him. The old man fumbled for a lamp chop.

Unsure what to do, Charlie was beginning to back away when Phineus raised his arm. 'Stay a moment, boy. I would like to speak to you. Give me your hand.'

Charlie sat down and held out his hand. Phineus felt for it. 'You have come a long way, boy — a world away.'

Charlie was surprised. 'Yes. That's right.'

'Hmm, and you have a question.' Phineus gripped his hand more tightly and pulled him close. 'You are in search of a cure?'

'Yes,' Charlie replied breathlessly. He could hardly contain himself. Did this Seer really have the answer to his prayers?

Phineus paused, for what seemed like an age. Charlie's heart was racing, the suspense almost killing him. Then Phineus pulled him even closer. 'Your cure lies at the end of this journey, in Colchis itself. Seek out the witch. She has more power than you know.' And with that Phineus let go of his hand.

Charlie couldn't believe it. The cure's location had finally been revealed. It lay in Colchis, the Argonaut's final destination. But was it true? Did Phineus really know? 'Are you sure?' he asked, immediately wishing he hadn't.

Phineus grabbed his hand again and squeezed it tightly. 'Never doubt a Seer's word, boy,' he replied quietly. 'Do you hear?'

'Sorry, yes,' said Charlie quickly, hoping he hadn't offended the man.

Phineus relaxed his grip slightly. 'The girl, she must be cured. She is vital to your success. The gift, it is for her,' he added.

'You mean Emily? But how? And what gift?' said Charlie, quite forgetting Phineus' warning.

Phineus scowled. 'Time will tell, boy,' he snapped. 'Now leave me to my food.' He dismissed Charlie with a wave. He would say no more.

Parseus, listening nearby, pulled Charlie away. 'Excellent news.' He patted Charlie on the shoulder. 'Typical, of course, why is everything always to be found at the end of a journey, rather than at the beginning? Never understood it.'

'What did he mean about the witch? Is she the one with the cure? And what about this gift?' asked Charlie, trying to make sense of what Phineus had told him.

'Not sure. But at least we now know where the cure lies…' Parseus paused. 'Interesting news about the witch though,' he muttered. 'Very interesting.'

'In what way?' pressed Charlie.

Parseus refused to be drawn and grabbing Charlie by the hand he pulled him back. They rejoined Max, who was avidly eyeing the platters of food which had been arriving in steady succession from the nearby village since Phineus' rescue from the Harpies.

'What did he say about the cure?' Max asked.

'It lies in Colchis apparently,' said Charlie. Then he relayed what else Phineus had said.

'Indeed, and since that is the case I can go and tell Jason we are leaving. We'll rejoin them later in Colchis,' said Parseus. 'Frankly I am relieved. Now you won't have to endure the Clashing Rocks.'

'But what was all that about Emily?' Charlie asked again.

'All in good time, Charlie.' Parseus patted his cloak pockets absent-mindedly. 'Now I must go and talk to Jason.'

He left the boys alone. Charlie was still unable to believe they had found out the cure's location. 'Glad we don't have to deal with those rocks now,' Max said, visibly relieved.

'Yeah, me too. And at least we know where the cure is. Wonder who this witch is though?' said Charlie. 'And what do you think he meant about Emily and this gift?'

Max shrugged. 'You're asking me?'

'I guess we'll find out soon enough. Seems to be how things work around here.' Charlie gestured to where the Argonauts were now enjoying the feast the villagers had laid out. 'Shall we?'

Max licked his lips. 'Another feast? Why not? You know how much I like my food.'

24. LOST AT SEA

CHARLIE and Max were happily tucking into the feast laid out by the villagers, when Parseus re-appeared. He did not look happy.

'What's the matter, Parseus?' asked Charlie.

'Trouble, I'm afraid. Jason says he needs all hands on deck. We're going to have to stay until we make it through the Clashing Rocks,' he said.

'WHAT?' both boys said at once.

'I pleaded with him but Jason was not to be persuaded and he has warned that if we don't stay we won't be allowed to return to the ship, even if it reaches Colchis. Without the Argonauts' help I doubt the cure can be secured.'

'So we have to stay?' Charlie's face fell.

'Yes, we must remain with the ship.'

'But Phineus said we will make it if we have the Gods' blessing,' said Charlie.

'The Argo will make it through, Charlie, for I know that to be a fact, but I cannot be sure that everyone in the crew will do so too. We can only hope for the best,' said Parseus.

'That's your advice?' said Charlie.

'Yes. But I'm sure you'll survive,' Parseus added.

'How sure?' said Max.

Parseus wouldn't say.

THE Argonauts started making their way back down to the ship. Charlie and Max followed with heavy hearts: for they faced their gravest threat yet — nature herself.

When they arrived back on board, the twins, Kalais and Zetes had returned from their chase, the Harpies now dispatched to the furthest reaches of the world. They were greeted warmly, especially by Charlie. Kalais had saved his life.

Lynkeus, the sharp-sighted one, was sent to search for a dove. Before long he spied one, hiding in a nearby wood and the twins were ordered to fetch it. They flew back triumphantly and, with the dove carefully caged, the Argo set sail once more. Next stop: the Clashing Rocks.

Several hours later, Lynkeus spotted them in the distance. 'Not far now,' he yelled.

However it was some time before the rest of the crew caught sight of them, though it did little to ease the growing tension.

Charlie was as anxious as everyone else. The closer they got the more ominous the task ahead.

The Clashing Rocks were two ridges of sheer black rock which rose up into the sky above. A narrow sea passage ran between them, cast in shadow. The water was as still as a pond and a deathly silence hung in the air. It was clear no birds made these rocks their home.

The Argo approached slowly until Jason gave the order to bank the oars and lower the anchor. The crew turned their attention towards the dimly-lit channel, the only way through to the Black Sea beyond.

Jason climbed up onto the stern and cleared his throat. 'Phineus has shown us the way, but do not doubt it will be hard. You will need all your strength now. When I give the order, take to your oars and row for your lives. We cannot afford to falter. Do you understand?'

A murmur ran through the crew. Everyone knew this would be their greatest test.

Jason beckoned Euphemos, who held the caged bird. 'Release the dove.' Euphemos opened the cage and the frightened dove escaped, soaring into the sky and flying directly into the narrow sea passage. For the first few seconds nothing happened. Charlie started to wonder whether it was true at all. He had never heard of rocks clashing together. Even here in this world such a phenomenon seemed unlikely.

Then he heard a strange rumbling. The waters around them started to bubble and the Argo began tipping and weaving from side to side. The rumbling grew louder and the rocks began to move. The waters rose. Boulders started tumbling down into the sea below, some splashing dangerously close to the Argo making it tip even more violently.

'Get to your oars,' shouted Jason.

But there was little need for such an order. Each Argonaut was already gripping his oar tightly, the waters frothing and boiling around them. The rocks moved steadily forwards, the gap narrowed and the light from the tunnel started disappearing.

Five minutes later, there was one last almighty crash. The rocks smashed together, causing a new shower of boulders to crash down and a wall of water to wash over the ship and crew, tipping the boat so much it almost capsized.

Then the waters settled down. 'Can you see the dove? Did it make it?' Jason bellowed.

Lynkeus climbed the mast and, shielding his eyes from the afternoon sun, peered into the sky. Everyone held their breath. For if the dove hadn't made it, neither would they.

Then Lynkeus shouted, 'IT MADE IT. I CAN SEE IT.'

He climbed down from the mast. Jason grabbed him by the shoulders. 'Are you certain? If not we are doomed,' he said.

'It may have lost its tail feathers. But it survived. I promise,' Lynkeus assured him.

Jason let go. 'Then if you say so, I will trust you.'

The rumbling began again and everyone knew they had little choice but to trust him. The rocks began separating and the waters rushed back in, forcing the Argo to rise up on the swelling sea.

Perikylemenos turned to Charlie. 'Get ready. You must row for your life now.'

Charlie didn't doubt that. He kept his eyes fixed on the narrow sea channel, the water surging back into the ever-widening passage.

The Argo rose up on the swell but it took a few minutes for the waters to settle and the sea to return to calm. Now that Charlie knew what they had to face, it was an even more daunting prospect. Max looked back at Charlie, he clearly felt the same. He was ashen-faced. If only they could have avoided this...if only, Charlie thought. But there was no time to think about 'what ifs' now.

Jason strapped himself to the mast and gave the final order. 'Row men, Row.'

The Argonauts grabbed their oars and pulling back they headed towards the sea passage. Rowing with all their might they entered the dark channel. The silence was unnerving.

The rumbling soon began again and the rocks closed in once more, the waters beginning to froth and boil. The Argonauts rowed furiously, each man drawing on every reserve of strength to try to force their way through the narrowing passage.

Charlie heaved on his oar too, the waves crashing across the deck, the force of the water so powerful he could feel it driving against his chest like a wall. Every second felt like an hour, his muscles burned furiously yet still he pulled back on his oar.

'You're doing fine, Charlie,' shouted Perikylemenos, trying to make himself heard over the din.

Charlie didn't feel fine. He was exhausted. His arms felt like they were being ripped from their sockets. He leaned forward to pull on his oar once more. Then he heard a noise dreaded by every Argonaut — the sound of his oar snapping in two.

A moment later he felt himself being launched into the air on the crest of a wave. He heard Max scream his name and the wave crashed down, smashing him into the wooden deck. He cried out in agony and tried to grab hold of something, anything, but there was nothing. Another wave crashed in from the side, sweeping him helplessly along in its wake, the sea water engulfing him. Choking and spluttering, his lungs began to fill up. The next thing he knew he was being swept overboard and sucked into the swirling sea channel — tossed about, spinning in circles, the churning sea dragging him further and further down into its black depths. The last thing he heard was Perikylemenos shout *'MAN OVERBOARD.'*

Charlie tried to gasp for air but there was none. The panic overwhelmed him. All was lost.

Almost as quickly the panic subsided and a strange calm descended. He was still spinning in circles but now he gave in to it, the darkness enveloping him. His life once again flashed before him. He was drowning, yet he no longer cared.

It was then that he felt something brush against him and the next thing he knew he was being pushed up out of the water. His head broke the surface and instinctively he gasped for air. This time he found it. Choking, he coughed up the sea water which had filled his lungs, the air taking its place instead.

The sea now seemed to spit him out and he landed with a thud back on board ship. Dazed, he felt someone grab him. When he opened his eyes he saw Jason, still tied to the mast, grasp his hand tightly and pull him close.

'Hold on boy, hold on,' he screamed.

So Charlie did, clinging on desperately, but with no idea how he had been plucked from the sea — or how it was that he was still alive.

THE Argonauts were still battling through the passage, the channel now plunged into darkness and the tunnel of light shrinking to a pinhole. The rocks were only feet apart, the oars almost touching the sides. The ship, it seemed was to be crushed.

'WE'RE DOOMED JASON.' The violent Idas cried out.

Jason looked up to the heavens. 'Help us, Athene,' he pleaded as he and Charlie watched the fast disappearing circle of light. 'Help us.'

And then it happened. The rocks stopped moving, the boulders stopped crashing down and the waters calmed. Charlie searched the skyline for any sign of a God but he saw none.

Silence descended. No one moved. No one dared. Then Jason bellowed, 'Row for your lives, men. ROW.'

The crew immediately took to their oars and rowed with all their might. They had almost reached the end of the passage when the rumbling started again. They gave it one final heave and the Argo spilled out of the narrow channel. The rocks clashed shut behind them. Their only loss, like the dove's tail feathers, was the tip of the stern.

It took several minutes for the crew to relax their grip, the adrenalin still coursing through them. The Argo drifted into the tranquil waters, they eased off their oars and slowly banked them. No one could quite believe they had made it through.

Parseus untied himself from the prow and ran across to Charlie. 'Are you OK?'

'Yes. But what happened?' Charlie asked.

'It was the work of Athene. I told you we had the Gods' blessing.'

'I'm not talking about that. I went overboard. How did I get back on ship?' said Charlie.

'Perikylemenos,' said Parseus. 'I saw him do it. He turned himself into a dolphin. Dived in and fished you out, so to speak. He saved your life,' he added. 'You really ought to thank him.'

Charlie was utterly astonished. 'I will.'

Max stumbled over, wincing in agony, yet grinning. 'Did you see what Perikylemenos did? He turned into...'

'I know,' said Charlie, 'a dolphin — Parseus told me. I thought I was dead.'

'I thought we all were,' said Max.

'Suffice it to say, we are all alive, and that is enough to be thankful for,' remarked Parseus casually.

'It's all right for you, Parseus. You're immortal,' said Max.

'Yes, quite. Still, I was very concerned for you two.'

'Gee, thanks,' said Max.

Charlie was still trying to catch his breath. 'I think I want to go home, Parseus. Surely Jason can cope without us now,' said Charlie. 'We need a break.'

'I second that,' added Max.

'Let's reach land first, Charlie. Then I'll ask Jason,' said Parseus. 'However now that we know where the cure lies, I think a break would be a good idea — although we cannot stay long in Hesper. When we return, we will be joining the Argonauts in Colchis.'

THE Argo reached the island of Thynias just before sunset. It was deserted. Charlie was relieved. He was in no mood for any more welcoming parties. The Argonauts disembarked, quickly made camp and prepared their sacrifice — this time to Athene to thank her for their safe passage through the Clashing Rocks.

Parseus took the boys aside. 'Jason has agreed to let us leave. We'll find a quiet spot out of sight and slip away,' he said.

'I want to thank Perikylemenos first,' said Charlie.

'Of course, but be quick,' Parseus replied.

Charlie found Perikylemenos. 'Thank you for saving me at the Clashing Rocks. I know what you did, and I won't forget it,' he said. 'I have to say goodbye now. We're leaving. Parseus says we'll join you again at Colchis.' Charlie took his hand. 'But thanks again for saving me.'

Perikylemenos squeezed Charlie's hand. 'Don't worry, boy. Anyway, something told me that I ought to save you. Don't know why.'

Charlie rejoined the others. Parseus was already plotting a course. A portal opened up and the next thing he knew they were back in the bar. It took a moment for Charlie to find his feet. Max was bent double, the nausea still taking its toll.

Parseus tucked the compass back in his pocket. 'A spot of lunch is in order, I think,' he announced brightly.

Charlie's father peeked out from behind the bar. He seemed

bewildered at the sight of Charlie standing there, his clothes torn, ragged and soaking wet.

'What on earth happened to you son — you look a wreck.' His father came over and inspected his bedraggled son.

Charlie grinned. 'We almost were Dad, we almost were.'

'Yeah and I'm starving,' said Max.

'But you only just had....' Charlie's father's voice trailed off. 'I just don't get it,' he muttered.

'How long are we going to stay this time, Parseus?' asked Charlie.

'Not long. Your essences have not faded that much. But I suggest you both get into some dry clothes. You can hang your tunics in front of the fire before we have something to eat. We will leave in an hour or so,' he said. 'Remember your sister has very little time.'

Charlie could hardly forget. Emily had hours, not days.

'And we're going directly to Colchis next time?' he asked.

'Yes, that's where the cure lies,' replied Parseus.

Charlie brightened. At least they were getting closer to it. His sister would be back to her annoying self soon enough. If only life would do the same, he thought.

'And after we cure her?' said Max.

'We will have to face the Dark One,' said Parseus.

Charlie stiffened. He hadn't wanted to think about that.

'But we don't know how to kill it yet,' he said. 'And what about Emily? How is she going to help?'

'Not sure yet,' said Parseus. 'But she is key, we know that.'

'I should go and see how she is.' Charlie started for the door.

'Very well. But remember in this world no time has passed. She'll be just the same as she was a few minutes ago.'

Charlie stopped. 'I know that Parseus. But I haven't seen her for over a week.'

'Indeed. I understand. I shall go to my room and see if there is anything else we need.'

Once upstairs, Charlie saw that his sister was, of course, exactly the same. Staring at her, Charlie remembered what Phineus had said about a gift. He wondered what he meant by that.

He left her room. Max appeared at the top of the stairs. 'I'm going to change,' he said.

Charlie looked down at his wet tunic. 'Good idea.'

The boys quickly changed, and Max took the tunics downstairs to dry out in front of the fire. Charlie wandered down the corridor to Parseus' room. The door was open. Parseus was kneeling by his trunk. A few of the little boxes were scattered on the floor around him.

'Got what you need?' asked Charlie.

'Almost,' said Parseus, rummaging around in his trunk.

Charlie knelt down and began inspecting some of the boxes. 'So are all of these potions of some sort?'

'Yes. Most of them are Intangibles,' said Parseus.

'Huh?' said Charlie.

'An Intangible is something like Strength. It cannot be seen or touched. The only way you can store and keep such powers is in these jars. They're very special.'

'So what other 'Intangibles' have you got?' said Charlie.

Parseus sat back. 'Aside from Strength, I've got some Sleep, which we used on Mrs. Payne, remember? And there's the potion of Lethe...'

Charlie interrupted, 'Is that the one that makes you forget? The one you gave Cheiron?'

'Yes, though he was probably right. No one would have believed him anyway.' Parseus picked up a jar, and held it up to the light. He frowned. 'Could do with a little more Strength.'

'We could have used some of that on the Argo,' said Max, appearing at the door.

'We use it when we need to use it, Max,' said Parseus. 'It's precious stuff and we cannot afford to waste it unnecessarily.'

Max knelt next to Charlie and picked up one of the boxes.

He opened it, took out the jar, uncorked it, and chanced a sniff. 'So what's this?'

Parseus' eyes narrowed. 'Be careful with that one, Max, it's a love potion. Just a few drops in a person's eyes and they will fall in love with the very next person they see.'

'Could come in handy one day. Max winked at Charlie.

Parseus scowled back. 'Do not underestimate the power of love, Max. People will go to extreme lengths for love. It can be a very powerful force — for both good and evil.'

Max shrugged. 'If you say so.'

'I don't say so, Max. I know so.' Parseus grabbed the potion from him and stopped the cork. 'This is not a plaything, believe me,' he said, waving it in the air.

Charlie spotted another box. It was different to the rest. It had a small jewel embedded in its centre. 'And this one?' he asked, inspecting it.

'Ah, that's Prophecy,' said Parseus.

'Prophecy? Why don't we open it then? It might tell us something.' Charlie tried to lift the lid but it wouldn't budge.

'No good, I'm afraid. Only the true recipient can open it.'

'Well, who's that?' asked Charlie.

'The box will know them when it sees them.'

'Sees them?' Charlie was mystified. 'How can a box see?'

'It's complicated. I had hoped it might be intended for you, but alas, no. Now let's get back downstairs,' said Parseus. He got to his feet and stuffed more of the potions into his various cloak pockets. 'Once, we've eaten, you can change back into your tunics — they should be dry by then.'

They all trooped back downstairs to the bar. The kitchen door opened and Charlie's father emerged with a plate piled high with grilled sausages. The boys quickly demolished them. That done, they grabbed their tunics, raced back upstairs and changed again.

Back in the bar, they found Parseus waiting, compass in hand. 'Almost time to go,' he declared.

'So you'll be back with the cure next time?' asked Mr Goodwin.

'Yes, we know where it lies now. We'll be back in no time,' said Parseus.

'No need to tell you to be careful is there, son?' Charlie's father hugged him. 'You're a brave boy. I'm proud of you. To think...' His father's lip quivered.

Charlie patted his arm. 'We'll be OK, Dad. You'll see.' Charlie was not about to tell his father how close he had already come to dying.

Charlie linked arms with Parseus and closed his eyes. Their next stop was Colchis — the cure's location.

'I suggest you get down again as before, Mr Goodwin. We're about to leave,' announced Parseus.

'Right you are,' Charlie's father replied, ducking back down as before.

Charlie watched his father disappear behind the bar. He could only pray that when his father stood up again it would be to find that they had brought back the cure to save Emily.

25. A WITCH IN TIME

OPENING his eyes, Charlie slowly got to his feet. They had landed on a cliff top. Black rocks rose up on all sides, sea gulls were squawking and a biting wind was blasting him in the face. Yet there was no sign of life. 'Are we lost, Parseus?' he asked.

'No, we are in the Caucasus Mountains,' he said, dusting his cloak down.

'But you said...'

'We are in Colchis. We just need to get to Aea.'

'Aea?' said Charlie.

'It's the capital city. I want to arrive at the same time as the Argo. All we need do is find a cloud and fly along until we spot her. Shouldn't take long. There's a path over there.' Parseus gestured towards a narrow, treacherous-looking track that ran down the side of the mountain.

'This witch, the one who has the cure, how do we know she's going to give it to us?' asked Charlie. He had been asking himself that since Phineus had first mentioned her.

'We don't. Although I'm sure we'll find a means of persuading her,' said Parseus. And with that he disappeared down the path.

Charlie and Max followed slowly. The black rock was so slippery that they had to hug the side of the mountain as they went, the sheer drop down so perilous that Charlie's heart was in his mouth every time his foot slipped.

Nearing the bottom of the cliff, the path at last widened and they found themselves in a lush green valley, sheltered from the wind. And there, on the far side of the meadow, stood a lone cypress tree.

'There's our bus stop,' shouted Max delightedly.

It was warmer in the valley, and once at the tree the boys sat down on the grass, waiting for a cloud to appear. It was a long wait.

'At last,' Parseus declared, a cloud finally heading their way before hovering beside them.

They climbed in and sat down. 'To Aea,' Parseus shouted.

The cloud shot off into the sky. They passed the occasional village with people going about their daily business, but there was no sign of the Argo.

They soon spotted a small tributary and the cloud turned and started following its line. Almost as soon as it did a foul smell engulfed the chariot making the boys retch. Charlie clasped his fingers over his nose to try to block it out.

'Urgh, what is that?' he asked.

'The dead. We're passing over the cemetery of Circe. It's the tradition here in Colchis. Only female bodies are buried. Male ones are left out here in the open to rot,' explained Parseus.

It sounded so gruesome, Charlie thought. He looked down and then immediately wished he hadn't. All along the river, on both its banks, were bodies in varying states of decomposition, haphazardly slung on the branches of the trees that lined the river. It was macabre. Charlie shrank back in his seat. If this was how Colchians treated their dead, how on earth did they treat their living?

The smell quickly dissipated and they left the cemetery behind flying further down the river. Ten minutes later, Parseus pointed. 'There she is — the Argo.'

Charlie sat up excitedly. 'Where?'

'In that bank of fog in the river. I can see her masthead.'

'Where did the fog come from?' Charlie asked.

'Hera is doing her work,' said Parseus.

'Hera?'

The queen of the Gods, remember? The patron of their quest. She has cloaked the ship in a fog so that the Colchians are not forewarned of its arrival.'

'Why is she the patron?' asked Charlie.

'Because Pelias, the king of Iolkus, snubbed her by refusing to make a sacrifice to her.'

'So?' said Max.

'Gods do not like to be snubbed, so Hera engineered this quest. She hoodwinked Pelias into believing that if he sent Jason on it, he would die. However, she knew Jason would actually succeed. When he returns he will overthrow Pelias and Hera will have her revenge.'

'All this for that? Seems like a lot of bother to get revenge,' said Charlie.

'Not to the Gods it isn't, and not to Hera. She is famed for her vengeance,' said Parseus.

'So why don't they want the Colchians to know of their arrival?' asked Max.

'Let's just say their king, Aeetes, is very suspicious and wary of anything he considers a threat to his throne, rather like Pelias in fact. If Aeetes knew the Argonauts were about to land, he would send soldiers to stop them. But don't worry. All will be well.'

'You're always saying that, and it never is,' muttered Max.

THEY neared the Argo and the cloud descended. Up ahead, Charlie could make out a harbour. 'Is that where we're going?'

'Yes, the city of Aea, the capital of Colchis,' said Parseus.

The bank of fog had now completely enveloped the Argo, mooring next to the city steps. High above and set back from the harbour, huge city walls rose up into the now darkening sky and beyond them lay a palace.

'Are we joining the Argonauts now?'

'Yes, Charlie.' Parseus pointed to a small jetty, tucked away on the far side of the harbour. 'We'll land over there. We should rejoin them shortly.'

The cloud came down to rest beside the jetty. They climbed out. The Argonauts were disembarking ahead, the ship still shrouded in fog.

'What about the witch, the one who has the cure? Who is she?' Charlie asked.

'Her name is Medea. She's the king's daughter. We'll be meeting her soon. Little does her father Aeetes know that she's the one who will betray him.'

'How?' asked Charlie.

'She is made to fall in love with Jason and helps him secure the Fleece. But I've got a slightly different plan for her.'

'What plan?'

Parseus tapped his nose. 'You'll see, Charlie.' A second later they slipped into the fog.

Polydeuces was the first to spot them. He was surprised. 'I thought we'd left you at the island of Thynias,' he said.

'We found our own way here,' said Parseus without further explanation.

Polydeuces left it at that. 'We're off to the city. Think we're going to get a hero's welcome,' he said.

'Why?' asked Charlie.

Polydeuces pointed to three men whom Charlie didn't recognise. They were leading the Argonauts towards the city. 'We rescued them. They're Colchians. Found them shipwrecked on an island nearby,' he said. 'And they're the king's grandsons,' Polydeuces added. 'Like I said, bound to be a hero's welcome for that.'

Charlie was relieved to hear it.

Trailing after the Argonauts they soon reached the city gates. They reminded Charlie of the palace of Ares and he wondered whether this had also been built by Hephaistos. Once inside he was certain of it.

An intricately-weaved canopy of vines lined the long avenue

which led to the palace and the great square in front of it — in its centre were four magnificent springs, made of bronze which towered up so high Charlie could barely see where they ended.

'What are they, Parseus?'

'The springs of Hephaistos — they're a marvel of engineering, Charlie — even by immortal standards.' Parseus pointed to each in turn. 'This one gushes milk, that one wine, the one over there water and the last one, honey.'

'But this king Aeetes — he's not a God, is he?' said Charlie.

'No. Although Hephaistos did build this palace — as a favour to Aeetes' father, the sun God, Helios,' said Parseus.

'Everyone seems to be the son of a God round here,' said Max. 'They certainly put themselves about, don't they?'

They left the springs behind and reached the palace a minute later. News of the Argonaut's arrival and their heroic rescue had spread quickly. People were emerging from rooms all over the place, eager to meet the men who had saved King Aeetes' grandsons. Within minutes the place was heaving.

'Now keep an eye out. We should see Eros soon,' said Parseus as he searched the ceiling above them.

'Who's he?' Charlie glanced up, puzzled.

'Surely you've heard of him — he's Aphrodite's son. He makes the witch, Medea, fall in love with Jason. It's the only way to get her to help. I told you, people will do almost anything for love,' said Parseus.

Charlie then recalled the name — of course, Eros. He had seen pictures of him: a cherubic god holding a bow and arrow.

'Ah — there he is.' Parseus pointed at a corner of the ceiling. There, hovering behind one of the columns, his bow at the ready, was a figure in a red tunic.

Charlie was surprised. He had thought of Eros as a chubby child but here he looked more like a teenager, with a mischievous face and long blonde hair.

'What's he doing, Parseus?'

'He's waiting for Medea. He's going to fire one of his arrows at her. Once struck, she will instantly fall in love with the very next person she sees.'

'But won't she notice — won't it hurt?' said Charlie.

'No. She won't feel a thing. Just an overwhelming desire for the first man she sets her eyes on — which if Eros gets it right — as we know he does — will be Jason. Come, let's get a little closer,' said Parseus.

They pushed forward. A woman emerged from one of the bedchambers. She was very beautiful with long black hair, pale porcelain skin and vivid green eyes. She wore a sumptuous red robe, trimmed with gold, while her neck and hair were adorned with all manner of jewels, which sparkled in the torchlight, giving her an ethereal glow.

'Medea?' said Charlie.

'Yes,' Parseus murmured. 'The witch herself.'

Charlie was astonished. He had expected someone haggard and ugly, like Mrs Payne, but this witch was entrancing. Charlie peered up at Eros, his bow still at the ready. He looked back down. Jason was standing in the middle of the hall, with Medea gliding directly towards him, clearly eager to meet the heroes.

She was only a few feet away when Jason stepped right in front of her. At that moment, Eros fired his arrow.

It was not the kind of arrow Charlie had imagined —just a beam of golden light shaped like an arrow. He saw it hit its mark and almost immediately Medea looked directly at Jason. Charlie saw her eyes flash brightly for an instant and then she stared at Jason as if unable to take her eyes off him.

Jason bowed, but seemed completely unaware that anything had happened.

'What next, Parseus?' Charlie asked.

'Medea will now do anything to help Jason. He doesn't know that yet, of course, but he's going to need it, believe me. Come along — we mustn't lose sight of her. We must try to speak with her,' said Parseus.

'About the cure?' After all, it was why they were here.

'Amongst other things, yes. I've got a plan though, so let's hurry.'

Parseus pushed his way through the jostling throng, the boys close behind.

Medea was being swept into the main chamber where a large crowd had already gathered. Following her into the room, servants rushed about carrying platters of food and jars of wine.

'What's everyone doing, Parseus?' asked Max.

'King Aeetes is on his way,' he replied.

As if on cue, a horn sounded and the king strode majestically into the chamber. Everyone fell silent. Charlie stood on tiptoe to get a better look.

King Aeetes was very old. He had short grey hair, a neatly-trimmed beard, and he was dressed in a richly-coloured purple robe, which hung down to the ground, its edges hemmed with gold thread. He planted himself down on his throne, silently surveying the room before his gaze came to rest on Jason, flanked by his three grandsons.

He stared at them coldly.

'Doesn't seem pleased to see them, does he?' Charlie said.

'Aeetes does not like his grandsons. You see he received a prophecy that he would be betrayed by a member of his own family. He thinks they were plotting his downfall. Indeed it was he who arranged their shipwreck. He wanted them to drown — though of course he cannot admit that. He will have to pretend to be glad they have been rescued,' whispered Parseus.

Aeetes cleared his throat. 'We are delighted to see you return so safely. Tell us what happened, and whom you have brought with you?'

One of his grandsons moved forward and relayed details of their rescue. He introduced Jason. 'Jason and his Argonauts are on a quest, your majesty.'

'Yes, we have heard something of that, but what is the purpose of this quest, and why does it bring them here?'

'They have come for the Golden Fleece,' his grandson replied.

With that, Aeetes exploded in rage and jumping to his feet, he glowered at Jason. 'Do you think me stupid? The Fleece has brought prosperity to our land. And you think I'm just going to give it to you?' he roared.

Jason bowed deeply. 'We come in peace, believe me. We can trade with you, offer our services. Your grandsons tell us you have numerous enemies. We could help. There are many among our crew of immortal birth. They are well-trained soldiers.'

'Soldiers? You come armed, but say you come in peace.' Aeetes' face twisted in fury.

'Yes, we are armed, but we have travelled a long way and it would be foolish not to have protection,' replied Jason.

Parseus leant over to Charlie. 'Aeetes realises he will have to tread carefully. The Argonauts have been hailed as heroes. He must treat them with respect. If anyone knew he had plotted his grandsons' deaths there would be rebellion.'

Aeetes sensing the mood of the crowd, calmed down. Sitting back on his throne he stroked his beard, his eyes never leaving Jason. There was a long silence. The king sat deep in thought for a while, then leaned forward.

'You ask of me a very great thing,' he said. 'However, in recognition of your heroism and the safe return of my beloved grandsons, I will let you have the fleece.' Aeetes slowly stared around the room then held up his hand. 'However, there is one condition.'

'Anything, your majesty,' said Jason.

'You must first complete a task. It is one that I myself have completed quite happily in just one day,' said Aeetes.

Parseus whispered to the boys. 'Beware, it's a trick,' he said. 'It's an impossible task. He knows Jason can never complete it.'

'So why set it?' asked Max.

'Because when Jason fails it, Aeetes can deny him the Fleece and expel him from the land without fear of reprisal. He fears Jason is here at the behest of his grandsons. He believes that they are plotting a coup,' said Parseus.

Aeetes stood up. 'The task is quite simple. You must first yoke the fire-breathing brazen-footed bulls and plough the field of Ares. Once you've done that, you must then sow the field with the teeth of Kadmos, the serpent's teeth,' said Aeetes. 'And you must complete this task in just one day.'

Jason hesitated, clearly unsure what to do. But since he had little choice but to agree, he thanked Aeetes politely. 'I will be more than happy to complete this task.'

'If you do, the fleece is yours.' Aeetes replied smiling, and with that, he rose and left the chamber.

'How's he going to manage that?' said Charlie.

'Medea will help him. Trust me. Jason will succeed.'

'But what about our cure? How are we going to get that?'

'We're going to use this situation to our advantage, Charlie,' said Parseus. 'Medea's sole concern is Jason — she's besotted with him. And we're the only ones who know that. Now follow me.'

With the crowd scattering after the withdrawal of the king, the Argonauts had gathered around Jason, discussing the challenge he faced and quietly suggesting alternative plans.

Medea watched them from a distance, her eyes fixed longingly on Jason. Parseus tiptoed over to her with the boys close behind. He bowed.'I bear a message from Jason,' he lied.

Medea's face lit up. 'A message?'

'Yes, I am to tell you that he is much taken with you. You have captured his heart.'

'And he has mine. But he's in danger. The task my father has set is impossible. I can help him though,' she said.

'Good, because he has asked if he might meet you in secret— very soon.'

'Very well. Tell him to meet me at the temple of Hecate. It's not far from here. Turn left out of the palace past the stables and follow the road until it forks in two. Take the right fork and you will reach the temple. Tell Jason I have potions that will help him complete the task,' she said.

'Excellent, he will be very grateful to you for that. However, there is also something else. Jason's sister has been wounded by an Ancient. Jason was told you possessed a cure,' Parseus lied again.

'An Ancient? But they no longer walk the earth. They're imprisoned in Tartaros.'

Parseus raised his arm. 'So it was thought. But it appears that at least one remains at large. Jason has been told you possess a cure. Is that so?'

Medea thought for a moment. 'Yes, I do, though I never thought I would ever have reason to use it. It is at the temple with my other potions.'

'I will tell Jason to meet you there in an hour?'

'I will be there,' replied Medea. And with one final look at Jason she disappeared into the crowd. Parseus turned around. He seemed pleased with himself.

'I think we are half-way home,' he said, rubbing his hands. 'All we need is the cure and the witch.'

'And the witch?' Charlie was confused.

'The Dark One is not our only problem, Charlie. Mrs Payne's power has grown. And who better to foil a witch, than another witch.' Parseus tapped the side of his head.

'So we're going to...'

'Get the cure and take it and the witch herself back to Hesper,' interrupted Parseus.

THEY left the palace and following Medea's instructions, turned left. Walking past the stables, they heard snorting coming from one of the stalls — a second later, a ball of flame shot towards them. Max and Charlie leapt back, falling to the ground, the flames missing them by inches.

Parseus glanced down. 'Sorry, should have told you to be careful. Those are the fire-breathing, brazen-footed bulls,' he remarked casually.

Charlie staggered to his feet and keeping his distance peered once again. He could just make out the bulls. They were jostling for space in the cramped confines of the stall, smoke pouring from their nostrils.

'Those are the bulls that Jason has to yoke?' he asked horrified.

'Yes, somewhat impossible wouldn't you say,' said Parseus.

'However, Medea possesses an extraordinary potion which, once spread over his whole body, will make him impervious to the flames. That's how he manages to complete the task.' Parseus walked on. 'Anyway enough of that, we've got our own potion to secure.'

Reaching the temple, they found Medea was already there. Her face fell when she saw Parseus entering with the two boys.

'Where is Jason?' she asked anxiously.

'He's on his way. However, perhaps we should wait for him in the temple. You could show us the potions,' Parseus suggested.

'Come then, all that Jason needs is in here,' she said. 'Follow me.'

The Temple of Hecate was quite small. A statue sat at the far end. Charlie assumed it was of the Witch Goddess herself. Columns ran down either side of the chamber. The flickering torches hanging on the walls gave off a warm glow.

They followed Medea to the back of the temple where long rows of jars, of various sizes, were neatly stored.

'Are all these potions?' Charlie asked.

Medea ignored him, addressing Parseus instead. 'Some yes, some are poisons.

But the most powerful potions are here,' she said, gesturing to a wooden casket sitting in the corner. It looked like a smaller version of Parseus' trunk, with a domed lid and bronze fastenings. 'Everything Jason needs is in here,' Medea said.

Charlie's heart started racing. 'The cure is in here, too?' he asked, quite forgetting his place. Parseus intervened. 'Jason will be most delighted to have found a cure for his sister. It is in here, isn't it?'

'Of course. The blood of Echidne, the mother of all monsters. She languishes in the hell realm of Tartaros. Only her blood can cure a wound from an Ancient,' said Medea.

Charlie could hardly contain himself. They had found the cure. It was in touching distance. Now all they had to do was get it home.

Medea looked towards the temple door, clearly eager to see Jason.

'Let us go outside. I can send one of the boys to find Jason, though I'm sure he's already on his way,' Parseus assured her.

Medea agreed and picked up her casket. 'Then we must hurry. My father's guards will come looking for me soon.' She followed them out of the temple.

Parseus carefully took out the compass and surreptitiously started fiddling with the dials, taking care to stand as close to Medea as possible while he did so.

Oblivious to this, she scanned the road for any sign of Jason, becoming increasingly impatient. 'I thought you were going to send one of your boys to find...'

Then Medea cried out in despair. Armed soldiers on horseback now appeared in the temple garden. 'What are you doing with the princess?' the leader demanded as he leapt from his horse, his men raising their bows and taking aim.

At that moment a portal opened up in the ground. Shocked, one of the soldiers fired, the arrow heading straight for Charlie. Max shouted a warning and dived in front of him. The last thing Charlie heard was Max scream.

26. THE END IS NIGH

THEY landed back in the inn. Charlie got to his feet and heard Max scream again, 'I've been hit. I've been hit.' Mr Goodwin, hiding behind the bar, leapt up in surprise. His jaw dropped at the sight of a wailing Max, and a strangely-dressed woman who had certainly not been there when he had ducked down a moment before.

Charlie looked over at Max, fearing the worst. Then he burst out laughing.

'What's so funny? I've been shot,' Max cried out.

Charlie tried to stifle his giggles. 'I know, I'm sorry, it's just that...that arrow, it's in your bottom,' he said, stifling another laugh.

'It's only a flesh wound, for goodness sake,' said Parseus, peering down to inspect it. 'Best place to get shot though, I can tell you,' he added.

'Still hurts you know,' groaned Max.

'I'm sure we can sort that out, can't we Medea?' said Parseus.

Medea was standing in the middle of the room weaving. 'Where am I?' she said, her head darting from side to side. 'And what is this place?' she added as she put her casket down on the floor.

'Don't worry, we can explain,' said Parseus.

Medea's face darkened. 'What did you do to me?' she hissed, her face twisted in fury. She looked around in disbelief and anger. 'Where is Jason?'

'Where on earth did she come from?' asked a bewildered Mr Goodwin.

'No time for explanations just yet, Mr Goodwin,' Parseus replied as Medea leapt towards him as if to strike him.

'You tricked me, didn't you? Where did you bring me?' she shook her fist at him. 'And where's Jason?'

'He's not here,' said Parseus. 'But if you do as I ask, you will see him shortly.'

'I want to see him now.' Medea crossed her arms, scowling.

'We need your help first,' said Charlie. 'My sister is wounded. Remember? You promised to help.'

'Your sister? I see, another trick. Well she can rot in Tartaros for all I care,' snarled Medea. She turned back to Parseus. 'Now take me home or I will use every power at my disposal. And I have a lot of power,' she added menacingly. 'I warn you, never cross a priestess of the Temple of Hecate.'

'Unfortunately, the only way you can return home is with my help,' replied Parseus quietly. 'So do what we ask or you will never see Colchis or your world again. Or Jason, for that matter.'

'My world?' said Medea.

Parseus held up his compass and waved it in the air. 'We brought you to another world, in the future. So you had better help us, or you will be staying here forever,' he said.

'In the future? That's impossible,' she spat.

'I think you know that it isn't. And that being so, without my help you cannot return to your world.' said Parseus.

'How come?'

'Because I am a Time God.' Parseus waved the compass again. 'And this is a Time Compass. Hephaistos made it for me. It is how you came to be here.'

Medea looked around the bar and through the window to the village square outside. She fell silent for a while as she slowly took in her strange new surroundings, then seemed to accept that what Parseus had said, however extraordinary, must somehow be true — after all, she was no longer in her temple garden. 'So where am I,' she asked.

'You're in a mortal world. This place is called Hesper. It's the gateway to Tartaros,' Parseus added.

Medea reeled back. 'Tartaros?' she whispered.

'Yes, and if you don't help us, I may even take you there instead. How would like to spend an eternity in hell?' Parseus tapped his Time Compass.

The threat seemed to work. Medea pursed her lips tightly. 'I see you have given me no choice.'

'Um, what's going on?' said Mr Goodwin. 'And who is that woman?'

'Dad, her name is Medea. She's a witch. We brought her back with us. She has the cure for Emily,' explained Charlie.

'A cure? That's wonderful,' said his father.

Medea stared at him, confused. 'What language is this man speaking?' she asked. 'I can't understand a word he says. And where did he come from?'

Parseus ignored her. 'Speaking of Emily, let's get upstairs. She has very little time left.'

'What about my *bottom*? I've got an arrow in it,' complained Max, still crouched on all fours.

'You're in no danger. We'll deal with you later,' said Parseus. 'We must cure Emily first.'

Charlie grabbed Medea by the hand and, dragging her behind him, led her out of the bar and up the stairs. Parseus picked up her casket and followed, Medea cursing them both as she stumbled behind Charlie.

Reaching his sister's room Charlie threw open the door. 'She's in here, Medea,' he said, pulling her inside. Parseus followed close behind, carrying her casket.

Emily was still much the same, pale and unconscious. Medea stood defiantly in the room for some moments, then curious she bent down and examined her. 'You used the potion of Thanatos?' she asked. She seemed surprised.

'Yes, Cheiron gave it to us,' said Charlie.

'Cheiron, the centaur?' Medea raised her eyebrows and glanced at Parseus. 'So *he's* helped you?' She stepped back from the bed, knelt down and opened her casket.

Charlie peered inside. It was full of little jars, many of which looked like the ones Parseus had in his trunk. Two were different though, cased in metal with little padlocks attached to them.

Medea picked one up and held it up to the light. 'Show me where the wound is,' she demanded.

Charlie pulled back Emily's shirt. The wound was now black and looked much worse than before.

Medea inspected it closely. Taking the jar she unlocked it and unstopped the cork. There was a loud hiss and a small trail of smoke rose out of it. Medea carefully applied the potion to the wound. It began bubbling.

'Are you sure this is going to work?' asked Charlie. The cure looked as if it might be doing more harm than good. He was worried that Medea had now tricked them.

'She'll soon recover,' said Medea as she stopped the cork and locked the padlock. 'But I saved her just in time.' She pointed. 'See where the flesh is turning green. The potion of Thanatos had worn off and the poison had begun to spread.'

'Thank goodness we got here then,' said Charlie. 'Is she really going to be OK?'

Medea stood up. 'Yes. But it will take some time for her strength to return.'

'Thank you, Medea. I really appreciate it,' said Charlie.

'Don't insult me with your thanks, boy. I was given no choice,' she snapped.

'I know.' Charlie backed away ever so slightly. 'But we had to save my sister. You would do the same, wouldn't you?'

Charlie saw a shadow cross Medea's face. He had a funny feeling she wouldn't.

'Now that's all done, I think we should deal with Max next,' declared Parseus, picking up Medea's casket.

Mr Goodwin appeared at the door. 'Is she OK?'

''She'll be just fine, Mr Goodwin. Give her a little time to come round.' Parseus ushered them out of the room. They slipped back downstairs to the bar. Max was still lying prone on the floor.

'How's Emily?' he asked, moaning slightly.

'She's going to be fine,' said Charlie.

Parseus beckoned Medea.

Kneeling next to Max, she ripped open his trousers.

Max wriggled in embarrassment. 'STOP MOVING,' Medea yelled. She opened her casket and took out another potion.

'This will numb it,' she said, applying a thin layer to the area. She waited a few seconds and then yanked out the arrowhead.

'OW,' screamed Max. 'I thought you said it would be numb.'

'Did I? Sorry. I meant to say it would hurt a lot,' replied Medea as she applied yet more of the potion on the wound. 'You should be fine in a few minutes. Might ache for a day or so but you'll live,' she said.

'Thank you, Medea,' said Parseus. 'However, there is just one more favour I have to ask of you.'

'What now?' sighed Medea.

'We need to deal with another witch.'

'Deal? In what way?'

'I'm not sure yet. But we need your help,' said Parseus.

Medea looked at him suspiciously. 'If you insist. But don't think I will forget this. I've a very long memory.'

'I know,' said Parseus. 'But so do I, and it's rather longer than yours,' he added, silencing Medea.

Parseus turned to Charlie. 'Now that your sister has been cured, I think you two should get some rest. We have a few hours left before sunset. Go upstairs and get some sleep.'

Charlie hadn't realised how tired he was, but now that Parseus had mentioned it, it washed over him like a wave. Max too looked exhausted. They slipped upstairs.

'She's really cured?' asked Max as they went inside Charlie's room.

'Yes. Not sure I trust that Medea one inch — but yes, she cured her.'

'Can't believe we did it,' said Max.

Neither did Charlie. They had endured so much to secure the cure: murderous women, monsters, armed soldiers, Harpies the Clashing Rocks — now it all seemed something of an anticlimax. Yet they still had no idea what part Emily was to play, or how to kill the Dark One. For now though Charlie was too tired to think about any of it.

'By the way, Max, I didn't thank you for saving me back in Colchis,' he said.

'Forget about it. It was only my pride that got hurt.'

Charlie grinned and patted him on the back.

Both boys collapsed on their beds and within a minute they were fast asleep.

PARSEUS woke them a few hours later. Charlie got up first. 'How long did I sleep?'

'Six hours or so. It will be sunset soon,' replied Parseus.

'I must check on Emily,' Charlie said. Still suspicious of Medea, he wanted to make sure that his sister was OK before he thought of anything else. He hurried to her room.

Thankfully Medea had been true to her word. Emily was awake.

'What happened to me?' she said as he walked in.

'You were injured by the Dark One,' said Charlie. 'You've been unconscious.'

Emily sat up, a shocked look on her face.

'It's alright Emily. It's not here. It's daylight,' he said.

'How long have I been out?'

'Not long,' said Charlie. 'But you need to take it easy. You're still weak. Can I get you anything?'

'Water. I'm really thirsty.'

'I'll go and get some,' said Charlie. He hurried downstairs to the bar.

'Emily is much better,' he said as he walked in. 'Thank you, Medea.'

Medea's face softened a little. 'Good. But now you are in my debt, do you hear?'

Charlie nodded and went behind the bar to fetch a glass of water. 'I'm just going to give Emily a drink,' he said.

'Ah, let me put a little Strength in that. She could probably do with it,' said Parseus. He slipped a couple of drops into the glass.

Charlie ran back upstairs and gave Emily the water. She drank the whole glass. Within seconds the colour had returned to her face. 'What was in that?' she asked. 'Tasted like strawberries.'

'Just a little Strength, that's all,' said Charlie.

'What, like the stuff you had?'

Charlie nodded.

'Wow, it's good isn't it?'

'Yeah, it really works.'

Emily tried to get out of bed.

'Are you sure that's wise,' said Charlie.

'I'm fine really. I need to stretch my legs.' She stood up unsteadily. 'So what's been going on?'

'You'd never believe me, Emily.'

'Try me.'

'Maybe later,' Charlie replied.

'OK. Well, I'm going to the bathroom.'

'Do you need any help?'

'I think I can manage, Charlie. I feel much better already,' she said. 'That Strength helped.'

Emily left the room and wandered down the corridor to the bathroom. Charlie waited in the hall. A few minutes later she re-emerged. She peered down the corridor towards Parseus' room. 'Is he in there?'

'No, don't think so,' said Charlie.

'Could have sworn I heard a voice,' she said as she started down the corridor to his room.

'What voice?' said Charlie.

'I swear I heard a voice.'

'But Parseus is downstairs,' said Charlie. 'Come on, let's go.'

Emily ignored him. Reaching Parseus' room she opened the door.

'This is no time for nosing around, Sis,' Charlie called out as he followed her into the room. But Emily appeared to have slipped into some kind of trance — she started searching through his trunk as if she were looking for something in particular.

'What are you doing?' asked Charlie.

Emily picked up the jewel-embedded box which Parseus had said was Prophecy. She turned it over in her hands, as if it meant something to her.

'Emily, put that back…'

The next moment the box opened. Charlie was taken aback.

'But that's…' Then it all came back: the Fates warning, what Phineus had said about the gift. It was obvious — the Prophecy was a gift — and it was intended for Emily.

Charlie looked inside. The box was lined with red silk and contained another little green jar surrounded in a metal mesh, like the one that had contained the Blood of Echidne: Emily's cure.

'It's telling me to drink it,' Emily whispered.

'Do you know what it is?' asked Charlie.

Emily shook her head.

'It's a gift for you.'

'What does it do?' she asked. But without waiting for an answer, Emily put the jar to her lips and started to drink.

As she finished, Parseus appeared in the doorway. 'I knew it. I knew it,' he said. 'It was meant for you.'

Emily looked down at the empty jar. 'What was?'

'You've been given a great and powerful gift,' Parseus said.

'But what does it do?'

'It makes you prophetic — able to foretell the future.' Parseus turned to Charlie. 'What did the Fates and Phineus say about Emily?'

'That without her, all is lost,' said Charlie.

'Exactly. And what do we need most of all?'

'A miracle?'

'Answers,' said Parseus.

'What do you mean?' said Charlie.

'We now have our very own prophet, Charlie.' Parseus paused. 'Now all we have to do is wait for a vision.'

'How long will that take?' asked Emily.

'Not sure. Minutes? Hours?' Parseus said.

Just then Emily cried out and fell to her knees.

'Or seconds,' he added.

Charlie jumped forward and helped her to the armchair.

He knelt next to her. 'Are you OK?'

Emily didn't answer. Then her eyes rolled into the back of her head.

'Is she OK, Parseus?' said Charlie.

'Perfectly all right. Be patient.'

'For what?'

Moments later, Emily sat up sharply and uttered just one word. 'ARES.'

'What about Ares?' said Charlie.

Emily shook her head. 'Sword — you must use it,' she added. 'Against the Dark One?'

'What sword?' asked Charlie.

Parseus clapped his hands. 'Of course, she means the sword of Ares.'

Emily started mumbling again. 'Must sever heads. Need wings, men with wings.'

Charlie looked at Parseus. 'The twins?'

Parseus' face brightened. 'Yes, why didn't I think of it earlier? We need help,' he said.

'You mean we need to go back to the Argo to fetch the twins?' asked Charlie.

'Dolphin?' muttered Emily.

'Dolphin?' Charlie was confused. Then it became clear. 'She must mean Perikylemenos,' he said.

'Why stop there,' said Parseus. 'Now I think of it, we could bring a handful of them. Lynkeus could prove useful. Polydeuces and Euphemos too,' he added.

Charlie was excited by the idea. Why face the Dark One alone when they could bring reinforcements?

Emily's eyes rolled back again and she sat up. 'What happened?' she mumbled, looking from one to the other.

'You don't remember?' said Charlie. 'A bit. I...I saw a sword and some men. It was weird. There were all these strange hazy images,' she said. 'Like a dream.'

'You had a vision, Emily. A prophetic vision,' said Charlie.

'Guess the gift works then, doesn't it?' she replied.

'It most definitely does, Emily,' said Parseus. He took out the compass. 'I'm going back to fetch the Argonauts. You two wait outside in the corridor. I don't want you involved in this. This time I go alone.'

Charlie and Emily stepped outside, closing the door behind them.

'I think I should go and see Dad. Bet he's been worried sick,' said Emily, before running along the corridor. As she disappeared down the main staircase, Charlie heard voices shouting and the sound of furniture falling over in the room behind him. He opened the door and stood back in astonishment.

Parseus' room was jammed with Argonauts. They had landed in a great heap and were noisily extricating themselves from the pile, cursing and shouting as they did so.

'What's going on?' shouted Lynkeus. 'Where are we?'

The Argonauts scrambled to their feet, shaking their heads, looking around in bemusement. Seeing them standing there in Parseus' room they looked so odd now that they were in

Charlie's world, so out of place, so much larger than life — even the more human-looking ones.

Parseus had brought seven Argonauts with him — Kalais and Zetes, the twins, Euphemos and Lynkeus, Perikylemenos, Polydeuces and Idas, the violent one. They were all shouting loudly, demanding to know what was going on and how it was that they had ended up there.

Parseus, hemmed into a corner, was doing his best to explain but it took some time to calm them down.

'And what was that spinning about?' asked Polydeuces.

'Forget that. What is this place?' said Lynkeus, surveying the room. Then he spotted Charlie standing in the doorway.

'By the Gods, it's Charlie.' The Argonauts turned to look. 'Where did you come from?' said Lynkeus.

'I was already here,' Charlie replied. 'We came with Medea.'

'The witch?' Periklylemenos was confused. 'But how could you, she's in the palace. I saw her myself.'

'Where exactly are we? And how did we get here?' demanded Euphemos, looking about him in utter bewilderment.

'What have you done to us?' shouted Idas. 'This is an outrage. Jason has a great task to complete. Our quest depends on it.'

'Well, wherever we are, we're nowhere near Colchis, I can tell you,' said Lynkeus.

Kalais glanced nervously around the room. 'Strange forces are at work. I can feel it.'

'Me too, brother,' said Zetes.

Periklylemenos dusted himself down and looked at Parseus suspiciously. 'You told us that you had important news, gathered us around, and then there was a flash of light. Explain yourself, Parseus — now.'

The other Argonauts joined in the chorus, protesting and demanding answers.

Parseus put the compass back in his pocket. 'I will explain everything, I promise,' he said. 'But why don't we all make ourselves more comfortable. It's far too crowded here.'

He pushed his way through the Argonauts and went into the corridor. Still grumbling, the mystified Argonauts filed out looking about them in surprise as they followed him downstairs.

Stooping to avoid the beams, the Argonauts entered the bar. They were stunned to find Medea standing in the middle of the room — she as amazed at the sight of them as they were of her.

'Is Jason here?' she asked breathlessly.

The Argonauts shook their heads. 'No. We were with him until...' Idas waved his arm around the room. 'Until we ended up here — wherever here is.'

Idas spotted Max. 'You're here too?' He was surprised. 'What's going on?'

Parseus held up his hand to silence them. 'As I explained to Medea, we're in another world.' He paused. 'In the future.'

'What?' said the Argonauts at once. They looked at Medea for explanation. She nodded glumly.

'He possesses some kind of Time Compass,' she said.

Parseus took it out once more and the Argonauts gathered round to inspect it.

'How does it work?' Euphemos asked.

'It's complicated,' replied Parseus. 'It was designed by Hephaistos.'

'Hephaistos?' Periklylemenos looked at the others. They seemed impressed, some now beginning to argue that Parseus must be telling the truth.

'Let me explain.' Then Parseus told them the story: his role in it, the Prophecy and the threat which faced Charlie from the Dark One.

The Argonauts listened in silence, occasionally glancing at Charlie as each new part of the story was related.

When Parseus finished, Polydeuces threw up his arms in disgust. 'You want us to help kill an Ancient. Are you mad?'

'Yes I do — and no, I'm not. There has been a prophecy and

each one of you has featured in it. You have to help us kill the Dark One. The Gods demand it.'

'Prophecy? Who saw this?' said Idas.

'The girl did,' said Parseus.

'This girl?' Polydeuces pointed at Emily.

'Yes. She has been given the gift of prophecy,' said Parseus.

A murmur ran through the group and they eyed Emily with interest.

Even Medea seemed impressed. 'She's prophetic?'

'Yes and now you must help Charlie defeat the threat. Then, I promise, I will take you back to Colchis. You will return to the exact moment you left, it will be like you had never gone,' said Parseus. 'And Jason will triumph — Medea will ensure that.'

The Argonauts looked at Medea.

'Of course, I want nothing more than to help him. Jason will succeed. I promise — you will secure the Fleece.' She paused. 'Provided Parseus keeps his promise.'

'You have my word on that as a Time God,' said Parseus.

Although the Argonauts seemed satisfied by his assurance, an awkward silence descended as they considered the proposal to help Charlie defeat the Dark One. Killing an Ancient it seemed was something they had never envisaged or even thought possible.

Perikylemenos was the first to speak. 'Very well. I agree. I will help the boy.'

Kalais looked at his brother, Zetes. He nodded. 'You can count us in.'

'Me, too,' said Idas. 'The boy did save my life.'

Polydeuces slapped Charlie on the back. 'You know me — always up for a fight.'

'Are we all in then?' asked Perikylemenos.

Lynkeus and Euphemos both nodded.

'Excellent,' said Parseus. 'Now all we need is a plan.'

Lynkeus snorted. 'You mean you don't have one? I thought there was a vision.'

'There is, but it's a little vague. We haven't quite worked out the details.'

'Oh, well do let us know when you have, Parseus,' sniped Polydeuces.

Charlie peered out of the window. The sun was already starting to set. Whatever the plan, they needed one fast.

'This is what we do know. The sword of Ares can kill the Dark One,' said Parseus. 'I have that sword.'

'The sword of Ares?' said Euphemos. 'You have that?'

The Argonauts were suitably impressed.

'And there's a secret chamber full of weapons,' piped up Charlie. 'There are enough weapons for everyone.'

'Marvellous — good to know. At least we'll be armed. That should help us face an Ancient,' sneered Idas.

Max now looked out of the window. 'You're going to face the Dark One tonight?'

'Yes,' said Charlie. But as he said it, the realisation hit him like a sledgehammer. His time had come. His moment of destiny.

He looked over at his father, who was standing behind the bar, watching the scene in utter bafflement.

'Are you OK, Dad?' Charlie had quite forgotten that his father couldn't understand a word anyone was saying.

'Think so,' said his father. He gestured towards the men. 'Who are they?'

'Argonauts — you know, Dad, heroes from the Ancient World. They're here to help me defeat the Dark One.'

'Defeat the Dark One?' Charlie's father gulped. 'Are you serious?' He surveyed the motley crew now assembled in his bar and shook his head. 'Does anyone want a drink?' He poured himself a large whisky, knocking it back in one go.

'Not now, Mr Goodwin. Maybe later,' said Parseus.

Mr Goodwin shook his head in disbelief and disappeared into the kitchen.

The Argonauts, curious at this strange new world, began inspecting the room, fiddling with everything.

'Look, some strange liquid comes out of this,' said Polydeuces, pulling down on one of the beer pumps. 'Did Hephaistos make this too?' he asked.

'No, it's just a beer pump,' said Charlie.

'Beer? What's that?' asked Polydeuces.

'It's a type of alcohol, like wine,' replied Charlie.

Excellent. Let's try some,' Polydeuces said. He bent down and put his mouth to the pump.

Parseus threw up his arms. 'What a good idea. Let's all get blind drunk, and then go and fight an Ancient, shall we?'

Polydeuces straightened. 'Good point,' he replied. 'Sorry.'

'Now listen. I think I have a plan,' Parseus said.

Everyone gathered round him.

'This is what we will do. The Dark One will be released at sunset,' he said.

'What's this Dark One look like?' asked Lynkeus.

'It has three serpent heads and the body of a giant scorpion. Its tail is poisonous, its bite and claws are poisonous and it can be both shadow and form.'

'Pretty harmless, then,' said Polydeuces.

The Argonauts laughed.

Parseus continued. 'First, we must lure it out into the open,' he said. 'This is where you come in, Max.'

'Huh? What do you mean— where I come in?' said Max.

'You're going to be the bait,' said Parseus.

'Bait? Again? Are you joking? Why do I always have to be bait?' said Max.

'You just do. We are going to use you to keep it distracted,' said Parseus. 'Kalais and Zetes, I want you two to fly the boys up to Hesper House. That's where the Dark One will be. The boys will show you the way.'

The twins nodded.

'Charlie, you're to take the helmet, so you'll be invisible.'

'Oh, he gets to be invisible does he?' said Max. 'This just get better and better.'

'You can't mean — the Helmet of Invisibility?' said Zetes, his eyes widening.

'The very same,' said Parseus.

'How did you get that?' asked Kalais, astonished.

'Hades leant it to us after we helped rescue Death,' said Parseus.

'Hades? Rescue Death?' Another murmur ran through the Argonauts.

'Got any other weapons from the Gods?' asked Lynkeus.

'Just the sword and shield which belonged to Ares.'

'Is there any God who hasn't helped?' shouted Polydeuces.

'Dionysos,' said Max.

The Argonauts burst out laughing. Polydeuces slapped Max on the back. 'Maybe the God of Wine can lend a hand later,' he winked.

'He'd better,' said Euphemos.

'Let's get back to the plan, shall we?' said Parseus.

'So what about everyone else?' said Charlie.

'We'll follow and wait in the shadows. Max will ride on Zetes' back and draw the Dark One out into the open. We'll be on hand and we'll give you all the help we can. But it's your destiny to defeat it, Charlie.'

'And Mrs Payne?' Charlie asked.

Parseus patted Lynkeus on the shoulder. 'That's where we need your eyes, Lynkeus. The witch will probably be somewhere in the tunnels under Hesper House.'

'There's a witch?' said Euphemos.

'Yes. That's why we need you too, Medea. You and Lynkeus must find the witch. You know what to do?' said Parseus.

'A binding spell will suffice,' she said.

'Good, because the witch's power has grown. Emily, you'll come with us, too. We need you close by in case you have another vision,' said Parseus. 'It could be decisive.'

He glanced out of the window. 'The sun will set soon. Let's get ready. I think we now have a plan which *can* work.'

'In which I'm bait,' protested Max again.

'You're a strong lad, Max, don't forget that. Remember your training. We need your help. I know you can do it,' Parseus assured him.

Max braced his shoulders. 'OK.'

'But you'll want to strap yourselves on. It could get dangerous up there,' Parseus added.

'Could?' said Max. 'We're about to fight a three-headed monster. There's no 'could' about it.'

'Have no fear, I will keep you safe,' said Zetes.

'Thanks,' said Max. 'And no offence but I am not entirely convinced.'

'What about our weapons?' said Idas.

'Max, take the others down to the cellar and get them equipped. I noticed some ropes down there too. Grab those as well,' said Parseus. 'Then fetch the helmet.'

Max disappeared down the hatch with the Argonauts.

Charlie looked out of the window again. The light was fading fast, and there was the faint sound of thunder in the distance. A storm was brewing.

He glanced at Emily in the armchair in the corner. Her eyes were rolling into the back of her head. She was having another vision.

'What can you see?' he said, rushing to her side. 'Tell me,' he pressed her again.

Emily's eyes rolled back and she looked up, terrified. 'It's dark, I couldn't see their face. I...'

'Don't worry, it will come,' said Parseus. 'The visions are never clear but you can learn to interpret their meaning.'

'I have,' said Emily. 'I saw someone die.'

27. VICTORY IN DEATH

CHARLIE heard the thunder in the distance. The storm was growing closer. Now though he had his own storm to weather. After everything that had happened, his destiny was at hand. But what if he failed? What if he couldn't kill the Dark One? He hadn't had enough training. He was only a boy. A mortal.

A moment later they heard gunshots.

Charlie rushed towards the hatch and threw it open. 'What happened?' he shouted down below.

'It's all right,' he heard Euphemos shout back. 'We're fine.'

Max climbed back through the hatch, the other Argonauts following behind. They were arguing.

'I told you not to touch those weapons. You don't know how to use them,' said Max as he and Polydeuces came back into the bar.

'I'm sorry — I just had no idea what would happen,' Polydeuces apologised.

'That's why I said not to touch them. You could have killed Lynkeus,' said Max.

'It's all right, boy,' said Lynkeus. 'I saw it just in time and dodged out of the way. They move pretty fast though. Nobody has better eyes than mine. It took even me by surprise.'

'Saw what just in time?' said Charlie.

'The...what did you call it, Max?' asked Lynkeus.

'Bullet,' said Max.

'Hey, no harm, no foul,' said Polydeuces, attaching a sword to his side.

'Yeah, whatever.' Max sighed. 'I'm going to get the helmet.' He left the bar.

The Argonauts were now fully armed. After Polydeuces' experience with the rifle, they had decided to pick more familiar weapons. Lynkeus and Euphemos had opted for bows and arrows, Perikylemenos, Polydeuces and Idas for swords.

Max reappeared with the helmet. Parseus beckoned everyone to gather round once more. 'It's time,' he said. 'Now Charlie will be invisible. He will also have the sword of Ares, so the plan is to protect him so that he can slay the Dark One. It is his destiny to do so.'

Charlie shuffled uncomfortably.

'According to Emily's vision, Charlie will need to sever its heads to kill it. We know that only the sword of Ares can do that,' Parseus added. He reached into his cloak and took out the jar of Strength.

'Everyone needs to take a sip of this.' He handed it round.

The jar was soon empty. Parseus pointed at the twins. 'You two will wait until sunset then fly the boys up to the house. The rest of us will set off first.'

Parseus turned to Charlie and Max. 'We'll see you at Hesper House. May the Gods be with you,' he said.

'Thanks,' said Charlie. 'Just hope that they are.'

Parseus shepherded the other Argonauts and Medea out of the bar, leaving the boys and the twins alone.

'Are you OK, Max?' asked Charlie.

'OK? I'm the bait. What's OK about that?' said Max.

Charlie could hear the fear in his voice. Who could blame him, he thought. He too was terrified.

Ten minutes later Max handed Charlie one of the ropes.

'Time to go then,' said Charlie. He fixed the sword to his side and Max strapped a bow to his back.

Charlie's father came back into the bar. Lost for words, he stared silently at the boys now armed for battle. Then he came over and hugged them both.

'Good luck, you two, you're brave boys. I know you'll be OK,' he said.

'Course we will, Dad. And we'll be back home soon,' said Charlie.

He took a deep breath and then he and Max slipped out through the side entrance, checking first to make sure the darkening square was deserted. Charlie gave the signal and ran as fast as he could, the others racing after him. He reached the oak tree beside the church gateway and checked the square behind them. There was no one about. They hadn't been spotted.

Charlie watched Max climb onto Zetes' back and tie himself securely with the rope. He climbed onto Kalais' back and did the same. A second later Zetes soared into the sky and they followed. In the fading light, Charlie could just see the turreted towers of Hesper House poking out above the trees in the distance.

'We're going there, Kalais,' he said, pointing ahead. They flew on, Charlie catching a brief glimpse of the others below before they turned up the drive to Hesper House. He could hear the thunder rolling in. The storm would soon be upon them. He wondered whether that would give them an advantage or not.

They soared over the top of the towers and landed on the lawn outside the west wing. The broken French windows lay in pieces all over the terrace, a reminder of Charlie's last visit. So much had happened since that he could hardly believe it.

A flash of lightning cracked across the sky, making him jump. A few seconds later he heard a clap of thunder. It was as if nature itself was there to bear witness to the impending battle.

Kalais glanced over his shoulder. 'What now?'

'We wait,' said Charlie.

Almost on cue, the Dark One — still in shadow form — slithered through the broken door frame and slunk onto the terrace. It had picked up Charlie's scent.

'Stay strong, Max,' Charlie called out. 'You're only the bait, remember that.'

'Yeah, that's what I always say to the worm when I hook it on the end of my line,' said Max.

'Don't worry. I'll do the rest,' Charlie said.

The Dark One, sensing Charlie's presence, hissed loudly and began its transformation. The plan was working.

'That's the Ancient?' said Kalais, watching the Dark One take solid form. 'We should have brought more Argonauts,' he added.

Kalais was probably right, thought Charlie as another bolt of lightning cracked across the sky, illuminating the Dark One in its glare. Charlie shuddered. He had forgotten how terrifying the monster was.

He took a deep breath, unsheathed his sword and readied himself. He went over the plan in his mind: sever the heads one by one and the Dark One would die. The plan was simple enough. Now though, staring down at the monstrous assassin, it didn't seem so simple.

A clap of thunder rang out. The storm was closing in. Charlie shouted to Max. 'Get into position. Just keep it distracted.'

'Distracted? That'll be easy.'

'Bug it like a fly,' Charlie called over his shoulder.

'Flies can be swatted you know,' Max shouted back.

The Dark One hissed again and Charlie and Kalais flew up into the air. Charlie put on the helmet. They immediately disappeared from view and the scent vanished. The Dark One stopped hissing. Confused, its heads darted about, looking in vain for Charlie.

It was then that Zetes and Max began their taunting. Flying this way and that they started flitting around the Dark One.

Keeping just out of reach, Zetes ducked and weaved around its heads. Distracted, The Dark One, its main target now vanished, desperately tried to strike at them, its serpent heads snapping in the air, determined to attack Max and Zetes. It jabbed furiously at them but Zetes was far too nimble to be caught.

Invisible to all, Charlie and Kalais waited for their moment. Charlie felt his heart thumping against his rib cage. 'We're going in for the head on the left,' he called out to Max and Zetes.

Kalais, with Charlie firmly secured to his back, dived down for an attack. Sweeping towards the Dark One, Charlie raised his sword and readied himself. He could feel its power coursing through him and remembered Herakles' words when he had been training him— strike hard, strike quickly. So as they closed in he brought the sword down sharply on the first head.

A large gash appeared in its neck and The Dark One hissed loudly. Spinning round, its other heads darting in all directions, it searched for its invisible attacker. But to no avail.

Kalais quickly soared back up into the air, just out of reach. 'Well done, Charlie. Let's go again,' he said.

This time, they flew down and came in from another angle. Charlie struck the neck even harder, the sword of Ares slicing through it like butter. The gash grew deeper. The first head was now hanging half-off.

'Once more,' Kalais urged Charlie.

Max and Zetes continued their taunts, ducking and weaving around it, the monster becoming more desperate, lashing out in fury and now pain.

Charlie and Kalais, hovering high in the sky above it, came in for another attack. Charlie's confidence was growing, and this time he struck the hardest blow yet. He and Kalais soared back into the air.

'You've done it. You've severed it,' Max shouted. He and Zetes cheered.

Charlie looked down. Max was right. The first head had fallen. The Dark One hissed again, but the sound no longer filled Charlie with fear.

'We're going for head number two,' Kalais called out to his brother and Max hovering nearby — their confidence growing, their taunts more daring. Max had even strung his bow and was pelting the Dark One with arrows, though to no effect.

Everything was going so well Charlie wondered why he had been so scared.

Then his face fell. Max and Zetes had grown a little too bold and neither of them had noticed the Dark One's tail. Flicking up in the air it cracked down like a whip, its poisonous barb heading straight for them.

'*Watch out for the tail*,' Charlie screamed as it sliced through the air towards them. He was certain Max and Zetes were doomed.

Fortunately Zetes, hearing the warning, back-flipped out of the way just in time, the tail missing them by inches.

Max wiped his brow in relief and Zetes, now more cautious, flew higher.

'We're going for the one on the right,' shouted Charlie. 'Distract the middle head.'

'Will do,' Max called back.

Diving down, Charlie was preparing to strike when he noticed something: the severed stem had begun to froth and boil, blood and gore were spurting out like an erupting volcano.

'What's that, Kalais?' he said. They flew in to take a closer look. Then Charlie realised what was happening. 'Quick, pull up now,' he yelled.

Kalais did so and they watched in disbelief as a new head started growing out of the severed stem. The Dark One, it seemed, was invincible. They had misinterpreted Emily's vision.

'What do we do, Kalais?' said Charlie.

'We retreat.' He waved to his brother. 'Zetes, fall back.' Zetes did as ordered. Charlie and Kalais followed. Flying round the west wing, they spotted the others coming up the drive.

'It's not working, Parseus,' shouted Charlie. 'The head re-grew.'

'Oh dear,' said Parseus.

Max and Zetes landed beside him. 'I don't like it when you say that,' said Max. 'It's never good.'

'Neither is our situation,' said Parseus.

A second later Emily cried out, clutching her stomach. Her eyes rolled back. 'Fire,' she whispered. 'You need fire.'

'Of course. Why didn't I think of that?' said Parseus. 'We have to cauterise the wounds. Come on, there's no time to lose. Max, as soon as Charlie severs a head, you and Zetes fly in and cauterise the wound.'

'But where do we get fire?' asked Max.

'The house. I've seen torches there before,' suggested Charlie.

'Good idea,' said Parseus. 'Get back to the fight, Charlie. Max and Zetes distract the Dark One. Lynkeus — we need your eyes. Look for a torch.'

Charlie and Kalais flew back round the side of the west wing. Max and Zetes followed, taunting the Dark One to distract it so the others could safely slip past.

Charlie saw a look of horror on the Argonauts' faces as they caught their first glimpse of the monster. Now that its head was fully re-grown, it was more vicious than ever.

Lynkeus stepped inside the house.

'Can you see any torches?' shouted Parseus.

Lynkeus scanned the building, his eyes penetrating the walls. 'I can see torches — they're in a room full of books.'

'It's the library. Tell Euphemos where it is,' said Parseus. 'He's the fastest. He can fetch it.'

Euphemos disappeared inside the house to fetch the torch while the other Argonauts positioned themselves as best they could. The Dark One now turned its attention on them.

Polydeuces nudged Idas. 'Starting to wish we had that gun thing.'

'Starting to wish we weren't here,' replied Idas as the Dark One came in for an attack.

Max and Zetes, seeing their predicament, dived down, Max pelting it with arrows so that Polydeuces and Idas could safely get out of the way. As they did so, Euphemos reappeared, torch in hand.

'Zetes — fly down and grab the torch,' Kalais shouted.

Zetes did so and Euphemos handed it to Max. 'When Charlie severs the head you must cauterise it, Max — get fire into it. Do you understand?'

'Yes, but I think I was better off when I was just bait,' replied Max. Then he and Zetes soared back into the air.

'Right — time for another attack, Charlie,' said Kalais. Swooping down once more, Charlie struck another blow at the first serpent head. Circling round they quickly came in for another strike. Moments later the first head fell again.

'NOW, Max,' shouted Parseus.

Max and Zetes flew straight at the Dark One, now flailing in pain. Max leaned over and shoved the flaming torch into the severed stem, cauterising the bleeding stump. The bubbling stopped. They flew back up and hovered high above it.

Everyone held their breath, hoping the plan had worked. Seconds later they realised it had. No new head grew back.

A cheer rang out from the Argonauts.

'Now sever the others and do the same,' ordered Parseus.

Just then another bolt of lightning lit up the sky, followed by a loud clap of thunder. The storm had arrived and with it the rain.

Charlie ignored it. He and Kalais were getting used to the attacks and flying in he struck at the second head. It fell crashing to the ground. They soared back up and another cheer rang out. Max and Zetes cauterised the second stump.

Meanwhile the other Argonauts started firing at the Dark One with arrows, or swiping at its legs with their swords.

Under attack from all sides, and hissing in pain, the Dark One had no idea where to turn.

Watching from above, Charlie breathed a huge sigh of relief. It would soon be dead.

The relief, however, was short-lived. With the rain pelting down, a bolt of lightning cracked across the sky, hitting Kalais squarely on the shoulder. Screaming in pain, he and Charlie fell like a stone. The helmet came off and Charlie came back into view. They tumbled to the ground with a thump.

The next moment the Dark One vanished from sight.

'Where did it go, Lynkeus?' Parseus shouted. Lynkeus shook his head. He couldn't see it.

'FALL BACK TO THE HOUSE,' yelled Parseus.

Polydeuces and Idas rushed forward and helped Charlie and Kalais to their feet. Stumbling, they all fled inside.

'Where did it go?' said Max.

'It must have stepped on the helmet,' replied Parseus.

Max groaned. 'Oh, that's just marvellous, that is. Now we've got an invisible monster. We're done for.'

Everyone shared his fears. It was the very worst predicament. Then Charlie noticed the torch in Max's hand. The driving rain had extinguished the flames. They didn't even have any fire. Every advantage they had possessed was gone. Now, even with only one head left, the Dark One had the upper hand.

PARSEUS examined Kalais' shoulder. It was badly burnt but he refused to complain.

Charlie glanced back at the lawn. The storm was raging hard and there was no sign of the Dark One. 'What now, Parseus?'

But before Parseus could answer they heard the Dark One crash through what remained of the French windows. Parseus screamed, 'WE RUN.'

Fleeing down the passage towards the west wing, pursued by the hissing but invisible Dark One, they made it to the library, slamming the heavy door behind them as they went inside.

'Where can we go?' cried Charlie, the Dark One now throwing itself against the door frame.

'The secret passage. We'll have to escape through that,' said Parseus.

'Then what? We don't know where it goes,' said Charlie.

'Yes we do. It leads to a river,' said Lynkeus.

'River?'

'Yes, Charlie. It's an underground river. I can see it leads back to the inn — amongst other places. There's a secret entrance at the back of the chamber where the weapons are kept. I was going to mention it earlier,' said Lynkeus.

'Then let's get to the river,' shouted Parseus.

At that moment the door frame crumbled into pieces and the Dark One crashed into the room. As it did so it dislodged the helmet and came back into view.

'Well at least we can see it now,' said Polydeuces as everyone immediately backed into the corner of the room.

Parseus leapt forward and grabbed Charlie by the shoulders. 'There's just one head left, Charlie. Just one,' he said.

Steeling himself, Charlie unsheathed his sword again and lifted it up. He went in to strike. The Dark One, now sensing his presence, lunged forward and bit him on the arm. Charlie could feel a sharp sting as the fangs pierced his skin.

He reeled back in agony but there was no time for pain. He had to keep fighting. Raising his sword he brought it down hard and another large gash appeared in The Dark One's neck. It hissed — but this time in fear.

'Keep striking, Charlie,' Parseus ordered.

Charlie did so. Swiping at the Dark One, he struck blow after blow. There was a final piercing hiss and the last head fell to the floor with a thud. Charlie stood for a second in disbelief, staring at the severed stem.

'Get the torch, Max,' Parseus shouted

'But it's gone out,' said Max. 'We can't cauterise it.'

Idas threw up his arms. 'Great. We're doomed — again. I say we flee,' he shouted, watching the stump starting to froth and boil.

'NO,' said Perikylemenos, stepping forward. 'Don't worry Max. I can do it.'

'How?' said Max.

'I can become anything I want to, remember?' he said.

But that means that you'll...' said Parseus.

Periklymenos smiled. 'Remember, there's no victory without death.'

'What do you mean by that?' said Charlie.

Perikylemenos didn't answer.

'Then let's finish this,' shouted Parseus.

With that, Perikylemenos transformed himself into a ball of fire.

'Light the torch, Max,' ordered Parseus.

Max did so and Zetes grabbed it from him. 'Let me do the honours,' he said. Leaping up into the air he flew towards the severed stem and pushed the flaming torch into the stump.

A deathly silence descended. Then The Dark One fell to the ground.

The Argonauts cheered. Kalais leapt up into the air whooping with delight. Emily rushed forward to hug Charlie — even Medea seemed thrilled. The Dark One had been vanquished.

'You did it Charlie. You did it,' yelled Max.

Everyone gathered round to congratulate him, the Argonauts slapping him on the back. They were right. Charlie had defeated the Dark One. The monster was dead.

Zetes flew down and patted a beaming Max on the shoulder. 'You're a hero, too, you know.' Max beamed with pride.

Charlie turned to thank Perikylemenos but he was nowhere to be seen. 'Where is he? Why hasn't he transformed back again?'

Parseus looked away. 'I'm sorry. He knew what he was doing, Charlie.'

'But he can transform at will,' said Charlie. 'Why isn't he back?'

Silence fell again. 'The wound was full of poison. Perikylemenos could not have survived that,' said Parseus. 'Not in his state.'

'He's...he's dead?' stammered Charlie.

'Yes,' said Parseus.

Charlie felt nausea and guilt wash over him in equal measure.

He didn't want to believe it, but as the seconds ticked by the truth dawned on him. Perikylemenos had made the ultimate sacrifice. He had saved them all.

Charlie stood looking at the lifeless creature now slumped in the doorway, its bloody stumps blackened with fire. He knew he should have been elated but he wasn't. There was no sweetness to their victory.

'UM, I think we have another problem,' said Lynkeus.

'What now?' said Parseus.

'I see gargoyles.'

'So what? They're dotted all over the roof,' said Max.

'Not any longer,' said Lynkeus.

Charlie spotted one of the books on the desk. It was the same book he had picked up when they had first visited the library — the book Parseus had slammed shut. It was now open.

Parseus came over and looked down at the pages. 'Ah,' he said. 'We do have another problem.'

'Problem?' Max stared blankly at the open book.

'It's a spell,' said Parseus. 'Mrs Payne has cast a spell. She's brought the gargoyles to life.'

'That doesn't sound good,' said Max.

'So what can we do?' asked Charlie. He could feel the poison starting to course through his veins. His arm felt heavy.

'We must find the witch and break the spell,' said Parseus. 'Lynkeus and Medea, take Emily. Find Mrs Payne. Use the binding spell. You have to stop her. It's the only way.'

'What are the rest of us going to do?' asked Max.

'Stand and fight,' said Parseus.

Max rolled his eyes. 'Of course. Why did I need to ask?'

Seconds later they heard howling.

'Get to the witch,' shouted Parseus.

Lynkeus and Emily raced over to the secret lever. Emily pulled it down, the door opened and they disappeared into the passage with Medea.

The others unsheathed their swords and strung their bows. 'Good luck,' said Parseus.

'Thought you said there was no such thing,' said Charlie, now wincing in agony, the pain growing worse.

'In this world there is,' replied Parseus.

'Good. Because I think we're going to need it,' added Max.

Moments later the gargoyles came. Clambering over the carcass of the Dark One they scurried into the library, crawling across the floor, running up the walls like cockroaches.

Charlie remembered their first visit to the house, looking up at them, perched on the roof. Yet now here they were as real as they had looked: some small and wiry with razor sharp talons, others huge with gaping jaws and jagged teeth — but all of them bent on destruction.

'Oh, great, some of them have got wings,' Max despaired, seeing another wave of gargoyles flying into the room.

'Just stay strong and stay focused,' shouted Parseus.

The battle began as the gargoyles, their eyes full of fury, started attacking from every angle. Charlie and Max stood shoulder to shoulder: Charlie striking with his sword, Max firing arrow upon arrow. But as each gargoyle fell, another took its place.

With their howls echoing round the room, they charged forward, lashing out with their claws from above and below. Kalais and Zetes fought the winged attackers while the others battled those on the ground.

Within minutes they were all starting to tire, their strength leaving them. Everyone was now backed up against the wall. Charlie, the Dark One's poison spreading, was finding it hard even to stand.

'We can't go on, Parseus. There are too many,' he groaned.

'There's only one thing to do,' shouted Parseus. 'RETREAT.' He threw himself against the secret door, pushed it open and they fled into the passage. 'We must get to the river,' he said. 'It's our only hope.'

Just then Charlie sank to his knees, clutching his arm.

'He's been injured, Parseus,' said Max. 'The Dark One struck him.'

'He needs that potion,' said Parseus. 'We must get him back to the inn.'

Helped up by Max and Idas, Charlie staggered into the passage. The gargoyles were close behind.

Idas, the violent one, pushed Charlie and Max in front of him. 'Save yourselves,' he shouted, and turning he squared his shoulders and raised his sword. Striking left and right, he held the gargoyles back.

Charlie stumbled forward, the pain growing with every step. A second later he felt his knees give way. Looking up he saw a gargoyle launch itself straight at him. He was done for. Closing his eyes tightly he prepared for the worst.

THEN there was silence. Charlie slowly opened his eyes. The gargoyle had turned back to stone — and so had all the others. 'She's done it,' Parseus cried out. 'Medea's done it. The spell worked. Thank the Gods.'

Charlie shouted for Idas. There was no reply.

'Come on. We must get to the river,' said Parseus, pulling him to his feet.

'What about Idas? We can't go without Idas.'

'Too late, I'm afraid. He didn't make it,' said Parseus.

Charlie looked down the passage but all he could see were stone gargoyles piled high along it. Idas was somewhere underneath them. There was no hope he had survived. He too had given his life.

Parseus and Max helped carry Charlie down the passage. Fifty yards on, they spotted a light in the tunnel up ahead. Not long afterwards, they reached a crossroads. There were two doors leading off it. Charlie recognised them: one led to the chamber where Emily and he had been held hostage.

Parseus was about to push open the door when Medea emerged. 'I see the spell worked,' he said.

'Eventually. She's in there.' Medea, a satisfied smile on her face, gestured behind her.

Charlie, struggling with the pain, looked up and peered into the room. Mrs Payne was suspended in mid-air, surrounded by a swirling mass of blue lights. She appeared to be unconscious.

'Didn't realise how strong she was. It took some time but she's bound,' said Medea. 'Won't last I'm afraid, but I've bought you a few days. You'll need to find something stronger to hold her. I'd try the library. There are some powerful spells in there. I'm sure you will find something,' she added.

'Thanks Medea. You saved us,' said Parseus.

'Just in time,' said Max, sighing with relief. 'Did you see how close they got?' He pointed to the line of gargoyles, now turned to stone, filling the passage behind them.

'Where's Idas though?' he asked.

'He didn't make it,' whispered Charlie.

Lynkeus and Emily appeared from the passage.

'CHARLIE?' Emily rushed to his side. Charlie was ashen-faced, sweat pouring down his temples.

'I'll be fine. Just need some of that potion you had, that's all Sis.' Charlie forced a smile.

'Indeed you do. We must get back to the inn,' said Parseus. 'We'll go by the river. How far is it, Lynkeus?'

'Not far,' he said. 'Follow me.'

Lynkeus led them down the passage until they reached the river. There was a small, stone jetty jutting out into it and two tunnels: one branching to the right, one to the left.

'Which way Lynkeus?' asked Parseus.

'We take the tunnel on the right. It leads to the inn. I have no idea where the tunnel to the left leads. Trust me though it's nowhere nice. I can feel it.'

'Kalais, Zetes can you take it in turns?' said Parseus.

The twins nodded.

'I can make my own way,' said Euphemos. 'I'll just skip across it.'

'Good, then I suggest you take Charlie and Medea first. You'll need to give him the cure, Medea. You two can come back for the rest of us,' said Parseus.

Half an hour later everyone was back in the inn again. Medea had administered the Blood of Echidne to Charlie's wound. The pain had vanished instantly.

'It was fortunate that you had taken some Strength or you'd have been unconscious within minutes,' she said. 'You'll be fine now.'

She took care of Kalais' shoulder next.

In the bar, exhausted from battle and grieving over the loss of both Perikylemenos and Idas, the celebrations were muted.

'It's all over, then?' said Max, collapsing into one of the armchairs.

'For the moment, Max, for the moment,' said Parseus.

Charlie's father, delighted to have the children back safe, brought out a bottle of whisky. 'How about a drink? You men look as if you all deserve it.'

'Indeed, let's have a toast,' said Parseus, taking the bottle from him. He held it up and translated the offer to the Argonauts.

'Excellent idea,' said Polydeuces, cheering up.

Parseus poured each of the Argonauts a drink. Charlie noticed him slip a few drops of one of his potions into their glasses before handing them round to the Argonauts and Medea.

'To lost friends,' they said, raising their glasses. They all drank.

Polydeuces raised his glass again. 'To Charlie and Max,' he said and they drank again.

Then they made a final toast to the Gods.

'What are we going to sacrifice?' asked Euphemos.

Parseus translated for Mr Goodwin.

'I've got a couple of chickens in the oven. Would they do?' he asked.

'Thank you Mr Goodwin, but sacrifices can wait for now,' said Parseus.

Charlie, now cured of his wound, started laughing. A moment later the inn door suddenly opened and his mother appeared with her suitcase.

'What's all the shouting about?' she said as she walked into the bar. She stopped and slowly surveyed the room, her mouth agape. Then she saw the twins, screamed and fainted on the spot. Charlie's father hurried to her side.

'Might be best if you took your wife upstairs for a bit, Mr Goodwin,' suggested Parseus.

'You're probably right, though what am I going to say to her when she comes round...' Mr Goodwin shook his head.

'Don't worry, you can leave that to me,' said Parseus. He picked up a glass at the bar, filled it with water and slipped a drop of potion into it. 'Just give her this,' he said. 'Oh, and you might want to close the bar for tonight. Don't want your regulars coming in, do we? Wouldn't want anyone else fainting.'

'Right you are,' replied Mr Goodwin. Euphemos went across to help him carry his wife upstairs to her own room.

He returned a minute later.

'It's time you all returned to Colchis. I'll take you back to the exact moment that you left — as promised,' said Parseus.

'I want to go too,' said Medea.

'Argonauts first,' said Parseus. 'Don't worry, I shall be back in an instant. You won't even notice I've gone. Then you can return to the temple garden.'

The remaining Argonauts said their goodbyes to Emily and the boys.

Lynkeus took Charlie's arm. 'Perikylemenos and Idas would have had it no other way. You know that. There's no greater way for a hero to die than in the heat of battle. They will be blessed by the Gods for this,' he said.

'I know,' said Charlie. 'But they died to save us and I can never repay that.'

'Yes, you can. Just make sure they didn't die in vain. Be worthy of their sacrifice.'

Kalais approached. 'I'll tell you something Charlie, this is one adventure I won't forget in a hurry,' he said. 'They're not going to believe me when I get back to the Argo and tell the others about this.'

Charlie laughed, but remembering the drops Parseus had put in the drinks, he knew that there would be no tale to tell. The potion of Lethe would soon work its magic. By the time the Argonauts were back in their own world they would have forgotten everything.

Parseus took out the compass and started plotting another course. The boys stood back. A portal opened up and Parseus and the Argonauts vanished into thin air.

Charlie wondered if he would ever see any of them again.

An instant later Parseus reappeared. He had a satisfied look on his face.

'Safely back,' he said. 'Now it's your turn, Medea.'

Medea came up to Charlie. 'I have decided to forgive you for tricking me. And I think you may have more need of this than I,' she said, handing over her casket. 'I have to keep the potion which Jason needs for his task, of course. But there are many potions here that may prove useful in the future. Use them wisely.'

Another portal opened up and she too vanished. A split second later Parseus was standing there alone.

'Is she back in the temple garden?' asked Charlie.

'Yes — to some confusion, though. The portal caused a bit of a stir. The soldiers fled in fear and their horses bolted. However, I think her reputation as a witch will be greatly enhanced as a consequence.' Parseus smiled. 'She won't remember any of us, of course. So all will be as it should be.'

Mr Goodwin came downstairs to the bar.

'How's Mum?' asked Charlie.

'She was in a complete state of shock then I gave her that water and she was fine. It was like she had forgotten it had ever happened.'

Charlie grinned. 'That's because Parseus gave her something to make her forget.'

'Well thank goodness, because I had no idea how I was going to explain it to her.' Mr Goodwin looked around the bar. 'So they've all gone?'

'Yes Mr Goodwin. You could probably open the bar if you want to,' said Parseus.

Mr Goodwin shook his head. 'I think I'll stay shut for tonight. Wednesday's are never busy anyway.'

'It's Wednesday?' said Max. 'Are you sure?'

'Of course I'm sure. Now how about those chickens?' Mr Goodwin said. 'They'll be ready soon.' He disappeared into the kitchen.

Max looked at Charlie. 'But that means it's only been two days since we first spotted…'

'The Shadow? I know. That was Monday afternoon. Then Monday night we brought back the helmet and we spent last night on the river,' said Charlie.

Only two days had passed in Hesper. Charlie could hardly believe it.

Neither could Max. 'But we've been away for weeks.' He frowned. 'Time certainly flies eh?' He shrugged. 'Anyway, at least everything's back to normal now.'

'Normal? Nothing's ever going to be normal again,' said Charlie.

At that very moment the room began to shake. Glasses crashed to the floor and pictures and ornaments fell from the walls.

Charlie staggered forward, grabbing hold of the side of the bar. 'What *is* that, Parseus?'

'An earthquake, Charlie.'

'Earthquake? But we don't have them here.'

'I'm afraid it isn't from earth,' replied Parseus.

The next moment Emily cried out and stumbled forward. Her eyes rolled back. Charlie took her by the shoulders.

'What is it now?'

Terrified, Emily looked up. 'GIANTS,' she cried out.

Parseus groaned. 'Oh dear.'

'What does she mean by Giants?' Charlie said, as more glasses tumbled to the floor.

'More importantly what do you mean by *oh dear*?' said Max.

The room stopped shaking. Parseus went over to the bar. He poured himself a large whisky and knocked it back in one swig. Then he put down his glass and turned to Charlie, a grim look on his face.

'The Giants have awakened.'

Postscript

Although *The Titan Prophecy — Rise of the Dark One* is first and foremost a fantasy novel centred on the adventures of Charlie and Max, the narrative is also rooted in Greek Mythology: its stories, characters and places. Indeed, the premise for the book — *The Titan Prophecy* — derives from the myth of the great ten-year war of the Gods and the Titans — the *Titanomachy*— which saw the Titans defeated and imprisoned for all eternity in the hell realm of Tartaros.

While this is not intended to be a book about classical mythology it does incorporate many well-known myths. Some readers may be more familiar with the Roman names for the Gods and heroes and for that reason the table below lists the Roman equivalents for the classical Greek names used in this book:

Zeus	*King of the Gods*	Jupiter
Hades	*God of the Underworld*	Pluto
Poseidon	*God of the Sea*	Neptune
Ares	*God of War*	Mars
Hephaistos	*Inventor or Smith God*	Vulcan
Apollo	*God of the Sun*	Apollo
Hermes	*Messenger God*	Mercury
Dionysos	*God of Wine*	Bacchus
Hera	*Wife of Zeus/Jupiter*	Juno
Aphrodite	*Goddess of Love*	Venus
Athene	*Goddess of Wisdom*	Minerva
Herakles	*Greatest of Greek heroes*	Hercules
Eros	*Son, Goddess of Love*	Cupid

www.thetitanprophecy.com